NEBULA
AWARDS
25

NEBULA AWARDS

25

*SFWA's Choices for the Best
Science Fiction and Fantasy*
—— *1989* ——

EDITED BY
Michael Bishop

Harcourt Brace Jovanovich, Publishers

San Diego   New York   London

Requests for permission to make copies of any part of the work should be mailed
to: Permissions Department, Harcourt Brace Jovanovich, Publishers, Orlando,
Florida 32887.

The Library of Congress has cataloged this serial as follows:

The Nebula awards.—No. 18—New York [N.Y.]: Arbor House, c1983–
v.; 22 cm.
Annual.
Published: San Diego, Calif.: Harcourt Brace Jovanovich, 1984–
Published for: Science Fiction Writers of America, 1983–
Continues: Nebula award stories (New York, N.Y.: 1982)
ISSN 0741-5567 = The Nebula awards
1. Science fiction, American—Periodicals. I. Science Fiction Writers of America.
PS648.S3N38   83-647399
813′.0876′08—dc19
AACR 2 MARC-S
Library of Congress   [8709r84]rev
ISBN 0-15-164933-2
ISBN 0-15-665473-3 (Harvest/HBJ: pbk)

Design by G. B. D. Smith
Printed in the United States of America

First edition   A B C D E

This twenty-fifth volume of the Nebula series is dedicated to
the memory of

Ed Emshwiller (1925–1990)
Karel Zeman (1911–1989)
William F. Temple (1914–1989)
Ross Rocklynne (1913–1988)
Michael Shaara (1929–1988)
C. L. Moore (1911–1987)

and is also in honor of Damon Knight (still very much alive),
who was instrumental in the founding of the Science Fiction
Writers of America a quarter century ago.

CONTENTS

INTRODUCTION

Michael Bishop

Every year, the members of the Science Fiction Writers of America recommend stories and novels for the annual Nebula Awards. The editor of SFWA's *Nebula Awards Report* lists all recommendations in a newsletter. Near the end of the year, the editor tallies the recommendations, draws up a preliminary ballot, and sends it to the membership. The top five novels (40,000 words or more), novellas (17,500–39,999 words), novelettes (7,500–17,499 words), and short stories (fewer than 7,500 words) earn a place on the final ballot, which also goes out to SFWA's eligible voters. Two Nebula Awards juries— one for the novel, one for short fiction—may add one nominee to each of their respective categories.

The following works made the final ballot in each category in the preliminary voting for the twenty-fifth annual awards. I have indicated the eventual winners with asterisks:

For Novel

The Boat of a Million Years by Poul Anderson (Tor)
Good News from Outer Space by John Kessel (Tor)
* *The Healer's War* by Elizabeth Ann Scarborough (Doubleday/
Foundation)
Ivory: A Legend of Past and Future by Mike Resnick (Tor)
Prentice Alvin by Orson Scott Card (Tor)
Sister Light, Sister Dark by Jane Yolen (Tor)

For Novella

"A Dozen Tough Jobs" by Howard Waldrop (Ziesing Books)
"Great Work of Time" by John Crowley (from *Novelty: Four
Stories*, Doubleday/Foundation)

"Marîd Changes His Mind" by George Alec Effinger (*Isaac Asimov's Science Fiction Magazine*, May 1989)
° "The Mountains of Mourning" by Lois McMaster Bujold (*Analog*, May 1989)
"Tiny Tango" by Judith Moffett (*Isaac Asimov's Science Fiction Magazine*, February 1989)
"A Touch of Lavender" by Megan Lindholm (*Isaac Asimov's Science Fiction Magazine*, February 1989)

For Novelette

° "At the Rialto" by Connie Willis (*Omni*, October 1989; *The Microverse*, Bantam Spectra)
"Enter a Soldier. Later: Enter Another" by Robert Silverberg (*Isaac Asimov's Science Fiction Magazine*, June 1989)
"Fast Cars" by Kristine Kathryn Rusch (*Isaac Asimov's Science Fiction Magazine*, October 1989)
"For I Have Touched the Sky" by Mike Resnick (*The Magazine of Fantasy & Science Fiction*, December 1989)
"Silver Lady and the Fortyish Man" by Megan Lindholm (*Isaac Asimov's Science Fiction Magazine*, January 1989)
"Sisters" by Greg Bear (from *Tangents*, Warner)

For Short Story

"The Adinkra Cloth" by Mary C. Aldridge (*Marion Zimmer Bradley's Fantasy Magazine*, Winter 1989)
"Boobs" by Suzy McKee Charnas (*Isaac Asimov's Science Fiction Magazine*, July 1989)
"Dori Bangs" by Bruce Sterling (*Isaac Asimov's Science Fiction Magazine*, September 1989)
"Lost Boys" by Orson Scott Card (*The Magazine of Fantasy & Science Fiction*, October 1989)
"The Ommatidium Miniatures" by Michael Bishop (*The Microverse*, Bantam Spectra)
° "Ripples in the Dirac Sea" by Geoffrey A. Landis (*Isaac Asimov's Science Fiction Magazine*, October 1988)

The appearance of six finalists in each of the four categories indicates that the two Nebula Awards juries chose to exercise their power to add titles. Astute SFWA members may occasionally deduce which finalists are jury choices, but the juries—to keep members from reacting to their intervention rather than to the merits of the added titles—do not publicly disclose them.

(My story, "The Ommatidium Miniatures," was a jury selection, and I have showcased it in this anthology as a runner-up because, rightly or wrongly, I am proud of what it attempts and of what I think it achieves. As Robert Silverberg wrote in his introduction to *Nebula Awards 18*, in which he ran a runner-up story of his own: "Not an apology; just an explanation.")

The novels on the 1989 final ballot leaned more toward fantasy than toward traditional science fiction. The winner, *The Healer's War* by Elizabeth Ann Scarborough, employs magic to take its wholly credible heroine through the literal and emotional mine fields of the Vietnam War. It is a powerful and satisfying work of the imagination.

It was also good to see nominated such fine and distinctive novels as Poul Anderson's *The Boat of a Million Years*, a genuine science fiction epic; John Kessel's *Good News from Outer Space*, a coolly literate examination of the role of chance in the human tragicomedy; and *Ivory* by Mike Resnick, an SF extravaganza dilating on the fate of the largest mammal ever to walk the earth. Like *The Healer's War*, the other two finalists were strong fantasies: Orson Scott Card's *Prentice Alvin*, the third novel in an alternative-history series about "the formation of the American community," and Jane Yolen's *Sister Light, Sister Dark*, which uses quest motifs and folklore to undergird its multiple tellings.

In the novella category, too, each nominee was so distinct it seemed folly to have to choose among them. John Crowley's elegant time-travel historical "Great Work of Time" bumped shins not only with Howard Waldrop's Mark Twainish reenvisioning of the Hercules legends, "Twelve Tough Jobs," but also with the eventual winner, "The Mountains of Mourning," in which Lois McMaster Bujold delivers up a whodunit with provocative consequences for its far-future society. But "Tiny Tango" by Judith Moffett, a brave look at AIDS anxiety, and "A Touch of Lavender" by Megan Lindholm, a poignant demonstration that choice rather than biology determines meaningful families, also earned well-deserved praise.

The nominated novelettes were likewise a heterogeneous bunch. My favorites included the highbrow slapstick of Connie Willis's "At the Rialto" and Mike Resnick's futuristic Kikuyu fable, "For I Have Touched the Sky." I also admired Robert Silverberg's expertly handled simulated meeting between Socrates and Pizarro in "Enter a Soldier. Later: Enter Another." Meanwhile, "Fast Cars" by newcomer Kristine Kathryn Rusch has a moody contemporary resonance, Megan Lindholm's "Silver Lady and the Fortyish Man" brings a spooky sort of magic into a lonely saleswoman's life, and Greg Bear's "Sisters" limns a future cause of teenage angst in a way that underscores the timelessness and universality of such feelings.

Forgive me, but in the short story category I voted for "The Ommatidium Miniatures." (I could lie about this, but I doubt that you would believe me.) Joe Haldeman once observed, maybe only half facetiously, that writers having a work on the final ballot needn't read any rival work. But I *did* read the other finalists, and my favorites among them included not only Geoffrey A. Landis's winning time-travel tale, "Ripples in the Dirac Sea," but also the ultrahip "Dori Bangs" by Bruce Sterling, which has already been reprinted in two other anthologies.

Meanwhile, Mary C. Aldridge's "The Adinkra Cloth" is a charming African fantasy, "Boobs" by Suzy McKee Charnas is a jazzy modern werewolf story with (of course) psychosexual overtones, and "Lost Boys" by Orson Scott Card is a horror story deploying the author, his wife, and their children as characters. "Lost Boys" occasioned both controversy (as its first readers tried to determine what in it was true, what fictional) and praise from those who saw it as an example of a subtle variety of experimentalism.

What the reader will discover in this twenty-fifth-anniversary volume, beyond the democratically dictated givens of the four award winners, is a celebration of the diversity and achievement of our field. And so this volume features runners-up or off-ballot works by writers as different, but as capable, as Mike Resnick, John Crowley, and Gardner Dozois, and opinion by writers of such varying mind-sets as Ian Watson, Damon Knight, Orson Scott Card, and Richard Grant. Also here are last year's winners of the Rhysling Awards for speculative poetry; Paul Di Filippo's witty send-up of Nebula Fever, "The Great Nebula Sweep," a satirical story original to this volume; and Bill Warren's annual survey of SF films.

My three-year run as editor of this series is over. I am left with decidedly mixed feelings. At times, the awards process seems to me an invasive waste of energy—contentious, frustrating, and infinitely second-guessable. At other times, it seems *almost* what its founders intended, namely, a visible and prestigious accolade for superior achievement in the writing of science fiction by other science fiction writers.

These annual volumes struggle to put the best possible face on the mess and mayhem of our awards process; indeed, they confer upon it a measure of validity. SFWA has duties and responsibilities beyond the awarding of prizes, true, but the *Nebula Awards* volumes remain the most visible manifestation of our organization to the general public. They perform a valuable service by affirming high standards, even if each reprinted story falls a little shy (as each invariably must) of the Platonic ideal toward which its author was gallantly, if hubristically, aiming.

So I hope that this series continues, that SFWA's members set themselves noble rather than trifling goals, and that readers do their part by refusing to support the facile, the colorless, the trite, the ill written, the unfelt, the downright dumb, or the intellectually and spiritually dead. There is little excuse for these failings in any sort of literature, and perhaps none in a literature whose noisiest advocates declare it, arguably, the one true voice of its time.

—*Pine Mountain, Georgia*
May 22, 1990

WHAT IS SCIENCE FICTION?

Damon Knight

If not for Damon Knight, SFWA would not exist. Neither would these annual *Nebula Awards* volumes. Born in 1922, Knight is one of the unsung heroes of contemporary science fiction. He has been short story writer, critic, editor, novelist, teacher, translator, and more. He was the founder and the first president of SFWA, the editor of *Nebula Award Stories, 1965* (the first volume in this series), and, for twenty-one numbers, the editor of the *Orbit* original anthologies, in which he broke new ground by publishing memorable, genre-expanding stories by Gardner Dozois, George Alec Effinger, R. A. Lafferty, Ursula K. Le Guin, Kate Wilhelm, and Gene Wolfe, among a raft of others. His most recent novels include *The Observers* and *A Reasonable World*, and he is now at work on "a comic novel about the destruction of the human race."

Here, from his essay in the *Contemporary Authors Autobiography Series*, volume 10, is the story of how SFWA came to be:

> Early in the sixties there had been several attempts to organize a science-fiction writers' association. What always happened was that the writers held meetings, passed resolutions, elected officers, and then everybody went home and forgot the whole thing. I thought I saw there was a better way, but it required somebody with more clout than I had then, and I waited.
>
> By 1965 I had accumulated a little more clout, meaning to say that I had published a few more stories and novels, and my patience was running short. One week I got three requests for flat-fee anthology rights, and I wrote an indignant flyer, mailed it to a hundred writers, and said, 'If you would like to receive more information like this, send your three dollars.' The checks rolled in. When I had seventy-eight writers signed up, I declared them the charter members of Science Fiction Writers of America, wrote a set of bylaws (adapted from those of the Mystery Writers of America), and held an election.
>
> I ran unopposed for President, feeling that it would be pointless to try to find an opponent that year. For Secretary-Treasurer I tapped Lloyd Biggle, Jr., whom I had met briefly when I lectured

at a college in Ann Arbor, Michigan. This was a lucky choice. Biggle turned out to be conscientious, steady, ingenious, and tenacious as a bulldog. He organized our bookkeeping and records system, took charge of mailings, saw the need for a board of trustees and established it, and served on it himself until 1973, long after I was out from under. It was his suggestion of an annual anthology of stories by members that led immediately to the Nebula Awards, which I had seen only as a remote future possibility.

I wanted a trophy for the SFWA awards that would be beautiful and distinctive, unlike the Hugo rocket ship and all other conventional trophies. When I told Katie [Knight's wife, Kate Wilhelm] about this, she came forward with a design she had thought of years before, a spiral nebula embedded in plastic above a quartz crystal. Judith Ann Lawrence, Jim Blish's wife, turned this into a finished design after many changes and much agony, and took it on herself to procure the crystals, make the nebulas out of acetate and glitter, and find a manufacturer to do the embedments.

I organized the first SFWA Awards banquet *ex officio*, although I hate banquets and considered this one a necessary evil. For the occasion I bought my first tuxedo and was reminded later of Thoreau's 'Beware of all enterprises that require new clothes.' On the way to New York we stopped at a red light and the truck behind us didn't. Our Dodge Dart was totaled and we both had sprained necks. Anne McCaffrey's VW bug was squeezed between two playful semis the same day, and *it* was totaled.

We got into New York somehow, and I wrestled with my studs and cummerbund. The banquet was held in the upstairs dining room of the Overseas Press Club, which turned out to be a rather depressing place. There was only one short speech, and I made that myself, explaining how to pronounce SFWA ("sefwa"). In order to avoid the necessity of other speeches, I had arranged for the first showing of Ed Emshwiller's later-award-winning film, *Relativity*.

Knight goes on to write about a later banquet and SFWA's first dramatic, and successful, showdown with an intransigent publisher. So it is far from outlandish to argue that every writer of science fiction at work today owes a significant debt of gratitude to Damon Knight, as does every reader who enjoys these annual anthologies. In assembling this twenty-fifth-anniversary volume, I felt that it would be an insult—indeed, no small crime—to fail either to acknowledge our collective indebtedness or to offer Damon a forum for his clear-eyed views about what science fiction is in practice and how we may with some certainty identify it.

"What Is Science Fiction?" first appeared in an anthology that Knight edited in 1977, *Turning Points: Essays on the Art of Science Fiction*. His essay remains pertinent today, and I applaud the word *art* in the volume's subtitle.

Once at a Milford Science Fiction Writers' Conference I said a colleague's punctuation was wrong; he replied that he didn't agree with me. I failed to ask him why he thought punctuation was a matter of opinion, but I brooded over this later, and finally realized that he was talking about what the rules of punctuation ought to be, while I was talking about what they are. One is arguable, the other not.

In a similar way, science fiction writers and critics have been trying without success for forty years to define science fiction, because each of them has been talking about his own idea of what the field ought to be, never about what it is. Intent on distinguishing the true s.f. from the false, they invariably find that most of it is false; thus Heinlein casts out "space opera," Bailey "scientific romance," Asimov social satire. De Camp divides fiction into imaginative stories (including science fiction) and realistic stories; Heinlein insists that s.f. is a branch, and the most important branch, of realistic fiction.

Here are some other attempts:

"Science fiction is the search for a definition of man and his status in the universe which will stand in our advanced but confused state of knowledge (science), and is characteristically cast in the Gothic or post-Gothic mode."—Brian W. Aldiss. (This admits *The Fountainhead*, by Ayn Rand, but excludes Hal Clement's *Mission of Gravity*.)

"The more powers above the ordinary that the protagonist enjoys, the closer the fiction will approach to hard-core science fiction. Conversely, the more ordinary and fallible the protagonist, the further from hard-core."—Aldiss. (This admits *Dracula* as hard-core science fiction, but excludes "Night," by John W. Campbell.)

"A handy short definition of almost all science fiction might read: realistic speculation about possible future events, based solidly on adequate knowledge of the real world, past and present, and on a thorough understanding of the scientific method. To make this definition cover all science fiction (instead of 'almost all') it is necessary only to strike out the word 'future.' "—Robert A. Heinlein. (This admits *Arrowsmith*, by Sinclair Lewis, but excludes the collected works of Robert Sheckley.)

"There is only one definition of science fiction that seems to make pragmatic sense: 'Science fiction is anything published as science fiction.' "—Norman Spinrad. (This admits Spinrad's "The Last Hurrah of the Golden Horde," but excludes the book version of Walter Miller's *A Canticle for Leibowitz*.)

Taken together (if anyone were idiot enough to try), these definitions would narrow the field of science fiction almost to invisibility. Yet nearly every critic claims an intuitive knowledge of what s.f. is, and I claim it myself. We do know the difference between stories that are perceived as science fiction and those that are not; the question is, how do we know?

In an attempt to find out, I wrote a list of promising definitions and checked them against works published as science fiction to see how well they matched. This is the list:

1. Science. (Gernsback.)
2. Technology and invention. (Heinlein, Miller.)
3. The future and the remote past, including all time travel stories. (Bailey.)
4. Extrapolation. (Davenport.)
5. Scientific method. (Bretnor.)
6. Other places—planets, dimensions, etc., including visitors from the above. (Bailey.)
7. Catastrophes, natural or manmade. (Bailey.)

I discarded other definitions, for instance Campbell's dictum that s.f. is predictive, which I thought were impossible to evaluate. (To find out how many s.f. stories contain accurate predictions I would have to wait until the results are all in, i.e., to the end of the universe.) I also discarded all negative definitions, e.g., that any story that contains fantasy elements is not s.f. (because that excludes Heinlein's "Waldo"), or that any story that is literature is not s.f. (because that excludes Le Guin's *The Left Hand of Darkness*).

For source material I used *Nebula Award Stories Eight*; *The Hugo Winners, Volume Two*; and *The Science Fiction Hall of Fame, Volume*

One, in the belief that any defect in the hypothesis would show up here first. I added recent issues of the three leading s.f. magazines, and recent volumes of three hardcover series, plus a one-shot anthology, Spinrad's *The New Tomorrows*, which I chose because it is devoted to "New Wave" s.f.°

On the basis of the results (see tables), I conclude that a story containing three or more of the elements listed above is usually perceived as science fiction; with two, it is perceived as borderline; with one or none, it is non-science fiction.

I had better emphasize that these scores say nothing about the quality of the stories, or about the quality of the science, the extrapolation, etc. If an element was present in a story, no matter how perfunctory or feeble, I scored it.

I also ran some test cases. The system held up well for these, with the single exception of *Gulliver's Travels*, which scored 4, although it is not usually perceived as s.f. To cure this, I would have to add the negative definition that nothing published before 1860 is science fiction, a perception due partly to tradition and, I think, partly to the desire to get rid of all the Lucians and Cyranos who have been dragged in by overanxious scholars.

In the course of this study my own perceptions were altered. At the end of it I found that I agreed with C. S. Lewis when he said that not all romances laid in the future are science fiction. I lost some (not all) of my dedication to a very broad definition of s.f., one which would include any work of fiction informed by a scientific attitude toward nature and man. I became more aware of the sleights practiced by commercial s.f. writers to ensure that their work will be perceived as science fiction, and to get work published which could as well have been written as mundane adventure fiction. I also became more aware of the number of non-s.f. stories regularly published in nearly all the magazines and hardcover series, including my own.

I offer this study as an extended definition of what science fiction is. Like other people, I have an opinion about what it should be. I

° I omit these from the tables because they will be out of date by the time this book is published, but, for the record, *Galaxy* scored an average of 3.8, *Analog* 3.2, *New Dimensions* 3.2, *Orbit* 3.2, *Universe* 3.2 (like a sampling of near beers), *F & SF* 1.4, and *The New Tomorrows* 1.3.

would like to see less dependence on conventional stage furniture and more on honestly worked out extrapolations. I am inclined to agree with Alexei and Cory Panshin when they say that s.f. and fantasy as we know them are two filled-in areas in a broad, largely empty field. I believe more strongly than before that science fiction has not yet found its limits.

"Science fiction" and "literature" are not mutually exclusive terms. I propounded this as a heresy in 1952, and it is still so regarded, not only by hostile critics but by many of s.f.'s defenders. The proposition "If it's s.f., it isn't literature" is self-proving: " 'But this looks good.' 'Well then, it's not s.f.' " And around we go again.

There is general agreement that science fiction has some essential attraction which is not easy to capture in words but which is unmistakable to a receptive reader. Kingsley Amis refers to this when he gives excerpts from two s.f. novels, and then remarks, ". . . anybody encountering such passages who fails to experience a peculiar interest, related to, but distinct from, ordinary literary interest, will never be an addict of science fiction." Basil Davenport, noting the argument as to whether *Arrowsmith* should be considered science fiction, says that he read the book at a time when he was avidly searching for s.f., and yet it never crossed his mind that this might be it. Isaac Asimov says that Plato, More and Swift are works of imagination, "but they do not have the *intent* of science fiction." I don't know what Isaac's version of the intent of s.f. is, but probably it has something to do with giving the same essential thrill of difference that Amis is talking about, and that Davenport failed to find in *Arrowsmith*.°

To say that this quality is characteristic of science fiction is not to say that it is always present, however, or that s.f. can have no other quality, no other way of appealing to its readers.

Science fiction, as C. S. Lewis points out, is not all one thing. Even in its commercial history in the United States, dating from the early years of the century, it has undergone repeated infusions from

° I read *Arrowsmith* for the first time recently, and concluded that in an odd way it is the antithesis of science fiction. In a realistic novel set in the past or present, nothing can happen that would conspicuously alter the real world as we know it; therefore Lewis's hero, although he develops a new serum, has no place in history because someone else (a real person) beats him to it. This is just the opposite of what happens in a science fiction story, where the *consequences* of the invention or discovery are all-important.

other kinds of fiction—dime-novel fiction beginning about 1900, pulp adventure fiction in the early thirties, slick fiction in the late thirties and forties, women's-magazine and little-magazine fiction in the early fifties, avant-garde fiction in the sixties and seventies.

Every one of these transformations has provoked cries of outrage from old-guard editors and writers, but not one of them has obliterated previous forms—the latter are all still alive, even the Gernsbackian story (see Isaac Asimov's "Take a Match" in *New Dimensions II*). Adventure s.f., now more than forty years old, accounts for more than half the science fiction on the newsstands.

Brian Stableford, in "Science Fiction: a Sociological Perspective" (*Fantastic*, March 1974), makes the interesting suggestion that "the identity of SF—the identity of the social phenomenon called SF—is not to be found in its content; it is to be found in the way people *use* it, the way people orient themselves towards it, and in the way which it orients *them* to matters external to it." What Stableford appears to overlook is that different people use s.f. in different ways. He identifies himself as a writer of trash, says that many such writers make a living at their trade, and therefore that s.f. must be "*useful* at a trash level." So far he is on safe ground, but he errs when he says that "with few exceptions, books labeled as SF tend to sell the same number of copies, regardless of literary merit or seriousness of intent." By and large, the first printings of s.f. books sell within a very narrow range. For the pure article of commerce, the kind of thing Stableford is talking about, that's the end—the book has had its one printing and will never be seen again. Science fiction books of unusual merit are reprinted over and over.

Earlier, Stableford argues that Verne and Wells are not part of "the same social phenomenon as science fiction," because the phenomenon did not exist when they wrote. "When *The Time Machine*—the Wells story which seems to live most meaningfully within the SF paradigm—was written, the paradigm did not exist. It did not then belong to the same subculture which SF belongs to, even to the same type of subculture. . . . It is now possible for us to *use The Time Machine* as SF, and to meaningfully speak of it as SF. We may also *use* as SF the works of Verne, of Cyrano de Bergerac, of Voltaire and of Lucian of Samosata, but . . . it is a conceptual mistake to think that because I, in 1973, can read *The Time Machine* as science fiction,

H. G. Wells, in 1895, *wrote The Time Machine* as science fiction."

This curious statement needs some interpretation. Let me approach it from the rear. During the recent wave of permissiveness, several paperback publishers put out lines of well-written erotic novels. They didn't sell. Hardcore pornography fans don't want good writing, characterization, vividness, insight, or any other literary quality—not only don't want it, but are actively annoyed by it. So with the lowest class of s.f. readers, and I think we ought to have a term for the crude, basic kind of s.f. that satisfies the appetite for pseudo-scientific marvels without appealing to any other portion of the intellect: I propose that we call it "sci-fi."*

Substitute this for "science fiction" in Stableford's essay: the argument then reads that since there was no audience of sci-fi readers when Wells wrote *The Time Machine*, it was not sci-fi when he wrote it. This makes perfect sense.

What is alarming is the suspicion that not only Stableford but other and more literate critics of the field are really sci-fi readers. Some of the most industrious promoters of science fiction, when they announce that s.f. is good, may only mean it is good junk. This is hardly more comforting than being told it is bad junk. Of the flock of pop culture enthusiasts who have descended on s.f. lately, how many are crypto-sci-fi-sniffers?

NOTE, 1990: The bulk of this essay is as it appeared in *Turning Points* in 1977; at Michael Bishop's request, I have added scores for the stories in *Nebula Awards 23*.

Although I tried my hardest to score these stories by the same standards I used thirteen years ago, I believe I detect a shift in my perceptions of what s.f. is, and I am certain I detect a shift in the perceptions of those who pick the Nebula winners and the stories in the anthology. The average score, 2.3, makes this collection borderline; four stories out of eleven are non-s.f.

I think it is a mistake of catastrophic proportions to bill the Nebula anthology as SFWA's choices for the best science fiction *and fantasy*. The Nebula was never intended to be and should not be an award for fantasy.

---

* Pronounced "skiffy."

It's true that there is no general agreement on where to draw the line. My solution to this problem when I was president of SFWA was to tell people, "If *you* think it's fantasy, don't nominate it and don't vote for it."

D.K

	science	technology, invention	future, past	extrapolation	scientific method	other places	catastrophes	total
Nebula Award Stories Eight								
"A Meeting with Medusa," Clarke	♦	♦	♦	♦	♦	♦		6
"Shaffery among the Immortals," Pohl	♦	♦			♦			3
"Patron of the Arts," Rotsler			♦	♦	♦			3
"When It Changed," Russ	♦	♦	♦			♦	♦	5
"On the Downhill Side," Ellison								0
"The Fifth Head of Cerberus," Wolfe	♦	♦	♦	♦	♦	♦		6
"When We Went to See the End of the World," Silverberg	♦	♦	♦	♦			♦	5
"Goat Song," Anderson	♦	♦	♦	♦				4
								average: 4.0
The Hugo Winners, Volume Two								
"The Dragon Masters," Vance	♦	♦	♦		♦			4
"No Truce with Kings," Anderson	♦	♦	♦		♦	♦		5
"Soldier, Ask Not," Dickson	♦	♦	♦		♦			4
"'Repent, Harlequin!' Said the Ticktockman," Ellison		♦	♦	♦				3
"The Last Castle," Vance	♦	♦	♦	♦		♦		5
"Neutron Star," Niven	♦	♦	♦	♦		♦		5
"Weyr Search," McCaffrey	♦	♦	♦	♦		♦		5
"Riders of the Purple Wage," Farmer	♦	♦	♦					3
"Gonna Roll the Bones," Leiber								0
"I Have No Mouth, and I Must Scream," Ellison	♦	♦	♦					3
"Nightwings," Silverberg	♦	♦	♦	♦				4
"The Sharing of Flesh," Anderson	♦	♦	♦	♦		♦		5

	science	technology, invention	future, past	extrapolation	scientific method	other places	catastrophes	total
"The Beast That Shouted Love at the Heart of the World," Ellison	♦					♦		2
"Time Considered as a Helix of Semiprecious Stones," Delany	♦	♦	♦	♦		♦		5

average: 3.8

The Science Fiction Hall of Fame, Volume One

	science	technology, invention	future, past	extrapolation	scientific method	other places	catastrophes	total
"A Martian Odyssey," Weinbaum	♦	♦	♦	♦	♦	♦		6
"Twilight," Campbell	♦	♦	♦	♦		♦	♦	6
"Helen O'Loy," del Rey			♦	♦	♦			3
"The Roads Must Roll," Heinlein			♦	♦	♦			3
"Microcosmic God," Sturgeon	♦	♦	♦		♦			4
"Nightfall," Asimov	♦				♦	♦	♦	4
"The Weapon Shop," van Vogt			♦	♦	♦		♦	4
"Mimsy Were the Borogoves," Padgett			♦	♦		♦		3
"Huddling Place," Simak			♦	♦	♦	♦	♦	5
"Arena," Brown		♦	♦	♦	♦	♦		5
"First Contact," Leinster		♦	♦	♦	♦	♦		5
"That Only a Mother," Merril			♦	♦	♦			3
"Scanners Live in Vain," Smith			♦	♦		♦		3
"Mars Is Heaven!," Bradbury			♦	♦	♦	♦		4
"The Little Black Bag," Kornbluth	♦	♦	♦	♦				4
"Born of Man and Woman," Matheson								0
"Coming Attraction," Leiber			♦	♦	♦		♦	4
"The Quest for Saint Aquin," Boucher			♦	♦	♦		♦	4
"Surface Tension," Blish	♦	♦	♦	♦		♦		5
"The Nine Billion Names of God," Clarke			♦		♦		♦	3
"It's a *Good* Life," Bixby						♦		1
"The Cold Equations," Goodwin			♦	♦	♦	♦		4
"Fondly Fahrenheit," Bester			♦	♦	♦			3
"The Country of the Kind," Knight			♦	♦	♦			3
"Flowers for Algernon," Keyes	♦		♦		♦			3
"A Rose for Ecclesiastes," Zelazny			♦	♦		♦	♦	4

average: 3.7

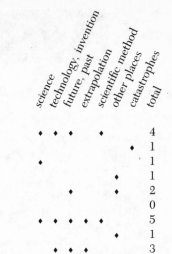

Nebula Awards 23

	science	technology, invention	future, past	extrapolation	scientific method	other places	catastrophes	total
"Forever Yours, Anna," Wilhelm	♦	♦	♦			♦		4
"Flowers of Edo," Sterling							♦	1
"Schwarzchild Radius," Willis	♦							1
"Witness," Williams						♦		1
"Judgment Call," Kessel				♦		♦		2
"The Glassblower's Dragon," Shepard								0
"Rachel in Love," Murphy	♦	♦	♦	♦	♦			5
"Angel," Cadigan						♦		1
"Freezeframe," Benford	♦	♦	♦					3
"The Blind Geometer," Robinson	♦	♦	♦					3
"Spelling God with the Wrong Blocks," Morrow	♦	♦	♦			♦		4

average: 2.3

Test Cases

	science	technology, invention	future, past	extrapolation	scientific method	other places	catastrophes	total
Gulliver's Travels, Swift	♦	♦		♦		♦		4
Walden Two, Skinner	♦				♦			2
1984, Orwell		♦	♦	♦				3
Watch the North Wind Rise, Graves				♦				1
"The Metamorphosis," Kafka								0
Winnie the Pooh, Milne						♦		1
The Wind in the Willows, Grahame								0
Alice in Wonderland, Carroll						♦		1
The Sword in the Stone, White	♦							1
Robinson Crusoe, Defoe				♦				1

RIPPLES IN THE DIRAC SEA

Geoffrey A. Landis

Geoff Landis has just completed a postdoctoral fellowship at NASA's Lewis Research Center in Cleveland. He writes science fiction grounded in the hard sciences, but his first story, "Elemental," a Hugo nominee for best novella of 1984, dealt with magical matters in a scientific context and appeared in *Analog*. Later work has been published in *Isaac Asimov's Science Fiction Magazine*, *Pulphouse*, and *Amazing Stories*.

About his award-winning short story, Geoff writes, " 'Ripples in the Dirac Sea' was an experimental story for me. Quite a number of disparate threads wove into the final narrative. One important thread was my feeling that a story involving time travel should have a nonlinear narrative to reflect the discontinuous way the characters experience time.

"I also wanted to see if it was possible to write a story in which real physics is presented. Very little of modern SF goes beyond the early quantum mechanics of Heisenberg and Schrödinger, work which is admittedly remarkable and beautiful, but by no means the end of the story. Here I tried to invoke some of the strangeness and beauty— I might even say sense of wonder—of the physics of Paul Adrien Maurice Dirac. In 'Ripples' I decided to explore the inconsistency between Dirac's relativistic quantum mechanics and the mathematics of infinity developed by Cantor and others (as far as I can tell, a quite real inconsistency). The Dirac sea is also real, not an invention of mine— despite the very science-fictional feel of an infinitely dense sea of negative energy that surrounds and permeates us.

"Among the other threads, one might distinguish my attempts to deal with a protagonist who has both great power and utter helplessness at the same time, my father's death of complications from a cerebral aneurysm in 1984, along with some of my thoughts about the philosophical implications of time travel, the sixties, dinosaurs, and various other things."

My death looms over me like a tidal wave, rushing toward me with an inexorable slow-motion majesty. And yet I flee, pointless though it may be.

I depart, and my ripples diverge to infinity, like waves smoothing out the footprints of forgotten travellers.

WE WERE SO CAREFUL to avoid any paradox, the day we first tested my machine. We pasted a duct-tape cross onto the concrete floor of a windowless lab, placed an alarm clock on the mark, and locked the door. An hour later we came back, removed the clock, and put the experimental machine in the room with a super-eight camera set in the coils. I aimed the camera at the X, and one of my grad students programmed the machine to send the camera back half an hour, stay in the past five minutes, then return. It left and returned without even a flicker. When we developed the film, the time on the clock was half an hour before we loaded the camera. We'd succeeded in opening the door into the past. We celebrated with coffee and champagne.

Now that I know a lot more about time, I understand our mistake, that we had not thought to put a movie camera in the room with the clock to photograph the machine as it arrived from the future. But what is obvious to me now was not obvious then.

I ARRIVE, and the ripples converge to the instant *now* from the vastness of the infinite sea.

To San Francisco, June 8, 1965. A warm breeze riffles across dandelion-speckled grass, while puffy white clouds form strange and wondrous shapes for our entertainment. Yet so very few people pause to enjoy it. They scurry about, diligently preoccupied, believing that if they act busy enough, they must be important. "They hurry so," I say. "Why can't they slow down, sit back, enjoy the day?"

"They're trapped in the illusion of time," says Dancer. He lies on his back and blows a soap bubble, his hair flopping back long and brown in a time when "long" hair meant anything below the ear. A puff of breeze takes the bubble down the hill and into the stream of pedestrians. They uniformly ignore it. "They're caught in the belief that what they do is important to some future goal." The bubble pops against a briefcase, and Dancer blows another. "You and I, we know how false an illusion that is. There is no past, no future, only the now, eternal."

He was right, more right than he could have possibly imagined.

Once I, too, was preoccupied and self-important. Once I was brilliant and ambitious. I was twenty-eight years old, and I made the greatest discovery in the world.

FROM MY hiding place I watched him come up the service elevator. He was thin almost to the point of starvation, a nervous man with stringy blond hair and an armless white T-shirt. He looked up and down the hall, but failed to see me hidden in the janitor's closet. Under each arm was a two-gallon can of gasoline, in each hand another. He put down three of the cans and turned the last one upside down, then walked down the hall, spreading a pungent trail of gasoline. His face was blank. When he started on the second can, I figured it was about enough. As he passed my hiding spot, I walloped him over the head with a wrench, and called hotel security. Then I went back to the closet and let the ripples of time converge.

I arrived in a burning room, flames licking forth at me, the heat almost too much to bear. I gasped for breath—a mistake—and punched at the keypad.

Notes on the Theory and Practice of Time Travel:

1. Travel is possible only into the past.
2. The object transported will return to exactly the time and place of departure.
3. It is not possible to bring objects from the past to the present.
4. Actions in the past cannot change the present.

ONE TIME I tried jumping back a hundred million years, to the Cretaceous, to see dinosaurs. All the picture books show the landscape as being covered with dinosaurs. I spent three days wandering around a swamp—in my new tweed suit—before catching even a glimpse of any dinosaur larger than a basset hound. That one—a theropod of some sort, I don't know which—skittered away as soon as it caught a whiff of me. Quite a disappointment.

MY PROFESSOR in transfinite math used to tell stories about a hotel with an infinite number of rooms. One day all the rooms are full, and another guest arrives. "No problem," says the desk clerk. He moves the person in room one into room two, the person in room two into room three, and so on. Presto! A vacant room.

A little later, an infinite number of guests arrive. "No problem," says the dauntless desk clerk. He moves the person in room one into room two, the person in room two into room four, the person in room three into room six, and so on. Presto! An infinite number of rooms vacant.

My time machine works on just that principle.

AGAIN I RETURN to 1965, the fixed point, the strange attractor to my chaotic trajectory. In years of wandering I've met countless people, but Daniel Ranien—Dancer—was the only one who truly had his head together. He had a soft, easy smile, a battered secondhand guitar, and as much wisdom as it has taken me a hundred lifetimes to learn. I've known him in good times and bad, in summer days with blue skies that we swore would last a thousand years, in days of winter blizzards with drifted snow piled high over our heads. In happier times we have laid roses into the barrels of rifles; we have laid our bodies across the city streets in the midst of riots, and not been hurt. And I have been with him when he died, once, twice, a hundred times over.

He died on February 8, 1969, a month into the reign of King Richard the Trickster and his court fool Spiro, a year before Kent State and Altamont and the secret war in Cambodia slowly strangled the summer of dreams. He died, and there was—is—nothing I can do. The last time he died I dragged him to a hospital, where I screamed and ranted until finally I convinced them to admit him for observation, though nothing seemed wrong with him. With X rays and arteriograms and radioactive tracers, they found the incipient bubble in his brain; they drugged him, shaved his beautiful long brown hair, and operated on him, cutting out the offending capillary and tying it off neatly. When the anesthetic wore off, I sat in the hospital room and held his hand. There were big purple blotches under his eyes. He gripped my hand and stared, silent, into space. Visiting hours or no, I didn't let them throw me out of the room. He just stared. In the gray hours just before dawn he sighed softly and died. There was nothing at all that I could do.

———

TIME TRAVEL is subject to two constraints: conservation of energy, and causality. The energy to appear in the past is only borrowed from the Dirac sea, and since ripples in the Dirac sea propagate in the negative t direction, transport is only into the past. Energy is conserved in the present as long as the object transported returns with zero time delay, and the principle of causality assures that actions in the past cannot change the present. For example, what if you went into the past and killed your father? Who, then, would invent the time machine?

Once I tried to commit suicide by murdering my father, before he met my mother, twenty-three years before I was born. It changed nothing, of course, and even when I did it, I knew it would change nothing. But you have to try these things. How else could I know for sure?

NEXT WE TRIED sending a rat back. It made the trip through the Dirac sea and back undamaged. Then we tried a trained rat, one we borrowed from the psychology lab across the green without telling them what we wanted it for. Before its little trip it had been taught to run through a maze to get a piece of bacon. Afterwards, it ran the maze as fast as ever.

We still had to try it on a human. I volunteered myself and didn't allow anyone to talk me out of it. By trying it on myself, I dodged the university regulations about experimenting on humans.

The dive into the negative-energy sea felt like nothing at all. One moment I stood in the center of the loop of Renselz coils, watched by my two grad students and a technician; the next I was alone, and the clock had jumped back exactly one hour. Alone in a locked room with nothing but a camera and a clock, that moment was the high point of my life.

The moment when I first met Dancer was the low point. I was in Berkeley, a bar called Trishia's, slowly getting trashed. I'd been doing that a lot, caught between omnipotence and despair. It was 1967. 'Frisco then—it was the middle of the hippy era—seemed somehow appropriate.

There was a girl, sitting at a table with a group from the university. I walked over to her table and invited myself to sit down. I told her she didn't exist, that her whole world didn't exist, it was all created by the fact that I was watching, and would disappear back into the sea of unreality as soon as I stopped looking. Her name was Lisa, and she argued back. Her friends, bored, wandered off, and in a while Lisa realized just how drunk I was. She dropped a bill on the table and walked out into the foggy night.

I followed her out. When she saw me following, she clutched her purse and bolted.

He was suddenly there under the streetlight. For a second I thought he was a girl. He had bright blue eyes and straight brown hair down to his shoulders. He wore an embroidered Indian shirt, with a silver and turquoise medallion around his neck and a guitar slung across his back. He was lean, almost stringy, and moved like a dancer or a karate master. But it didn't occur to me to be afraid of him.

He looked me over. "That won't solve your problem, you know," he said.

And instantly I was ashamed. I was no longer sure exactly what I'd had in mind or why I'd followed her. It had been years since I'd first fled my death, and I had come to think of others as unreal, since nothing I could do would permanently affect them. My head was spinning. I slid down the wall and sat down, hard, on the sidewalk. What had I come to?

He helped me back into the bar, fed me orange juice and pretzels, and got me to talk. I told him everything. Why not, since I could unsay anything I said, undo anything I did? But I had no urge to. He listened to it all, saying nothing. No one else had ever listened to the whole story before. I can't explain the effect it had on me. For un-countable years I'd been alone, and then, if only for a moment . . . It hit me with the intensity of a tab of acid. If only for a moment, I was not alone.

We left arm in arm. Half a block away, Dancer stopped, in front of an alley. It was dark.

"Something not quite right here." His voice had a puzzled tone.

I pulled him back. "Hold on. You don't want to go down there—" He pulled free and walked in. After a slight hesitation, I followed.

The alley smelled of old beer, mixed with garbage and stale vomit. In a moment, my eyes became adjusted to the dark.

Lisa was cringing in a corner behind some trash cans. Her clothes had been cut away with a knife, and lay scattered around. Blood showed dark on her thighs and one arm. She didn't seem to see us. Dancer squatted down next to her and said something soft. She didn't respond. He pulled off his shirt and wrapped it around her, then cradled her in his arms and picked her up. "Help me get her to my apartment."

"Apartment, hell. We'd better call the police," I said.

"Call the pigs? Are you crazy? You want them to rape her, too?"

I'd forgotten; this was the sixties. Between the two of us, we got her to Dancer's VW bug and took her to his apartment in The Hashbury. He explained it to me quietly as we drove, a dark side of the summer of love that I'd not seen before. It was greasers, he said. They come down to Berkeley because they heard that hippie chicks gave it away free, and get nasty when they met one who thought otherwise.

Her wounds were mostly superficial. Dancer cleaned her, put her in bed, and stayed up all night beside her, talking and crooning and making little reassuring noises. I slept on one of the mattresses in the hall. When I woke up in the morning, they were both in his bed. She was sleeping quietly. Dancer was awake, holding her. I was aware enough to realize that that was all he was doing, holding her, but still I felt a sharp pang of jealousy, and didn't know which one of them it was that I was jealous of.

Notes for a Lecture on Time Travel

The beginning of the twentieth century was a time of intellectual giants, whose likes will perhaps never again be equaled. Einstein had just invented relativity, Heisenberg and Schrödinger quantum mechanics, but nobody yet knew how to make the two theories consistent with each other. In 1930, a new person tackled the problem. His name was Paul Dirac. He was twenty-eight years old. He succeeded where the others had failed.

His theory was an unprecedented success, except for one small detail. According to Dirac's theory, a particle could have either positive or negative energy. What did this mean, a particle of negative energy? How could something have negative energy? And why don't ordinary—positive energy—particles fall down into these negative energy states, releasing a lot of free energy in the process?

You or I might have merely stipulated that it was impossible for an ordinary positive energy particle to make a transition to negative energy. But Dirac was not an ordinary man. He was a genius, the greatest physicist of all, and he had an answer. If every possible negative energy state was already occupied, a particle couldn't drop into a negative energy state. Ah ha! So Dirac postulated that the entire universe is entirely filled with negative energy particles. They surround us, permeate us, in the vacuum of outer space and in the center of the earth, every possible place a particle could be. An infinitely dense "sea" of negative energy particles. The Dirac sea.

His argument had holes in it, but that comes later.

ONCE I WENT to visit the crucifixion. I took a jet from Santa Cruz to Tel Aviv, and a bus from Tel Aviv to Jerusalem. On a hill outside the city, I dove through the Dirac sea.

I arrived in my three-piece suit. No way to help that, unless I wanted to travel naked. The land was surprisingly green and fertile, more so than I'd expected. The hill was now a farm, covered with grape arbors and olive trees. I hid the coils behind some rocks and walked down to the road. I didn't get far. Five minutes on the road, I ran into a group of people. They had dark hair, dark skin, and wore clean white tunics. Romans? Jews? Egyptians? How could I tell? They spoke to me, but I couldn't understand a word. After a while two of them held me, while a third searched me. Were they robbers, searching for money? Romans, searching for some kind of identity papers? I realized how naive I'd been to think I could just find appropriate dress and somehow blend in with the crowds. Finding nothing, the one who'd done the search carefully and methodically beat me up. At last he pushed me face down in the dirt. While the other two held me down, he pulled out a dagger and slashed through the tendons on the back of each leg. They were merciful, I guess. They left me with my life. Laughing and talking incomprehensibly among themselves, they walked away.

My legs were useless. One of my arms was broken. It took me four hours to crawl back up the hill, dragging myself with my good arm. Occasionally people would pass by on the road, studiously ignoring me. Once I reached the hiding place, pulling out the Renselz coils and wrapping them around me was pure agony. By the time I entered return on the keypad I was wavering in and out of consciousness. I finally managed to get it entered. From the Dirac sea the ripples converged

and I was in my hotel room in Santa Cruz. The ceiling had started to fall in where the girders had burned through. Fire alarms shrieked and wailed, but there was no place to run. The room was filled with dense, acrid smoke. Trying not to breathe, I punched out a code on the keypad, somewhen, anywhen other than that one instant

and I was in the hotel room, five days before. I gasped for breath. The woman in the hotel bed shrieked and tried to pull the covers up. The man screwing her was too busy to pay any mind. They weren't real anyway. I ignored them and paid a little more attention to where to go next. Back to '65, I figured. I punched in the combo

and was standing in an empty room on the thirtieth floor of a hotel just under construction. A full moon gleamed on the silhouettes of silent construction cranes. I flexed my legs experimentally. Already the memory of the pain was beginning to fade. That was reasonable, because it had never happened. Time travel. It's not immortality, but it's got to be the next best thing.

You can't change the past, no matter how you try.

IN THE MORNING I explored Dancer's pad. It was crazy, a small third-floor apartment a block off Haight Ashbury that had been converted into something from another planet. The floor of the apartment had been completely covered with old mattresses, on top of which was a jumbled confusion of quilts, pillows, Indian blankets, stuffed animals. You took off your shoes before coming in—Dancer always wore sandals, leather ones from Mexico with soles cut from old tires. The radiators, which didn't work anyway, were spray painted in Day-Glo colors. The walls were plastered with posters: Peter Max prints, brightly colored Eschers, poems by Allen Ginsberg, record album covers, peace-rally posters, a "Haight Is Love" sign, FBI ten-most-wanted posters torn down from a post office with the photos of famous antiwar activists circled in magic marker, a huge peace symbol in passion-pink. Some of the posters were illuminated with black light and luminesced in impossible colors. The air was musty with incense and the banana-sweet smell of dope. In one corner a record player played *Sergeant Pepper's Lonely Hearts Club Band* on infinite repeat. Whenever one copy of the album got too scratchy, inevitably one of Dancer's friends would bring in another.

He never locked the door. "Somebody wants to rip me off, well, hey, they probably need it more than I do anyway, okay? It's cool." People dropped by any time of day or night.

I let my hair grow long. Dancer and Lisa and I spent that summer together, laughing, playing guitar, making love, writing silly poems and sillier songs, experimenting with drugs. That was when LSD was blooming onto the scene like sunflowers, when people were still unafraid of the strange and beautiful world on the other side of reality. That was a time to live. I knew that it was Dancer that Lisa truly loved, not me, but in those days free love was in the air like the scent of poppies, and it didn't matter. Not much, anyway.

Notes for a Lecture on Time Travel (continued)

Having postulated that all of space was filled with an infinitely dense sea of negative energy particles, Dirac went further and asked if we, in the positive-energy universe, could interact with this negative-energy sea. What would happen, say, if you added enough energy to an electron to take it out of the negative-energy sea? Two things: first, you would create an electron, seemingly out of nowhere. Second, you would leave behind a "hole" in the sea. The hole, Dirac realized, would act as if it were a particle itself, a particle exactly like an electron except for one thing: it would have the opposite charge. But if the hole ever encountered an electron, the electron would fall back into the Dirac sea, annihilating both electron and hole in a bright burst of energy. Eventually they gave the hole in the Dirac sea a name of its own: "positron." When Anderson discovered the positron two years later to vindicate Dirac's theory, it was almost an anticlimax.

And over the next fifty years, the reality of the Dirac sea was almost ignored by physicists. Antimatter, the holes in the sea, was the important feature of the theory; the rest was merely a mathematical artifact.

Seventy years later, I remembered the story my transfinite math teacher told and put it together with Dirac's theory. Like putting an extra guest into a hotel with an infinite number of rooms, I figured out how to borrow energy from the Dirac sea. Or, to put it another way: I learned how to make waves.

And waves on the Dirac sea travel backward in time.

NEXT WE HAD to try something more ambitious. We had to send a human back farther into history, and obtain proof of the trip. Still we were afraid to make alterations in the past, even though the mathematics stated that the present could not be changed.

We pulled out our movie camera and chose our destinations carefully.

In September of 1853 a traveler named William Hapland and his family crossed the Sierra Nevadas to reach the California coast. His daughter Sarah kept a journal, and in it she recorded how, as they reached the crest of Parker's Ridge, she caught her first glimpse of the distant Pacific ocean exactly as the sun touched the horizon, "in a blays of cryms'n glorie," as she wrote. The journal still exists. It was easy enough for us to conceal ourselves and a movie camera in a cleft of rocks above the pass, to photograph the weary travelers in their ox-drawn wagon as they crossed.

The second target was the great San Francisco earthquake of 1906. From a deserted warehouse that would survive the quake—but not the following fire—we watched and took movies as buildings tumbled down around us and embattled firemen in horse-drawn fire-trucks strove in vain to quench a hundred blazes. Moments before the fire reached our building, we fled into the present.

The films were spectacular.

We were ready to tell the world.

There was a meeting of the AAAS in Santa Cruz in a month. I called the program chairman and wangled a spot as an invited speaker without revealing just what we'd accomplished to date. I planned to show those films at the talk. They were to make us instantly famous.

THE DAY that Dancer died we had a going-away party, just Lisa and Dancer and I. He knew he was going to die; I'd told him and somehow he believed me. He always believed me. We stayed up all night, playing Dancer's secondhand guitar, painting psychedelic designs on each other's bodies with greasepaint, competing against each other in a marathon game of cutthroat Monopoly, doing a hundred silly, ordinary things that took meaning only from the fact that it was the last time. About four in the morning, as the glimmer of false-dawn began to show in the sky, we went down to the bay and, huddling together for warmth, went tripping. Dancer took the largest dose, since he wasn't going to return. The last thing he said, he told us not to let our dreams die; to stay together.

We buried Dancer, at city expense, in a welfare grave. We split up three days later.

I kept in touch with Lisa, vaguely. In the late seventies she went back to school, first for an MBA, then law school. I think she was married for a while. We wrote each other cards on Christmas for a while, then I lost track of her. Years later, I got a letter from her. She said that she was finally able to forgive me for causing Dan's death.

It was a cold and foggy February day, but I knew I could find warmth in 1965. The ripples converged.

ANTICIPATED QUESTIONS from the audience:

Q (old, stodgy professor): It seems to me this proposed temporal jump of yours violates the law of conservation of mass/energy. For example, when a transported object is transported into the past, a quantity of mass will appear to vanish from the present, in clear violation of the conservation law.

A (me): Since the return is to the exact time of departure, the mass present is constant.

Q: Very well, but what about the arrival in the past? Doesn't this violate the conservation law?

A: No. The energy needed is taken from the Dirac sea, by the mechanism I explain in detail in the *Phys Rev* paper. When the object returns to the "future," the energy is restored to the sea.

Q (intense young physicist): Then doesn't Heisenberg uncertainty limit the amount of time that can be spent in the past?

A: A good question. The answer is yes, but because we borrow an infinitesimal amount of energy from an infinite number of particles, the amount of time spent in the past can be arbitrarily large. The only limitation is that you must leave the past an instant before you depart from the present.

IN HALF AN HOUR I was scheduled to present the paper that would rank my name with Newton's and Galileo's—and Dirac's. I was twenty-eight years old, the same age as Dirac when he announced his theory. I was a firebrand, preparing to set the world aflame. I was nervous, rehearsing the speech in my hotel room. I took a swig out of an old Coke that one of my grad students had left sitting on top of the television. The evening news team was babbling on, but I wasn't listening.

I never delivered that talk. The hotel had already started to burn; my death was already foreordained. Tie neat, I inspected myself in the mirror, then walked to the door. The doorknob was warm. I opened it onto a sheet of fire. Flame burst through the opened door like a ravening dragon. I stumbled backward, staring at the flames in amazed fascination.

Somewhere in the hotel I heard a scream, and all at once I broke free of my spell. I was on the thirtieth story; there was no way out. My thought was for my machine. I rushed across the room and threw open the case holding the time machine. With swift, sure fingers I pulled out the Renselz coils and wrapped them around my body. The carpet had caught on fire, a sheet of flame between me and any possible escape. Holding my breath to avoid suffocation, I punched an entry into the keyboard and dove into time.

I return to that moment again and again. When I hit the final key, the air was already nearly unbreathable with smoke. I had about thirty seconds left to live, then. Over the years I've nibbled away my time down to ten seconds or less.

I live on borrowed time. So do we all, perhaps. But I know when and where my debt will fall due.

DANCER DIED on February 9, 1969. It was a dim, foggy day. In the morning he said he had a headache. That was unusual, for Dancer. He never had headaches. We decided to go for a walk through the fog. It was beautiful, as if we were alone in a strange, formless world. I'd forgotten about his headache altogether, until, looking out across the sea of fog from the park over the bay, he fell over. He was dead before the ambulance came. He died with a secret smile on his face. I've never understood that smile. Maybe he was smiling because the pain was gone.

Lisa committed suicide two days later.

YOU ORDINARY PEOPLE, you have the chance to change the future. You can father children, write novels, sign petitions, invent new machines, go to cocktail parties, run for president. You affect the future with everything you do. No matter what I do, I cannot. It is too late for that, for me. My actions are written in flowing water. And having no effect, I have no responsibilities. It makes no difference what I do, not at all.

When I first fled the fire into the past, I tried everything I could to change it. I stopped the arsonist, I argued with mayors, I even went to my own house and told myself not to go to the conference.

But that's not how time works. No matter what I do, talk to a governor or dynamite the hotel, when I reach that critical moment— the present, my destiny, the moment I left—I vanish from whenever I was, and return to the hotel room, the fire approaching ever closer. I have about ten seconds left. Every time I dive through the Dirac sea, everything I changed in the past vanishes. Sometimes I pretend that the changes I make in the past create new futures, though I know this is not the case. When I return to the present, all the changes are wiped out by the ripples of the converging wave, like erasing a blackboard after a class.

Someday I will return and meet my destiny. But for now, I live in the past. It's a good life, I suppose. You get used to the fact that nothing you do will ever have any effect on the world. It gives you a feeling of freedom. I've been places no one has ever been, seen things no one alive has ever seen. I've given up physics, of course. Nothing I discover could endure past that fatal night in Santa Cruz. Maybe some people would continue for the sheer joy of knowledge. For me, the point is missing.

But there are compensations. Whenever I return to the hotel room, nothing is changed but my memories. I am again twenty-eight, again wearing the same three-piece suit, again have the fuzzy taste of stale cola in my mouth. Every time I return, I use up a little bit of time. One day I will have no time left.

Dancer, too, will never die. I won't let him. Every time I get to that final February morning, the day he died, I return to 1965, to that perfect day in June. He doesn't know me, he never knows me. But we meet on that hill, the only two willing to enjoy the day doing nothing. He lies on his back, idly fingering chords on his guitar, blowing bubbles and staring into the clouded blue sky. Later I will introduce him to Lisa. She won't know us either, but that's okay. We've got plenty of time.

"Time," I say to Dancer, lying in the park on the hill. "There's so much time."

"All the time there is," he says.

THE AVALANCHE: A VIEW ON THE SF AND FANTASY NOVELS OF 1989

Ian Watson

Ian Watson has written the annual survey essay in these volumes ever since *Nebula Awards 23*. He is the author of such idea-rich science-fiction novels as, among many others, *The Embedding*, *Alien Embassy*, *Miracle Visitors*, *Deathhunter*, *Whores of Babylon*, and *The Flies of Memory*, as well as a trio of unsettling, idiosyncratic, issue-driven horror novels, *The Power*, *The Fire Worm*, and *Meat*. His most recent books are *Inquisitor* (the first volume in a trilogy entitled *The Inquisition War*, set in the gothic Warhammer universe of the forty-first millennium) and a new story collection, *Stalin's Teardrops*.

This year, Ian writes exclusively about 1989's novels. Had Ian also tried to read a major portion of 1989's short fiction, he would have gone mad. By focusing on novels, however, he retained both his sanity and his critical acumen. The following essay offers a fast-paced and cogent overview of the more conspicuous, controversial, and/or distinguished science-fiction and fantasy novels of 1989.

The winners of the Nebula Award for the best science fiction and fantasy of 1989 are co-celebrants in a significant anniversary, for this is the twenty-fifth year of those awards. So it would seem timely to praise Caesar (as it were)—except that Caesar looks in some danger of being buried, beneath an avalanche of books.

Once upon a time, *Locus*—the "newspaper of the science fiction field"—consisted of a few duplicated pages held by a humble staple. A typical issue in 1973 took twenty-odd lines of largish type to list the new books scheduled for the month of July. Nowadays *Locus* is a fully professional glossy magazine of eighty-odd pages packed with advertising. The September 1989 issue devoted no less than *eight* whole pages of tiny type to listing the output of SF and fantasy promised by American publishers during the next several months. An avalanche indeed.

And an avalanche causes casualties.

Good books are buried. Out of print before the reviews can appear, they are shoved aside to make way for the next consignment of titles, and are stripped of their covers, or remaindered. Like stags in rut, compelled by their glands to roar and display macho, editors compete for prominence, paying some hysterically high advances that are very unlikely to be recouped, with the result that a book receiving such an advance must be a dramatic rapid success or it is a disaster. The "mid-list"—formerly the home of much that was original and meritorious, though not blatantly commercial—is cramped and given short economic shrift. Meanwhile, brand-name books are concocted in order to ape past successes. The "worlds" of classic authors are franchised. Hype teaches readers to consume processed fodder. The stick-and-carrot routine trains authors to supply such and to imagine that they are genuinely pursuing a successful career in the field of imaginative fiction. Early fame can ruin an author, causing burnout or turning that author into a circus animal, yet insufficient fame can swiftly relegate an author to frustrating obscurity. As Greg Bear said in a recent interview in *Vector*, the journal of the British Science Fiction Association, "Science fiction eats its authors."

To parody Charles Dickens rather than Shakespeare, for science fiction and fantasy literature this is at once the best of times and the worst of times.

Joe Haldeman's novel *Buying Time* inadvertently provides a telling metaphor for the circumstances of science-fiction authors. Haldeman's 1974 novel *The Forever War* propelled him to stardom, and his second offering, *Mindbridge*, netted what was in terms of the mid-1970s the Big Advance. *Buying Time* signals a loud return after a period of something resembling eclipse for this author. The frisson of the million-dollar advance, not to mention immortality—of the literary kind—is perhaps the actual psychological subtext of *Buying Time*.

The Stileman process offers medical rejuvenation for a period of ten years provided that the purchaser hands over all assets—minimum, a cool one million pounds sterling. The nominal reason for this price is to prevent huge amounts of money from accumulating in the hands of immortals. At the same time, as Scott Fitzgerald might have put it, Stileman immortals are different from you and me. Reduced to poverty, any such former millionaire knows how to make another million easily, wherewith to buy a subsequent rejuvenation. This run-for-your-life thriller exposes the ten-year limit as a deliberate fix. However, the megalomaniac conspiracy to deny immortality to everybody is basically pointless. As an artificial intelligence finally points out, there would never be enough surgeons to meet the demand.

The world of Haldeman's hero is a *Playboy* wet dream, with hard-boiled edges. Ultimately, the hero achieves transcendence, courtesy of a trick with time similar to that used in Herbert's *Heretics of Dune* to redeem the plot line, and he becomes a superhuman immortal, paragon of a new elite. What more could one wish for? Meanwhile, the majority of the human race will continue to die of starvation.

Alas, the sums don't add up. In a world where major trading nations went down the tube, a 10 percent inflation rate over *seven decades* is unbelievable; and in a crucial scene where the hero must bargain for a spaceship, the author forgets his own inflation factor. The vendor simply wouldn't receive enough money to buy another Stileman treatment. Such is the dazzling magic of the figure one million. Lacking the requisite million, by the way, Nobel laureates receive immortality free. One is tempted to ask whether Nebula laureates should likewise receive immortality. Thus, if we read *Buying Time* metaphorically.

Nor, in today's publishing world, do the sums seem to add up, either, a lot of the time.

The new superstar of 1989 was undoubtedly Dan Simmons, though without too much accompanying hoo-ha, perhaps because Simmons's four novels to date are so remarkably different from one another in tone and theme. Nineteen eighty-nine saw publication of a horror epic, *Carrion Comfort*; a virtuoso far-future SF novel, *Hyperion*; and the peculiarly quiet *Phases of Gravity*. This last concerns an astronaut who once walked on the moon and whose subsequent life has seemed hollow. Simmons hardly adopts the usual American approach to the space adventure, being quite Ballardian in mood—melancholy, though intense. Eventually, the astronaut Baedeker (whose name is that of an old-fashioned guidebook) achieves transcendence and a vision of a future moon base, the *real* Real Stuff, courtesy of an Indian place of power. En route, young Maggie (of the pale, heavy breasts) dispenses sex and wisdom, rekindling the fire in the ageing Baedeker. For no very logical reason this girlfriend of Baedeker's dropout son plays the role of the goddess who sleeps with the mortal. The son seems deeply alienated from his dad, yet he conspires in this ploy, and eventually turns into a neat, straight citizen who is determined to join the armed forces. Simmons mixes a peculiar cocktail of motivations, unless we view events as being nudged by some numinous power.

Hyperion is a prodigy of a book: luminous, erotic, exotic, nightmarish, and much else. A small band of pilgrims journey towards the enigmatic time-tombs on a planet named after a poem by Keats, to an encounter with the deadly, worshipped Shrike, which defies physical laws. In turn diplomat, poet, priest, soldier, detective, and scholar tell very different "Canterbury Tales" redolent of film noir, of theo-anthropological SF, of Delany, of Gibson. These build towards revelations of the most terrible manipulations that lurk behind the seemingly benign facade of galactic society. Some aspects of this lustrous, eloquent novel are self-indulgent, yet Simmons has ample justification for indulging himself.

Every dog will have its day—including dead dogs. In my essay on the SF and fantasy of 1988 ("Themes and Variations" in *Nebula Awards 24*), I remarked how some authors seem almost to be involved in collective research projects. In *Hyperion*, we visit a simulation of early nineteenth-century Rome re-created by cyberminds and inhabited by a "cybrid" John Keats. The same venue and author also feature in Tim Powers's wondrously gonzo reinterpretation of the "romantic agony," *The Stress of Her Regard*. Keats—and Byron and Shelley, who form the main focus of this daring, and moving, exercise in Grand Guignol—were actually kin to a very peculiar variety of vampires. After the minimal female characterization in Powers's *On Stranger Tides* (1987), the schizoid automaton sister who hunts, then redeems, the hero of his new novel is even more remarkable than the other remarkable characters; moreover, there are few jarring modernist notes.

The illustrious dead enjoy no rest, either, in Robert Silverberg's *To the Land of the Living*, a streetwisely lyrical version of that synchrony—or coexistence in time—whereby Earth's past and present and future increasingly seem liable to meld and mutate and permutate in SF. Gilgamesh, Helen of Troy, Picasso, Lenin, and the prototype of Conan: the gang's all here, in an afterlife offering an alternative type of immortality, together with a chance to step through a mystic portal into twentieth-century New York.

Immortality is likewise the theme of veteran Poul Anderson's big-screen return, in *The Boat of a Million Years*. Romantically heroic, almost bardic at times, though with an eye firmly fixed on the space-time cosmos and the dynamics of social evolution, Anderson conducts his little band of freak immortals out to the stars to encounter alien civilizations and to discover that they themselves are unique in their questing. As biological civilizations mature, these may well become inward-looking. Even if not, there's simply no point in venturing much farther than a hundred light-years from home due to sheer data overload. Machine civilizations are not constrained thus; yet by the same token there's no mutual threat between bio-cultures and cyber-cultures.

Such a threat does exist in Gregory Benford's *Tides of Light*, where machine civilization is determined to exterminate biological life including the pathetic remnants of the once-great human race. More incandescent than its predecessor, *Great Sky River* (1987), *Tides of Light* expands beyond that earlier minimalist terrain, evoking wonders and enigmas. In this well-integrated, cunningly nested tale, Benford elegantly and vividly evokes the way an alien views a human being. Descriptions of spacescapes are painterly, while science becomes lyrical, thrilling narrative. There's often a certain irritatingly mandarin tone to Benford's narratives; and his art hardly lies in the concealment of art but rather in exquisite consciousness of how well he is deploying words and wisdom, fusing fiction and science. By concentrating on cameo scenes—some of them mega-cameos—*Tides of Light* avoids pomposity.

Benford writes much about fighting without in any sense writing military science fiction, which forms a sizable sub-genre these days. If Joel Rosenberg's *Not for Glory* represents a well-crafted specimen of that rather routine ilk—starring extraterrestrial Israeli mercenaries— Jack McDevitt's *A Talent for War* is a novel about mega-violence that deploys little direct violence at all, save for a bomb planted on an aircraft with the aim of scaring, not slaughtering. We observe simulated, reconstructed conflict, and wonder for a while whether anyone will even be genuinely wounded in this tale of a terrible bygone war. Libraries, museums, and brandies abound; the style is "mature," like a malt scotch. McDevitt lends a new meaning to archaeology, with his perfectly plausible future archaeology of spaceships. It is as though the Henry James of "The Author of Beltrafio" has written a historical detective story set in the future, to probe the nature of lonely and perhaps futile heroism—the brooding, sacrificial, elegiac nobility of battle against superior odds.

Jeffrey Carver's *From a Changeling Star* also offers a sophisticated treatment of future galactic conflict. As in Delany's *Babel-17*, one set of conspirators has turned the hero into a sabotage weapon, in this case by using nanotechnology to reconfigure his neural structures. Thus the hero cannot trust his own thoughts. Nanotechnology, the possible future science of atom-size machines, is of course the newest entrée on the SF menu. The superscience plot involves blowing up the star Betelguese by snaring a cosmic string, such strings being another fashionable device taken from the cutting edge of theoretical physics. (Benford uses one as an apple corer to quarry a planet.) The explosion of Betelguese will open a dimensional gateway, thus increasing the volume of habitable space, this project being the cause of the conflict. Multiple betrayals movingly crescendo to a deathly yet transcendent climax, with stars revealed as conscious beings, and with victim and assassin, betrayer and betrayed united in a new metalife.

Cosmic skulduggery and detective story provide the skeleton for Mike Resnick's episodic *Ivory*, wherein the last Masai searches for sacred elephant tusks lost for thousands of years. Unlike in *A Talent for War*, the places, battles, and artifacts are cut from colored cardboard, and the narrative dances along like a zombie, jerking vigorously but dead at heart. There are rattling good yarns, and there are yarns that merely rattle noisily.

Charles Sheffield's *Proteus Unbound* is one of the former. Where Resnick has cartoonlike space pirates and absurd 300-strong starship convoys transporting gold, Sheffield's space pirates—and his mysterious Dancing Man, and secret weapon—recapture the frisson of early Bester allied to Varley. Sheffield's superscience is "form control," the ability to alter the body radically; and his revelation is that black-hole kernels are intelligent.

The current maestro of superscience is perhaps Greg Bear. Following on from *Eon* (1985), *Eternity* posits children constructed in the memory of a supercity prior to incarnation, should they prove of high enough caliber. The enemy aliens, the Jarts, turn out to be single-minded crusaders obeying a teleological imperative to study and store life in service of the ends of knowledge, thus assisting the Final Mind, the Godhead in which evolution will culminate. The Final Mind will ultimately harvest all life, so as to impose a pattern on the next cycle of the universe. It sends an avatar back in time to persuade our superhuman (though hypocritical and confused) descendants to re-open the superscience superhighway through space-time and then destroy it because that "tapeworm" is preventing the universe from ending suitably. Big issues! And of course a Final Mind can do almost anything in space and time, so the author holds an unbeatable trump card. In my survey essay in *Nebula Awards 23*, "The World Renews Itself," I suggested that total cosmic answers can reduce awesome mystery to childishness. *Eternity* does indulge somewhat in shorthand and miracles, besides being in large part static compared with its predecessor due to the burden of unfolding explanation. Nor does superscience, in its plot-rescuing role of *deus ex machina*, necessarily boost a book into persuasive overdrive. Bob Shaw's *The Fugitive Worlds*, conclusion to his Ragged Astronauts trilogy, recaptures the quaintly heroic magic of low-tech balloon flights through space only to toss this virtue away by allowing silly superior aliens to pull tricks out of hats, a case of superscience "underdrive." The hero's doughty sword becomes a supersword, and soon he is miraculously invulnerable to boot. At the critical moment, Greg Bear also unwraps a cache of secret superweapons, but *Eternity* remains numinous, a nova in the same constellation as *Childhood's End*.

Hypocrisy, confused motives, and elegant chicanery permeate the galaxy of Iain Banks's *The Player of Games*, in which a games master with a streak of dishonesty in his world-weary soul is blackmailed by a delightfully idiosyncratic machine into competing against the games gurus of an alien empire. An extraordinarily complex game structures the power politics and social mores of the alien society, which rather satirizes our own. As opposed to the luxurious, laissez-faire "Culture" from which the player hails, these aliens conduct their affairs op-pressively, with sex and torture on TV and skid row around the corner. However, our player has been set up by his own Culture, and though he does not end up destroyed, as does the protagonist of *Consider Phlebas* (1987), Banks's previous novel set in another zone of the same milieu, he is distinctly disenchanted. In a further exercise of guile, the identity of the narrator remains masked until the very end. *The Player of Games* is ingenious, sophisticated, socially incisive, and energetically paced.

Still spanning galaxies, David Zindell's debut novel, *Neverness*, is a radiant, passionate, tormented, and questing book exploring the wonders and tragedies of being human, and somewhat other than human. From its wonderful city with color-coded streets of ice, via its ice age Neanderthal community, to its vividly envisioned mathematical spaces, the book enchants. In a sense it's an everything book, which the most ambitious of first novels often tend to be, and there are strong echoes of other major SF authors whom Zindell admires. Here are reflections of Wolfe, Bishop, Silverberg, Herbert, yet never in a merely imitative way. The black gamma-phages that resist the light of the supernova are close cousin to the antibodies in Farmer's *The Unreasoning Mask*. The macrolifers are heavily into nanotechnology because that's in the wind at the moment. But Zindell's synthesis is very stylishly his own. Perhaps the reprogramming and immortalizing of none other than Gilgamesh (who is already hard at work in the Silverberg studio) by ancient "UFOs" is a shade iffy. Yet Zindell manages to fit everything into a grand affirmative cosmic jigsaw, darkly shaded with an almost Dostoevskian hue of crime and horror. One appealing grace note is a remark by the none-too-perfect narrator: "Even we pilots may not talk about those things that we may not talk about." So what *hasn't* he talked about? Ah ha.

Whitley Strieber's recent lurid, ambiguous, and lucrative revelations about contact by what might or might not be Ufonauts, in *Communion* (1987) and *Transformation* (1989), have rendered the topic of UFOs more intellectually suspect than for quite some while. Nevertheless Garfield-Reeves Stevens, in *Nighteyes*, bravely charts this peculiar terrain fictionally and comes up with a satisfying science-fictional rationale, of our altered descendants traveling back through time to a catastrophic epoch—ours. On the one hand, *Nighteyes* is a vigorous, eerie, fast-paced, and intelligent espionage thriller that begins like something by Strieber and ends in a way reminiscent of Greg

Bear's *The Forge of God*; its impact is brooding and hallucinatory. On the other hand, with its short sentences, its surplus of decor as in the stage directions of a film script, its huge type, and its bulked-out blank spaces, it resembles a TelePrompTer script. Actually dense as regards concepts, *Nighteyes* features a design that irritatingly dilutes its impact; one mourns the trees felled simply to make margins.

Iain Banks's short *The State of the Art* also has aliens in our midst, visiting from his sophisticated yet playful Culture. The result is a Socratic reprise of Voltaire's *Candide*. The mother-ship is virtually omniscient, yet capricious and mischievous too. Shall Earth be erased because human society is such a chaotic mess? Or does its bubbling busy-ness present qualities that the superior Culture has lost—ultimately, a sense of wonder, and of sin? A defector opts for the latter interpretation, though the book itself is a satire on human follies.

Other, surgically altered aliens keep covert watch on human activities in preparation for contact in Rebecca Ore's *Being Alien*, sequel to *Becoming Alien* (1988), in which one human being, Tom, is spirited away in tragic, xenophobic circumstances to become a cadet of the very believable Interstellar Federation of Sapients. *Being Alien* offers a fascinating account of human and alien relationships and feelings of profound alienation and bigotry, which can painfully be overcome, though only just. Tom's primary sensation, on return to Earth, is not one of happy homecoming but of terror. Ore is a fine explorer of psychology, both human and alien.

Wrapping up her Xenogenesis trio, Octavia Butler concludes *her* exploration of the fatal genetic flaw in the human species—the co-existence in us of intelligence and hierarchical behavior—and of the ongoing fusion between human and alien engineered by the gene-trading Oankali. *Imago* focuses on the development of a mixed-gene child belonging to the Ooloi third sex. More domestic than the epochal first volume, *Imago* is a highly sensual, somatic narrative of poly-morphous sexuality, though also serious and duty-bound in tone. A joke in this text comes as a surprise.

James Patrick Kelly's *Look into the Sun* likewise deploys the twin themes of alien visitors and alienation, when a high-flying human architect is cajoled into designing a mausoleum for an alien goddess who communes with her local star. To which end, he must be surgically altered. This is one of those exemplary novels that blend aliens, the alienation of the hero, anthropological theology, science, and art, seamlessly.

In *Good News from Outer Space*, John Kessel offers no good news at all. Are trickster aliens—or angels—in our midst working at God's behest to bring about Judgment Day? Is God using subversion and disinformation like some cosmic CIA director? A charismatic religious revivalist works hectically towards a national Armageddon while an insane female private detective high on a language-scrambling drug hunts the obsessed newshound who is trying to hunt the alien angel. In the process Kessel exposes America's "lethal innocence" and paints a powerful new streak of savage satire—similar to that laid down by James Morrow in *Only Begotten Daughter* (1990) and in his various subversive rewritings of Bible stories. To be sure, Kessel is right on target; but to a secular European—notwithstanding the parallel rise of militant Islam and its abhorrent death sentence against the author of *The Satanic Verses*—there seems something almost provincial, even culturally isolationist, about such stress on the importance of fundamentalist American Christianity, dire though its products are—almost as though, at root, it may be valid. *Bugs* by John Sladek, an American deculturized by years of residence in Britain, though back home in Middle America again, is a hilarious satire on consumerism, jargon, and contemporary corniness. Intercut with a cybernetic Frankenstein theme whereby an epistemological robot misbehaves, *Bugs* culminates in slapstick bedroom farce that makes the reader laugh out loud. Interestingly, Sladek chooses a Briton as protagonist, and what there is of religion is hardly handled with any high seriousness. Sladek writes with zany brio; Kessel ultimately induces a sense of cultural claustrophobia, worthy though his aim is.

Quite out of culture, and askew from the author's usual style, Kim Stanley Robinson's *Escape from Kathmandu* is a memorably wacky travelogue, wonderfully lived-in like a muddy anorak, evoking Yetis, the truth behind Shangri-la, an accidental ascent of Everest, not to mention all the weirdest mysteries of Himalayan shamanism, played for laughs though with a serious underbelly. The crazy capers and the Kafkaesque surrealism of the Nepalese bureaucracy are one side of the coin. The other is the sleazy, if amiable, corruptness of a third-world country rife with political shenanigans and beset by inefficient aid agencies. What emerges most is Robinson's affection for a quirky and unique part of the world, distant and dirty but full of life and spirit, as well as mystic spirits. Here is squalor, intricate corruption, and hope springing eternal in the guise of an Illuminati-like "underground" government unlike any other . . .

. . . or perhaps second cousin several times removed to the anarchist postcatastrophe administration by artists of San Francisco in Pat Murphy's *The City, Not Long After*. After her dour Mayan trip in *The Falling Woman* (1987), Murphy joins the SF school of magical surrealism epitomized by Lisa Goldstein's *A Mask for the General* with its artist-revolutionaries. Mermaids and wolves wearing kerchiefs appear from out of the city's dreams, and flowers rain to confuse another general bent on occupying San Francisco. Elegiac, offbeat, and poignant, this is a tender love story full of beautiful poetical touches and bittersweet tragedy. Lurking—far off in the Himalayas—is a magical science-fictional rationale, of sorts. Of course, inhabitants of San Francisco already know that their city is uniquely magical. Would such magic also apply to Middletown, U.S.A.—or to Poughkeepsie? Set in the latter, Rachel Pollack's *Unquenchable Fire* liberates magic from the earth to overthrow the reign of cold science, though without dispensing with shopping malls, TV game shows, and such. You can become pregnant from a dream, and a curse will cause frogs and lizards to leap from a victim's mouth; but equally, the blades of a helicopter can chop up your astral body. Myth and miracle have broken through into the modern world, transfiguring it. Murphy's magic has no religious overtones and operates for the most part benignly; Pollack's has a strongly manipulative edge—Martin Luther school of magic rather than Zen magic. *Unquenchable Fire* won the Arthur C. Clarke Award, which must have been puzzling to the staunch scientific rationalist Arthur Clarke himself, who specifically funded this award for *science* fiction.

Is *Unquenchable Fire* science fiction at all, when it denies science so radically? Is it fantasy, magical realism, or a harbinger of some new mythic vision? Certainly, myth falls within the compass of works deemed Nebula-worthy, as witnessed by the nomination of Jane Yolen's *Sister Light, Sister Dark*, which eloquently evokes the upbringing of a savior figure in a unique feminist community—part heroic age, part medieval (yet plainly never of this world)—where people's alter egos emerge as separate living individuals. Yolen ingeniously parallels the myth of her heroine, the legend, the true story, the ballads sung about her (which are lovely verse in their own right), and the later scholarly commentary by folklorists and social anthropologists—at which point, perhaps, the book is indeed science fiction, since here are the findings of fictitious social scientists.

Ellen Kushner's *Swordspoint* is another wholly unsciencefictional novel that won many Nebula recommendations without actually reaching the final ballot. A fairy tale for grown-ups, a comedy of manners almost in the style of Ronald Firbank, this playful book is set in an androgynous Regency-type domain. Here is clever chatter and snobbery, here is wooing and conniving; also, hired swords, power ploys, and casual murder, high life and low life. Kushner's is a closed mini-world like one of those snowstorm scenes in plastic. Give it a shake, it invites. In itself, *Swordspoint* is perfect, with not a false note or turn of phrase.

Judith Tarr's *A Wind in Cairo* is also set in its own, this time arabesque, domain, telling of a reprobate prince who rapes a magician's daughter and is sentenced to redeem himself as a stallion. The story is lively and mettlesome, yet flawed by semiarchaic parlance. "Enmity had waxed for that Ali Mousa had prospered in her despite." Yolen, by contrast, is pellucid, conjuring up the mood of legend without affectation.

Another fantasy novel that we might have expected to succumb fatally to the parameters of its own peculiar world of special rules, but that triumphantly transcends them, is *Drachenfels*, by Kim Newman writing as Jack Yeovil. This stylish, witty tale is the debut volume from Games Workshop's new publishing arm, set in their Warhammer universe. Both as a classy publishing product and as a genuine novel of characterization as well as of action, *Drachenfels* bodes well for subsequent Warhammer fiction; and indeed quality literature is the aim. (Ironically, Games Workshop's models factory is now the largest employer in Eastwood, D. H. Lawrence's hometown.)

From military fiction and fantasy conflict . . . to real war, with parapsychological implications. Two remarkable novels, Bruce McAllister's *Dream Baby* and Elizabeth Scarborough's *The Healer's War*, explore the Vietnam War from a perspective that perhaps only science fiction could offer, both focusing upon a nurse who develops paranormal powers induced by the stresses of the combat zone. McAllister has based his book on research among veterans; Scarborough has based hers upon her own memories of Vietnam. Successor to several humorous fantasy novels, *The Healer's War* is powerful, moving, horrific, and ultimately cathartic. The nurse in question inherits from a dying Vietnamese shaman a magic amulet that lets her perceive human auras and heal with her touch. Scarborough writes evocatively—"high cheekbones jutting through the shiny flesh like carnival apples bleeding through caramel." McAllister's nurse is dragged into a nightmarish military special operation to exploit the wild talents that the pressure of that terrible war is breeding. Fraught with Machiavellian deceit, the expedition she joins to blow up the Red Dikes is intended to fail; in fact, it is really a test of the wild talents to see how long their possessors can survive. Intensely powerful too, and intercut with seemingly authentic interviews with veterans regarding ESP experiences, *Dream Baby* climaxes with the nurse and three fellow survivors of the doomed expedition fusing into a gestalt with awesome powers, including the ability to see alternate historical timelines and visions of alternative futures. However, these powers fade after nurse Mary kills the sinister, ruthless officer who was in control of the special covert operation.

Manipulation, the paranormal, and a fundamentalist preacher feature in Mike McQuay's *Nexus*, a kind of hybrid of Spinrad's *Bug Jack Barron* (1969) and Le Guin's *The Lathe of Heaven* (1971). An ace newsman, who has been downgraded because of a very combative interview with the President, begins to exploit an autistic girl whose wishes for anything whatever will invariably come true. He reasons that his own emotional ennui—his lack of commitment to any cause but the "truth"—makes him the best custodian of this once-in-a-lifetime story, and of the girl. She fixates on him, and he begins to cause miracles, fiercely opposed by a televangelist. *Nexus* is moving and terrifying in its portrayal of this newsman's descent into hell, as he becomes twisted and doomed, discovering at last his own essential dishonesty. McQuay offers huge TV script-style sections, tailored into narrative. Well, the book *is* about TV. As the newsman enters the girl's hallucinatory world of enhanced feeling, daringly unrestrained erotic effects abound. Ultimately, he abreacts Amy from out of her autistic, omnipotent Godhead back into ordinary humanity—but not before the whole human race, having experienced the pangs of the most wretched famine victims, rejigs the global economy virtually overnight to eradicate hunger. This is perhaps a bigger logistical miracle than the climactic miracle that Amy produces. Thus, eventually, *Nexus* becomes a song to the potential of beauty and goodness. As in *Dream Baby*, however, the paranormal must needs vanish in the end, otherwise reality would be meaningless and the novel would lose its ultimate rationale.

Orson Scott Card's saga of an alternate America where magic works reaches volume three with *Prentice Alvin*, narrated by Tale-swapper, this world's folksy, homespun William Blake. After the really heavy Indian magic of the preceding volume, *Red Prophet* (1988), Card necessarily shows more restraint—even if an absconding African slave turns into a bird, Alvin transmutes a plow into gold, and more besides. Otherwise, reality might become quite unstrung. Nevertheless, it is the aim of Alvin's opponent, the Unmaker, that precisely this should happen; for Alvin, who is still patiently discovering the true nature of his mighty knack and how to use it responsibly (unlike Amy), is destined to become the greatest Maker, whatever a Maker actually might be and whatever he might be destined to make or remake.

Remaking a whole world technologically rather than magically is the theme of Pamela Sargent's epic *Venus of Shadows*, the second volume of an epic account of the colonization of that planet, which at the same time is humane, tragic, and family oriented, at once gigantic and domestic. A new mystery religion of Ishtar arises and proceeds to totalitarian excesses, devaluing itself. The fundamental ideological dispute remains that between the pragmatic, secular habitat dwellers and the Koranic rulers of Earth, who view the former as impeding the universality of Islam. In this ill-starred year of the *fatwa* against Salman Rushdie, Pamela Sargent manages coincidentally to say some remarkably interesting, even controversial, things about a future Islam.

To be paradoxical, there exists a secret alternate history of Rushdie too, for he submitted his first novel, *Grimus* (1975), to a first-SF-novel competition organized by Gollancz and the *Observer* newspaper back in the early 1970s, reportedly with the condition that if he did not win and if Gollancz nevertheless wished to publish his novel, then it should not have the SF label attached to it. He did not win; Gollancz did indeed publish *Grimus*. Had he won, perhaps exactly the same *Satanic Verses* might in due course have appeared as a fantasy title . . . and no one would have paid very much undue attention. For there is an avalanche of books in our SF-fantasy genre, and many excellent works are simply swept under.

Shall we speak of George Alec Effinger's *A Fire in the Sun* and Michael Bishop's *The Secret Ascension*? The former is a richly humorous, tough, ultimately romantic intrigue at the end of which our pill-popper turned silicon superman reforms the police department and starts to pray seriously to Allah; the latter is a wonderful homage to Philip Dick in which Richard Nixon is exorcised on the moon. These two fine novels have in no sense been swept under. But a score, two score more novels deserve mention for one reason or another. Only an entire book could do justice to the SF and fantasy output of 1989. Furthermore, there is also an annual avalanche of excellent short stories, novelettes, and novellas.

One remarkable nonfiction volume—the love-labor of ten years and more—that organizes the science-fictional heritage of the past in visionary, crusading, analytic style is *The World Beyond the Hill* by Alexei and Cory Panshin. Its 685 pages carry the story of SF up to 1945. At the end the authors hint that they may have a further story to tell.

What latter-day Panshins of the twenty-first century will chronicle our own years of the avalanche half as comprehensively?

"SNAKE CHARM":
THE HEALER'S WAR, CHAPTER 16

Elizabeth Ann Scarborough

In 1979, Elizabeth Ann Scarborough began writing fantasy. Her first novel, *Song of Sorcery*, appeared in 1982. Her second and third novels, *The Unicorn Creed* and *Bronwyn's Bane*, followed the next year, and *The Christening Quest* in the summer of 1985—four books later reprinted by Bantam in two volumes under the title *Songs from the Seashell Archives*. More recent fantasies include *The Harem of Aman Akbar*, *The Drastic Dragon of Draco, Texas*, and *The Goldcamp Vampire*, the last two of which star "a female Ned Buntline wannabe calling herself Valentine Lovelace." Ms. Scarborough has published short fiction in Jane Yolen's *Werewolves*, Andre Norton's *Cat Fantastic*, Susan Shwartz's *Arabesques*, and Parke Godwin's *Invitation to Camelot*. She is at work on a contemporary trilogy called *The Songkiller Saga* as well as another "more serious" novel (somewhat in the mode of 1989's Nebula winner) set in a POW camp in Tibet, *Nothing Sacred*.

Here, however, is "Snake Charm," a suspenseful chapter from Ms. Scarborough's award-winning Vietnam novel, *The Healer's War*. It can be read on its own without vitiating either its impact or that of the extraordinary fantasy from which it is taken. After "Snake Charm," the reader will find an insightful personal essay about the writing of *The Healer's War*, the real-life experiences undergirding it, its startling but ultimately superficial resemblances to the TV series "China Beach," and its liberating effects on a wide variety of readers, including Vietnam vets.

Synopsis: Army nurse Kitty McCulley has tried to save a young Vietnamese boy, Ahn, an amputee who has been under her care for several months, by transferring him to a different hospital. A former boyfriend agrees to fly Ahn and Kitty to this hospital, but the chopper is shot down in the jungle, the pilot and crew chief are killed, and

Ahn and Kitty are stranded with nothing between them and death but a strange amulet given to Kitty by a Vietnamese shaman.

Kitty already knows that the amulet can magnify the auras of living things; she uses this power to avoid Viet Cong and other hazards. As they seek safety, a shock-crazed foot soldier named William sometimes helps and sometimes threatens them, for William, who has witnessed the slaughter of his entire platoon, is subject to murderous flashbacks in which he cannot differentiate between his American companions and the enemy. Kitty soon realizes that she and Ahn would be safer seeking refuge in a nearby village than staying with William.

Chapter 16 opens as Kitty follows Ahn to the outskirts of this village, where the people are battling a monstrous snake. Before the war, such snakes were frequent threats to Vietnamese villages. Although most constrictors do not possess venom, a venomous giant constrictor does exist in Vietnam. One authority calls it a "horse snake" because it can crush and ingest a horse.

When I first saw the snake I thought, What's that fireman's hose doing here? I thought it might be something the villagers used for irrigation. Ahn sat at the edge of the paddy, very still, and I wondered if he was having second thoughts about being with his people again. I thought he was scared of something that insubstantial. Then I saw the fire hose more clearly, noticed that it had a distinct aura pulsing from it, the dark red of old blood, anger, malice, and hunger brewed together.

The villagers swarmed across the paddy and then stood watching uncertainly. The snake reared up like a self-motivated Indian rope trick to about two and a half yards above the ground. That made it taller than any of them.

They were very small people, short and lean from hard work and hunger and intestinal parasites, and there wasn't an able-bodied man among them. Ancient men, ancient women, pregnant girls who looked too young to have periods, and tiny children stood with their hoes and knives and watched the snake. It watched them too, swaying, and I thought its aura flickered with satisfaction as it eyed an infant on its sister's hip. The snake thought it was one badass motherfucker, and it swaggered toward the people as if they were so many mice.

For their part, they prudently backed up, considering, but looked at it mainly as if it was a curiosity. They chatted at one another, as if expecting one of their number to come up with an answer. The snake lay back as if it was about to strike, and the slimmest of the pregnant girls leaped out well beyond striking range and taunted it, flapping her arms and trying to draw attention away from the others. Meanwhile, a few of the others circled back toward the snake's tail.

The snake was a no-nonsense-type creature. It decided that if the damn-fool girl wanted to get eaten so badly, it would accommodate her. It didn't so much strike as fling itself upon her. The others hacked at it as it flew past them, but it grabbed her in its coils and she cried out as it squeezed. Its jaws snapped onto her thigh and she abruptly stopped thrashing with her machete and collapsed within the coils. The other villagers tried to pull the coils loose, but the snake just squeezed more tightly. One of the babies, sensing the panic of its elders, bawled.

Ahn grabbed his stick and hobbled forward. I hadn't said anything as I came up behind him, and he still didn't know I was there. He grabbed the nearest old lady and held on with one hand and felt around the snake with the other until he found the tail, took it in his mouth, and bit. The snake stopped biting and the coils relaxed so that snake, girl, and Ahn all tumbled to the ground in a heap.

I couldn't just squat in the bushes and watch. There was already one corpse lying in the grass, near where the snake had risen. An old woman or an old man, I couldn't tell—just a mass of mottled skin and a hank of long gray hair in the midst of a bundle of rags. The snake was trying to free its head to reach Ahn. The others were pulling on various parts of the snake while an old man and a girl of about eight tried to whack at the reptile's head without whacking the victim or Ahn in the process. Ahn continued to chow down on the snake's tail.

I knew that however frail these folks looked, they were quite strong from years of work that would have killed me. I knew that they were much quicker than I was, and that I would likely get myself snake-bit or hacked if I tried to help. I also knew that I weighed almost double what any one of them did, and that maybe dragging with all my weight behind it might help. And I had a hell of a big machete. I also didn't think I would be able to live with myself, for however long I was going to be able to live anyhow, if I just sat there and watched that goddamn snake kill people who had survived bombs and bullets for so many years.

I waded into the paddy, my boots shedding pounds of accumulated mud into the watery muck beneath the rice shoots.

Ahn sneezed, releasing his hold on the tail, and it whipped away from the girl, sending Ahn flying. The snake's head reared up about six inches from the girl's body to watch the kid and lunge for the nearest spectator. It had to uncoil a length of itself from the girl to make the lunge, and when it did, I hit it with my machete, not even sure I was using the right end.

The snake's body was bigger around than my neck, bigger around than my thighs even, so at first I wasn't sure I had done any good. But the blade had bitten deeply into the body just behind the snake's head and the snake hissed, shaking a head the shape and size of a spade, blood spattering into its eyes, and over me and several surrounding feet. I straddled it and bent over double so I could bear down on the blade, which was hard to do. The snake's writhing knocked first one of my boots and then the other sliding in the mud of the paddy, but I held on. I had to. The machete jerked in my hands, but I held it clenched in both fists. I heard a crack and knew one or more of the girl's bones were being crushed. She couldn't even scream with her breath cut off like that. The other villagers tried frantically to pull the coils from her. I leaned more heavily into my machete. There wasn't enough room between me and the girl for me to get good leverage on the snake's head. Any moment now it would crush her to death and round on me.

"Push her away from me. Ahn, tell them push her away."

Ahn started yammering in Vietnamese and the other people began rolling the girl's shoulders and legs away from my back as if they unrolled people from snakes all the time. I dropped to my knees and used them like a vise against the snake, and it bucked like a rodeo bronc beneath me. But from this vantage point I could put most of my weight onto the machete. If I let go and the snake's head snapped free, the war would be over for me.

I cringed inwardly every time the snake undulated, afraid the girl was being pulverized. I didn't dare look back to see, and that almost got me killed.

Ahn's tail biting, though I didn't know it at the time, had caused the snake to loosen its grip somewhat, and the people were able to roll the girl out of its grip. But as soon as she was free of the tail, the tail was also free of her, and the tip whipped up and around my shoulders, jerking me, machete, snake head, and all, backward.

As the coils started constricting around me, my grip on my machete started to loosen. I felt the people mass behind me, grabbing armfuls of slippery snake.

Then Ahn's head was beside mine, and his mouth grabbed an end section of tail and lightly chomped. The coils loosened and the villagers redoubled their efforts at straightening out the snake. That allowed me to keep hanging on to the machete and with it to bear the great head back to the ground.

"Got him," I gasped, and wanted to laugh in spite of everything, because anybody looking on would have seen that I was a little confused about who had whom. William was right. I did think I was Sheena, Queen of the Jungle, serpent slayer extraordinaire. But the truth was, I didn't exactly see a lot of other options. I was a big, strapping girl then and accustomed to wrestling three-hundred-pound ladies in body casts onto bedpans, having knockdown drag-outs with grown men with the DTs, and subduing hysterical three-year-olds while giving them injections. The snake was bigger and more dangerous and more powerful than any of the situations I was used to, but not by all that much.

"Somebody chop off his fuckin' head, for Christsake!" I rasped. It was in English, no one should have been able to understand me, and Ahn's mouth was full of snake, but the old grandfather with the hoe hit the creature a blow on the noggin and the coils fell from me like a feather boa. I fell back against a pile of villagers and lay panting for a moment. The old man kept hacking, his aura as blood-red as the snake's had been, his face a calm, almost kindly mask.

I crawled over to the girl who had been bitten. Her aura was very dim, gray and muddy except for the part around where her leg had been bitten. That was deep black and spreading.

The bite was larger than any snakebite I had ever seen—the snake's mouth was bigger than mine, and almost bigger than my entire head. The standard treatment for rattlesnake bites was going to be useless, I knew it, but nevertheless I grabbed a knife out of the nearest hand and sliced at the wounds. The girl took her breath in sharply and her hand shot toward me, a knife in her fist. I dropped my knife and caught her hand, barely keeping her from stabbing both me and herself. She was looking at me with what I would normally have interpreted as hatred, aura and all, but considering what she'd been through, I just figured she was a little unhinged, probably confusing me with her former assailant.

"Come on, you guys, hang on to her or I'm not going to be able to help her," I said, and shoved her wrist into the bony hands of the nearest grandmother. I must have made my point clear enough, because three children and another pregnant woman rushed to help restrain her hands. Her eyes rolled in terror as she looked down at me and she moaned and squirmed under the blade. "Sssh, sssh, sssh," I told her, as I'd heard Vietnamese women shush their babies. I sat on her leg to keep it from wiggling, so I could do just a little incision instead of major surgery. "I know this hurts, but I have to try to get the poison out."

All around me the women were shushing her, hissing louder than the late snake. Hoping I didn't have any new cavities or canker sores I'd forgotten about, I bent over her leg and made like a vampire, sucking up mouthfuls of venom and blood and spitting it out again— sort of a reverse artificial respiration. It was a huge snake and there was a lot of venom. Even as I sucked I could see the blackness spreading through her pelvis, up her torso, toward her heart, down her knee.

I knew I was getting nowhere, and now the adrenaline was wearing off and I was feeling the effects of exhaustion, starvation, and exertion all at once. Helplessly I spread my hands along the perimeters of the spreading blackness of the venom, mumbling senselessly at it to stop, dammit. I was tired, muddy, and frustrated and about to lose this brave if somewhat screwy young girl in spite of everything. The venom on my tongue made it tingle, and I was starting to turn from her and try to wash my mouth out when I noticed that where the bright mauve of my aura touched the blackness, it gathered before my hands as if I were herding it. I stared at it stupidly, then ran my hands down her trunk, up her leg, and across her pelvis, as if I were sweeping the venom out of her system. Where I touched the black, it retreated before my palms, until it gathered at the wound and bubbled up out of it, like an artesian spring. When it was gone I kept staring at where it had been for a moment, then ran my hand across my tongue. A sheen of black appeared on my palm, and I wiped it off against the rice.

The girl lay still, panting, her eyes wide and her face still terrified. "Ahn, tell her I think it's going to be all right," I said, my tongue so thick I had to repeat it. "Tell her I think the poison is gone."

I hoped I wasn't raising false hopes. I hoped I wasn't hallucinating. My head seemed too heavy to lift as I looked up at the faces around me: the girl herself, as pretty as Xinhdy had been, except for a gold tooth in the front of her mouth; the old man who had hacked the snake, most of his teeth gone; the children, wide-eyed and looking half-scared, half-excited. Finally the old man picked up the snake's head and the children followed, trying to lift portions of the body. When I got to my feet, the man shifted his grip farther back and tried to hand me the head. I declined, and emptied my breakfast of stewed monkey into the rice paddy. I hate snakes. I can't stand to look at them, much less touch them.

One of the girls helped the injured woman to her feet, while Ahn leaned on his stick and supervised. I felt the wounded girl flinch as I put my arm around her waist to support her on her injured side, but among us we got her back to the village. No mines, no booby traps. Just mud and rice and a concertina-wire barrier.

Later, four of the girls took a mat back out to the field and dragged home the snake's first victim. I watched mutely as they laid the body out. She was not as old as I thought, just very gray. Her face was purpled from suffocation and her body had been crushed, her features so ugly with her death that I had to look away. The injured girl cried out and argued at length with one of the women who was attending the body, but was finally persuaded to lie back. Her aura radiated grieving, a gray as cold and empty as a midwinter sky.

As they cleaned the body and arranged the features back to a semblance of normalcy before laying a banyan leaf across the face, it seemed to me that the dead woman looked nearly like the live one. No wonder the girl had been so ready to kill the snake.

Ahn wasn't allowed in while they dressed the corpse, and the injured woman looked at me, still angrily, as if I were committing a terrible breach of manners, but the truth was I didn't have the strength to drag myself out of there. I fell asleep while they were finishing the preparation of the corpse.

I awoke some time later to the groans of the girl beside me. She was on the mat and I lay beside her on the dirt floor. I was so stiff I could scarcely move, and it flashed across my mind that perhaps the snake had done me more damage than I realized.

But the girl's groan gave way to a sudden, panicky scream. I sat up and automatically reached for her pulse and stared at my watch, counting. Her stomach was rolling beneath the light cotton of her pajama top, and she clutched it with both hands.

This time she looked at me entreatingly. "Dau quadi," she breathed. "Dau quadi."

She was aborting, of course. It was actually inevitable. Even if the venom had never crossed the placental membrane, being squeezed in the coils of a giant snake was bound to be damaging to any growing fetus. I stretched out to the door of the hut and yelled, to whom it might concern, "La dai, la dai," and hoped the urgency in my voice would make up for the lack of explanation.

It was almost over before anyone else could reach her. Blood and water gushed from between her thighs, soaking her pajamas and the mat before I could turn away from the door again. As the first village woman ducked into the house, the fetus, a very small fetus, delivered. It was not well developed. It could almost have been any sort of a baby creature, poor pathetic little thing. It hadn't had a chance. The women brought cloths and we wiped her clean and I wrapped the fetus in one. She grabbed my wrist. She wanted to see it. I shook my head at first and she persisted, so I showed it to her. It helps sometimes when you know what you're mourning.

She began to cry, then to wail, and one of the other women touched me on the shoulder and nodded that I should leave the hut. I rose ponderously to my feet, feeling like an out-of-shape water buffalo behind the small lithe figure ahead of me. We hadn't far to go—just to a hut a few yards away, which was blessedly empty except for Ahn, who was tucking into a bowl of rice. He looked up long enough to nod at me and went back to eating.

The woman showed me a mat with a roll of cloth at the head for a pillow. I sat down gratefully and started to go to sleep, but she sat on her heels and reached for my bootlaces, as if she thought she was my maid or something.

"No, no," I said, and tried to wave her away. "Ahn, please tell this woman I don't need a maid, just some sleep. She should get some sleep herself or she could lose her baby too."

"I tell her, co, but she be mad—lose face."

I compromised by sitting back up again and helping her take my boots off. A little girl brought me a rice bowl and a bottle of hot Pepsi, which I opened with the church key William had given me. She took the bottle from me and poured the Pepsi into a bowl.

The little girl put her hands together and backed off, leaving the Pepsi beside me. I put my hands together and bowed at her too. I was going to receive a crash course in Vietnamese customs, I supposed. But tired as I was, I was elated. William had been wrong and I was right. These people seemed no more threatening than my patients. I hadn't walked into the clutches of the enemy, I thought, just into a strenuous one-woman medcap mission, with a side dish of indigenous prehistoric wildlife.

Ahn stirred and coughed in his sleep. I felt his forehead. He was burning again. The rice and the Pepsi were something I wouldn't have touched ordinarily, but I had to have something in my stomach if I was going to renew my strength. As the food took effect, my perception of his aura deepened. Blackness spread from the stump up his leg. I was sure that if I disturbed him to do so, I'd find a knot in his groin. Well, now that I'd gotten the hang of the old faith healer bit by trying it out on a perfect stranger, the amulet's power was bound to work on Ahn too. I spread my fingers so that each touched the end of one of the threads of infection and concentrated on thinking of the veins as being clean and clear, with nothing but healthy blood flowing through them. The black threads knotted near the stump and, with a little urging, drained out the end. While I was working, the little girl was on the ball. She brought me water in what looked suspiciously like the same sort of basin we used for patients at the 83rd. I supposed it was just another of the instances of the black market moving in mysterious ways.

I went through the bowing routine again and smiled at her. The poor kid had fought that snake just as hard as I had and she must be just as tired. I unwrapped Ahn's stump and he woke up, hissing. My old fatigue shirt sleeve was thoroughly be-nastied.

I turned back to the little girl, who was sitting on her heels watching with the expression of a nursing instructor checking to see if I was doing everything right. Disinfectant was too much to hope for, but I made motions of pouring some over Ahn's wound and bandaging it up again. My other fatigue shirt sleeve was grimy and slimy from the snake fight.

She dipped out of the house, and a few minutes later, an elderly man dipped back in and sat down on *his* heels. He was holding a bottle, from which he took a swig before handing it to me. It was Jim Beam. He passed it over, indicating that I should take a swig. I only pretended to, because the last thing I needed was a drink that would knock me on my can, and wiped off the bottle mouth before pouring a good inch of the stuff over Ahn's stump. He winced and hissed and started to cry.

The old man winced and hissed and started to cry when I poured his booze over Ahn's stump. I handed it back to him and made the steepled-hands bow again. I couldn't remember how to say thank you in Vietnamese.

He nodded wisely and looked me up and down in the manner of dirty old men everywhere. "Mamasan beaucoup," he said. He sounded a little awestricken.

"No," I said, grinning and shaking my head. "No, papasan tete." Which was perfectly true, of course. Walking along beside me on the way back to the village, he stood only as high as my bust line, which might have been what led to the personal remarks. He laughed and shook his head at my incomparable wit and he and the Jim Beam disappeared.

The little girl was gone a long time and I began to think that bandages were too much to hope for. People probably didn't have any spare clothing that was in better shape than mine, which was pretty sad. I used the rest of the basin of water to rinse the mud off myself and tossed the thick residue into the ditch surrounding the house. A regular moat. Well, I'd already met the monster.

The old man was out in front of the house, admiring the snake again. He had technically killed the thing, though he'd never have made it without the rest of the village, Ahn, and me. But he walked around it and nodded to himself. I thought he was preening until I paid attention to his aura. It was the gray I was coming to associate with grief. I left Ahn for a moment and stepped across the ditch.

"Some snake, eh, papasan?" I asked, nodding to our kill, which still made my vertebrae stand at attention.

"Yes, numbah one snake," he said sadly, pronouncing snake uncertainly, a new English word.

"I've never seen one that big," I said inanely. He continued staring down at the snake as if I hadn't spoken. "Beaucoup snake," I said and spread my arms and rolled my eyes for emphasis. "Are there more like that around?" I asked, and indicated our snake, plus another beside it and another.

The old man shook his head sadly. "Snake fini," he said and repeated my gesture to indicate that he meant all the snakes were gone, then threw his arms up like a child imitating a bomb, making the appropriate explosive noises. It should have been funny, but the grieving gray and sparks of red in the aura belied his smile, and the whole demonstration was as grotesque as if he had plucked out his eye and asked me to laugh at him.

I looked down and nodded. Bombs might make you nostalgic for the comparative harmlessness of enormous snakes at that. He picked up a stick and drew a few deft lines in the mud and a hungry crocodile slithered within them, mouth open and tail lashing. The old man threw his arms in the air, miming the bomb again, and tapped the picture of the crocodile. "Fini."

As the mud oozed back together and the crocodile sank into the mire, he flourished his stick again and eels, otters, huge fish, and a hungry tiger populated the mud. "Fini," the old man said each time, his voice grimmer with the vanishing of each species. The tiger had figured in our word games on the ward, however, and I thought I might use it to change the topic to a lighter one.

"Mao bey?" I asked, pointing at the picture.

He looked at me as if I'd done something astonishing and now his smile deepened and some of the gray sank back into him in the same way his pictures sank into the mud. He nodded enthusiastically. An educable American. How astonishing.

I drew a picture of a house cat. "Mao?"

He nodded. I was on safe ground. Maos had come up frequently in the word games Xinhdy, Mai, Ahn, and I had played.

I said, "In English, Mao same-same cat same-same Kitty same-same me," and pointed to myself.

He thought that was pretty funny and catcalled at me.

The little girl ran toward us, her black hair flying like a scarf behind her. In her hot little hand was a roll of gauze bandage, still in its white wrapper with the red cross in the blue circle.

"Co, co, see, see!" she cried. She was such a gorgeous child, like a doll with that Kewpie mouth and little pointed chin and that shining hair.

"Co Mao, Co Mao," the old man said.

It was no good trying to get him to go ahead and say my name untranslated. I ducked back inside the house to bandage Ahn's leg. He was sitting up now, and supervised while I wrapped his stump. The little girl again watched as if her life depended on it. I smiled at her when I was done.

"Ahn, we should introduce ourselves."

He looked dubious but said his name and a string of words after, looking as if he had just been elected to the dubiously honorable office of President of South Vietnam.

The little girl pointed to herself and said, "Hoa," and bowed to me and said, "Co Mao."

Ahn shook his head furiously. "Mamasan Kitty, chu—" I shook my head at him before he could say "chung wi." These people didn't need to know me by my rank any more than American civilians did.

"Ahn, I have Vietnamese name here. I like Mao."

"Okay, okay," he said, as if I were very upset about it, and looked at Hoa as if to say, Americans, who can tell what they're going to want next?

She nodded gravely, as if, because of his advanced age, his position and wisdom were unquestionable.

I wanted to rest a little longer, but thought I should first check on my other patient. She seemed to be asleep as I poked my head in the doorway, but as soon as I set foot in the room she jerked awake and glowered at me. Ignoring the glower, I knelt beside her.

Her aura was mostly a muddy jumble of anger, grief, fear, and pain, but the basis of it was an appealing brilliant aqua and clear yellow, with tendrils of spring green and a bloom of pink. The brighter colors were smothered beneath the layer of muddy ones, like the rainbow in an oil slick. She looked at me with a rebellious hatred that struck me as totally unfair, considering I'd helped save her life twice.

"Okay, be that way," I said aloud. She looked healthy enough now, her aura bright and strong despite all the muddiness surrounding it. This village had managed its ob. problems before I came along and I wasn't about to intrude on the privacy of a woman who obviously didn't want me there.

I was turning to leave when the woman who had brought me to the hut stepped into the doorway. Ahn squeezed in beside her. She seemed chagrined and bowed two or three times. I reciprocated. She started speaking rapidly to Ahn, gesturing toward the woman on the bed with lifts of her chin, watching me anxiously. Clearly, she had expected the girl to be rude and was apologizing for it.

"What did she say, Ahn?" I asked.

"This one name Tran Thi Truong, very please to meet you," Ahn said, inclining his head to the woman beside him. "Truong say that one Dinh Thi Hue."

Dinh Thi Hue interrupted suddenly, with a spate of imperious questions, her words sounding harsh and accusing.

"Well, what did she say?"

"She want to know where are other American soldiers."

I started to say there weren't any more and then thought maybe that wasn't such a good idea.

"What's it to her?" I asked Ahn.

Truong pulled us outdoors and started talking again, in low, emphatic tones, her eyes full of apology, but also some anger.

Ahn looked wise and said, "Last time Americans here they boom-boom Dinh Thi Hue." He made a graphic gesture with a circle of the forefinger and thumb and the forefinger of his other hand as casually as an American eight-year-old might wave hi. "Make babysan. She no like American soldiers."

No wonder. I turned back to her with more sympathy, which I had no idea how to express. I murmured, "Sin loi, Dinh Thi Hue."

Ahn was defensive on my behalf, however, and hobbled over to Hue's bedside and regaled the girl for several minutes, nodding at me, slapping the thigh above his stump with a gesture that said it was now sound as a dollar owing to my expert intervention, and clearly told her I was a GI of a different kind than she had known before. I hoped he wasn't telling her I was the only one of my kind.

She let out a long sigh and lay back against the pillow, her face sweaty and her hair still matted with mud and blood. Her face seemed familiar to me, but I thought that was because she reminded me of one of the patients. She had a banty toughness about her that reminded me of Cammy Dover, a four-foot-eleven biker I'd met at a folk club in Denver.

Ahn picked up her hand and la daied me over to her, and put our hands together. She didn't look into my eyes but inclined her head a bare half inch and muttered something in English.

"She say, 'Thank you, Mao,' for helping her when big snake have her. She say thank you to Ahn also, because Ahn *bite* big snake, make him let her go. She say Ahn and Mao numbah one team and she love us too much."

I laughed and patted his shoulder. "I say Ahn numbah one bull-shitter and full of wishful thinking, but thanks for trying."

"Com bic? What means 'wishful thinking'?" he asked.

But about then Hoa came to the door and gestured urgently to Ahn to la dai. He turned away from the peace conference and hobbled toward the door, negotiating the ditch with more agility than I would have thought possible. I wished we'd been able to save his crutch during the crash.

The little girl appeared in the doorway again and this time la daied me. Truong frowned at her, but the child didn't notice.

Dinh Thi Hue watched all of this through slitted eyes, as if taking notes.

"It's been great having such a warm friendly chat with you," I said, "but I gotta go now. Kids. You know how it is. Probably want me to car-pool them to the Little League game or take them to the Dairy Queen."

She blinked, mildly puzzled. Her aura looked a little less muddied now. I thought I would be able to tell from it if she was losing blood. It would be dimmer surely. The way she felt about Americans, I didn't want to invade her privacy to check under the Army blanket someone had laid across her. Truong bent over her, murmuring something.

The rain started again, a thin gray drizzle. It made a pewter backdrop for the wet brilliance of the jungle.

As soon as I was outside, Hoa took off at a run, leaving me standing beside Ahn.

In a few minutes, Hoa returned, her pace slow and solemn this time, her arms cradling something that turned out to be a puppy.

"This Hoa's friend, very fierce tete guard dog, Bao Phu," Ahn told me. "Protecting Hoa, Bao Phu is hurt. Hoa want Mao to make better."

Wow. Snake charming, faith healing, and veterinary medicine all in one day. Ought to look great on my résumé.

SOME REFLECTIONS ON THE HEALER'S WAR

Elizabeth Ann Scarborough

Never tell your editor a war story. He'll assume you've been holding out on him. I forget which cleaned-up-for-prime-time Vietnam vignette I was telling Lou Aronica, my editor at Bantam, when he said, "Why don't you write a novel set in Vietnam?"

I said very condescendingly, "Lou, just because everybody else is jumping off that particular bridge right now doesn't mean I'm going to. I learned my lesson about that kind of conformity by going to Vietnam in the first place. There wasn't a bit of fantasy or magic there. If there had been, people would have used it to keep themselves alive."

Not long before this conversation, Jack and Jeanne Van Buren Dann had sent out an all-points bulletin for SF or fantasy stories for their Vietnam anthology, *In the Fields of Fire*, and I began thinking about doing a fantasy story set in 'Nam. At last, though, I wrote the Danns a vaguely apologetic letter explaining that, although I was well qualified to write such a story, having served a year in I Corps as an army nurse, I was unable to think of one. If I did, I would let them know. I didn't want to be left out, but for eighteen years I hadn't been able to stand reading or watching anything about Vietnam. How could I *write* about it?

Of course, once I'd told Lou I couldn't write a Vietnam book, I thought of several ways I might. For about two weeks, I called him every other day or so with a complicated scenario set on another planet, or in another world, or in another time, anything to remove my war story from the reality I had known. Finally, I thought, Well, I've done quest stories before. Maybe *this* should be a quest story— a couple of strange companions (about the only kind anyone had in

Vietnam) and a magic enabling device providing a framework for talking about what I did in the war, Daddy.

I gave Kitty McCulley, my heroine, most of my own motives for joining the army. I wanted to get out of Kansas, but didn't think I ever would unless someone made me. I was curious about the war. Also, I had always felt that the only way to solve world problems was to start with the basics—health care, food, shelter, and so on. Briefly, however, the army seemed like a game. The band at Fort Sam Houston played "Thank Heaven for Little Girls" as marching music for us nurses. When I went to Fitzsimmons Army Hospital and later to 'Nam, it was no longer a game.

Years later, when I first visited the Vietnam War Memorial, I, unlike a lot of veterans, didn't recognize the names I remembered most vividly from 'Nam. My GI patients were in and out of our MUST unit hospital in Da Nang so fast that I never really got to know them. When they left, they went back to "The World"—to Okinawa or Japan to stabilize, and then back to the United States.

The names I remember are unlikely to appear on any memorials, although the people they belong to may now be dead—names like Ahn and Chi, Lan and Xuan, the names of Vietnamese civilians with whom I worked for many months because the only safe place for them to heal was our hospital. I doubt that any of my patients, even if they wanted to, made it to the States as refugees. They weren't officials or people with jobs important to the American presence; they were mostly farmers, shopkeepers, people caught in the middle, people with terrible wounds that, even after treatment, kept them from competing for seats on outgoing aircraft.

One name that remains sharp in my memory is that of Dang Thi Thai, a civilian patient lost through a variety of circumstances that never, in a sane world, should have cost a woman her life. What happened to her—and to people like her, both military and civilian—lies at the core of *The Healer's War*.

The Healer's War is as much about Dang Thi Thai, and my other civilian patients, as it is about American nurses, helicopter pilots, and ground troops. I told the story from the perspective of a girl like the one I used to be because I felt that even in fiction it would be difficult for me to express exactly the depths of pain, fear, and conflict experienced by my patients and by other Vietnamese people. Especially because so many Vietnamese refugees now live in this country, I wanted to share what I knew of their stories—to give homebound Americans, their new neighbors, some insight into the world that the refugees have left. In fact, the only parts of the novel not heavily fictionalized are the stories of my Vietnamese patients.

I chose to write a novel because fiction is supposed to make sense of real life, and I *needed* to make sense of this episode of my life, of my experiences in Vietnam. In a nonfiction account, I would have been able to write only about myself, what I had seen and felt. I wasn't very clear about that when I started writing. At the University of Alaska in Fairbanks, I studied Asian history, but the first time my professor pointed to Vietnam on the map, I was immediately nauseated. Like many veterans, I had deliberately distanced the entire experience.

If friends had not started asking questions and saying, "You never told me you were a nurse in Vietnam," I might never have realized what a black hole in my spirit the war had become. I looked at it sideways, with shame and dread, sharing only the funny stories. I remembered how uncomfortable, and sometimes hostile, even people very close to me had been when, after first returning to the United States, I had tried to talk about my life in 'Nam. Researching *The Healer's War*—to give it, as fiction, a broader perspective—I began to realize how many other people in all capacities shared my feelings. Foot soldiers, helicopter pilots, and nurses alike spoke of the tragedies still haunting them twenty years later. Further, Vietnamese refugees, former Viet Cong, and protesters for peace, as well as foot soldiers, were as full of conflicts about the war as I was. And the children and relatives of veterans, not to mention those who chose not to go, just didn't understand.

In *The Healer's War*, then, I tried to weave my own story into the stories I had heard in 'Nam and, later, from veterans here in the States. I tried to be fair—to show both the good and the bad, the help and the damage, the kindness and the cruelty, the strange bonds formed with an enemy and the equally inexplicable hostility of friends. These conflicts made it impossible to deck out everyone in either black hats or white hats, to know what was the right thing to do and when to do it (always supposing that a person *wanted* to do the "right thing").

Writing my novel as a fantasy helped me focus these conflicts: I realized that many of my feelings about Vietnam, much of my emotional experience, derived not from what I had seen myself but from others' reports of their undertow of despair at not being able to make any discernible difference. I wanted to send Kitty into the jungle not to show what a heroine she was, or *I* wanted to be, but to provide more vivid pictures of the terror felt by the villagers (who, to stay alive, had to try to please both Viet Cong and U.S./ARVN troops) and of the fear and bewilderment of American troops (who wanted to be like their World War II vet fathers, giving candy and nylons to the nice Vietnamese and killing the bad ones, but who had no way of knowing which were which). In a straight realistic novel, honest writing would have required that an unarmed American woman in hostile territory, with a Vietnamese child amputee as her only companion, be killed within the first few pages after the helicopter crash. That would have made for a damn short book.

Writing a fantasy allowed me to keep my protagonists alive by creating a wise old Vietnamese healer who gives Kitty a variation on the standard magical enabling device. Unfortunately, the device cannot help Kitty destroy evil, as most magical enabling devices do. It can, however, help her recognize danger, and try to avoid it; help her recognize sickness and woundedness, and try to reverse them. My most grandiose hope is that *The Healer's War* may serve a similar function for some of its readers.

Many people have asked my opinion of "China Beach," a television drama centering on women in Vietnam. I've seen only two episodes. Despite some very good acting and some powerful scenes, it strikes me as another example of Hollywood playing dress-up with real life. The show's gratuitous cheesecake may appeal to a segment of its audience, but it has nothing to do with the hard realities of nursing or of being one of a very few "round-eye" women among thousands of angry, horny men. (Incidentally, I grew sick of the term "round eye"; it is as perjorative as any other intentionally derogatory racial designation.) Teasing was not only not very nice, it was not very safe.

A more profound objection to "China Beach" is that it premiered about three months before my book was released. People who read *The Healer's War* and saw the TV show assumed that my book was based on it—a drama performed by actresses who hadn't even been born during my tour in 'Nam. Some reviewers dismissed my novel as being "too much like 'China Beach.'" Certain superficial resemblances do exist. The setting, for example. However, China Beach was not the site of a hospital, but an R&R center near the hospital where I worked in Da Nang. We swam there during the summer, but the rest of the wild social life depicted on the series had to go on hold while we worked twelve-hour shifts six or seven days a week at the hospital. When we got off night shift and it was 120 degrees inside our tin-roofed hooches, we sometimes slept on China Beach.

The name of the show's central character is Colleen McMurphy, a nurse from Kansas. My protagonist's name is Kitty McCulley, also a nurse from Kansas. Oddly enough, I'm from Kansas, too. But many conservatively raised midwestern girls with Irish names served in Vietnam. My own name is not Irish, but I certainly didn't want to christen my character after me. I borrowed the surname of one of my maternal cousins, McCulley, and the first name of another cousin—to keep Kitty "in the family," so to speak, and to continue to feel connected with her without having her *be* me.

Although the TV series touches on some of the problems I myself faced in Vietnam, the writers have used the stories of many women who served there, inevitably dolling them up for prime time—but, of course, many of us nurses had similar experiences. *Tour of Duty, Platoon, Full Metal Jacket*, and several other 'Nam movies have been about soldiers—guys—with similar experiences, suggesting that you can have an endless, fascinating stream of stories about men at war, but that if you've seen one army nurse, you've seen 'em all. My final objection to "China Beach," or any other TV show about the war, is that the dialogue just doesn't ring true without a single "fuck."

Besides its superficial similarity to "China Beach," *The Healer's War* incurred negative critical comment with its fantasy-supported episodes in Part Two, "The Jungle"—those distinguishing my novel from any other Vietnam story.

One scene in this section has particular significance for me. Drained by her trek and her battle with an enormous snake, Kitty no longer has enough energy to funnel through the amulet to heal villagers wounded in an air strike. Unable to heal the injured herself, Kitty must channel the energy of the other villagers so that they can help their own people. This scene dramatizes what I feel is the myth sold to American participants in the Vietnam conflict—that we were not there as invaders or oppressors but as a means to help the Vietnamese heal themselves. Today, most of us realize that that goal was no more the real one than freeing the slaves was the real issue in the War Between the States. But for the idealistic—and, some may think, the blind—it was a goal that some of us set ourselves.

A friend, a former cop on whom I leaned for emotional support, told me that one reason the Vietnam experience was especially tough for medical people was that we exhausted ourselves trying to save lives and limbs, rebuild health, and preserve minds in the face of a vast war machine that mowed down and plowed under everything and everybody in its path. Our patients were blades of grass under a tank tread. We would no sooner help them stand tall again than the damned tank would back over them, flattening them for good.

The Healer's War addresses these concerns. In its own way, so does "China Beach." If either my novel or the TV show helps people see that war is not a healthy or a sane occupation, good. But more important to me than a media deal, or even a Nebula Award, are the approving letters of people touched by my book—men acknowledging that it helped them face up to their own conflicts about Vietnam, women writing to say that they now understand something about how their loved ones felt when they came home, teachers and social workers admitting that my novel has given them new insights into the Vietnamese people they're trying to help. My most rewarding compliment was from a surgical triage nurse during Tet who said that *The Healer's War* was the best story written about women's experience in Vietnam, period. Money and awards pale before such heartfelt responses.

It's common medical folk belief that anything that's good for you is supposed to hurt or to taste bad. Writing *The Healer's War* hurt almost as bad as going through 'Nam the first time—for I was determined that although my novel was going to be a fantasy, it was not going to be bullshit. It's not.

Gardner Dozois

Currently the fiction editor of *Isaac Asimov's Science Fiction Magazine*, Gardner Dozois produces too little fiction of his own. What he does write, he crafts lovingly and sells to prestigious markets. He is the co-author of a novel with George Alec Effinger, *Nightmare Blue*. Other books include *The Visible Man*, a collection of groundbreaking stories; the poignant human-and-alien love story *Strangers*, a Nebula finalist in 1978; and *Slow Dancing Through Time*, a collection of collaborative stories written, in a dizzying variety of combinations, with Jack Dann, Michael Swanwick, Jack C. Haldeman, and/or Susan Casper, Dozois's wife. He has won two Nebulas for short story, in 1983 for "The Peacemaker" and in 1984 for "Morning Child." Dozois is also an indefatigable editor, both at *Asimov's* and of independent projects, producing reprint theme anthologies with Jack Dann (*Aliens!*, *Magicats!*, *Dog Tales!*, etc.) and annually assembling a best-SF-of-the-year volume that critics and readers alike often hail as definitive.

"Solace" appeared in *Omni's* February 1989 issue. It gathered recommendations steadily throughout the year and finished high on the 1989 preliminary ballot. Although it failed to nudge its way onto the final ballot, it is a high-impact extrapolation written in Dozois's characteristically intense and vivid prose.

" 'Solace,' " Dozois observes, "began as a dream. In the dream, I was reading a story in a book, and the story that I was *reading* was essentially what happens between Kleisterman and Dr. Au in Dr. Au's office in 'Solace.' I awoke, fumbled for a piece of paper, and blurrily jotted down the essential details.

"The next morning, looking over what I had written, I decided that I could actually, with a little tinkering, turn this dream fragment into a real story—something not often true of dreams, which tend to fall apart when reviewed in the cold and logical light of day.

"I first thought to have the story begin with Kleisterman's arrival at Dr. Au's office, as it had in the dream, but I decided that the reader needed more time to get a feel for Kleisterman's personality and character and I to establish the story's mood and tone—so I began instead with a distance shot at high resolution and slowly zoomed in as Kleisterman travels from the edge of things closer and closer to the story's center, Dr. Au's office.

"Once I'd started, the details of the world through which Kleisterman travels became arbitrary. I wanted a certain kind of color and a sort of low-rent, hard-edged tone. I finally worked out the scenario present in 'Solace' because *I* had once covered the ground between Denver and Santa Fe and knew the route, and because the values implicit in the society depicted made it seem the kind of place where Kleisterman would have inevitably plied his craft—and Dr. Au, for that matter, his."

Kleisterman took a zeppelin to Denver, a feeder line to Pueblo, then transferred to a clattering local bus to Santa Fe. The bus was full of displaced Anglos who preferred the life of migrant field-worker to the Oklahoma refugee camps, a few Cambodians, a few Indians, and a number of the poorer Hispanics, mostly mestizos—unemployables who had hoped that the liberation would mean the fulfillment of all their dreams but who had instead merely found themselves working for rich Mexican caudillos rather than for millionaire Anglos. Most of the passengers had been across the border to blow their work vouchers in Denver or Cañon City and were now on their way back into Aztlan for another week's picking. They slouched sullenly in their seats, some passed out from drink or God Food and already snoring, many wrapped in ponchos or old Army blankets against the increasing chill of the evening. They ignored Kleisterman, even though, in spite of his carefully anonymous clothes, he was clearly no field hand— and Kleisterman preferred it that way.

The bus was spavined and old, the seats broken in, the sticky vinyl upholstery smelling of sweat and smoke and ancient piss. A Greyhound logo had been chipped off the side and replaced by VIAJANDO AZTLAN. The bus rattled through the cold prairie night with exquisite slowness, farting and lurching, the transmission groaning and knocking every time the driver shifted gears. The heat didn't work, or the interior lights, but Kleisterman sat stoically, not moving, as one by one the blaring radios faded and the crying babies quieted, until Kleisterman alone was awake in the chill darkness, his eyes gleaming in the shadows, shifting restlessly, never closing. At some point they passed the Frontera Libertad, the Liberty Line, and its largely symbolic chain-link fence and stopped at a checkpoint. A cyborg looked in, his great blank oval face glowing with sullen heat, like a dull rufous moon; he peered eyelessly at them for a thoughtful moment, then waved them on.

South of the border, in what had once been Colorado, they began to crawl up the long steep approach to the Raton Pass, the bus jittering and moaning like a soul in torment. Kleisterman was being washed by waves of exhaustion now, but in spite of them he slept poorly, fitfully, as he always did. It seemed as if every time his head dropped, his eyes closed, faces would spring to vivid life behind his eyelids, faces he did not want to encounter or consider, and his head would jerk up again, and his eyes would fly open, like suddenly released window shades. As always, he was afraid to dream . . . which only increased the bitter irony of his present mission. So he pinched himself cruelly to stay awake as the old bus inched painfully up and over the high mountain pass and onto the Colorado Plateau.

At Raton the bus stopped to take on more methane. The town was dark and seemingly deserted, the only light a dim bulb in the window of a ramshackle building that was being used as a fuel dump. Kleisterman stepped out of the bus and walked away from the circle of light to piss. It was very cold, and the inverted black bowl of sky overhead blazed with a million icy stars, more than Kleisterman had ever seen at once before. There was no sound except for a distant riverine roar of cold wind through the trees on the surrounding hillsides. His piss steamed in the milky starlight. As he watched, one of the stars overhead suddenly, noiselessly flared into diamond brilliance, a dozen times as bright as it had been, and then faded, guttering, and was gone. Kleisterman knew that somewhere out there a killer satellite had found its prey, out there where the multinationals and the great conglomerates fought their silent and undeclared war, with weapons more obvious than those they usually allowed themselves to use on Earth. The wind shifted, blowing through the high valley now, cutting him to the bone with chill and bringing with it the howling of wolves, a distant, feral keening that put the hair up along his spine in spite of himself. They were only the distant cousins of dogs, after all; just dogs, talking to one another on the wind. Still, the hairs stayed up.

Feet crunching gravel, Kleisterman went back to the bus and climbed aboard, found his iron-hard seat again in the darkness. In spite of the truly bitter cold, the air inside the bus was thick and stale, heavy with sleep, exhaled breath, spilled wine, sweat, the smell of cigarette smoke and marijuana and garlic. He huddled in his overcoat, shivering, and wondered whose satellite or station had just been lost and if any of his old colleagues had had anything to do with the planning or execution of the strike. Possibly. Probably, even. Once again he had to fight sleep, in spite of the cold. Once he turned his head and looked out of the window, and Melissa was there in the burnished silver moonlight, standing alongside the bus, staring up at him, and he knew that he had failed to stay awake and jerked himself up out of sleep and into the close, stuffy darkness of the bus once again. The other passengers tossed and murmured and farted. The moon *had* come out, a fat pale moon wading through a boiling river of smoky clouds, but Melissa was gone. Had not been there. Would not ever be anywhere anymore. Kleisterman found himself nodding again and pressed his face against the cold window glass, fighting it off. He would not dream. Not now. Not yet.

The bus sat unmoving in the silent town for an hour, two hours, three, for no reason Kleisterman could ascertain, and then the driver appeared again, from who knows where, climbed aboard muttering and swearing, slammed the door, twisted the engine into noisy, coughing life.

They rattled on through the night, winding down slowly out of the mountains, stopping here and there at small villages and communes to discharge passengers, the hung-over field hands climbing wordlessly from the bus and disappearing like spirits into the darkness, Kleisterman sleeping in split-second dozes. He woke from one such doze to see that the windows had turned red, red as though washed with new blood, and thought that he still slept; but it was the dawn, coming up from the broken badlands to the east, and they went down through the blood-red dawn to Santa Fe.

Kleisterman climbed stiffly down from the bus at Santa Fe. The sun had not yet warmed the air. It was still cold. The streets were filled with watery gray light, through which half-perceived figures moved with the stiff precision of early risers on a brisk morning. Kleisterman found a shabby café a block away from the bus station, ordered *huevos rancheros* and a bowl of green chili, was served the food by a sullen old Anglo woman wearing a faded Grateful Dead

T-shirt. Unusually for Santa Fe, the food was terrible, tasting of rancid grease and ashes. Kleisterman spooned it up anyway, mechanically, taking it medicinally almost. As fuel. How long had it been since he'd really enjoyed a meal? All food seemed to taste dreadful to him these days. How long since he'd really had a full night's sleep? His hand shook as he spooned beet sugar into his bitter chicory coffee. He'd always been a tall, thin, bony man, but the reflection the inside of the café window showed him was gaunt, emaciated, almost cadaverous. He'd lost a lot of weight. This could not go on. . . . Grimly he checked through his preparations once again. This time he'd been very careful about being traced. He'd made his contacts with exquisite care. There should be no trouble.

He left the café. The light had become bluer, the shadows oil-black and sharp, the sky clear and cerulean. The sun was not yet high, but the streets were already full of people. Mexican soldiers were everywhere, of course, in their comic-opera uniforms, so absurdly ornate that it was difficult to tell a private from a general. Touring Swedish nationals, each with the scarlet King's Mark tattoo on the right cheek, indicating that they were above most local law. Gangs of skinny Cambodian kids on skateboards whizzed by, threading their way expertly through the crowds, calling to one another in machine-gun-fast bursts of Spanish. A flat-faced Indian leaned from a storefront and swore at them in Vietnamese, shaking his fist. Two chimeras displayed for Kleisterman, inflating their hoods and hissing in playful malice, then sliding aside as he continued to walk toward them unperturbed. This was the kind of unregulated, wide-open town where he could find what he needed, out on the fringes, in the interstices of the worldwide networks, where things would not be watched so closely as elsewhere—no longer part of the United States but not really well integrated into Old Mexico either, with a limited official presence of the multinationals but plenty of black-market money circulating anyway.

He crossed the plaza, with its ancient Palace of the Governors, which had seen first Spanish, then Anglo, now Mexican conquerors come and go. There were slate-gray thunderheads looming over the peaks of the Sangre de Cristo mountains, which in turn loomed over the town. There was a New Town being built to the southeast, on the far side of the mostly dry Santa Fe River, a megastructure of bizarre geometric shapes, all terraces and tetrahedrons; but here in the Old Town the buildings were still made of adobe or mock adobe, colored white or salmon or peach. He threaded a maze of little alleyways and enclosed courtyards on the far side of the plaza, the noise of the plaza fading away behind, and came at last to a narrow building of sun-faded adobe that displayed a small brass plaque that read DR. AU—CONSULTATIONS.

Trembling a little, Kleisterman climbed a dusty stairwell to a third-floor office at the back of a long, dim hallway. Dr. Au turned out to be one of those slender, ageless Oriental men of indeterminate nationality who might have been fifty or eighty. Spare, neat, dry, phlegmatic. The name was Chinese, but Kleisterman suspected that he might actually be Vietnamese, as his English held the slightest trace of a French accent. He had a sad face and hard eyes. An open, unscreened window looked out through the thick adobe wall to an enclosed courtyard with a cactus garden below. The furniture was nondescript, well used, and the carpet dusty and threadbare, but an exquisite hologram of Botticelli's *Adoration of the Magi* moved and glittered in muted colors on the bare white walls, and the tastefully discreet ankh earring in the doctor's left earlobe might well have been real silver. There was no receptionist, just a desk with a complex of office terminals, a few faded armchairs, and Dr. Au.

Kleisterman could feel his heart pounding and his vision blurring as he and Dr. Au engaged in an intricate pavane of hints and innuendo and things not quite said, code words and phrases being mentioned in passing with artful casualness, contacts named, references mentioned and discussed. Dr. Au moved with immense wariness and delicacy, at every stage ready to instantly disengage, always phrasing things so that there was a completely innocent interpretation that could be given his words, while Kleisterman was washed by alternate waves of impatience, fear, rage, despair, muddy black exhaustion, ennui. At last, however, they reached a point beyond which it would no longer be possible to keep up the pretense that Kleisterman had come here for some legal purpose, a point beyond which both men could not proceed without committing themselves. Dr. Au sighed, made a fatalistic gesture, and said, "Well, then, Mr."—glancing at the card on his desk—"Ramirez, what can I do for you?"

Terror rose up in Kleisterman then. Almost, almost, he got up and fled. But he mastered himself. And as he pushed instinctual fear down, guilt and self-hate and anger rose, black and bristling and strong. None of this had reached his face.

"I want you to destroy me," Kleisterman said calmly.

Dr. Au looked first surprised, then wary—reassessing the situation for signs of potential entrapment—then, after a pause, almost regretful. "I must say, this is somewhat out of our line. We're usually asked to supply illicit fantasies, clandestine perversions, occasionally a spot of nonconsensual behavior modification." He looked at Kleisterman with curiosity. "Have you thought about this? Do you really mean what you say?"

Kleisterman was as cool as ice now, although his hands still trembled. "Yes, I mean it. I used to be in the business; I used to be an operator myself, so I can assure you that I understand the implications perfectly. I want to die. I want you to kill me. But that's not *all*. Oh, no." Kleisterman leaned forward, his gaunt face intense. His voice rose. "I want you to destroy me. I want you to make me suffer. You're an operator, an adept, you know what I mean. Not just pain; anybody can do that. I want you to make me *pay*." Kleisterman slumped back in his chair, made a tired gesture. "I know you can do it; I know you've *done* it. I know you are discreet. And when you're done with me, a hundred years subjective from now, you can get rid of my body, discreetly, and no one will ever know what happened to me. It will be as if I had never existed." His voice roughened. "As if I had never been born. Would to God I had not been."

Dr. Au made a noncommittal noise, tapped his fingers together thoughtfully. His face was tired as though in his life he had been made to see more deeply than he cared to into the human soul. His eyes glittered with interest. After a polite pause he said, "You must be quite certain of this, for later there will be no turning back. Are you sure you won't reconsider?"

Kleisterman made an impatient, despairing gesture. "I could have put a bullet in my head at any time, but that means nothing. It's not enough, not nearly enough. There must be retribution. There must be restitution. I must be made to *pay* for what I have done. Only this way can I find solace."

"Even so—" Dr. Au said, doubtfully.

Kleisterman held up his hand. Moving with slow deliberation, he reached into an inner pocket, produced a coded credit strip. "All my assets," he said, "and they are considerable." He held the credit slip up for display, then proffered it to Dr. Au. "I want you to destroy me," he said.

Dr. Au sighed. He looked left, he looked right, he looked down, he looked up. His face was suffused with dull embarrassment. But he took the credit strip.

Dr. Au ushered Kleisterman politely into an adjacent room, stood by with sad patience while Kleisterman removed his clothing. At a touch, a large metal egg rose from the floor, opened like a five-petaled flower, extruded a narrow metal bench or shelf. Dr. Au gestured brusquely; Kleisterman lay down on the bench, wincing at the touch of cold metal on his naked skin. Dr. Au leaned close over him, his face remote now and his movements briskly efficient, as though to get it all over with quickly. He taped soft cloth pads first over Kleisterman's left eye, then over his right. There was a feeling of motion, and Kleisterman knew that the metal shelf was sliding back into the machine, which would be retracting around it, the petals closing tight to form a featureless steel egg, with him inside.

Darkness. Silence.

At first, Kleisterman was aware of a sense of enclosure, was aware of the feel of the metal under his back, could even stir a little, move his fingers impatiently. But then his skin began to prickle over every inch of his body, as feathery probes made contact with his nerve endings, and as the prickling began to fade, with it went all other sensation. He could no longer feel his body, no longer move; no longer wanted to move. He didn't have a body anymore. There was nothing. Not even darkness, not even silence. Nothing. Nonexistence. Kleisterman floated in the void, waiting for the torment to begin.

This kind of machine had many names—simulator, dream machine, iron maiden, imager, shadow box. It fed coded impulses through the subject's nerves, directly into the brain. With it, the operator could make the subject experience anything. Pain, of course. Any amount of pain. With a simulator you could torture someone to death again and again, for years of subjective time, without doing them any actual physical harm—not much comfort for the subject in that, though, since to them the experience would be indistinguishable from objective reality. Of course, the most expert operators scorned this sort of thing as hopelessly crude, lacking in all finesse. Not artistic. Pain was only one key that could be played. There were many others. The subject had no secrets, and with access to the subject's deepest longings and most hidden fears, the skilled operator, the artisan, the clever craftsman could devise cunning scenarios much more effective than pain.

Kleisterman had been such an operator, one of the best, admired by his colleagues for his subtlety and ingenuity and skill. He had clandestinely "processed" thousands of subjects for his multinational and had never felt a qualm, until suddenly one day, for no particular reason, he began to sicken. After Donaldson, Ramaswamy, and Kole, three especially difficult and unpleasant jobs, he had sickened further and, for the first time in his life, began to have difficulty sleeping— and, when he did sleep, began to have unquiet dreams. Then Melissa had somehow become the target of corporate malice and had been sent to him for his ministrations. By rights he should have declined the job, since he knew Melissa and had even had a brief affair with her once, years before. But he had had his professional pride. He did not turn down the job. And somewhere deep in her mind, he had found himself, an ennobled and idealized version of himself as he had never been, and he realized that while for him their affair had been unimportant, for her it had been much more intensely charged— that, in fact, she had loved him deeply and still did.

This discovery brought out the very worst in him, and in a fever of sick excitement, he created scenario after scenario for her, life after life, each scenario working some variation on the theme of her love for him; and each time, "his" treatment of her in the scenario became worse, his betrayal of her uglier and more humiliating, the pain and shame and anguish he visited on her more severe. He turned the universe against her in grotesque ways, too, so that in one life she died in a car wreck on the way to her own wedding, and in another life she died slowly and messily of cancer, and in another she was hideously disfigured in a fire, and in another she had a stroke and lingered on for years as a semiaware paralytic in a squalid nursing home, and so on. Each life began to color the next, not with specific memories of other existences but with a dark emotional residue, an unspoken, instinctual conviction that life was drab and bitter and harsh, with nothing to look forward to but defeat and misery and pain, that the dice were stacked hopelessly against you—as, in fact, they were. Then, tiring of subtlety, irresistibly tempted to put aside his own aesthetic precepts, he began to hit her, in the scenarios—at first just slapping her around in drunken rages, then beating her severely enough to put her in the hospital. Then, in one scenario, he picked up a knife. Several lifetimes subjective later, the heart in her physical body finally gave out, and she died in a way that was no more real to her than the dozens of times she'd died before but which put her at last beyond his reach. He had been dismayed to discover that in the deepest recesses of her mind, below the fear and hate and bitterness and grief, she loved him still, even at the last. He switched off the machine, and he awoke, as from a fever dream, as though he had been possessed by a demon of perversity that had only now been exorcised, to find himself alone in his soundproofed cubicle with the simulator and Melissa's cooling body. He betrayed the corporation on his next assignment, freeing the subject rather than "processing" him, and from then on he had been on the run. He had found that he could successfully hide from the multinational. Hiding from himself had proved more difficult.

Light exploded in his head, and it took a second for his vision to adjust and to realize that the patch over his left eye had been removed. Dr. Au leaned in over him again, filling his field of vision like a god, and this time Kleisterman felt the painful yank of tape against skin as Dr. Au ripped the other eye patch free. More light. Kleisterman blinked, disoriented and confused. He was out of the machine. Dr. Au was tugging at him, getting him to sit up. Dr. Au was saying something, but it was a blare of noise, harsh and hurtful to the ears. He pawed at Kleisterman again, and Kleisterman shook him off. Kleisterman sat, head down, on the edge of the metal bench until his senses readjusted to the world again, and his mind cleared. His skin prickled as sensation returned.

Dr. Au tugged at Kleisterman's arm. "A red security flag came up on your credit account," Dr. Au said. His voice was anxious, and his face was pinched with fear. "There was a security probe; I barely avoided it. You must leave. I want you out of here right away."

Kleisterman stared at him. "But you agreed—" he said thickly.

"I want nothing to do with you, Mr. Ramirez," Dr. Au said apprehensively. "Here, take your clothes, get dressed. You have some very ruthless forces opposed to you, Mr. Ramirez. I want nothing to do with them, either. No trouble. Leave now. Take your business elsewhere."

Slowly Kleisterman dressed, manipulating the clothes with stiff, clumsy fingers while Dr. Au hovered anxiously. The office was filled with watery gray light that seemed painfully bright after the darkness inside the simulator. Dust motes danced in suspension in the light, and a fly hopped along the adobe edge of the open window before darting outside again. A dog was barking out there somewhere, a flat, faraway sound, and a warm breeze puffed in for a second to ruffle his hair and bring him the smell of pine and juniper. He was perceiving every smallest detail with exquisite clarity.

Kleisterman pushed wordlessly by Dr. Au, walked through the outer office and out into the dusty hallway beyond. The floor was scuffed, grime between the tiles, and there were peeling water stains on the ceiling. A smell of cooking food came up the stairwell. *This is real*, Kleisterman told himself fiercely. *This is real, this is really happening, this is the real world. The multinational boys aren't subtle enough for this; they wouldn't be satisfied with just denying me solace. Letting me go on. They're not that subtle.*

Are they? Are they?

Kleisterman went down the narrow stairs. He dragged his fist against the rough adobe wall until his knuckles bled, but he couldn't convince himself that any of it was real.

THE MOUNTAINS OF MOURNING

Lois McMaster Bujold

Lois McMaster Bujold, a resident of Marion, Ohio, won the 1988 Nebula Award for her novel *Falling Free* and appeared in last year's anthology with an informal essay about the writing of that novel. Her most recent titles include *Borders of Infinity*, of which "The Mountains of Mourning" is an integral part; *The Vor Game*, a novel featuring Miles Vorkosigan; *The Enchanted Saltcellar*, a stand-alone fantasy; and a direct sequel to her acclaimed first novel, *Shards of Honor*. The sequel, titled *Barrayar*, dramatizes Miles's mother Cordelia's first year on the planet Barrayar.

In 1989, Ms. Bujold won her second Nebula for "The Mountains of Mourning." Of it, she writes, "My deformed hero Miles, as son of the local lord, must travel into the backcountry to solve a sticky, indeed personally excruciating, infanticide for birth defects. I enjoyed trying out the mystery forms—the woman with a problem, the parade of red herrings, a salute to Judge Dee—as Miles became caught up in his temporary role as detective. But the solution to the mystery, Miles discovers, is not the solution to the problem, and he must reach deeply into a larger sense of his humanity and his history to find justice. As an idealistic young officer sworn to service, he must also learn the subtle difference between serving an empire and serving a people."

Ms. Bujold likes the flexibility, intensity, independence, and novelistic roominess of the novella—good news for both admirers of her work and devotees of the form.

Miles heard the woman weeping as he was climbing the hill from the long lake. He hadn't dried himself after his swim, as the morning already promised shimmering heat. Lake water trickled cool from his hair onto his naked chest and back, more annoyingly down his legs from his ragged shorts. His leg braces chafed on his damp skin as he pistoned up the faint trail through the scrub, military double-time. His feet squished in his old wet shoes. He slowed curiously as he became conscious of the voices.

The woman's voice grated with grief and exhaustion. "Please, lord, please. All I want is m'justice. . . ."

The front gate guard's voice was irritated and embarrassed. "I'm no lord. C'mon, get *up*, woman. Go back to the village and report it at the district magistrate's office."

"I tell you, I just came from there!" The woman did not move from her knees as Miles emerged from the bushes and paused to take in the tableau across the paved road. "The magistrate's not to return for weeks, weeks. I walked four days to get here. I only have a little money. . . ." A desperate hope rose in her voice, and her spine bent and straightened as she scrabbled in her skirt pocket and held out her cupped hands to the guard. "A mark and twenty pence, it's all I have, but—"

The exasperated guard's eye fell on Miles, and he straightened abruptly, as if afraid Miles might suspect him of being tempted by so pitiful a bribe. "Be off, woman!" he snapped.

Miles quirked an eyebrow, and limped across the road to the main gate. "What's all this about, Corporal?" he inquired easily.

The guard corporal was on loan from Imperial Security, and wore the high-necked dress greens of the Barrayaran Service. He was sweating and uncomfortable in the bright morning light of this southern district, but Miles fancied he'd be boiled before he'd undo his collar on this post. His accent was not local, he was a city man from the capital, where a more or less efficient bureaucracy absorbed such problems as the one on her knees before him.

The woman, now, was local and more than local—she had back-country written all over her. She was younger than her strained voice had at first suggested. Tall, fever-red from her weeping, with stringy blonde hair hanging down across a ferret-thin face and protuberant gray eyes. If she were cleaned up, fed, rested, happy and confident, she might achieve a near-prettiness, but she was far from that now, despite her remarkable figure. Lean but full-breasted—no, Miles revised himself as he crossed the road and came up to the gate. Her bodice was all blotched with dried milk leaks, though there was no baby in sight. Only temporarily full-breasted. Her worn dress was factory-woven cloth, but hand-sewn, crude and simple. Her feet were bare, thickly callused, cracked and sore.

"No problem," the guard assured Miles. "Go *away*," he hissed to the woman.

She lurched off her knees and sat stonily.

"I'll call my sergeant," the guard eyed her warily, "and have her removed."

"Wait a moment," said Miles.

She stared up at Miles from her cross-legged position, clearly not knowing whether to identify him as hope or not. His clothing, what there was of it, offered her no clue as to what he might be. The rest of him was all too plainly displayed. He jerked up his chin and smiled thinly. Too-large head, too-short neck, back thickened with its crooked spine, crooked legs with their brittle bones too often broken, drawing the eye in their gleaming chromium braces. Were the hill woman standing, the top of his head would barely be even with the top of her shoulder. He waited in boredom for her hand to make the back-country hex sign against evil mutations, but it only jerked and clenched into a fist.

"I must see my lord count," she said to an uncertain point halfway between Miles and the guard. "It's my right. My daddy, he died in the Service. It's my right."

"Prime Minister Count Vorkosigan," said the guard stiffly, "is on his country estate to rest. If he were working, he'd be back in Vorbarr Sultana." The guard looked like *he* wished he were back in Vorbarr Sultana.

The woman seized the pause. "You're only a city man. He's *my* count. My right."

"What do you want to see Count Vorkosigan for?" asked Miles patiently.

"Murder," growled the girl/woman. The security guard spasmed slightly. "I want to report a murder."

"Shouldn't you report to your village speaker first?" inquired Miles, with a hand-down gesture to calm the twitching guard.

"I did. He'll do *nothing*." Rage and frustration cracked her voice. "He says it's over and done. He won't write down my accusation, says it's nonsense. It would only make trouble for everybody, he says. I don't care! I want my justice!"

Miles frowned thoughtfully, looking the woman over. The details checked, corroborated her claimed identity, added up to a solid if subliminal sense of truth which perhaps escaped the professionally paranoid security man. "It's true, Corporal," Miles said. "She has a right to appeal, first to the district magistrate, then to the Count's court. And the district magistrate won't be back for two weeks."

This sector of Count Vorkosigan's native district had only one overworked district magistrate, who rode a circuit that included the lakeside village of Vorkosigan Surleau but one day a month. Since the region of the Prime Minister's country estate was crawling with Imperial Security when the great lord was in residence, and closely monitored even when he was not, prudent troublemakers took their troubles elsewhere.

"Scan her, and let her in," said Miles. "On my authority."

The guard was one of Imperial Security's best, trained to look for assassins in his own shadow. He now looked scandalized, and lowered his voice to Miles. "Sir, if I let every country lunatic wander the estate at will—"

"I'll take her up. I'm going that way."

The guard shrugged helplessly, but stopped short of saluting; Miles was decidedly not in uniform. The gate guard pulled a scanner from his belt and made a great show of going over the woman. Miles wondered if he'd have been inspired to harass her with a strip-search without Miles's inhibiting presence. When the guard finished demonstrating how alert, conscientious, and loyal he was, he palmed open the gate's lock, entered the transaction, including the woman's retina scan, into the computer monitor, and stood aside in a pose of rather pointed parade rest. Miles grinned at the silent editorial, and steered the bedraggled woman by the elbow through the gates and up the winding drive.

She twitched away from his touch at the earliest opportunity, yet still refrained from superstitious gestures, eyeing him with a strange and hungry curiosity. Time was, such openly repelled fascination with the peculiarities of his body had driven Miles to grind his teeth; now he could take it with a serene amusement only slightly tinged with acid. They would learn, all of them. They would learn.

"Do you serve Count Vorkosigan, little man?" she asked cautiously.

Miles thought about that one a moment. "Yes," he answered finally. The answer was, after all, true on every level of meaning but the one she'd asked it. He quelled the temptation to tell her he was the court jester. From the look of her, this one's troubles were much worse than his own.

She had apparently not quite believed in her own rightful destiny, despite her mulish determination at the gate, for as they climbed unimpeded toward her goal a nascent panic made her face even more drawn and pale, almost ill. "How—how do I talk to him?" she choked. "Should I curtsey . . . ?" She glanced down at herself as if conscious for the first time of her own dirt and sweat and squalor.

Miles suppressed a facetious set-up starting with, *Kneel and knock your forehead three times on the floor before speaking, that's what the General Staff does,* and said instead, "Just stand up straight and speak the truth. Try to be clear. He'll take it from there. He does not, after all," Miles's lips twitched, "lack experience."

She swallowed.

A hundred years ago, the Vorkosigans' summer retreat had been a guard barracks, part of the outlying fortifications of the great castle on the bluff above the village of Vorkosigan Surleau. The castle was now a burnt-out ruin, and the barracks transformed into a comfortable low stone residence, modernized and remodernized, artistically landscaped and bright with flowers. The arrow slits had been widened into big glass windows overlooking the lake, and comm-link antennae bristled from the roof. There was a new guard barracks concealed in the trees downslope, but it had no arrow slits.

A man in the brown and silver livery of the Count's personal retainers exited the residence's front door as Miles approached with the strange woman in tow. It was the new man, what was his name? Pym, that was it.

"Where's m'lord Count?" Miles asked him.

"In the upper pavilion, taking breakfast with m'lady." Pym glanced at the woman, waited on Miles in a posture of polite inquiry.

"Ah. Well, this woman has walked four days to lay an appeal before the district magistrate's court. The court's not here, but the Count is, so she now proposes to skip the middlemen and go straight to the top. I like her style. Take her up, will you?"

"During *breakfast?*" said Pym.

Miles cocked his head at the woman. "Have you had breakfast?"

She shook her head mutely.

"I thought not." Miles turned his hands palm-out, dumping her, symbolically, on the retainer. "Now, yes."

"My daddy, he died in the Service," the woman repeated faintly. "It's my right." The phrase seemed as much to convince herself as anyone else, now.

Pym was, if not a hill man, district-born. "So it is," he sighed, and gestured her to follow him without further ado. Her eyes widened, as she trailed him around the house, and she glanced back nervously over her shoulder at Miles. "Little man . . . ?"

"Just stand straight," he called to her. He watched her round the corner, grinned, and took the steps two at a time into the residence's main entrance.

AFTER A SHAVE and cold shower, Miles dressed in his own room overlooking the long lake. He dressed with great care, as great as he'd expended on the Service Academy ceremonies and Imperial Review two days ago. Clean underwear, long-sleeved cream shirt, dark green trousers with the side piping. High-collared green tunic tailor-cut to his own difficult fit. New pale blue plastic Ensign's rectangles aligned precisely on the collar and poking most uncomfortably into his jaw. He dispensed with the leg braces and pulled on mirror-polished boots to the knee, and swiped a bit of dust from them with his pajama pants, ready to hand on the floor where he'd dropped them before going swimming.

He straightened and checked himself in the mirror. His dark hair hadn't even begun to recover from that last cut before the graduation ceremonies. A pale, sharp-featured face, not too much dissipated bag under the gray eyes, nor too bloodshot—alas, the limits of his body compelled him to stop celebrating well before he could hurt himself.

Echoes of the late celebration still boiled up silently in his head, twitching his mouth into a grin. He was on his way now, had his hand clamped firmly around the lowest rung of the highest ladder on Barrayar, Imperial Service itself. There were no giveaways in the Service even for sons of the old Vor. You got what you earned. His brother officers could be relied on to know that, even if outsiders wondered. He was in position at last to prove himself to all doubters. Up and away and never look down, never look back.

One last look back. As carefully as he'd dressed, Miles gathered up the necessary objects for his task. The white cloth rectangles of his former, Academy cadet's rank. The hand-calligraphed second copy, purchased for this purpose, of his new officer's commission in the Barrayaran Imperial Service. A copy of his Academy three-year scholastic transcript on paper, with all its commendations (and demerits). No point in anything but honesty in this next transaction. In a cupboard downstairs he found the brass brazier and tripod, wrapped in its polishing cloth, and a plastic bag of very dry juniper bark. Chemical firesticks.

Out the back door and up the hill. The landscaped path split, the right branch going up to the pavilion overlooking it all. Miles took the left fork to a garden-like area surrounded by a low fieldstone wall. He let himself in by the gate. "Good morning, crazy ancestors," he called, then quelled his humor. It might be true, but lacked the respect due the occasion.

He strolled over and around the graves until he came to the one he sought, knelt, and set up the brazier and tripod, humming. The stone was simple, GENERAL COUNT PIOTR PIERRE VORKOSIGAN, and the dates. If they'd tried to list all the accumulated honors and accomplishments, they'd have had to go to microprint.

He piled in the bark, the very expensive papers, the cloth bits, a clipped mat of dark hair from that last cut. He set it alight and rocked back on his heels to watch it burn. He'd played a hundred versions of this moment over in his head, over the years, ranging from solemn public orations with musicians in the background, to dancing naked on the old man's grave. He'd settled on this private and traditional ceremony, played straight. Just between the two of them.

"So, Grandfather," he purred at last. "And here we are after all. Satisfied now?"

All the chaos of the graduation ceremonies behind, all the mad efforts of the last three years, all the pain, came to this point; but the grave did not speak, did not say, *Well done; you can stop now*. The ashes spelled out no messages, there were no visions to be had in the rising smoke. The brazier burned down all too quickly. Not enough stuff in it, perhaps.

He stood, and dusted his knees, in the silence and the sunlight. So what had he expected? Applause? Why was he here, in the final analysis? Dancing out a dead man's dreams—who did his Service really serve? Grandfather? Himself? Pale Emperor Gregor? Who cared?

"Well, old man," he whispered, then shouted: "ARE YOU SAT-ISFIED YET?" The echoes rang from the stones.

A throat cleared behind him, and Miles whirled like a scalded cat, heart pounding.

"Uh . . . my lord?" said Pym carefully. "Pardon me, I did not mean to interrupt . . . anything. But the Count your father requires you to attend on him in the upper pavilion."

Pym's expression was perfectly bland. Miles swallowed, and waited for the scarlet heat he could feel in his face to recede. "Quite," he shrugged. "The fire's almost out. I'll clean it up later. Don't . . . let anybody else touch it."

He marched past Pym and didn't look back.

THE PAVILION was a simple structure of weathered silver wood, open on all four sides to catch the breeze, this morning a few faint puffs from the west. Good sailing on the lake this afternoon, maybe. Only ten days precious home leave left, and much Miles wanted to do, including the trip to Vorbarr Sultana with his cousin Ivan to pick out his new lightflyer. And then his first assignment would be coming through—ship duty, Miles prayed. He'd had to overcome a major temptation, not to ask his father to make sure it was ship duty. He would take whatever assignment fate dealt him, that was the first rule of the game. And win with the hand he was dealt.

The interior of the pavilion was shady and cool after the glare outside. It was furnished with comfortable old chairs and tables, one of which bore the remains of a noble breakfast—Miles mentally marked two lonely-looking oil cakes on a crumb-scattered tray as his own. Miles's mother, lingering over her cup, smiled across the table at him.

Miles's father, casually dressed in an open-throated shirt and shorts, sat in a worn armchair. Aral Vorkosigan was a thickset, gray-haired man, heavy-jawed, heavy-browed, scarred. A face that lent itself to savage caricature—Miles had seen some, in Opposition press, in the histories of Barrayar's enemies. They had only to draw one lie, to render dull those sharp penetrating eyes, to create everyone's parody of a military dictator.

And how much is he haunted by Grandfather? Miles wondered. He doesn't show it much. But then, he doesn't have to. Admiral Aral Vorkosigan, space master strategist, conquerer of Komarr, hero of Escobar, for sixteen years Imperial Regent and supreme power on Barrayar in all but name. And then he'd capped it, confounded history and all self-sure witnesses and heaped up honor and glory beyond all that had gone before by voluntarily stepping *down* and transferring command smoothly to Emperor Gregor upon his majority. Not that the Prime Ministership hadn't made a dandy retirement from the Regency, and he was showing no signs yet of stepping down from *that*.

And so Admiral Aral's life took General Piotr's like an over-powering hand of cards, and where did that leave Ensign Miles? Holding two deuces and the joker. He must surely either concede or start bluffing like crazy. . . .

The hill woman sat on a hassock, a half-eaten oil cake clutched in her hands, staring open-mouthed at Miles in all his power and polish. As he caught and returned her gaze her lips pressed closed and her eyes lit. Her expression was strange—anger? Exhilaration? Embarrassment? Glee? Some bizarre mixture of all? *And what did you think I was, woman?*

Being in uniform (showing off his uniform?), Miles came to attention before his father. "Sir?"

Count Vorkosigan spoke to the woman. "That is my son. If I send him as my Voice, would that satisfy you?"

"Oh," she breathed, her wide mouth drawing back in a weird, fierce grin, the most expression Miles had yet seen on her face, "*yes*, my lord."

"Very well. It will be done."

What will be done? Miles wondered warily. The Count was leaning back in his chair, looking satisfied himself, but with a dangerous tension around his eyes hinting that something had aroused his true anger. Not anger at the woman, clearly they were in some sort of agreement, and—Miles searched his conscience quickly—not at Miles himself. He cleared his throat gently, cocking his head and baring his teeth in an inquiring smile.

The Count steepled his hands and spoke to Miles at last. "A most interesting case. I can see why you sent her up."

"Ah . . ." said Miles. What had he got hold of? He'd only greased the woman's way through Security on a quixotic impulse, for God's sake, and to tweak his father at breakfast. ". . . ah?" he continued noncommittally.

Count Vorkosigan's brows rose. "Did you not know?"

"She spoke of a murder, and a marked lack of cooperation from her local authorities about it. Figured you'd give her a lift on to the district magistrate."

The Count settled back still farther, and rubbed his hand thoughtfully across his scarred chin. "It's an infanticide case."

Miles's belly went cold. *I don't want anything to do with this.* Well, that explained why there was no baby to go with the breasts. "Unusual . . . for it to be reported."

"We've fought the old customs for twenty years and more," said the Count. "Promulgated, propagandized . . . In the cities, we've made good progress."

"In the cities," murmured the Countess, "people have access to alternatives."

"But in the backcountry—well—little has changed. We all know what's going on, but without a report, a complaint—and with the family invariably drawing together to protect its own—it's hard to get leverage."

"What," Miles cleared his throat, nodded at the woman, "what was your baby's mutation?"

"The cat's mouth." The woman dabbed at her upper lip to demonstrate. "She had the hole inside her mouth, too, and was a weak sucker, she choked and cried, but she was getting enough, she was. . . ."

"Harelip," the Count's off-worlder wife murmured half to herself, translating the Barrayaran term to the galactic standard, "and a cleft palate, sounds like. Harra, that's not even a mutation. They had that back on Old Earth. A . . . a normal birth defect, if that's not a contradiction in terms. Not a punishment for your Barrayaran ancestors' pilgrimage through the Fire. A simple operation could have corrected—" Countess Vorkosigan cut herself off. The hill woman was looking anguished.

"I'd heard," the woman said. "My lord had made a hospital to be built at Hassadar. I meant to take her there, when I was a little stronger, though I had no money. Her arms and legs were sound, her head was well-shaped, anybody could see—surely they would have"—her hands clenched and twisted, her voice went ragged—"but Lem killed her first."

A seven-day walk, Miles calculated, from the deep Dendarii Mountains to the lowland town of Hassadar. Reasonable, that a woman newly risen from child-bed might delay that hike a few days. An hour's ride in an aircar . . .

"So one is reported as a murder at last," said Count Vorkosigan, "and we will treat it as exactly that. This is a chance to send a message to the farthest corners of my own district. You, Miles, will be my Voice, to reach where it has not reached before. You will dispense Count's justice upon this man—and not quietly, either. It's time for the practices that brand us as barbarians in galactic eyes to end."

Miles gulped. "Wouldn't the district magistrate be better qualified . . . ?"

The Count smiled slightly. "For this case, I can think of no one better qualified than yourself."

The messenger and the message all in one: *Times have changed.* Indeed. Miles wished himself elsewhere, anywhere—back sweating blood over his final examinations, for instance. He stifled an unworthy wail, *My home leave . . . !*

Miles rubbed the back of his neck. "Who, ah . . . who is it killed your little girl?" *Meaning, who is it I'm expected to drag out, put up against a wall, and shoot?*

"My husband," she said tonelessly, looking at—through—the polished silvery floorboards.

I knew this was going to be messy. . . .

"She cried and cried," the woman went on, "and wouldn't go to sleep, not nursing well—he shouted at me to shut her up—"

"Then?" Miles prompted, sick to his stomach.

"He swore at me, and went to go sleep at his mother's. He said at least a working man could sleep there. I hadn't slept either. . . ."

This guy sounds like a real winner. Miles had an instant picture of him, a bull of a man with a bullying manner—nevertheless, there was something missing in the climax of the woman's story.

The Count had picked up on it too. He was listening with total attention, his strategy-session look, a slit-eyed intensity of thought you could mistake for sleepiness. That would be a grave mistake. "Were you an eyewitness?" he asked in a deceptively mild tone that put Miles on full alert. "Did you actually see him kill her?"

"I found her dead in the midmorning, lord."

"You went into the bedroom—" Count Vorkosigan led her on.

"We've only got one room." She shot him a look as if doubtful for the first time of his total omniscience. "She had slept, slept at last. I went out to get some brillberries, up the ravine a way. And when I came back . . . I should have taken her with me, but I was so glad she slept at last, didn't want to risk waking her—" Tears leaked from the woman's tightly closed eyes. "I let her sleep when I came back, I was glad to eat and rest, but I began to get full," her hand touched a breast, "and I went to wake her. . . ."

"What, were there no marks on her? Not a cut throat?" asked the Count. That was the usual method for these backcountry infanticides, quick and clean compared to, say, exposure.

The woman shook her head. "Smothered, I think, lord. It was cruel, something cruel. The village Speaker said I must have overlain her, and wouldn't take my plea against Lem. I did not, I did not! She had her own cradle, Lem made it with his own hands when she was still in my belly. . . ." She was close to breaking down.

The Count exchanged a glance with his wife, and a small tilt of his head. Countess Vorkosigan rose smoothly.

"Come, Harra, down to the house. You must wash and rest before Miles takes you home."

The hill woman looked taken aback. "Oh, not in your house, lady!"

"Sorry, it's the only one I've got handy. Besides the guard barracks. The guards are good boys, but you'd make 'em uncomfortable. . . ." The Countess eased her out.

"It is clear," said Count Vorkosigan as soon as the women were out of earshot, "that you will have to check out the medical facts before, er, popping off. And I trust you will also have noticed the little problem with a positive identification of the accused. This could be the ideal public-demonstration case we want, but not if there's any ambiguity about it. No bloody mysteries."

"I'm not a coroner," Miles pointed out immediately. If he could wriggle off this hook . . .

"Quite. You will take Dr. Dea with you."

Lieutenant Dea was the Prime Minister's physician's assistant. Miles had seen him around—an ambitious young military doctor, in a constant state of frustration because his superior would never let him touch his most important patient—oh, he was going to be thrilled with this assignment, Miles predicted morosely.

"He can take his osteo kit with him, too," the Count went on, brightening slightly, "in case of accidents."

"How economical," said Miles, rolling his eyes. "Look, uh—suppose her story checks out and we nail this guy. Do I have to, personally . . . ?"

"One of the liveried men will be your bodyguard. And—if the story checks—the executioner."

That was only slightly better. "Couldn't we wait for the district magistrate?"

"Every judgment the district magistrate makes, he makes in my place. Every sentence his office carries out is carried out in my name. Someday, it will be done in your name. It's time you gained a clear understanding of the process. Historically, the Vor may be a military caste, but a Vor lord's duties were never only military ones."

No escape. Damn, damn, damn. Miles sighed. "Right. Well . . . we could take the aircar, I suppose, and be up there in a couple of hours. Allow some time to find the right hole. Drop out of the sky on 'em, make the message loud and clear . . . be back before bedtime." Get it over with quickly.

The Count had that slit-eyed look again. "No . . ." he said slowly, "not the aircar, I don't think."

"No roads for a groundcar, up that far. Just trails." He added uneasily—surely his father could not be thinking of—"I don't think I'd cut a very impressive figure of central Imperial authority on foot, sir."

His father glanced up at his crisp dress uniform and smiled slightly. "Oh, you don't do so badly."

"But picture this after three or four days of beating through the bushes," Miles protested. "You didn't see us in Basic. Or smell us."

"I've been there," said the Admiral dryly. "But no, you're quite right. Not on foot. I have a better idea."

MY OWN CAVALRY TROOP, thought Miles ironically, turning in his saddle, *just like Grandfather*. Actually, he was pretty sure the old man would have had some acerbic comments about the riders now strung out behind Miles on the wooded trail, once he'd got done rolling on the ground laughing at the equitation being displayed. The Vorkosigan stables had shrunk sadly since the old man was no longer around to take an interest, the polo string sold off, the few remaining ancient and ill-tempered ex-cavalry beasts put permanently out to pasture. The handful of riding horses left were retained for their sure-footedness and good manners, not their exotic bloodlines, and kept exercised and gentle for the occasional guest by a gaggle of girls from the village.

Miles gathered his reins, tensed one calf, and shifted his weight slightly, and Fat Ninny responded with a neat half turn and two precise back steps. The thick-set roan gelding could not have been mistaken by the most ignorant urbanite for a fiery steed, but Miles adored him, for his dark and liquid eye, his wide velvet nose, his phlegmatic disposition equally unappalled by rushing streams or screaming air-cars, but most of all for his exquisite dressage-trained responsiveness. Brains before beauty. Just being around him made Miles calmer, the beast was an emotional blotter, like a purring cat. Miles patted Fat Ninny on the neck. "If anybody asks," he murmured, "I'll tell them your name is Chieftain." Fat Ninny waggled one fuzzy ear, and heaved a wooshing, barrel-chested sigh.

Grandfather had a great deal to do with the unlikely parade Miles now led. The great guerrilla general had poured out his youth in these mountains, fighting the Cetagandan invaders to a standstill and then reversing their tide. Anti-flyer heatless seeker-strikers smuggled in at bloody cost from off-planet had a lot more to do with the final victory than cavalry horses, which, according to Grandfather, had saved his forces through the worst winter of that campaign mainly by being edible. But through retroactive romance, the horse had become the symbol of that struggle.

Miles thought his father was being overly optimistic, if he thought Miles was going to cash in thusly on the old man's residual glory. The guerrilla caches and camp clearings were shapeless lumps of rust and *trees*, dammit, not just weeds and scrub anymore—they had passed some, earlier in today's ride—the men who had fought that war had

long since gone to ground for the last time, just like Grandfather.
What was he doing here? It was Jump ship duty he wanted, taking him high, high above all this. The future, not the past, held his
destiny.

Miles's meditations were interrupted by Dr. Dea's horse, which,
taking exception to a branch lying across the logging trail, planted all
four feet in an abrupt stop and snorted loudly. Dr. Dea toppled off
with a faint cry.

"Hang on to the *reins*," Miles called, and pressed Fat Ninny back
down the trail.

Dr. Dea was getting rather better at falling off, he'd landed more
or less on his feet this time. He made a lunge at the dangling reins,
but his sorrel mare shied away from his grab. Dea jumped back as
she swung on her haunches and then, realizing her freedom, bounced
back down the trail, tail bannering, horse body language for *Nyah,
nyah, ya can't catch me!* Dr. Dea, red and furious, ran swearing in
pursuit. She broke into a canter.

"No, no, don't run after her!" called Miles.

"How the hell am I supposed to catch her if I don't run after
her?" snarled Dea. The space surgeon was not a happy man. "My
medkit's on that bloody beast!"

"How do you think you can catch her if you do?" asked Miles.
"She can run faster than you can."

At the end of the little column, Pym turned his horse sideways,
blocking the trail. "Just wait, Harra," Miles advised the anxious hill
woman in passing. "Hold your horse still. Nothing starts a horse
running faster than another running horse."

The other two riders were doing rather better. The woman Harra
Csurik sat her horse wearily, allowing it to plod along without interference, but at least riding on balance instead of trying to use the
reins as a handle like the unfortunate Dea. Pym, bringing up the rear,
was competent if not comfortable.

Miles slowed Fat Ninny to a walk, reins loose, and wandered
after the mare, radiating an air of calm relaxation. *Who, me? I don't
want to catch you. We're just enjoying the scenery, right. That's it,
stop for a bite.* The sorrel mare paused to nibble at a weed, but kept
a wary eye on Miles's approach.

At a distance just short of starting the mare bolting off again,

Miles stopped Fat Ninny and slid off. He made no move toward the mare, but instead stood still and made a great show of fishing in his pockets. Fat Ninny butted his head against Miles eagerly, and Miles cooed and fed him a bit of sugar. The mare cocked her ears with interest. Fat Ninny smacked his lips and nudged for more. The mare snuffled up for her share. She lipped a cube from Miles's palm as he slid his other arm quietly through the loop of her reins.

"Here you go, Dr. Dea. One horse. No running."

"No fair," wheezed Dea, trudging up. "You had sugar in your pockets."

"Of course I had sugar in my pockets. It's called foresight and planning. The trick of handling horses isn't to be faster than the horse, or stronger than the horse. That pits your weakness against his strengths. The trick is to be smarter than the horse. That pits your strength against his weakness, eh?"

Dea took his reins. "It's snickering at me," he said suspiciously.

"That's nickering, not snickering." Miles grinned. He tapped Fat Ninny behind his left foreleg, and the horse obediently grunted down onto one knee. Miles clambered up readily to his conveniently lowered stirrup.

"Does mine do that?" asked Dr. Dea, watching with fascination.

"Sorry, no."

Dea glowered at his horse. "This animal is an idiot. I shall lead it for a while."

As Ninny lurched back to his four feet Miles suppressed a riding-instructorly comment gleaned from his Grandfather's store such as, *Be smarter than the horse, Dea.* Though Dr. Dea was officially sworn to Lord Vorkosigan for the duration of this investigation, Space Surgeon Lieutenant Dea certainly outranked Ensign Vorkosigan. To command older men who outranked one called for a certain measure of tact.

The logging road widened out here, and Miles dropped back beside Harra Csurik. Her fierceness and determination of yesterday morning at the gate seemed to be fading even as the trail rose toward her home. Or perhaps it was simply exhaustion catching up with her. She'd said little all morning, been sunk in silence all afternoon. If she was going to drag Miles all the way up to the back of beyond and then wimp out on him . . .

"What, ah, branch of the Service was your father in, Harra?" Miles began conversationally.

She raked her fingers through her hair in a combing gesture more nervousness than vanity. Her eyes looked out at him through the straw-colored wisps like skittish creatures in the protection of a hedge.

"District Militia, m'lord. I don't really remember him, he died when I was real little."

"In combat?"

She nodded. "In the fighting around Vorbarr Sultana, during Vordarian's Pretendership."

Miles refrained from asking which side he had been swept up on—most footsoldiers had had little choice, and the amnesty had included the dead as well as the living.

"Ah . . . do you have any, sibs?"

"No, lord. Just me and my mother left."

A little anticipatory tension eased in Miles's neck. If this judgment indeed drove all the way through to an execution, one misstep could trigger a blood feud among the in-laws. *Not* the legacy of justice the Count intended him to leave behind. So the fewer in-laws involved, the better. "What about your husband's family?"

"He's got seven. Four brothers and three sisters."

"Hm." Miles had a mental flash of an entire team of huge, menacing hill hulks. He glanced back at Pym, feeling a trifle understaffed for his task. He had pointed out this factor to the Count, when they'd been planning this expedition last night.

"The village Speaker and his deputies will be your backup," the Count had said, "just as for the district magistrate on court circuit."

"What if they don't want to cooperate?" Miles had asked nervously.

"An officer who expects to command Imperial troops," the Count had glinted, "should be able to figure out how to extract cooperation from a backcountry headman."

In other words, his father had decided this was a test, and wasn't going to give him any more clues. Thanks, Dad.

"You have no sibs, lord?" said Harra, snapping him back to the present.

"No. But surely that's known, even in the backbeyond."

"They *say* a lot of things about you." Harra shrugged.

Miles bit down on the morbid question in his mouth like a wedge of raw lemon. He would not ask it, he would not . . . he couldn't help himself: "Like what?" forced out past his stiff lips.

"Everyone knows the Count's son is a mutant." Her eyes flicked defiant-wide. "Some said it came from the off-worlder woman he married. Some said it was from radiation from the wars, or a disease from, um, corrupt practices in his youth among his brother-officers—"

That last was a new one to Miles. His brow lifted.

"—but most say he was poisoned by his enemies."

"I'm glad most have it right. It was an assassination attempt using soltoxin gas, when my mother was pregnant with me. But it's not—" *A mutation*, his thought hiccoughed through the well-worn grooves— how many times had he explained this?—*it's teratogenic, not genetic, I'm not a mutant, not . . .* What the hell did a fine point of biochemistry matter to this ignorant, bereaved woman? For all practical purposes— for her purposes—he might as well be a mutant. "—important," he finished.

She eyed him sideways, swaying gently in the clop-a-clop rhythm of her mount. "Some said you were born with no legs, and lived all the time in a float chair in Vorkosigan House. Some said you were born with no bones—"

"—and kept in a jar in the basement, no doubt," Miles muttered.

"But Karal said he'd seen you with your grandfather at Hassadar Fair, and you were only sickly and undersized. Some said your father had got you into the Service, but others said no, you'd gone off-planet to your mother's home and had your brain turned into a computer and your body fed with tubes, floating in a liquid—"

"I knew there'd be a jar turn up in this story somewhere," Miles grimaced. *You knew you'd be sorry you asked, too, but you went and did it anyway.* She was baiting him, Miles realized suddenly. How *dare* she . . . but there was no humor in her, only a sharp-edged watchfulness.

She had gone out, way out on a limb to lay this murder charge, in defiance of family and local authorities alike, in defiance of established custom. And what had her Count given her for a shield and support, going back to face the wrath of all her nearest and dearest? Miles. Could he handle this? She must be wondering indeed. Or would he botch it, cave and cut and run, leaving her to face the whirlwind of rage and revenge alone?

He wished he'd left her weeping at the gate.

The woodland, fruit of many generations of terraforming forestry, opened out suddenly on a vale of brown native scrub. Down the middle of it, through some accident of soil chemistry, ran a half-kilometer-wide swathe of green and pink—feral roses, Miles realized with astonishment as they rode nearer. Earth roses. The track dove into the fragrant mass of them and vanished.

He took turns with Pym, hacking their way through with their Service bush knives. The roses were vigorous and studded with thick thorns, and hacked back with a vicious elastic recoil. Fat Ninny did his part by swinging his big head back and forth and nipping off blooms and chomping them down happily. Miles wasn't sure just how many he ought to let the big roan eat—just because the species wasn't native to Barrayar didn't mean it wasn't poisonous to horses. Miles sucked at his wounds and reflected upon Barrayar's shattered ecological history.

The fifty thousand Firsters from Earth had only meant to be the spearhead of Barrayar's colonization. Then, through a gravitational anomaly, the wormhole jump through which the colonists had come shifted closed, irrevocably and without warning. The terraforming which had begun, so careful and controlled in the beginning, collapsed along with everything else. Imported Earth plant and animal species had escaped everywhere to run wild, as the humans turned their attention to the most urgent problems of survival. Biologists still mourned the mass extinctions of native species that had followed, the erosions and droughts and floods, but really, Miles thought, over the centuries of the Time of Isolation the fittest of both worlds had fought it out to a perfectly good new balance. If it was alive and covered the ground who cared where it came from?

We are all here by accident. Like the roses.

THEY CAMPED that night high in the hills, and pushed on in the morning to the flanks of the true mountains. They were now out of the region Miles was personally familiar with from his childhood, and he checked Harra's directions frequently on his orbital survey map.

They stopped only a few hours short of their goal at sunset of the second day. Harra insisted she could lead them on in the dusk from here, but Miles did not care to arrive after nightfall, unannounced, in a strange place of uncertain welcome.

He bathed the next morning in a stream, and unpacked and dressed carefully in his new officer's Imperial dress greens. Pym wore the Vorkosigan brown and silver livery, and pulled the Count's standard on a telescoping aluminum pole from the recesses of his saddlebag and mounted it on his left stirrup. *Dressed to kill*, thought Miles joylessly. Dr. Dea wore ordinary black fatigues and looked uncomfortable. If they constituted a message, Miles was damned if he knew what it was.

They pulled the horses up at midmorning before a two-room cabin set on the edge of a vast grove of sugar maples, planted who-knew-how-many centuries ago but now raggedly marching up the vale by self-seeding. The mountain air was cool and pure and bright. A few chickens stalked and bobbed in the weeds. An algae-choked wooden pipe from the woods dribbled water into a trough, which overflowed into a squishy green streamlet and away.

Harra slid down and smoothed her skirt and climbed the porch. "Karal?" she called. Miles waited high on horseback for the initial contact. Never give up a psychological advantage.

"Harra? Is that you?" came a man's voice from within. He banged open the door and rushed out. "Where have you been, girl? We've been beating the bushes for you! Thought you'd broke your neck in the scrub somewhere—" He stopped short before the three silent men on horseback.

"You wouldn't write down my charges, Karal," said Harra rather breathlessly. Her hands kneaded her skirt. "So I walked to the district magistrate at Vorkosigan Surleau to Speak them myself."

"Oh, girl," Karal breathed regretfully, "that was a *stupid* thing to do. . . ." His head lowered and swayed, as he stared uneasily at the riders. He was a balding man of maybe sixty, leathery and worn, and his left arm ended in a stump. Another veteran.

"Speaker Serg Karal?" began Miles sternly. "I am the Voice of Count Vorkosigan. I am charged to investigate the crime Spoken by Harra Csurik before the Count's court, namely the murder of her infant daughter Raina. As Speaker of Silvy Vale, you are requested and required to assist me in all matters pertaining to the Count's justice."

At this point Miles ran out of prescribed formalities, and was on his own. That hadn't taken long. He waited. Fat Ninny snuffled. The silver-on-brown cloth of the standard made a few soft snapping sounds, lifted by a vagrant breeze.

"The district magistrate wasn't there," put in Harra, "but the Count was."

Karal was gray-faced, staring. He pulled himself together with an effort, came to a species of attention, and essayed a creaking half-bow. "Who—who are you, sir?"

"Lord Miles Vorkosigan."

Karal's lips moved silently. Miles was no lipreader, but he was pretty sure it came to a dismayed variant of *Oh, shit*. "This is my liveried man Sergeant Pym, and my medical examiner, Lieutenant Dea of the Imperial Service."

"You are my lord Count's son?" Karal croaked.

"The one and only." Miles was suddenly sick of the posing. Surely that was a sufficient first impression. He swung down off Ninny, landing lightly on the balls of his feet. Karal's gaze followed him down, and down. *Yeah, so I'm short. But wait'll you see me dance.* "All right if we water our horses in your trough, here?" Miles looped Ninny's reins through his arm and stepped toward it.

"Uh, that's for the people, m'lord," said Karal. "Just a minute and I'll fetch a bucket." He hitched up his baggy trousers and trotted off around the side of the cabin. A minute's uncomfortable silence, then Karal's voice floating faintly, "Where'd you put the goat bucket, Zed?"

Another voice, light and young. "Behind the woodstack, Da." The voices fell to a muffled undertone. Karal came trotting back with a battered aluminum bucket, which he placed beside the trough. He knocked out a wooden plug in the side and a bright stream arced out to plash and fill. Fat Ninny flickered his ears and snuffled and rubbed his big head against Miles, smearing his tunic with red and white horsehairs and nearly knocking him off his feet. Karal glanced up and smiled at the horse, though his smile fell away as his gaze passed on to the horse's owner. As Fat Ninny gulped his drink Miles caught a glimpse of the owner of the second voice, a boy of around twelve who flitted off into the woods behind the cabin.

Karal fell to, assisting Miles and Harra and Pym in securing the horses. Miles left Pym to unsaddle and feed, and followed Karal into his house. Harra stuck to Miles like glue, and Dr. Dea unpacked his medical kit and trailed along. Miles's boots rang loud and unevenly on the wooden floorboards.

"My wife, she'll be back in the nooning," said Karal, moving uncertainly around the room as Miles and Dea settled themselves on a bench and Harra curled up with her arms around her knees on the floor beside the fieldstone hearth. "I'll . . . I'll make some tea, m'lord." He skittered back out the door to fill a kettle at the trough before Miles could say, *No, thank you.* No, let him ease his nerves in ordinary movements. Then maybe Miles could begin to tease out how much of this static was social nervousness and how much was (perhaps) guilty conscience. By the time Karal had the kettle on the coals he was noticeably better controlled, so Miles began.

"I'd prefer to commence this investigation immediately, Speaker. It need not take long."

"It need not . . . take place at all, m'lord. The baby's death was natural—there were no marks on her. She was weakly, she had the cat's mouth, who knows what else was wrong with her? She died in her sleep, or by some accident."

"It is remarkable," said Miles dryly, "how often such accidents happen in this district. My father the Count himself has . . . remarked on it."

"There was no call to drag you up here." Karal looked exasperation at Harra. She sat silent, unmoved by his persuasion.

"It was no problem," said Miles blandly.

"Truly, m'lord," Karal lowered his voice, "I believe the child might have been overlain. 'S no wonder, in her grief, that her mind rejected it. Lem Csurik, he's a good boy, a good provider. She really doesn't want to do this, her reason is just temporarily overset by her troubles."

Harra's eyes, looking out from her hair-thatch, were poisonously cold.

"I begin to see." Miles's voice was mild, encouraging.

Karal brightened slightly. "It all could still be all right. If she will just be patient. Get over her sorrow. Talk to poor Lem. I'm sure he didn't kill the babe. Not rush to something she'll regret."

"I begin to see," Miles let his tone go ice cool, "why Harra Csurik found it necessary to walk four days to get an unbiased hearing. 'You think.' 'You believe.' 'Who knows what?' Not you, it appears. I hear speculation—accusation—innuendo—assertion. I came for *facts*, Speaker Karal. The Count's justice doesn't turn on guesses. It doesn't have to. This isn't the Time of Isolation. Not even in the backbeyond.

"My investigation of the facts will begin now. No judgment will be—rushed into, before the facts are complete. Confirmation of Lem Csurik's guilt or innocence will come from his own mouth, under fast-penta, administered by Dr. Dea before two witnesses—yourself and a deputy of your choice. Simple, clean, and quick." *And maybe I can be on my way out of this benighted hole before sundown.* "I require you, Speaker, to go now and bring Lem Csurik for questioning. Sergeant Pym will assist you."

Karal killed another moment pouring the boiling water into a big brown pot before speaking. "I'm a traveled man, lord. A twenty-year Service man. But most folks here have never been out of Silvy Vale. Interrogation chemistry might as well be magic to them. They might say it was a false confession, got that way."

"Then you and your deputy can say otherwise. This isn't exactly like the good old days, when confessions were extracted under torture, Karal. Besides, if he's as innocent as you *guess*—he'll clear himself, no?"

Reluctantly, Karal went into the adjoining room. He came back shrugging on a faded Imperial Service uniform jacket with a corporal's rank marked on the collar, the buttons of which did not quite meet across his middle anymore. Preserved, evidently, for such official functions. Even as in Barrayaran custom one saluted the uniform, and not the man in it, so might the wrath engendered by an unpopular duty fall on the office and not the individual who carried it out. Miles appreciated the nuance.

Karal paused at the door. Harra still sat wrapped in silence by the hearth, rocking slightly.

"M'lord," said Karal. "I've been Speaker of Silvy Vale for sixteen years now. In all that time nobody has had to go to the district magistrate for a Speaking, not for water rights or stolen animals or swiving or even the time Neva accused Bors of tree piracy over the maple sap. We've not had a blood feud in all that time."

"I have no intention of starting a blood feud, Karal. I just want the facts."

"That's the thing, m'lord. I'm not so in love with facts as I used to be. Sometimes, they bite." Karal's eyes were urgent.

Really, the man was doing everything but stand on his head and juggle cats—one-handed—to divert Miles. How overt was his obstruction likely to get?

"Silvy Vale cannot be permitted to have its own little Time of Isolation," said Miles warningly. "The Count's justice is for everyone, now. Even if they're small. And weakly. And have something wrong with them. And cannot even speak for themselves—*Speaker.*"

Karal flinched, white about the lips—point taken, evidently. He trudged away up the trail, Pym following watchfully, one hand loosening the stunner in his holster.

They drank the tea while they waited, and Miles pottered about the cabin, looking but not touching. The hearth was the sole source of heat for cooking and washwater. There was a beaten metal sink for washing up, filled by hand from a covered bucket but emptied through a drainpipe under the porch to join the streamlet running down out of the trough. The second room was a bedroom, with a double bed and chests for storage. A loft held three more pallets; the boy around back had brothers, apparently. The place was cramped, but swept, things put away and hung up.

On a side table sat a government-issue audio receiver, and a second and older military model, opened up, apparently in process of getting minor repairs and a new power pack. Exploration revealed a drawer full of old parts, nothing more complex than for simple audio sets, unfortunately. Speaker Karal must double as Silvy Vale's commlink specialist, how appropriate. They must pick up broadcasts from the station in Hassadar, maybe the high-power government channels from the capital as well.

No other electricity, of course. Powersat receptors were expensive pieces of precision technology. They would come even here, in time; some communities almost as small, but with strong economic co-ops, already had them. Silvy Vale was obviously still stuck in subsistence-level, and must needs wait till there was enough surplus in the district to gift them, if the surplus was not grabbed off first by some competing want. If only the city of Vorkosigan Vashnoi had not been obliterated by Cetagandan atomics, the whole district could be years ahead, economically. . . .

Miles walked out on the porch and leaned on the rail. Karal's son had returned. Down at the end of the cleared yard Fat Ninny was standing tethered, hip-shot, ears aflop, grunting with pleasure as the grinning boy scratched him vigorously under his halter. The boy looked up to catch Miles watching him, and scooted off fearfully to vanish again in the scrub downslope. "Huh," muttered Miles.

Dr. Dea joined him. "They've been gone a long time. About time to break out the fast-penta?"

"No, your autopsy kit, I should say. I fancy that's what we'll be doing next."

Dea glanced at him sharply. "I thought you sent Pym along to enforce the arrest."

"You can't arrest a man who's not there. Are you a wagering man, Doctor? I'll bet you a mark they don't come back with Csurik. No, hold it—maybe I'm wrong. I hope I'm wrong. Here are three coming back. . . ."

Karal, Pym, and another were marching down the trail. The third was a hulking young man, big-handed, heavy-browed, thick-necked, surly. "Harra," Miles called, "is this your husband?" He looked the part, by God, just what Miles had pictured. And four brothers just like him—only bigger, no doubt. . . .

Harra appeared by Miles's shoulder, and let out her breath. "No, m'lord. That's Alex, the Speaker's deputy."

"Oh." Miles's lips twitched in silent frustration. *Well, I had to give it a chance to be simple.*

Karal stopped beneath him and began a wandering explanation of his empty-handed state. Miles cut him off with a lift of his eyebrows. "Pym?"

"Bolted, m'lord," said Pym laconically. "Almost certainly warned."

"I agree." He frowned down at Karal, who prudently stood silent. Facts first. Decisions, such as how much deadly force to pursue the fugitive with, second. "Harra. How far is it to your burying place?"

"Down by the stream, lord, at the bottom of the valley. About two kilometers."

"Get your kit, Doctor, we're taking a walk. Karal, fetch a shovel."

"M'lord, surely it isn't needful to disturb the peace of the dead," began Karal.

"It is entirely needful. There's a place for the autopsy report right in the Procedural I got from the district magistrate's office. Where I will file my completed report upon this case when we return to Vorkosigan Surleau. I have permission from the next-of-kin—do I not, Harra?"

She nodded numbly.

"I have the two requisite witnesses, yourself and your . . ."— *gorilla*—". . . deputy, we have the doctor and the daylight—if you don't stand there arguing till sundown. All we need is the shovel. Unless you're volunteering to dig with your hand, Karal." Miles's voice was flat and grating and getting dangerous.

Karal's balding head bobbed in his distress. "The—the father is the legal next-of-kin, while he lives, and you don't have his—"

"Karal," said Miles.

"M'lord?"

"Take care the grave you dig is not your own. You've got one foot in it already."

Karal's hand opened in despair. "I'll . . . get the shovel, m'lord."

THE MIDAFTERNOON was warm, the air golden and summer-sleepy. The shovel bit with a steady *scrunch-scrunch* through the soil at the hands of Karal's deputy. Downslope, a bright stream burbled away over clean rounded stones. Harra hunkered watching, silent and grim.

When big Alex levered out the little crate—so little!—Sergeant Pym went off for a patrol of the wooded perimeter. Miles didn't blame him. He hoped the soil at that depth had been cool, these last eight days. Alex pried open the box, and Dr. Dea waved him away and took over. The deputy too went off to find something to look at at the far end of the graveyard.

Dea looked the cloth-wrapped bundle over carefully, lifted it out and set it on his tarp laid out on the ground in the bright sun. The instruments of his investigation were arrayed upon the plastic in precise order. He unwrapped the brightly patterned cloths in their special folds, and Harra crept up to retrieve them, straighten and fold them ready for re-use, then crept back.

Miles fingered the handkerchief in his pocket, ready to hold over his mouth and nose, and went to watch over Dea's shoulder. Bad, but not too bad. He'd seen and smelled worse. Dea, filter-masked, spoke procedurals into his recorder, hovering in the air by his shoulder, and made his examination first by eye and gloved touch, then by scanner.

"Here, my lord," said Dea, and motioned Miles closer. "Almost certainly the cause of death, though I'll run the toxin tests in a moment. Her neck was broken. See here on the scanner where the spinal cord was severed, then the bones twisted back into alignment."

"Karal, Alex." Miles motioned them up to witness; they came reluctantly.

"Could this have been accidental?" said Miles.

"Very remotely possible. The re-alignment had to be deliberate, though."

"Would it have taken long?"

"Seconds only. Death was immediate."

"How much physical strength was required? A big man's or . . ."

"Oh, not much at all. Any adult could have done it, easily."

"Any sufficiently motivated adult." Miles's stomach churned at the mental picture Dea's words conjured up. The little fuzzy head would easily fit under a man's hand. The twist, the muffled cartilaginous crack—if there was one thing Miles knew by heart, it was the exact tactile sensation of breaking bone, oh yes.

"Motivation," said Dea, "is not my department." He paused. "I might note, a careful external examination could have found this. Mine did. An experienced layman"—his eye fell cool on Karal—"paying attention to what he was doing, should not have missed it."

Miles too stared at Karal, waiting.

"Overlain," hissed Harra. Her voice was ragged with scorn.

"M'lord," said Karal carefully, "it's true I suspected the possibility—"

Suspected, hell. You knew.

"But I felt—and still feel, strongly," his eye flashed a wary defiance, "that only more grief would come from a fuss. There was nothing I could do to help the baby at that point. My duties are to the living."

"So are mine, Speaker Karal. As, for example, my duty to the next small Imperial subject in mortal danger from those who should be his or her protectors, for the grave fault of being," Miles flashed an edged smile, "physically different. In Count Vorkosigan's view this is not just a case. This is a test case, fulcrum of a thousand cases. Fuss . . ." He hissed the sibilant; Harra rocked to the rhythm of his voice. "You haven't begun to see *fuss* yet."

Karal subsided as if folded.

There followed an hour of messiness yielding mainly negative data; no other bones were broken, the infant's lungs were clear, her gut and bloodstream free of toxins except those of natural decomposition. Her brain held no secret tumors. The defect for which she had died did not extend to spina bifida, Dea reported. Fairly simple plastic surgery would indeed have corrected the cat's mouth, could she somehow have won access to it. Miles wondered what comfort this confirmation was to Harra; cold, at best.

Dea put his puzzle back together, and Harra rewrapped the tiny body in intricate, meaningful folds. Dea cleaned his tools and placed them in their cases and washed his hands and arms and face thoroughly in the stream, for rather a longer time than needed for just hygiene, Miles thought, while the gorilla reburied the box.

Harra made a little bowl in the dirt atop the grave and piled in some twigs and bark scraps and a sawed-off strand of her lank hair.

Miles, caught short, felt in his pockets. "I have no offering on me that will burn," he said apologetically.

Harra glanced up, surprised at even the implied offer. "No matter, m'lord." Her little pile of scraps flared briefly and went out, like her infant Raina's life.

But it does matter, thought Miles.

Peace to you, small lady, after our rude invasions. I will give you a better sacrifice, I swear by my word as Vorkosigan. And the smoke of that burning will rise and be seen from one end of these mountains to the other.

MILES CHARGED Karal and Alex straightly with producing Lem Csurik, and gave Harra Csurik a ride home up behind him on Fat Ninny. Pym accompanied them.

They passed a few scattered cabins on the way. At one a couple of grubby children playing in the yard loped alongside the horses, giggling and making hex signs at Miles, egging each other on to bolder displays, until their mother spotted them and ran out and hustled them indoors with a fearful look over her shoulder. In a weird way it was almost relaxing to Miles, the welcome he'd expected, not like Karal's and Alex's strained, self-conscious, careful not-noticing. Raina's life would not have been an easy one.

Harra's cabin was at the head of a long draw, just before it narrowed into a ravine. It seemed very quiet and isolated, in the dappled shade.

"Are you sure you wouldn't rather go stay with your mother?" asked Miles dubiously.

Harra shook her head. She slid down off Ninny, and Miles and Pym dismounted and followed her in.

The cabin was of standard design, a single room with a fieldstone fireplace and a wide roofed front porch. Water apparently came from the rivulet in the ravine. Pym held up a hand and entered first behind Harra, his hand on his stunner. If Lem Csurik had run, might he have run home first? Pym had been making scanner checks of perfectly innocent clumps of bushes all the way here.

The cabin was deserted. Although not long deserted; it did not have the lingering, dusty silence one would expect of eight days mournful disoccupation. The remains of a few hasty meals sat on the sinkboard. The bed was slept-in, rumpled and unmade. A few man's garments were scattered about. Automatically Harra began to move about the room, straightening it up, reasserting her presence, her existence, her worth. If she could not control the events of her life, at least she might control one small room.

The one untouched item was a cradle that sat beside the bed, little blankets neatly folded. Harra had fled for Vorkosigan Surleau just a few hours after the burial.

Miles wandered about the room, checking the view from the windows. "Will you show me where you went to get your brillberries, Harra?"

She led them up the ravine; Miles timed the hike. Pym divided his attention unhappily between the brush and Miles, alert to catch any bone-breaking stumble. After flinching away from about three aborted protective grabs Miles was ready to tell him to go climb a tree. Still, there was a certain understandable self-interest at work here; if Miles broke a leg it would be Pym who'd be stuck with carrying him out.

The brillberry patch was nearly a kilometer up the ravine. Miles plucked a few seedy red berries and ate them absently, looking around, while Harra and Pym waited respectfully. Afternoon sun slanted through green and brown leaves, but the bottom of the ravine was already gray and cool with premature twilight. The brillberry vines clung to the rocks and hung down invitingly, luring one to risk one's neck reaching. Miles resisted their weedy temptations, not being all that fond of brillberries. "If someone called out from your cabin, you couldn't hear them up here, could you?" remarked Miles.

"No, m'lord."

"About how long did you spend picking?"

"About," Harra shrugged, "a basketful."

The woman didn't own a chrono. "An hour, say. And a twenty-minute climb each way. About a two-hour time window, that morning. Your cabin was not locked?"

"Just a latch, m'lord."

"Hm."

Method, motive, and opportunity, the district magistrate's Procedural had emphasized. Damn. The method was established, and almost anybody could have used it. The opportunity angle, it appeared, was just as bad. Anyone at all could have walked up to that cabin, done the deed, and departed, unseen and unheard. It was much too late for an aura detector to be of use, tracing the shining ghosts of movements in and out of that room, even if Miles had brought one.

Facts, hah. They were back to motive, the murky workings of men's minds. Anybody's guess.

Miles had, as per the instructions in the district magistrate's Procedural, been striving to keep an open mind about the accused, but it was getting harder and harder to resist Harra's assertions. She'd been proved right about everything so far.

They left Harra reinstalled in her little home, going through the motions of order and the normal routine of life as if they could somehow re-create it, like an act of sympathetic magic.

"Are you sure you'll be all right?" Miles asked, gathering Fat Ninny's reins and settling himself in the saddle. "I can't help but think that if your husband's in the area, he could show up here. You say nothing's been taken, so it's unlikely he's been here and gone before we arrived. Do you want someone to stay with you?"

"No, m'lord." She hugged her broom, on the porch. "I'd . . . I'd like to be alone for a while."

"Well . . . all right. I'll, ah, send you a message if anything important happens."

"Thank you, m'lord." Her tone was unpressing; she really did want to be left alone. Miles took the hint.

At a wide place in the trail back to Speaker Karal's, Pym and Miles rode stirrup to stirrup. Pym was still painfully on the alert for boogies in the bushes.

"My lord, may I suggest that your next logical step be to draft all the able-bodied men in the community for a hunt for this Csurik? Beyond doubt, you've established that the infanticide was a murder."

Interesting turn of phrase, Miles thought dryly. *Even Pym doesn't find it redundant. Oh, my poor Barrayar.* "It seems reasonable at first glance, Sergeant Pym, but has it occurred to you that half the able-bodied men in this community are probably relatives of Lem Csurik's?"

"It might have a psychological effect. Create enough disruption, and perhaps someone would turn him in just to get it over with."

"Hm, possibly. Assuming he hasn't already left the area. He could have been halfway to the coast before we were done at the autopsy."

"Only if he had access to transport." Pym glanced at the empty sky.

"For all we know one of his sub-cousins had a rickety lightflyer in a shed somewhere. But . . . he's never been out of Silvy Vale. I'm not sure he'd know how to run, where to go. Well, if he has left the district it's a problem for Imperial Civil Security, and I'm off the hook." Happy thought. "But—one of the things that bothers me, a lot, are the inconsistencies in the picture I'm getting of our chief suspect. Have you noticed them?"

"Can't say as I have, m'lord."

"Hm. Where did Karal take you, by the way, to arrest this guy?"

"To a wild area, rough scrub and gullies. Half a dozen men were out searching for Harra. They'd just called off their search and were on their way back when we met up with them. By which I concluded our arrival was no surprise."

"Had Csurik actually been there, and fled, or was Karal just ring-leading you in a circle?"

"I think he'd actually been there, m'lord. The men claimed not, but as you point out they were relatives, and besides, they did not, ah, lie well. They were tense. Karal may begrudge you his cooperation, but I don't think he'll quite dare disobey your direct orders. He is a twenty-year man, after all."

Like Pym himself, Miles thought. Count Vorkosigan's personal guard was legally limited to a ceremonial twenty men, but given his political position their function included very practical security. Pym was typical of their number, a decorated veteran of the Imperial Service who had retired to this elite private force. It was not Pym's fault that when he had joined he had stepped into a dead man's shoes, replacing the late Sergeant Bothari. Did anyone in the universe besides himself miss the deadly and difficult Bothari? Miles wondered sadly.

"I'd like to question *Karal* under fast-penta," said Miles morosely. "He displays every sign of being a man who knows where the body's buried."

"Why don't you, then?" asked Pym logically.

"I may come to that. There is, however, a certain unavoidable degradation in a fast-penta interrogation. If the man's loyal it may not be in our best long-range interest to shame him publicly."

"It wouldn't be in public."

"No, but he would remember being turned into a drooling idiot. I need . . . more information."

Pym glanced back over his shoulder. "I thought you had all the information, by now."

"I have facts. Physical facts. A great big pile of—meaningless, useless facts." Miles brooded. "If I have to fast-penta every back-beyonder in Silvy Vale to get to the bottom of this, I will. But it's not an elegant solution."

"It's not an elegant problem, m'lord," said Pym dryly.

THEY RETURNED to find Speaker Karal's wife back and in full possession of her home. She was running in frantic circles, chopping, beating, kneading, stoking, and flying upstairs to change the bedding on the three pallets, driving her three sons before her to fetch and run and carry. Dr. Dea, bemused, was following her about trying to slow her down, explaining that they had brought their own tent and food, thank you, and that her hospitality was not required. This produced a most indignant response from Ma Karal.

"My lord's own son come to my house, and I to turn him out in the fields like his horse! I'd be ashamed!" And she returned to her work.

"She seems rather distraught," said Dea, looking over his shoulder.

Miles took him by the elbow and propelled him out onto the porch. "Just get out of her way, Doctor. We're doomed to be Entertained. It's an obligation on both sides. The polite thing to do is sort of pretend we're not here till she's ready for us."

Dea lowered his voice. "It might be better, in light of the circumstances, if we were to eat only our packaged food."

The chatter of a chopping knife, and a scent of herbs and onions, wafted enticingly through the open window. "Oh, I would imagine anything out of the common pot would be all right, wouldn't you?" said Miles. "If anything really worries you, you can whisk it off and check it, I suppose, but—discreetly, eh? We don't want to insult anyone."

They settled themselves in the homemade wooden chairs, and were promptly served tea again by a boy draftee of ten, Karal's youngest. He had apparently already received private instructions in manners from one or the other of his parents, for his response to Miles's deformities was the same flickering covert not-noticing as the adults', not quite as smoothly carried off.

"Will you be sleeping in my bed, m'lord?" he asked. "Ma says we got to sleep on the porch."

"Well, whatever your Ma says, goes," said Miles. "Ah . . . do you like sleeping on the porch?"

"Naw. Last time, Zed kicked me and I rolled off in the dark."

"Oh. Well, perhaps, if we're to displace you, you would care to sleep in our tent by way of trade."

The boy's eyes widened. "Really?"

"Certainly. Why not?"

"Wait'll I tell Zed!" He danced down the steps and shot away around the side of the house. "Zed, hey, Zed . . . !"

"I suppose," said Dea, "we can fumigate it, later. . . ."

Miles's lips twitched. "They're no grubbier than you were at the same age, surely. Or than I was. When I was permitted." The late afternoon was warm. Miles took off his green tunic and hung it on the back of his chair, and unbuttoned the round collar of his cream shirt.

Dea's brows rose. "Are we keeping shopman's hours, then, m'lord, on this investigation? Calling it quits for the day?"

"Not exactly." Miles sipped tea thoughtfully, gazing out across the yard. The trees and treetops fell away down to the bottom of this feeder valley. Mixed scrub climbed the other side of the slope. A crested fold, then the long flanks of a backbone mountain, beyond, rose high and harsh to a summit still flecked with dwindling dirty patches of snow.

"There's still a murderer loose out there somewhere," Dea pointed out helpfully.

"You sound like Pym." Pym, Miles noted, had finished with their horses and was taking his scanner for another walk. "I'm waiting."

"What for?"

"Not sure. The piece of information that will make sense of all this. Look, there's only two possibilities. Csurik's either innocent or he's guilty. If he's guilty, he's not going to turn himself in. He'll certainly involve his relations, hiding and helping him. I can call in reinforcements by comm link from Imperial Civil Security in Hassadar, if I want to. Any time. Twenty men, plus equipment, here by aircar in a couple of hours. Create a circus. Brutal, ugly, disruptive, exciting—could be quite popular. A manhunt, with blood at the end.

"Of course, there's also the possibility that Csurik's innocent, but scared. In which case . . ."

"Yes?"

"In which case, there's still a murderer out there." Miles drank more tea. "I merely note, if you want to catch something, running after it isn't always the best way."

Dea cleared his throat, and drank his tea too.

"In the meantime, I have another duty to carry out. I'm here to be seen. If your scientific spirit is yearning for something to do to while away the hours, try keeping count of the number of Vor-watchers that turn up tonight."

MILES'S PREDICTED PARADE began almost immediately. It was mainly women, at first, bearing gifts as to a funeral. In the absence of a comm-link system Miles wasn't sure by what telepathy they managed to communicate with each other, but they brought covered dishes of food, flowers, extra bedding, and offers of assistance. They were all introduced to Miles with nervous curtseys, but seldom lingered to chat; apparently a look was all their curiosity desired. Ma Karal was polite, but made it clear that she had the situation well in hand, and set their culinary offerings well back of her own.

Some of the women had children in tow. Most of these were sent to play in the woods in back, but a small party of whispering boys sneaked back around the cabin to peek up over the rim of the porch at Miles. Miles had obligingly remained on the porch with Dea, remarking that it was a better view, without saying for whom. For a few moments Miles pretended not to notice his audience, restraining Pym with a hand signal from running them off. *Yes, look well, look your fill*, thought Miles. *What you see is what you're going to get, for the rest of your lives or at any rate mine. Get used to it. . . .* Then he caught Zed Karal's whisper, as self-appointed tour guide to his cohort—"That big one's the one that's come to kill Lem Csurik!"

"Zed," said Miles.

There was an abrupt frozen silence from under the edge of the porch. Even the animal rustlings stopped.

"Come here," said Miles.

To a muted background of dismayed whispers and nervous giggles, Karal's middle boy slouched warily up on to the porch.

"You three—" Miles's pointing finger caught them in mid-flight, "wait there." Pym added his frown for emphasis, and Zed's friends stood paralyzed, eyes wide, heads lined up at the level of the porch floor as if stuck up on some ancient battlement as a warning to kindred malefactors.

"What did you just say to your friends, Zed?" asked Miles quietly. "Repeat it."

Zed licked his lips. "I jus' said you'd come to kill Lem Csurik, lord." Zed was clearly now wondering if Miles's murderous intent included obnoxious and disrespectful boys as well.

"That is not true, Zed. That is a dangerous lie."

Zed looked bewildered. "But Da—said it."

"What is true, is that I've come to catch the person who killed Lem Csurik's baby daughter. That may be Lem. But it may not. Do you understand the difference?"

"But Harra said Lem did it, and she ought to know, he's her husband and all."

"The baby's neck was broken by someone. Harra thinks Lem, but she didn't see it happen. What you and your friends here have to understand is that I won't make a mistake. I *can't* condemn the wrong person. My own truth drugs won't let me. Lem Csurik has only to come here and tell me the truth to clear himself, if he didn't do it.

"But suppose he did. What should I do with a man who would kill a baby, Zed?"

Zed shuffled. "Well, she was only a mutie . . ." Then shut his mouth and reddened, not-looking at Miles.

It was, perhaps, a bit much to ask a twelve-year-old boy to take an interest in any baby, let alone a mutie one . . . *no*, dammit. It wasn't too much. But how to get a hook into that prickly defensive surface? And if Miles couldn't even convince one surly twelve-year-old, how was he to magically transmute a whole District of adults? A rush of despair made him suddenly want to rage. These people were so bloody *impossible*. He checked his temper firmly.

"Your Da was a twenty-year man, Zed. Are you proud that he served the Emperor?"

"Yes, lord." Zed's eyes sought escape, trapped by these terrible adults.

Miles forged on. "Well, these practices—mutie-killing—shame the Emperor, when he stands for Barrayar before the galaxy. I've been out there. I know. They call us all savages, for the crimes of a few. It shames the Count my father before his peers, and Silvy Vale before the District. A soldier gets honor by killing an armed enemy, not a baby. This matter touches my honor as a Vorkosigan, Zed. Besides," Miles's lips drew back on a mirthless grin, and he leaned forward intently in his chair—Zed recoiled as much as he dared— "you will all be astonished at what *only a mutie* can do. *That* I have sworn on my grandfather's grave."

Zed looked more suppressed than enlightened, his slouch now almost a crouch. Miles slumped back in his chair and released him with a weary wave of his hand. "Go play, boy."

Zed needed no urging. He and his companions shot away around the house as though released from springs.

Miles drummed his fingers on the chair arm, frowning into the silence that neither Pym nor Dea dared break.

"These hill-folk are ignorant, lord," offered Pym after a moment.

"These hill-folk are *mine*, Pym. Their ignorance is . . . a shame upon my house." Miles brooded. How had this whole mess become his anyway? He hadn't created it. Historically, he'd only just got here himself. "Their continued ignorance, anyway," he amended in fairness. It still made a burden like a mountain. "Is the message so complex? So difficult? 'You don't have to kill your children anymore.' It's not like we're asking them all to learn—5-Space navigational math." That had been the plague of Miles's last Academy semester.

"It's not easy for them," shrugged Dea. "It's easy for the central authorities to make the rules, but these people have to live every minute of the consequences. They have so little, and the new rules force them to give their margin to marginal people who can't pay back. The old ways were wise, in the old days. Even now you have to wonder how many premature reforms we can afford, trying to ape the galactics."

And what's your definition of a marginal person, Dea? "But the margin is growing," Miles said aloud. "Places like this aren't up against famine every winter anymore. They're not isolated in their disasters, relief can get from one district to another under the Imperial seal . . . we're all getting more connected, just as fast as we can. Besides," Miles paused, and added rather weakly, "perhaps you underestimate them."

Dea's brows rose ironically. Pym strolled the length of the porch, running his scanner in yet another pass over the surrounding scrubland. Miles, turning in his chair to pursue his cooling teacup, caught a slight movement, a flash of eyes, behind the casement-hung front window swung open to the summer air—Ma Karal, standing frozen, listening. For how long? Since he'd called her boy Zed, Miles guessed, arresting her attention. She raised her chin as his eyes met hers, sniffed, and shook out the cloth she'd been holding with a snap. They exchanged a nod. She turned back to her work. Dea, watching Pym, didn't notice her.

KARAL AND ALEX returned, understandably, around suppertime.

"I have six men out searching," Karal reported cautiously to Miles on the porch, now well on its way to becoming Miles's official HQ. Clearly, Karal had covered ground since mid-afternoon. His face was sweaty, lined with physical as well as the underlying emotional strain. "But I think Lem's gone into the scrub. It could take days to smoke him out. There's hundreds of places to lie low out there."

Karal ought to know. "You don't think he's gone to some relative's?" asked Miles. "Surely, if he intends to evade us for long, he has to take a chance on resupply, on information. Will they turn him in when he surfaces?"

"It's hard to say." Karal turned his hand palm-out. "It's . . . a hard problem for 'em, m'lord."

"Hm."

How long would Lem Csurik hang around out there in the scrub, anyway? His whole life—his blown-to-bits life—was all here in Silvy Vale. Miles considered the contrast. A few weeks ago, Csurik had been a young man with everything going for him; a home, a wife, a family on the way, happiness; by Silvy Vale standards, comfort and security. His cabin, Miles had not failed to note, though simple, had been kept with love and energy, and so redeemed from the potential squalor of its poverty. Grimmer in the winter, to be sure. Now Csurik was a hunted fugitive, all the little he had torn away in the twinkling of an eye. With nothing to hold him, would he run away and keep running? With nothing to run to, would he linger near the ruins of his life?

The police force available to Miles a few hours away in Hassadar was an itch in his mind. Was it not time to call them in, before he fumbled this into a worse mess? But . . . if he were meant to solve this by a show of force, why hadn't the Count let him come by aircar on the first day? Miles regretted that two-and-a-half-day ride. It had sapped his forward momentum, slowed him down to Silvy Vale's walking pace, tangled him with time to doubt. Had the Count foreseen it? What did he know that Miles didn't? What *could* he know? Dammit, this test didn't need to be made harder by artificial stumbling blocks, it was bad enough all on its own. *He wants me to be clever*, Miles thought morosely. *Worse, he wants me to be seen as clever, by everyone here*. He prayed he was not about to be spectacularly stupid instead.

"Very well, Speaker Karal. You've done all you can for today. Knock off for the night. Call your men off too. You're not likely to find anything in the dark."

Pym held up his scanner, clearly about to volunteer its use, but Miles waved him down. Pym's brows rose, editorially. Miles shook his head slightly.

Karal needed no further urging. He dispatched Alex to call off the night search with torches. He remained wary of Miles. Perhaps Miles puzzled him as much as he puzzled Miles? Dourly, Miles hoped so.

Miles was not sure at what point the long summer evening segued into a party. After supper the men began to drift in, Karal's cronies, Silvy Vale's elders. Some were apparently regulars who shared the evening government news broadcasts on Karal's audio set. Too many names, and Miles daren't forget a one. A group of amateur musicians arrived with their homemade mountain instruments, rather breathless, obviously the band tapped for all the major weddings and wakes in Silvy Vale; this all seemed more like a funeral to Miles every minute.

The musicians stood in the middle of the yard and played. Miles's porch-HQ now became his aristocratic box seat. It was hard to get involved with the music when the audience was all so intently watching him. Some songs were serious, some—rather carefully at first—funny. Miles's spontaneity was frequently frozen in mid-laugh by a faint sigh of relief from those around him; his stiffening froze them in turn, self-stymied like two people trying to dodge each other in a corridor.

But one song was so hauntingly beautiful—a lament for lost love—

that Miles was struck to the heart. *Elena. . . .* In that moment, old pain transformed to melancholy, sweet and distant; a sort of healing, or at least the realization that a healing had taken place, unwatched. He almost had the singers stop there, while they were perfect, but feared they might think him displeased. But he remained quiet and inward for a time afterward, scarcely hearing their next offering in the gathering twilight.

At least the piles of food that had arrived all afternoon were thus accounted for. Miles had been afraid Ma Karal and her cronies had expected him to get around that culinary mountain all by himself.

At one point Miles leaned on the rail and glanced down the yard to see Fat Ninny at tether, making more friends. A whole flock of pubescent girls were clustered around him, petting him, brushing his fetlocks, braiding flowers and ribbons in his mane and tail, feeding him tidbits, or just resting their cheeks against his warm silky side. Ninny's eyes were half-closed in smug content.

God, thought Miles jealously, *if I had half the sex appeal of that bloody horse I'd have more girlfriends than my cousin Ivan.* Miles considered, very briefly, the pros and cons of making a play for some unattached female. The striding lords of old and all that . . . no. There were some kinds of stupid he didn't have to be, and that was definitely one of them. The service he had already sworn to one small lady of Silvy Vale was surely all he could bear without breaking; he could feel the strain of it all around him now, like a dangerous pressure in his bones.

He turned to find Speaker Karal presenting a woman to him, far from pubescent; she was perhaps fifty, lean and little, work-worn. She was carefully clothed in an aging best-dress, her graying hair combed back and bound at the nape of her neck. She bit at her lips and cheeks in quick tense motions, half-suppressed in her self-consciousness.

" 'S Ma Csurik, m'lord. Lem's mother." Speaker Karal ducked his head and backed away, abandoning Miles without aid or mercy— *Come back, you coward!*

"Ma'am," Miles said. His throat was dry. Karal had set him up, dammit, a public play—no, the other guests were retreating out of earshot too, most of them.

"M'lord," said Ma Csurik. She managed a nervous curtsey.

"Uh . . . do sit down." With a ruthless jerk of his chin Miles evicted Dr. Dea from his chair and motioned the hill woman into it. He turned his own chair to face hers. Pym stood behind them, silent as a statue, tight as a wire. Did he imagine the old woman was about to whip a needler-pistol from her skirts? No—it was Pym's job to imagine things like that for Miles, so that Miles might free his whole mind for the problem at hand. Pym was almost as much an object of study as Miles himself. Wisely, he'd been holding himself apart, and would doubtless continue to do so till the dirty work was over.

"M'lord," said Ma Csurik again, and stumbled again to silence. Miles could only wait. He prayed she wasn't about to come unglued and weep on his knees or some damn thing. This was excruciating. *Stay strong, woman*, he urged silently.

"Lem, he . . ." She swallowed. "I'm sure he didn't kill the babe. There's never been any of that in our family, I swear it! He says he didn't, and I believe him."

"Good," said Miles affably. "Let him come say the same thing to me under fast-penta, and I'll believe him too."

"Come away, Ma," urged a lean young man who had accompanied her and now stood waiting by the steps, as if ready to bolt into the dark at a motion. "It's no good, can't you see." He glowered at Miles.

She shot the boy a quelling frown—another of her five sons?— and turned back more urgently to Miles, groping for words. "My Lem. He's only twenty, lord."

"*I'm* only twenty, Ma Csurik," Miles felt compelled to point out. There was another brief impasse.

"Look, I'll say it again," Miles burst out impatiently. "And again, and again, till the message penetrates all the way back to its intended recipient. I *cannot* condemn an innocent person. My truth drugs won't let me. Lem can clear himself. He has only to come in. Tell him, will you? Please?"

She went stony, guarded. "I . . . haven't seen him, m'lord."

"But you might."

She tossed her head. "So? I might not." Her eyes shifted to Pym and away, as if the sight of him burned. The silver Vorkosigan logos embroidered on Pym's collar gleamed in the twilight like animal eyes, moving only with his breathing. Karal was now bringing lighted lamps onto the porch, but keeping his distance still.

"Ma'am," said Miles tightly. "The Count my father has ordered me to investigate the murder of your granddaughter. If your son means so much to you, how can his child mean so little? Was she . . . your first grandchild?"

Her face was sere. "No, lord. Lem's older sister, she has two. *They're* all right," she added with emphasis.

Miles sighed. "If you truly believe your son is innocent of this crime, you must help me prove it. Or—do you doubt?"

She shifted uneasily. There was doubt in her eyes—she didn't know, blast it. Fast-penta would be useless on her, for sure. As Miles's magic wonder drug, much counted-upon, fast-penta seemed to be having wonderfully little utility in this case so far.

"Come away, Ma," the young man urged again. "It's no good. The mutie lord came up here for a killing. They have to have one. It's a show."

Damn straight, thought Miles acidly. He was a perceptive young lunk, that one.

Ma Csurik let herself be persuaded away by her angry and embarrassed son plucking at her arm. She paused on the steps, though, and shot bitterly over her shoulder, "It's all so easy for you, isn't it?"

My head hurts, thought Miles.

There was worse to come before the evening ended.

The new woman's voice was grating, low and angry. "Don't you talk down to me, Serg Karal. I got a right for one good look at this mutie lord."

She was tall and stringy and tough. *Like her daughter*, Miles thought. She had made no attempt to freshen up. A faint reek of summer sweat hung about her working dress. And how far had she walked? Her gray hair hung in a switch down her back, a few strands escaping the tie. If Ma Csurik's bitterness had been a stabbing pain behind the eyes, this one's rage was a wringing knot in the gut.

She shook off Karal's attempted restraint and stalked up to Miles in the lamplight. "So."

"Uh . . . this is Ma Mattulich, m'lord," Karal introduced her. "Harra's mother."

Miles rose to his feet, managed a short formal nod. "How do you do, madam." He was very conscious of being a head shorter than her. She had once been of a height with Harra, Miles estimated, but her aging bones were beginning to pull her down.

She merely stared. She was a gum-leaf chewer, by the faint black-ish stains around her mouth. Her jaw worked now on some small bit, tiny chomps, grinding too hard. She studied him openly, without subterfuge or the least hint of apology, taking in his head, his neck, his back, his short and crooked legs. Miles had the unpleasant il-lusion that she saw right through to all the healed cracks in his brittle bones as well. Miles's chin jerked up twice in the twitchy, nervous-involuntary tic that he was sure made him look spastic, before he controlled it with an effort.

"All right," said Karal roughly, "you've seen. Now come away, for God's sake, Mara." His hand opened in apology to Miles. "Mara, she's been pretty distraught over all this, m'lord. Forgive her."

"Your only grandchild," said Miles to her, in an effort to be kind, though her peculiar anguish repelled kindness with a scraped and bleeding scorn. "I understand your distress, ma'am. But there will be justice for little Raina. That I have sworn."

"How can there be justice *now*?" she raged, thick and low. "It's too late—a world too late—for justice, mutie lordling. What use do I have for your damned justice *now*?"

"Enough, Mara!" Karal insisted. His brows drew down and his lips thinned, and he forced her away and escorted her firmly off his porch.

The last lingering remnant of visitors parted for her with an air of respectful mercy, except for two lean teenagers hanging on the fringes who drew away as if avoiding poison. Miles was forced to revise his mental image of the Brothers Csurik. If those two were another sample, there was no team of huge menacing hill hulks after all. They were a team of little skinny menacing hill squirts instead. Not really an improvement, they looked like they could move as fast as striking ferrets if they had to. Miles's lips curled in frustration.

THE EVENING'S entertainments ended finally, thank God, close to midnight. Karal's last cronies marched off into the woods by lantern light. The repaired and repowered audio set was carried off by its owner with many thanks to Karal. Fortunately it had been a mature and sober crowd, even somber, no drunken brawls or anything. Pym got the Karal boys settled in the tent, took a last patrol around the cabin, and joined Miles and Dea in the loft. The pallets' stuffing had been spiked with fresh scented native herbs, to which Miles hoped devoutly he was not allergic. Ma Karal had wanted to turn her own bedroom over to Miles's exclusive lordly use, exiling herself and her husband to the porch too, but fortunately Pym had been able to persuade her that putting Miles in the loft, flanked by Dea and himself, was to be preferred from a security standpoint.

Dea and Pym were soon snoring, but sleep eluded Miles. He tossed on his pallet as he turned his ploys of the day, such as they had been, over and over in his mind. Was he being too slow, too careful, too conservative? This wasn't exactly good assault tactics, surprise with a superior force. The view he'd gained of the terrain from Karal's porch tonight had been ambiguous at best.

On the other hand, it did no good to charge off across a swamp, as his fellow cadet and cousin Ivan Vorpatril had demonstrated so memorably once on summer maneuvers. It had taken a heavy hovercab with a crane to crank the six big, strong, healthy, fully fieldequipped young men of Ivan's patrol out of the chest-high, gooey black mud. Ivan had got his revenge simultaneously, though, when the cadet "sniper" they had been attacking fell out of his tree and broke his arm while laughing hysterically as they sank slowly and beautifully into the ooze. Ooze that the little guy, with his laser rifle wrapped in his loincloth, had swum across like a frog. The war games umpire had ruled it a draw. Miles rubbed his forearm and grinned in memory, and faded out at last.

MILES AWOKE abruptly and without transition deep in the night with a sense of something wrong. A faint orange glow shimmered in the blue darkness of the loft. Quietly, so as not to disturb his sleeping companions, he rose on his pallet and peered over the edge into the main room. The glow was coming through the front window.

Miles swung onto the ladder and padded downstairs for a look outdoors. "Pym," he called softly.

Pym shot awake with a snort. "M'lord?" he said, alarmed.

"Come down here. Quietly. Bring your stunner."

Pym was by his side in seconds. He slept in his trousers with his stunner holster and boots by his pillow. "What the hell—?" Pym muttered, looking out too.

The glow was from fire. A pitchy torch, flung to the top of Miles's tent set up in the yard, was burning quietly. Pym lurched toward the door, then controlled his movements as the same realization came to him as had to Miles. Theirs was a Service-issue tent, and its combat-rated synthetic fabric would neither melt nor burn.

Miles wondered if the person who'd heaved the torch had known that. Was this some arcane warning, or a singularly inept attack? If the tent had been ordinary fabric, and Miles in it, the intended result might not have been trivial. Worse with Karal's boys in it—a bursting blossom of flame—Miles shuddered.

Pym loosened his stunner in his holster and stood poised by the front door. "How long?"

"I'm not sure. Could have been burning like that for ten minutes before it woke me."

Pym shook his head, took a slight breath, raised his scanner, and vaulted into the fire-gilded darkness.

"Trouble, m'lord?" Speaker Karal's anxious voice came from his bedroom door.

"Maybe. Wait—" Miles halted him as he plunged for the door. "Pym's running a patrol with a scanner and a stunner. Wait'll he calls the all-clear, I think. Your boys may be safer inside the tent."

Karal came up to the window, caught his breath, and swore.

Pym returned in a few minutes. "There's no one within a kilometer, now," he reported shortly. He helped Karal take the goat bucket and douse the torch. The boys, who had slept through the fire, woke at its quenching.

"I think maybe it was a bad idea to lend them my tent," said Miles from the porch in a choked voice. "I am profoundly sorry, Speaker Karal. I didn't think."

"This should never . . ." Karal was spluttering with anger and delayed fright. "This should *never* have happened, m'lord. I apologize for . . . for Silvy Vale." He turned helplessly, peering into the darkness. The night sky, star-flecked, lovely, was threatening now.

The boys, once the facts penetrated their sleepiness, thought it was all just great, and wanted to return to the tent and lie in wait for the next assassin. Ma Karal, shrill and firm, herded them indoors instead and made them bed down in the main room. It was an hour before they stopped complaining at the injustice of it and went back to sleep.

Miles, keyed up nearly to the point of gibbering, did not sleep at all. He lay stiffly on his pallet, listening to Dea, who slept breathing heavily, and Pym, feigning sleep for courtesy and scarcely seeming to breathe at all.

Miles was about to suggest to Pym that they give up and go out on the porch for the rest of the night when the silence was shattered by a shrill squeal, enormously loud, pain-edged, from outside.

"The horses!" Miles spasmed to his feet, heart racing, and beat Pym to the ladder. Pym cut ahead of him by dropping straight over the side of the loft into an elastic crouch, and beat him to the door. There, Pym's trained bodyguard's reflexes compelled him to try to thrust Miles back inside. Miles almost bit him. "Go, dammit! I've got a weapon!"

Pym, good intentions frustrated, swung out the cabin door with Miles on his heels. Halfway down the yard they split to each side as a massive snorting shape loomed out of the darkness and nearly ran them down; the sorrel mare, loose again. Another squeal pierced the night from the lines where the horses were tethered.

"Ninny?" Miles called, panicked. It was Ninny's voice making those noises, the like of which Miles had not heard since the night a shed had burned down at Vorkosigan Surleau with a horse trapped inside. "Ninny!"

Another grunting squeal, and a thunk like someone splitting a watermelon with a mallet. Pym staggered back, inhaling with difficulty, a resonant deep stutter, and tripped to the ground where he lay curled up around himself. Not killed outright, apparently, because between gasps he was managing to swear lividly. Miles dropped to the ground beside him, checked his skull—no, thank God it had been Pym's chest Ninny's hoof had hit with that alarming sound. The bodyguard only had the wind knocked out of him, maybe a cracked rib. Miles more sensibly ran around to the *front* of the horse lines. "Ninny!"

Fat Ninny was jerking his head against his rope, attempting to rear. He squealed again, his white-rimmed eyes gleaming in the darkness. Miles ran to his head. "Ninny, boy! What is it?" His left hand slid up the rope to Ninny's halter, his right stretched to stroke Ninny's shoulder soothingly. Fat Ninny flinched, but stopped trying to rear, and stood trembling. The horse shook his head. Miles's face and chest were suddenly spattered with something hot and dark and sticky.

"Dea!" Miles yelled. *"Dea!"*

Nobody slept through this uproar. Six people tumbled off the porch and down the yard, and not one of them thought to bring a light . . . no, the brilliant flare of a cold light sprang from between Dr. Dea's fingers, and Ma Karal was struggling even now to light a lantern. "Dea, get that damn light over here!" Miles demanded, and stopped to choke his voice back down an octave to its usual carefully cultivated deeper register.

Dea galloped up and thrust the light toward Miles, then gasped, his face draining. "My lord! Are you shot?" In the flare the dark liquid soaking Miles's shirt glowed suddenly scarlet.

"Not me," Miles said, looking down at his chest in horror himself. A flash of memory turned his stomach over, cold at the vision of another blood-soaked death, that of the late Sergeant Bothari whom Pym had replaced. Would never replace.

Dea spun. "Pym?"

"He's all right," said Miles. A long inhaling wheeze rose from the grass a few meters off, the exhalation punctuated with obscenities. "But he got kicked by the horse. Get your medkit!" Miles peeled Dea's fingers off the cold light, and Dea dashed back to the cabin.

Miles held the light up to Ninny, and swore in a sick whisper. A huge cut, a third of a meter long and of unknown depth, scored Ninny's glossy neck. Blood soaked his coat and runneled down his foreleg. Miles's fingers touched the wound fearfully; his hands spread on either side, trying to push it closed, but the horse's skin was elastic and it pulled apart and bled profusely as Fat Ninny shook his head in pain. Miles grabbed the horse's nose—"Hold still, boy!" Somebody had been going for Ninny's jugular. And had almost made it; Ninny—tame, petted, friendly, trusting Ninny—would not have moved from the touch until the knife bit deep.

Karal was helping Pym to his feet as Dr. Dea returned. Miles waited while Dea checked Pym over, then called, "Here, Dea!"

Zed, looking quite as horrified as Miles, helped to hold Ninny's head as Dea made inspection of the cut. "I took tests," Dea complained *sotto voce* as he worked. "I beat out twenty-six other applicants, for the honor of becoming the Prime Minister's personal physician. I have practiced the procedures of seventy separate possible medical emergencies, from coronary thrombosis to attempted assassination. Nobody—*nobody*—told me my duties would include sewing up a damned horse's neck in the middle of the night in the middle of a howling wilderness. . . ." But he kept working as he complained, so Miles didn't quash him, but kept gently petting Ninny's nose, and hypnotically rubbing the hidden pattern of his muscles, to soothe and still him. At last Ninny relaxed enough to rest his slobbery chin on Miles's shoulder.

"Do horses get anesthetics?" asked Dea plaintively, holding his medical stunner as if not sure just what to do with it.

"This one does," said Miles stoutly. "You treat him just like a person, Dea. This is the last animal that the Count my grandfather personally trained. He named him. I watched him get born. We trained him together. Grandfather had me pick him up and hold him every day for a week after he was foaled, till he got too big. Horses are creatures of habit, Grandfather said, and take first impressions to heart. Forever after Ninny thought I was bigger than he was."

Dea sighed and made busy with anesthetic stun, cleansing solution, antibiotics, muscle relaxants, and biotic glue. With a surgeon's touch he shaved the edges of the cut and placed the reinforcing net. Zed held the light anxiously.

"The cut is clean," said Dea, "but it will undergo a lot of flexing— I don't suppose it can very well be immobilized, in this position? No, hardly. This should do. If he were a human, I'd tell him to rest at this point."

"He'll be rested," Miles promised firmly. "Will he be all right now?"

"I suppose so. How the devil should I know?" Dea looked highly aggrieved, but his hand sneaked out to recheck his repairs.

"General Piotr," Miles assured him, "would have been very pleased with your work." Miles could hear him in his head now, snorting, *Damned technocrats. Nothing but horse doctors with a more expensive set of toys.* Grandfather would have loved being proved right. "You, ah . . . never met my grandfather, did you?"

"Before my time, my lord," said Dea. "I've studied his life and campaigns, of course."

"Of course."

Pym had a hand-light now, and was limping with Karal in a slow spiral around the horse lines, inspecting the ground. Karal's eldest boy had recaptured the sorrel mare and brought her back and re-tethered her. Her tether had been torn loose, not cut; had the mysterious attacker's choice of equine victim been random, or calculated? How calculated? Was Ninny attacked as a mere symbol of his master, or had the person known how passionately Miles loved the animal? Was this vandalism, a political statement, or an act of precisely directed, subtle cruelty?

What have I ever done to you? Miles's thought howled silently to the surrounding darkness.

"They got away, whoever it was," Pym reported. "Out of scanner range before I could breathe again. My apologies, m'lord. They don't seem to have dropped anything on the ground."

There had to have been a knife, at least. A knife, its haft gory with horse blood in a pattern of perfect fingerprints, would have been extremely convenient just now. Miles sighed.

Ma Karal drifted up and eyed Dea's medkit, as he cleaned and re-packed it. "All that," she muttered under her breath, "for a horse. . . ."

Miles refrained, barely, from leaping to a hot defense of the value of this particular horse. How many people in Silvy Vale had Ma Karal seen suffer and die, in her lifetime, for lack of no more medical technology than what Dea was carrying under his arm just now?

GUARDING HIS HORSE, Miles watched from the porch as dawn crept over the landscape. He had changed his shirt and washed off. Pym was inside getting his ribs taped. Miles sat with his back to the wall and a stunner on his lap as the night mists slowly grew gray. The valley was a gray blur, fog-shrouded, the hills darker rolls of fog beyond. Directly overhead, gray thinned to a paling blue. The day would be fine and hot once the fog burned away.

It was surely time now to call out the troops from Hassadar. This was getting just too weird. His bodyguard was half out of commission—true, it was Miles's horse that had rendered him so, not the mystery attacker. But just because the attacks hadn't been fatal didn't mean they hadn't been intended so. Perhaps a third attack would be brought off more expertly. Practice makes perfect.

Miles felt unstrung with nervous exhaustion. How had he let a mere horse become such a handle on his emotions? Bad, that, almost unbalanced—yet Ninny's was surely one of the truly innocent pure souls Miles had ever known. Miles remembered the other innocent in the case then, and shivered in the damp. *It was cruel, lord, something cruel. . . .* Pym was right, the bushes could be crawling with Csurik assassins right now.

Dammit, the bushes *were* crawling—over there, a movement, a damping wave of branch lashing in recoil from—what? Miles's heart lurched in his chest. He adjusted his stunner to full power, slipped silently off the porch, and began his stalk, crouching low, taking advantage of cover wherever the long grasses of the yard had not been trampled flat by the activities of the last day, and night. Miles froze like a predatory cat as a shape seemed to coalesce out of the mist.

A lean young man, not too tall, dressed in the baggy trousers that seemed to be standard here, stood wearily by the horse lines, staring up the yard at Karal's cabin. He stood so for a full two minutes without moving. Miles held a bead on him with his stunner. If he dared make one move toward Ninny . . .

The young man walked back and forth uncertainly, then crouched on his heels, still gazing up the yard. He pulled something from the pocket of his loose jacket—Miles's finger tightened on the trigger— but he only put it to his mouth and bit. An apple. The crunch carried clearly in the damp air, and the faint perfume of its juices. He ate about half, then stopped, seeming to have trouble swallowing. Miles checked the knife at his belt, made sure it was loose in its sheath. Ninny's nostrils widened, and he nickered hopefully, drawing the young man's attention. He rose and walked over to the horse.

The blood pulsed in Miles's ears, louder than any other sound. His grip on the stunner was damp and white-knuckled. The young man fed Ninny his apple. The horse chomped it down, big jaw rippling under his skin, then cocked his hip, dangled one hind hoof, and sighed hugely. If he hadn't seen the man eat off the fruit first Miles might have shot him on the spot. It couldn't be poisoned. . . . The man made to pet Ninny's neck, then his hand drew back in startlement as he encountered Dea's dressing. Ninny shook his head uneasily. Miles rose slowly and stood waiting. The man scratched Ninny's ears instead, looked up one last time at the cabin, took a deep breath, stepped forward, saw Miles, and stood stock still.

"Lem Csurik?" said Miles.

A pause, a frozen nod. "Lord Vorkosigan?" said the young man. Miles nodded in turn.

Csurik swallowed. "Vor lord," he quavered, "do you keep your word?"

What a bizarre opening. Miles's brows climbed. Hell, go with it. "Yes. Are you coming in?"

"Yes and no, m'lord."

"Which?"

"A bargain, lord. I must have a bargain, and your word on it."

"If you killed Raina . . ."

"No, lord. I swear it. I didn't."

"Then you have nothing to fear from me."

Lem Csurik's lips thinned. What the devil could this hill man find ironic? How dare he find irony in Miles's confusion? Irony, but no amusement.

"Oh, lord," breathed Csurik, "I wish that were so. But I have to prove it to Harra. Harra must believe me—you have to make her believe me, lord!"

"You have to make me believe you first. Fortunately, that isn't hard. You come up to the cabin and make that same statement under fast-penta, and I will rule you cleared."

Csurik was shaking his head.

"Why not?" said Miles patiently. That Csurik had turned up at all was strong circumstantial indication of his innocence. Unless he somehow imagined he could beat the drug. Miles would be patient for, oh, three or four seconds at least. Then, by God, he'd stun him, drag him inside, tie him up till he came round, and get to the bottom of this before breakfast.

"The drug—they say you can't hold anything back."

"It would be pretty useless if you could."

Csurik stood silent a moment.

"Are you trying to conceal some lesser crime on your conscience? Is that the bargain you wish to strike? An amnesty? It . . . might be possible. If it's short of another murder, that is."

"No, lord. I've never killed anybody!"

"Then maybe we can deal. Because if you're innocent, I need to know as soon as possible. Because it means my work isn't finished here."

"That's . . . that's the trouble, m'lord." Csurik shuffled, then seemed to come to some internal decision and stood sturdily. "I'll come in and risk your drug. And I'll answer anything about me you want to ask. But you have to promise—swear!—you won't ask me about . . . about anything else. Anybody else."

"Do you know who killed your daughter?"

"Not for sure." Csurik threw his head back defiantly. "I didn't see it. I have guesses."

"I have guesses too."

"That's as may be, lord. Just so's they don't come from my mouth. That's all I ask."

Miles holstered his stunner, and rubbed his chin. "Hm." A very slight smile turned one corner of his lip. "I admit, it would be more—elegant—to solve this case by reason and deduction than brute force. Even so tender a force as fast-penta."

Csurik's head lowered. "I don't know elegant, lord. But I don't want it to be from my mouth."

Decision bubbled up in Miles, straightening his spine. Yes. He *knew*, now. He had only to run through the proofs, step by chained step. Just like 5-Space math. "Very well. I swear by my word as Vorkosigan, I shall confine my questions to the facts to which you were an eyewitness. I will not ask you for conjectures about persons or events for which you were not present. There, will that do?"

Csurik bit his lip. "Yes, lord. If you keep your word."

"Try me," suggested Miles. His lips wrinkled back on a vulpine smile, absorbing the implied insult without comment.

Csurik climbed the yard beside Miles as if to an executioner's block. Their entrance created a tableau of astonishment among Karal and his family, clustered around their wooden table where Dea was treating Pym. Pym and Dea looked rather blanker, till Miles made introduction: "Dr. Dea, get out your fast-penta. Here's Lem Csurik come to talk with us."

Miles steered Lem to a chair. The hill man sat with his hands clenched. Pym, a red and purpling bruise showing at the edges of the white tape circling his chest, took up his stunner and stepped back.

Dr. Dea muttered under his breath to Miles as he got out the hypospray. "How'd you *do* that?"

Miles's hand brushed his pocket. He pulled out a sugar cube and held it up, and grinned through the C of his thumb and finger. Dea snorted, but pursed his lips with reluctant respect.

Lem flinched as the hypospray hissed on his arm, as if he expected it to hurt.

"Count backwards from ten," Dea instructed. By the time Lem reached three, he had relaxed; at zero, he giggled.

"Karal, Ma Karal, Pym, gather round," said Miles. "You are my witnesses. Boys, stay back and stay quiet. No interruptions, please."

Miles ran through the preliminaries, half a dozen questions designed to set up a rhythm and kill time while the fast-penta took full effect. Lem Csurik grinned foolishly, lolling in his chair, and answered them all with sunny good will. Fast-penta interrogation had been part of Miles's military intelligence course at the Service Academy. The drug seemed to be working exactly as advertised, oddly enough.

"Did you return to your cabin that morning, after you spent the night at your parents'?"

"Yes, m'lord," Lem smiled.

"About what time?"

"Midmorning."

Nobody here had a chrono, that was probably as precise an answer as Miles was likely to get. "What did you do when you got there?"

"Called for Harra. She was gone, though. It frightened me that she was gone. Thought she might've run out on me." Lem hiccoughed. "I want my Harra."

"Later. Was the baby asleep?"

"She was. She woke up when I called for Harra. Started crying again. It goes right up your spine."

"What did you do then?"

Lem's eyes widened. "I got no milk. She wanted Harra. There's nothing I could do for her."

"Did you pick her up?"

"No, lord, I let her lay. There was nothing I could do for her. Harra, she'd hardly let me touch her, she was that nervous about her. Told me I'd drop her or something."

"You didn't shake her, to stop her screaming?"

"No, lord, I let her lay. I left to look down the path for Harra."

"Then where did you go?"

Lem blinked. "My sister's. I'd promised to help haul wood for a new cabin. Bella—m'other sister—is getting married, y'see, and—"

He was beginning to wander, as was normal for this drug. "Stop," said Miles. Lem fell silent obediently, swaying slightly in his chair. Miles considered his next question carefully. He was approaching the fine line, here. "Did you meet anyone on the path? Answer yes or no."

"Yes."

Dea was getting excited. "Who? Ask him who!"

Miles held up his hand. "You can administer the antagonist now, Dr. Dea."

"Aren't you going to ask him? It could be vital!"

"I can't. I gave my word. Administer the antagonist now, Doctor!"

Fortunately, the confusion of two interrogators stopped Lem's mumbled willing reply to Dea's question. Dea, bewildered, pressed his hypospray against Lem's arm. Lem's eyes, half-closed, snapped open within seconds. He sat up straight and rubbed his arm, and his face.

"Who did you meet on the path?" Dea asked him directly.

Lem's lips pressed tight; he looked for rescue to Miles.

Dea looked too. "Why won't you ask him?"

"Because I don't need to," said Miles. "I know precisely who Lem met on the path, and why he went on and not back. It was Raina's murderer. As I shall shortly prove. And—witness this, Karal, Ma Karal—that information did not come from Lem's mouth. Confirm!"

Karal nodded slowly. "I . . . see, m'lord. That was . . . very good of you."

Miles gave him a direct stare, his mouth set in a tight smile. "And when is a mystery no mystery at all?"

Karal reddened, not replying for a moment. Then he said, "You may as well keep on like you're going, m'lord. There's no stopping you now, I suppose."

"No."

MILES SENT RUNNERS to collect the witnesses, Ma Karal in one direction, Zed in a second, Speaker Karal and his eldest in a third. He had Lem wait with Pym, Dea, and himself. Having the shortest distance to cover, Ma Karal arrived back first, with Ma Csurik and two of her sons in tow.

His mother fell on Lem, embracing him and then looking fearfully over her shoulder at Miles. The younger brothers hung back, but Pym had already moved between them and the door.

"It's all right, Ma." Lem patted her on the back. "Or . . . anyway, I'm all right. I'm clear. Lord Vorkosigan believes me."

She glowered at Miles, still holding Lem's arm. "You didn't let the mutie lord give you that poison drug, did you?"

"Not poison," Miles denied. "In fact, the drug may have saved his life. That damn near makes it a medicine, I'd say. However," he turned toward Lem's two younger brothers, and folded his arms sternly, "I would like to know which of you young morons threw the torch on my tent last night?"

The younger one whitened; the elder, hotly indignant, noticed his brother's expression and cut his denial off in mid-syllable. "You didn't!" he hissed in horror.

"Nobody," said the white one. "Nobody did."

Miles raised his eyebrows. There followed a short, choked silence.

"Well, *nobody* can make his apologies to Speaker and Ma Karal, then," said Miles, "since it was their sons who were sleeping in the tent last night. I and my men were in the loft."

The boy's mouth opened in dismay. The youngest Karal stared at the pale Csurik brother, his age-mate, and whispered importantly, "You, Dono! You idiot, didn't ya know that tent wouldn't burn? It's real Imperial Service issue!"

Miles clasped his hands behind his back, and fixed the Csuriks with a cold eye. "Rather more to the point, it was attempted assassination upon your Count's heir, which carries the same capital charge of treason as an attempt upon the Count himself. Or perhaps Dono didn't think of that?"

Dono was thrown into flummoxed confusion. No need for fast-penta here, the kid couldn't carry off a lie worth a damn. Ma Csurik now had hold of Dono's arm too, without letting go of Lem's; she looked as frantic as a hen with too many chicks, trying to shelter them from storm.

"I wasn't trying to kill you, lord!" cried Dono.

"What were you trying to do, then?"

"You'd come to kill Lem. I wanted to . . . make you go away. Frighten you away. I didn't think anyone would really get hurt—I mean, it was only a tent!"

"You've never seen anything burn down, I take it. Have you, Ma Csurik?"

Lem's mother nodded, lips tight, clearly torn between a desire to protect her son from Miles, and a desire to beat Dono till he bled for his potentially lethal stupidity.

"Well, but for a chance, you could have killed or horribly injured three of your friends. Think on that, please. In the meantime, in view of your youth and ah, apparent mental defectiveness, I shall hold the treason charge. In return, Speaker Karal and your parents shall be responsible for your good behavior in future, and decide what punishment is appropriate."

Ma Csurik melted with relief and gratitude. Dono looked like he'd rather have been shot. His brother poked him, and whispered, "Mental defective!" Ma Csurik slapped the taunter on the side of his head, effectively suppressing him.

"What about your horse, m'lord?" asked Pym.

"I . . . do not suspect them of the business with the horse," Miles replied slowly. "The attempt to fire the tent was plain stupidity. The other was . . . a different order of calculation altogether."

Zed, who had been permitted to take Pym's horse, returned then with Harra up behind him. Harra entered Speaker Karal's cabin, saw Lem, and stopped with a bitter glare. Lem stood open-handed, his eyes wounded, before her.

"So, lord," Harra said. "You caught him." Her jaw was clenched in joyless triumph.

"Not exactly," said Miles. "He came here and turned himself in. He's made his statement under fast-penta, and cleared himself. Lem did not kill Raina."

Harra turned from side to side. "But I saw he'd been there! He'd left his jacket, and took his good saw and wood planer away with him. I knew he'd been back while I was out! There must be something wrong with your drug!"

Miles shook his head. "The drug worked fine. Your deduction was correct as far as it went. Lem did visit the cabin while you were out. But when he left, Raina was still alive, crying vigorously. It wasn't Lem."

She swayed. "Who, then?"

"I think you know. I think you've been working very hard to deny that knowledge, hence your excessive focus on Lem. As long as you were sure it was Lem, you didn't have to think about the other possibilities."

"But who else would care?" Harra cried. "Who else would bother?"

"Who, indeed?" sighed Miles. He walked to the front window and glanced down the yard. The fog was clearing in the full light of morning. The horses were moving uneasily. "Dr. Dea, would you please get a second dose of fast-penta ready?" Miles turned, paced back to stand before the fireplace, its coals still banked for the night. The faint heat was pleasant on his back.

Dea was staring around, the hypospray in his hand, clearly wondering to whom to administer it. "My lord?" he queried, brows lowering in demand for explanation.

"Isn't it obvious to you, Doctor?" Miles asked lightly.

"*No*, my lord." His tone was slightly indignant.

"Nor to you, Pym?"

"Not . . . entirely, m'lord." Pym's glance, and stunner aim, wavered uncertainly to Harra.

"I suppose it's because neither of you ever met my grandfather," Miles decided. "He died just about a year before you entered my father's service, Pym. He was born at the very end of the Time of Isolation, and lived through every wrenching change this century has dealt to Barrayar. He was called the last of the Old Vor, but really, he was the first of the new. He changed with the times, from the tactics of horse cavalry to that of flyer squadrons, from swords to atomics, and he changed *successfully*. Our present freedom from the Cetagandan occupation is a measure of how fiercely he could adapt, then throw it all away and adapt again. At the end of his life he was called a conservative, only because so much of Barrayar had streamed past him in the direction he had led, prodded, pushed, and pointed all his life.

"He changed, and adapted, and bent with the wind of the times. Then, in his age—for my father was his youngest and sole surviving son, and did not himself marry till middle-age—in his age, he was hit with me. And he had to change again. And he couldn't.

"He begged for my mother to have an abortion, after they knew more or less what the fetal damage would be. He and my parents were estranged for five years after I was born. They didn't see each other or speak or communicate. Everyone thought my father moved us to the Imperial Residence when he became Regent because he was angling for the throne, but in fact it was because the Count my grandfather denied him the use of Vorkosigan House. Aren't family squabbles jolly fun? Bleeding ulcers run in my family, we give them to each other." Miles strolled back to the window and looked out. Ah, yes. Here it came.

"The reconciliation was gradual, when it became quite clear there would be no other son," Miles went on. "No dramatic denouement. It helped when the medics got me walking. It was essential that I tested out bright. Most important of all, I never let him see me give up."

Nobody had dared interrupt this lordly monologue, but it was clear from several expressions that the point of it was escaping them. Since half the point was to kill time, Miles was not greatly disturbed by their failure to track. Footsteps sounded on the wooden porch outside. Pym moved quietly to cover the door with an unobscured angle of fire.

"Dr. Dea," said Miles, sighting through the window, "would you be so kind as to administer that fast-penta to the first person through the door, as they step in?"

"You're not waiting for a volunteer, my lord?"

"Not this time."

The door swung inward, and Dea stepped forward, raising his hand. The hypospray hissed. Ma Mattulich wheeled to face Dea, the skirts of her work dress swirling around her veined calves, hissing in return—"You dare!" Her arm drew back as if to strike him, but slowed in mid-swing and failed to connect as Dea ducked out of her way. This unbalanced her, and she staggered. Speaker Karal, coming in behind, caught her by the arm and steadied her. "You dare!" she wailed again, then turned to see not only Dea but all the other witnesses waiting, Ma Csurik, Ma Karal, Lem, Harra, Pym. Her shoulders sagged, and then the drug cut in and she just stood, a silly smile fighting with anguish for possession of her harsh face.

The smile made Miles ill, but it was the smile he needed. "Sit her down, Dea, Speaker Karal."

They guided her to the chair lately vacated by Lem Csurik. She was fighting the drug desperately, flashes of resistance melting into flaccid docility. Gradually the docility became ascendant, and she sat draped in the chair, grinning helplessly. Miles sneaked a peek at Harra. She stood white and silent, utterly closed.

For several years after the reconciliation Miles had never been left with his grandfather without his personal bodyguard. Sergeant Bothari had worn the Count's livery, but been loyal to Miles alone, the one man dangerous enough—some said, crazy enough—to stand up to the great General himself. There was no need, Miles decided, to spell out to these fascinated people just what interrupted incident had made his parents think Sergeant Bothari a necessary precaution. Let General Piotr's untarnished reputation serve—Miles, now. As *he* willed. Miles's eyes glinted.

Lem lowered his head. "If I had known—if I had guessed—I wouldn't have left them alone together, m'lord. I thought—Harra's mother would take care of her. I couldn't have—I didn't know *how*—"

Harra did not look at him. Harra did not look at anything.

"Let us conclude this," Miles sighed. Again, he requested formal witness from the crowd in the room, and cautioned against interruptions, which tended to unduly confuse a drugged subject. He moistened his lips and turned to Ma Mattulich.

Again, he began with the standard neutral questions, name, birthdate, parents' names, checkable biographical facts. Ma Mattulich was harder to lull than the cooperative Lem had been, her responses scattered and staccato. Miles controlled his impatience with difficulty. For all its deceptive ease, fast-penta interrogation required skill, skill and patience. He'd got too far to risk a stumble now. He worked his questions up gradually to the first critical ones.

"Were you there, when Raina was born?"

Her voice was low and drifting, dreamy. "The birth came in the night. Lem, he went for Jean the midwife, the midwife's son was supposed to go for me but he fell back to sleep. I didn't get there till morning, and then it was too late. They'd all seen."

"Seen what?"

"The cat's mouth, the dirty mutation. Monsters in us. Cut them out. Ugly little man." This last, Miles realized, was an aside upon himself. Her attention had hung up on him, hypnotically. "Muties make more muties, they breed faster, overrun . . . I saw you watching the girls. You want to make mutie babies on clean women, poison us all . . ."

Time to steer her back to the main issue. "Were you ever alone with the baby after that?"

"No. Jean she hung around. Jean knows me, she knew what I wanted. None of her damn business. And Harra was always there. Harra must not know. Harra must not . . . why should she get off so soft? The poison must be in her. Must have come from her Da, I lay only with her Da and they were all wrong but the one."

Miles blinked. "What were all wrong?" Across the room Miles saw Speaker Karal's mouth tighten. The headman caught Miles's glance and stared down at his own feet, absenting himself from the procedings. Lem, his lips parted in absorption, and the rest of the boys were listening with alarm. Harra hadn't moved.

"All my babies," Ma Mattulich said.

Harra looked up sharply at that, her eyes widening.

"Was Harra not your only child?" Miles asked. It was an effort to keep his voice cool, calm; he wanted to shout. He wanted to be gone from here. . . .

"No, of course not. She was my only clean child, I thought. I thought, but the poison must have been hidden in her. I fell on my knees and thanked God when she was born clean, a clean one at last, after so many, so much pain. . . . I thought I had finally been punished enough. She was such a pretty baby, I thought it was over at last. But she must have been mutie after all, hidden, tricksy, sly. . . ."

"How many," Miles choked, "babies did you have?"

"Four, besides Harra my last."

"And you killed all four of them?" Speaker Karal, Miles saw, gave a slow nod to his feet.

"No!" said Ma Mattulich. Indignation broke through the fast-penta wooze briefly. "Two were born dead already, the first one, and the twisted-up one. The one with too many fingers and toes, and the one with the bulgy head, those I cut. Cut out. My mother, she watched over me to see I did it right. Harra, I made it soft for Harra. I did it for her."

"So you have in fact murdered not one infant, but three?" said Miles frozenly. The younger witnesses in the room, Karal's boys and the Csurik brothers, looked horrified. The older ones, Ma Mattulich's contemporaries, who must have lived through the events with her, looked mortified, sharing her shame. Yes, they all must have known.

"Murdered?" said Ma Mattulich. "No! I cut them out. I had to. I had to do the right thing." Her chin lifted proudly, then drooped. "Killed my babies, to please, to please . . . I don't know who. And now you call me a murderer? Damn you! What use is your justice to me *now*? I needed it then—where were you *then*?" Suddenly, shockingly, she burst into tears, which wavered almost instantly into rage. "If mine must die then so must hers! Why should she get off so soft? Spoiled her . . . I tried my best, I did my best, it's not fair. . . ."

The fast-penta was not keeping up with this . . . no, it was working, Miles decided, but her emotions were too overwhelming. Upping the dose might level her emotional surges, at some risk of respiratory arrest, but it would not elicit any more complete a confession. Miles's belly was trembling, a reaction he trusted he concealed. It had to be completed now.

"Why did you break Raina's neck, instead of cutting her throat?"

"Harra, she must not know," said Ma Mattulich. "Poor baby. It would look like she just died. . . ."

Miles eyed Lem, Speaker Karal. "It seems a number of others shared your opinion that Harra should not know."

"I didn't want it to be from my mouth," repeated Lem sturdily.

"I wanted to save her double grief, m'lord," said Karal. "She'd had so much. . . ."

Miles met Harra's eyes at that. "I think you all underestimate her. Your excessive tenderness insults both her intelligence and will. She comes from a tough line, that one."

Harra inhaled, controlling her own trembling. She gave Miles a short nod, as if to say, *Thank you, little man.* He returned her a slight inclination of the head, *Yes, I understand.*

"I'm not sure yet where justice lies in this case," said Miles, "but this I swear to you, the days of cooperative concealment are over. No more secret crimes in the night. Daylight's here. And speaking of crimes in the night," he turned back to Ma Mattulich, "*was* it you who tried to cut my horse's throat last night?"

"I tried," said Ma Mattulich, calmer now in a wave of fast-penta mellowness, "but it kept rearing up on me."

"Why my *horse?*" Miles could not keep exasperation from his voice, though a calm, even tone was enjoined upon fast-penta inter-rogators by the training manual.

"I couldn't get at you," said Ma Mattulich simply.

Miles rubbed his forehead. "Retroactive infanticide by proxy?" he muttered.

"You," said Ma Mattulich, and her loathing came through even the nauseating fast-penta cheer, "*you* are the worst. All I went through, all I did, all the grief, and you come along at the end. A mutie made lord over us all, and all the rules changed, betrayed at the end by an off-worlder woman's weakness. You make it all for *nothing.* Hate you. Dirty mutie . . ." Her voice trailed off in a drugged mumble.

Miles took a deep breath, and looked around the room. The stillness was profound, and no one dared break it.

"I believe," he said, "that concludes my investigation into the facts of this case."

The mystery of Raina's death was solved.

The problem of justice, unfortunately, remained.

MILES TOOK a walk.

The graveyard, though little more than a crude clearing in the woodland, was a place of peace and beauty in the morning light. The stream burbled endlessly, shifting green shadows and blinding brilliant reflections. The faint breeze that had shredded away the last of the night fog whispered in the trees, and the tiny, short-lived creatures

that everyone on Barrayar but biologists called bugs sang and twittered
in the patches of native scrub.

"Well, Raina," Miles sighed, "and what do I do now?" Pym lingered by the borders of the clearing, giving Miles room. "It's all right,"
Miles assured the tiny grave, "Pym's caught me talking to dead people
before. He may think I'm crazy, but he's far too well-trained to say
so."

Pym in fact did not look happy, nor altogether well. Miles felt
rather guilty for dragging him out, by rights the man should be resting
in bed, but Miles had desperately needed this time alone. Pym wasn't
just suffering the residual effect of having been kicked by Ninny. He
had been silent ever since Miles had extracted the confession from
Ma Mattulich. Miles was unsurprised. Pym had steeled himself to
play executioner to their imagined hill bully; the substitution of a mad
grandmother as his victim had clearly given him pause. He would
obey whatever order Miles gave him, though, Miles had no doubt of
that.

Miles considered the peculiarities of Barrayaran law, as he wandered about the clearing, watching the stream and the light, turning
over an occasional rock with the toe of his boot. The fundamental
principle was clear; the spirit was to be preferred over the letter,
truth over technicalities. Precedent was held subordinate to the judgment of the man on the spot. Alas, the man on the spot was himself.
There was no refuge for him in automated rules, no hiding behind
the law says as if the law were some living overlord with a real Voice.
The only voice here was his own.

And who would be served by the death of that half-crazed old
woman? Harra? The relationship between mother and daughter had
been wounded unto death by this, Miles had seen that in their eyes,
yet still Harra had no stomach for matricide. Miles rather preferred
it that way; having her standing by his ear crying for bloody revenge
would have been enormously distracting just now. The obvious justice
made a damn poor reward for Harra's courage in reporting the crime.
Raina? Ah. That was more difficult.

"I'd like to lay the old gargoyle right there at your feet, small
lady," Miles muttered to her. "Is it your desire? Does it serve you?
What *would* serve you?" Was this the great burning he had promised
her?

What judgment would reverberate along the entire Dendarii mountain range? Should he indeed sacrifice these people to some larger political statement, regardless of their wants? Or should he forget all that, make his judgment serve only those directly involved? He scooped up a stone and flung it full force into the stream. It vanished invisibly in the rocky bed.

He turned to find Speaker Karal waiting by the edge of the graveyard. Karal ducked his head in greeting and approached cautiously.

"So, m'lord," said Karal.

"Just so," said Miles.

"Have you come to any conclusion?"

"Not really." Miles gazed around. "Anything less than Ma Mattulich's death seems . . . inadequate justice, and yet . . . I cannot see who her death would serve."

"Neither could I. That's why I took the position I did in the first place."

"No . . ." said Miles slowly, "no, you were wrong in that. For one thing, it very nearly got Lem Csurik killed. I was getting ready to pursue him with deadly force at one point. It almost destroyed him with Harra. Truth is better. Slightly better. At least it isn't a fatal error. Surely I can do . . . something with it."

"I didn't know what to expect of you, at first," admitted Karal.

Miles shook his head. "I meant to make changes. A difference. Now . . . I don't know."

Speaker Karal's balding forehead wrinkled. "But we are changing."

"Not enough. Not fast enough."

"You're young yet, that's why you don't see how much, how fast. Look at the difference between Harra and her mother. God—look at the difference between Ma Mattulich and *her* mother. *There* was a harridan." Speaker Karal shuddered. "I remember her, all right. And yet, she was not so unusual, in her day. So far from having to make change, I don't think you could stop it if you tried. The minute we finally get a powersat receptor up here, and get on the comm net, the past will be done and over. As soon as the kids see the future— their future—they'll be mad after it. They're already lost to the old ones like Ma Mattulich. The old ones know it, too, don't believe they don't know it. Why d'you think we haven't been able to get at least a small unit up here yet? Not just the cost. The old ones are fighting it. They call it off-planet corruption, but it's really the future they fear."

"There's so much still to be done."

"Oh, yes. We are a desperate people, no lie. But we have hope. I don't think you realize how much you've done, just by coming up here."

"I've done nothing," said Miles bitterly. "Sat around, mostly. And now, I swear, I'm going to end up doing more nothing. And then go home. Hell!"

Speaker Karal pursed his lips, looked at his feet, at the high hills. "You are doing something for us every minute. Mutie lord. Do you think you are invisible?"

Miles grinned wolfishly. "Oh, Karal, I'm a one-man band, I am. I'm a parade."

"As you say, just so. Ordinary people need extraordinary examples. So they can say to themselves, well, if he can do *that*, I can surely do *this*. No excuses."

"No quarter, yes, I know that game. Been playing it all my life."

"I think," said Karal, "Barrayar needs you. To go on being just what you are."

"Barrayar will eat me, if it can."

"Yes," said Karal, his eyes on the horizon, "so it will." His gaze fell to the graves at his feet. "But it swallows us all in the end, doesn't it? You will outlive the old ones."

"Or in the beginning." Miles pointed down. "Don't tell *me* who I'm going to outlive. Tell Raina."

Karal's shoulders slumped. "True. S'truth. Make your judgment, lord. I'll back you."

MILES ASSEMBLED them all in Karal's yard for his Speaking, the porch now become his podium. The interior of the cabin would have been impossibly hot and close for this crowd, suffocating with the afternoon sun beating on the roof, though outdoors the light made them squint. They were all here, everyone they could round up, Speaker Karal, Ma Karal, their boys, all the Csuriks, most of the cronies who had attended last night's funereal festivities, men, women, and children.

Harra sat apart. Lem kept trying to hold her hand, though from the way she flinched it was clear she didn't want to be touched. Ma Mattulich sat displayed by Miles's side, silent and surly, flanked by Pym and an uncomfortable-looking Deputy Alex.

Miles jerked up his chin, settling his head on the high collar of his dress greens, as polished and formal as Pym's batman's expertise could make him. The Imperial Service uniform that Miles had earned. Did these people know he had earned it, or did they all imagine it a mere gift from his father, nepotism at work? Damn what they thought. He knew. He stood before his people, and gripped the porch rail.

"I have concluded the investigation of the charges laid before the Count's Court by Harra Csurik of the murder of her daughter Raina. By evidence, witness, and her own admission, I find Mara Mattulich guilty of this murder, she having twisted the infant's neck until it broke, and then attempted to conceal that crime. Even when that concealment placed her son-in-law Lem Csurik in mortal danger from false charges. In light of the helplessness of the victim, the cruelty of the method, and the cowardly selfishness of the attempted concealment, I can find no mitigating excuse for the crime.

"In addition, Mara Mattulich by her own admission testifies to two previous infanticides, some twenty years ago, of her own children. These facts shall be announced by Speaker Karal in every corner of Silvy Vale, until every subject has been informed."

He could feel Ma Mattulich's glare boring into his back. *Yes, go on and hate me, old woman. I will bury you yet, and you know it.* He swallowed, and continued, the formality of the language a sort of shield before him.

"For this unmitigated crime, the only proper sentence is death. And I so sentence Mara Mattulich. But in light of her age and close relation to the next-most-injured party in the case, Harra Csurik, I choose to hold the actual execution of that sentence. Indefinitely." Out of the corner of his eye Miles saw Pym let out, very carefully and covertly, a sigh of relief. Harra combed at her straw-colored bangs with her fingers and listened intently.

"But she shall be as dead before the law. All her property, even to the clothes on her back, now belongs to her daughter Harra, to dispose of as she wills. Mara Mattulich may not own property, enter contracts, sue for injuries, nor exert her will after death in any testament. She shall not leave Silvy Vale without Harra's permission. Harra shall be given power over her as a parent over a child, or as in senility. In Harra's absence Speaker Karal will be her deputy. Mara Mattulich shall be watched to see she harms no other child.

"Further. She shall die without sacrifice. No one, not Harra nor any other, shall make a burning for her when she goes into the ground at last. As she murdered her future, so her future shall return only death to her spirit. She will die as the childless do, without remembrance."

A low sigh swept the older members of the crowd before Miles. For the first time, Mara Mattulich bent her stiff neck.

Some, Miles knew, would find this only spiritually symbolic. Others would see it as literally lethal, according to the strength of their beliefs. The literal-minded, such as those who saw mutation as a sin to be violently expiated. But even the less superstitious, Miles saw in their faces, found the meaning clear. So.

Miles turned to Ma Mattulich, and lowered his voice. "Every breath you take from this moment on is by my mercy. Every bite of food you eat, by Harra's charity. By charity and mercy—such as you did not give—you shall live. Dead woman."

"Some mercy. Mutie lord." Her growl was low, weary, beaten.

"You get the point," he said through his teeth. He swept her a bow, infinitely ironic, and turned his back on her. "I am the Voice of Count Vorkosigan. This concludes my Speaking."

MILES MET Harra and Lem afterwards, in Speaker Karal's cabin.

"I have a proposition for you." Miles controlled his nervous pacing and stood before them. "You're free to turn it down, or think about it for a while. I know you're very tired right now." *As are we all*. Had he really been in Silvy Vale only a day and a half? It seemed like a century. His head ached with fatigue. Harra was red-eyed too. "First of all, can you read and write?"

"Some," Harra admitted. "Speaker Karal taught us some, and Ma Lannier."

"Well, good enough. You wouldn't be starting completely blind. Look. A few years back Hassadar started a teacher's college. It's not very big yet, but it's begun. There are some scholarships. I can swing one your way, if you will agree to live in Hassadar for three years of intense study."

"Me!" said Harra. "I couldn't go to a college! I barely know . . . any of that stuff."

"Knowledge is what you're supposed to have coming out, not going in. Look, they know what they're dealing with in this district. They have a lot of remedial courses. It's true, you'd have to work harder, to catch up with the town-bred and the lowlanders. But I know you have courage, and I know you have will. The rest is just picking yourself up and ramming into the wall again and again until it falls down. You get a bloody forehead, so what? You can do it, I swear you can."

Lem, sitting beside her, looked worried. He captured her hand again. "Three years?" he said in a small voice. "Gone away?"

"The school stipend isn't that much," said Miles. "But Lem, I understand you have carpenter's skills. There's a building boom going on in Hassadar right now. Hassadar's going to be the next Vorkosigan Vashnoi, I think. I'm certain you could get a job. Together, you could live."

Lem looked at first relieved, then extremely worried. "But they all use power tools—computers—robots. . . ."

"By no means. And they weren't all born knowing how to use that stuff either. If they can learn it, you can. Besides, the rich pay well for hand-work, unique one-of items, if the quality's good. I can see you get a start, which is usually the toughest moment. After that you should be able to figure it out all right."

"To leave Silvy Vale . . ." said Harra in a dismayed tone.

"Only in order to return. That's the other half of the bargain. I can send a comm unit up here, a small one with a portable power pack that lasts a year. Somebody'd have to hump down to Vorkosigan Surleau to replace it annually, no big problem. The whole setup wouldn't cost much more than oh, a new lightflyer." Such as the shiny red one Miles had coveted in a dealer's showroom in Vorbarr Sultana, very suitable for a graduation present, he had pointed out to his parents. The credit chit was sitting in the top drawer of his dresser in the lake house at Vorkosigan Surleau right now. "It's not a massive project like installing a powersat receptor for the whole of Silvy Vale or anything. The holovid would pick up the educational satellite broadcasts from the capital; set it up in some central cabin, add a couple of dozen lap-links for the kids, and you've got an instant school. All the children would be required to attend, with Speaker Karal to enforce it, though once they'd discovered the holovid you'd probably have to beat them to make them go home. I, ah," Miles cleared his throat, "thought you might name it the Raina Csurik Primary School."

"Oh," said Harra, and began to cry for the first time that grueling day. Lem patted her clumsily. She returned the grip of his hand at last.

"I can send a lowlander up here to teach," said Miles. "I'll get one to take a short-term contract, till you're ready to come back. But he or she won't understand Silvy Vale like you do. Wouldn't understand *why*. You—you already know. You know what they can't teach in any lowland college."

Harra scrubbed her eyes, and looked up—not very far up—at him. "You went to the Imperial Academy."

"I did." His chin jerked up.

"Then I," she said shakily, "can manage . . . Hassadar Teacher's College." The name was awkward in her mouth. At first. "At any rate—I'll try, m'lord."

"I'll bet on you," Miles agreed. "Both of you. Just, ah," a smile sped across his mouth and vanished, "stand up straight and speak the truth, eh?"

Harra blinked understanding. An answering half-smile lit her tired face, equally briefly. "I will. Little man."

FAT NINNY rode home by air the next morning, in a horse van, along with Pym. Dr. Dea went along with his two patients, and his nemesis the sorrel mare. A replacement bodyguard had been sent with the groom who flew the van from Vorkosigan Surleau, who stayed with Miles to help him ride the remaining two horses back down. Well, Miles thought, he'd been considering a camping trip in the mountains with his cousin Ivan as part of his home leave anyway. The liveried man was the laconic veteran Esterhazy, whom Miles had known most of his life; excellent company for a man who didn't want to talk about it, unlike Ivan you could almost forget he was there. Miles wondered if Esterhazy's assignment had been random chance, or a mercy of the Count's. Esterhazy was good with horses.

They camped overnight by the river of roses. Miles walked up the vale in the evening light, desultorily looking for the spring of it; indeed, the floral barrier did seem to peter out a couple of kilometers upstream, merging into slightly less impassable scrub. Miles plucked a rose, checked to make sure that Esterhazy was nowhere in sight, and bit into it curiously. Clearly, he was not a horse. A cut bunch would probably not survive the trip back as a treat for Ninny. Ninny could settle for oats.

Miles watched the evening shadows flowing up along the backbone of the Dendarii range, high and massive in the distance. How small those mountains looked from space! Little wrinkles on the skin of a globe he could cover with his hand, all their crushing mass made invisible. Which was illusory, distance or nearness? Distance, Miles decided. Distance was a damned lie. Had his father known this? Miles suspected so.

He contemplated his urge to throw all his money, not just a lightflyer's worth, at those mountains; to quit it all and go teach children to read and write, to set up a free clinic, a powersat net, or all of these at once. But Silvy Vale was only one of hundreds of such communities buried in these mountains, one of thousands across the whole of Barrayar. Taxes squeezed from this very district helped maintain the very elite military school he'd just spent—how much of their resources in? How much would he have to give back just to make it even, now? He was himself a planetary resource, his training had made him so, and his feet were set on their path.

What God means you to do, Miles's theist mother claimed, could be deduced from the talents He gave you. The academic honors, Miles had amassed by sheer brute work. But the war games, outwitting his opponents, staying one step ahead—a necessity, true, he had no margin for error—the war games had been an unholy joy. War had been no game here once, not so long ago. It might be so again. What you did best, that was what was wanted from you. God seemed to be lined up with the Emperor on that point, at least, if no other.

Miles had sworn his officer's oath to the Emperor less than two weeks ago, puffed with pride at his achievement. In his secret mind he had imagined himself keeping that oath through blazing battle, enemy torture, what-have-you, even while sharing cynical cracks afterwards with Ivan about archaic dress swords and the sort of people who insisted on wearing them.

But in the dark of subtler temptations, those which hurt without heroism for consolation, he foresaw, the Emperor would no longer be the symbol of Barrayar in his heart.

Peace to you, small lady, he thought to Raina. *You've won a twisted poor modern knight, to wear your favor on his sleeve. But it's a twisted poor world we were both born into, that rejects us without mercy and ejects us without consultation. At least I won't just tilt at windmills for you. I'll send in sappers to mine the twirling suckers, and blast them into the sky. . . .*

He knew who he served now. And why he could not quit. And why he must not fail.

RHYSLING AWARD WINNERS

The Rhysling Awards are presented annually by the Science Fiction Poetry Association for "excellence in speculative, science-oriented, science fiction, fantasy, horror and related poetry published during the preceding year." The name derives from that of the blind poet in Robert Heinlein's story "The Green Hills of Earth," and is used with his permission. Suzette Haden Elgin established the awards, along with the SFPA, in 1978, and a tradition has arisen of showcasing the Rhysling winners in these annual *Nebula Awards* volumes.

The competition for the 1989 Rhyslings produced a tie in the long-poem category (over fifty lines) between "In the Darkened Hours" by Bruce Boston and "Winter Solstice, Camelot Station" by John M. Ford. The winner in the short-poem category (under fifty lines) was "Salinity" by Robert Frazier.

Robert Frazier appeared in *Nebula Awards 24* with a long poem called "The Daily Chernobyl." Although he sometimes writes prose science fiction, his poetry has made his reputation. He has also edited an influential small-press journal, *T.A.S.P.* (*The Anthology of Speculative Poetry*), and a landmark collection of speculative poems, *Burning with a Vision* (1984). His poems have appeared in *Fantasy & Science Fiction, Isaac Asimov's Science Fiction Magazine, Amazing Stories, Fantasy Book*, a host of original anthologies, and—a difficult market for any SF poet to crack—*Omni*.

Of "Salinity," his short-poem winner, Frazier writes that it has its origins "in my family life, and in the way people use and comprehend science in their everyday experience. My father was a cryptologist who helped break the Nazi code in Bletchly, England, during World War II."

Bruce Boston has now won three Rhyslings. The previous two were for "For Spacers Snarled in the Hair of Comets" (best short poem, 1985) and "The Nightmare Collector" (best short poem, 1988, in a tie with a work by Suzette Haden Elgin). With Robert Frazier, he has written *Chronicles of the Mutant Rain Forest*. In addition to *Chronicles*, other works appearing in 1990 included *After Magic* (prose poems), *Short Circuits*, and *Faces of the Beast* (a collection of dark-fantasy poetry). Also a short story writer, Boston is a frequent contributor not only to science-fiction markets but to the American small press.

"To call something 'just a dream' is equivalent to saying, 'Forget it. It's not important,'" Boston notes. "In the Darkened Hours," however, tries "to embody this contradiction critically, at the same time portraying the compulsive-retentive nature of dreams by the manipulation of symbols from my own unconscious that struck me as having wider significance."

John M. Ford has written poems, essays, games, reviews, children's books, and comics. He has won two World Fantasy Awards, one for his fine historical fantasy, *The Dragon Waiting*, in 1984, and one for the poem that you are about to read, not as a poem per se but as "Best Short Fiction, 1989." Moreover, "Winter Solstice, Camelot Station"— which I was fortunate enough to receive as a Christmas greeting a few years back—has already been anthologized in Ellen Datlow and Terri Windling's *Year's Best Fantasy, 1989*.

"If I remember right," Ford tells us, "I was reading Charles Williams's Arthurian poetry (a wonderful book, much neglected among the middenheaps of inert matter of Britain). Much of Williams's imagery is mechanical—ships, coins, stones—and somewhere something gave me the image of an armored man as a steam locomotive. (Yes, I like trains. I'm sure that's a great surprise to everyone.)

"From there it was a process of extending the metaphor; you know, just like pulling teeth. (If you're going to explain the magic trick, never let 'em think just anyone can do it.)

"At any rate, 'Camelot Station' was my holiday card for 1986, and that was where it would have ended, except that Jane Yolen liked it enough to show it to Parke Godwin, who had a closed Arthurian anthology, and Parke liked it enough to unclose the book. Since then, other people seem to have liked it too."

Salinity
Robert Frazier

Sweating in the full glare of August,
my father taught me a bittersweet truth
on a beach day, when he was restless
to be holding something
other than me—
a surf casting rod perhaps,
or the glow of health that eluded him and
corroded year by year like his station wagon

from halite poured on New England's icy roads.
He taught me that we preserved our heritage,
our only heritage really,
in the saltiness of our blood.
A striped bass can't live out of the sea,
he said, or in fresh water either.
Yet we carry our oceans with us from birth to beyond.
And as he cut short this speech,
fully knowing what carcinomas ate at him,
he let tears drop into the sea spraying on me.
Unmindful, I sucked the salt from my wrist.
Now they haunt my veins
those molecules of his within me,
that ocean within the head of a pin.
There whole ecologies of salinity,
of the evolution of things
once left unsaid,
await evaporation and condensation
and distillation.
Worlds reduced within worlds.
Lives within lives.
Yesterdays.

In the Darkened Hours
Bruce Boston

So you are lost again
beneath the turning hub
of the fire flecked sky
and you call it a dream
as you wander the labyrinth
of streets and causeways,
past the shadow barges,
over the ice cloaked river,

down the rugged gullies
where you left behind
the satchels which hold
the weapons and the maps.

So you are lost again
where the night prevails
and you call it a dream
in the oldest city of all,
where the lighted towers
rise and fall like spokes
against the churning sky,
where the voices wail,
where you are engaged
in senseless conversation
with a host of familiar
strangers whose directions
lead you further astray.

So you must travel alone
without weapons or maps
to the house of your father,
past the wrought iron fences,
past the shores and lakes
of the naked arboretum,
past the fallen hillsides
and the deserted air field
where the burning engines
of destruction have fed.
So you climb the stairs
and discover the rooms
of your childhood have
blurred and shifted
like a moldering text,
door frames twisted
at elusive angles,
windows collapsed,
unbounded hallways

and shredded chambers
lifting off into space.

So you are lost again
in the night of the city.
So you must travel alone
to a house drawn from
your flesh and bones.
So you must do this
as the landscape changes.
So you must descend
the rugged gullies
while you forge
the faces of dead lovers.
So you must reassemble
the broken statuary
in your mother's garden
and leave your father's
books upon their shelves.
So you must speak with
the familiar strangers
who know your name.
So you must recite
from the annals
of your stillborn brother,
maniacal and devoted,
who takes your wrist
upon the stairs.
So you call it a dream:
this house you inhabit,
this city you traverse
with blind expectancy,
these faces you fashion
from the imperfect cloth
of memory transfigured,
these visions you conjure
in the darkened hours
with haunting replication.

Winter Solstice, Camelot Station
John M. Ford

Camelot is served
By a sixteen-track stub terminal done in High Gothick Style,
The tracks covered by a single great barrel-vaulted glass roof
　　framed upon iron,
At once looking back to the Romans and ahead to the Brunels.
Beneath its rotunda, just to the left of the ticket windows,
Is a mosaic floor depicting the Round Table
(Where all knights, regardless of their station of origin
Or class of accommodation, are equal),
And around it murals of knightly deeds in action
(Slaying dragons, righting wrongs, rescuing maidens tied to the
　　tracks).
It is the only terminal, other than Gare d'Avalon in Pais,
To be hung with original tapestries,
And its lavatories rival those at Great Gate of Kiev Central.
During a peak season such as this, some eighty trains a day pass
　　through,
Five times the frequency at the old Londinium Terminus,
Ten times the number the Druid towermen knew.
(The Official Court Christmas Card this year displays
A crisp black-and-white Charles Clegg photograph from the King's
　　own collection,
Showing a woad-blued hogger at the throttle of "Old XCVII,"
The Fast Mail overnight to Eboracum. Those were the days.)
The first of a line of wagons has arrived,
Spilling footmen and pages in Court livery,
And old thick Kay, stepping down from his Range Rover,
Tricked out in a bush coat from Swaine, Adeney, Brigg,
Leaning on his shooting stick as he marshalls his company,
Instructing the youngest how to behave in the station,
To help mature women that they may encounter,
Report pickpockets, gather up litter,

And of course no true Knight of the Table Round (even in
    training)
Would do a station porter out of Christmas tips.
He checks his list of arrival times, then his watch
(A moon-phase Breguet, gift from Merlin):
The seneschal is a practical man, who knows trains do run late,
And a stolid one, who sees no reason to be glad about it.
He dispatches pages to posts at the tracks,
Doling out pennies for platform tickets,
Then walks past the station buffet with a dyspeptic snort,
Goes into the bar, checks the time again, orders a pint.
The patrons half-turn—it's the fella from Camelot, innit?
And Kay chuckles soft to himself, and the Court buys a round.
He's barely halfway when a page tumbles in,
Seems the knights are arriving, on time after all,
So he tips the glass back (people stare as he guzzles),
Then plonks it down hard with five quid for the barman,
And strides for the doorway (half Falstaff, half Hotspur)
To summon his liveried army of lads.

Bors arrives behind steam, riding the cab of a heavy Mikado.
He shakes the driver's hand, swings down from the footplate,
And is like a locomotive himself, his breath clouding white,
Dark oil sheen on his black iron mail,
Sword on his hip swinging like siderods at speed.
He stamps back to the baggage car, slams mailed fist on steel door
With a clang like jousters colliding.
The handler opens up and goes to rouse another knight.
Old Pellinore has been dozing with his back against a crate,
A cubical chain-bound thing with FRAGILE tags and air holes,
BEAST says the label, *Questing, 1* the bill of lading.
The porters look doubtful but ease the thing down.
It grumbles. It shifts. Someone shouts, and they drop it.
It cracks like an egg. There is nothing within.
Elayne embraces Bors on the platform, a pelican on a rock,
Silently they watch as Pelly shifts the splinters,
Supposing aloud that Gutman and Cairo have swindled him.

A high-drivered engine in Northern Lines green
Draws in with a string of side-corridor coaches,
All honey-toned wood with stained glass on their windows.
Gareth steps down from a compartment, then Gaheris and
    Agravaine,
All warmly tucked up in Orkney sweaters;
Gawain comes after in Shetland tweed.
Their Gladstones and steamers are neatly arranged,
With never a worry—their Mum does the packing.
A redcap brings forth a curious bundle, a rude shape in red
    paper—
The boys did that themselves, you see, and how *does* one wrap a
    unicorn's head?
They bustle down the platform, past a chap all in green,
He hasn't the look of a trainman, but only Gawaine turns to look at
    his eyes,
And sees written there *Sir, I shall speak with you later.*

Over on the first track, surrounded by reporters,
All glossy dark iron and brass-bound mystery,
The Direct-Orient Express, ferried in from Calais and Points East.
Palomides appears. Smelling of patchouli and Russian leather,
Dripping Soubranie ash on his astrakhan collar,
Worry darkening his dark face, though his damascene armor shows
    no tarnish,
He pushes past the press like a broad-hulled icebreaker.
Flashbulbs pop. Heads turn. There's a woman in Chanel black,
A glint of diamonds, liquid movements, liquid eyes.
The newshawks converge, but suddenly there appears
A sharp young man in a crisp blue suit
From the Compagnie Internationale des Wagons-Lits,
That elegant, comfortable, decorous, close-mouthed firm:
He's good at his job, and they get not so much as a snapshot.
Tomorrow's editions will ask who she was, and whom with. . . .

Now here's a silver train, stainless steel, Vista-Domed,
White-lighted grails on the engine (running no extra sections)
The *Logres Limited*, extra fare, extra fine,

(Stops on signal at Carbonek to receive passengers only).
She glides to a Timken-borne halt (even her grease is clean),
Galahad already on the steps, flashing that winning smile,
Breeze mussing his golden hair, but not his Armani tailoring,
Just the sort of man you'd want finding your chalice.
He signs an autograph, he strikes a pose.
Someone says, loudly, "Gal! Who serves the Grail?"
He looks—no one he knows—and there's a silence,
A space in which he shifts like sun on water;
Look quick and you may see a different knight,
A knight who knows that meanings can be lies,
That things are done not knowing why they're done,
That bearings fail, and stainless steel corrodes.
A whistle blows. Snow shifts on the glass shed roof. That knight is
     gone.
This one remaining tosses his briefcase to one of Kay's pages,
And, golden, silken, careless, exits left.

Behind the carsheds, on the business car track, alongside the
     private varnish
Of dukes and smallholders, Persian potentates and Cathay princes
(James J. Hill is here, invited to bid on a tunnel through the
     Pennines)
Waits a sleek car in royal blue, ex-B&O, its trucks and fittings
     chromed,
A black-gloved hand gripping its silver platform rail;
Mordred and his car are both upholstered in blue velvet and black
     leather.
He prefers to fly, but the weather was against it.
His DC-9, with its video system and Quotron and waterbed, sits
     grounded at Gatwick.
The premature lines in his face are a map of a hostile country,
The redness in his eyes a reminder that hollyberries are poison.
He goes inside to put on a look acceptable for Christmas Court;
As he slams the door it rattles like strafing jets.

Outside the Station proper, in the snow,
On a through track that's used for milk and mail,

A wheezing saddle-tanker stops for breath;
A way-freight mixed, eight freight cars and caboose,
Two great ugly men on the back platform, talking with a third on
    the ballast.
One, the conductor, parcels out the last of the coffee;
They drink. A joke about grails. They laugh.
When it's gone, the trainman pretends to kick the big hobo off,
But the farewell hug spoils the act.
Now two men stand on the dirty snow,
The conductor waves a lantern and the train grinds on.
The ugly men start walking, the new arrival behind,
Singing "Wenceslas" off-key till the other says stop.
There are two horses waiting for them. Rather plain horses,
Considering. The men mount up.
By the roundhouse they pause,
And look at the locos, the water, the sand, and the coal,
They look for a long time at the turntable,
Until the one who is King says "It all seemed so simple, once,"
And the best knight in the world says "It is. We make it hard."
They ride on, toward Camelot by the service road.

The sun is winter-low. Kay's caravan is rolling.
He may not run a railroad, but he runs a tight ship:
By the time they unload in the Camelot courtyard,
The wassail will be hot and the goose will be crackling,
Banners snapping from the towers, fir logs on the fire, drawbridge
    down,
And all that sackbut and psaltery stuff.
Blanchefleur is taking the children caroling tonight,
Percivale will lose to Merlin at chess,
The young knights will dally and the damsels dally back,
The old knights will play poker at a smaller Table Round.
And at the great glass station, motion goes on,
The extras, the milk trains, the varnish, the limiteds,
The *Pindar of Wakefield*, the *Lady of the Lake*,
The *Broceliande Local*, the *Fast Flying Briton*,
The nerves of the kingdom, the lines of exchange,
Running to schedule as the world ought,

Ticking like a hot-fired hand-stoked heart,
The metal expression of the breaking of boundaries,
The boilers that turn raw fire into power,
The driving rods that put the power to use,
The turning wheels that make all places equal,
The knowledge that the train may stop but the line goes on;
The train may stop
But the line goes on.

FOR I HAVE TOUCHED THE SKY

Mike Resnick

With his wife, Carol, Mike Resnick operates the second-largest boarding and grooming kennel in the United States. He is also a prolific and popular science fiction novelist. Among his nearly thirty titles are *Ivory* (a Nebula finalist this year), *Santiago, Paradise, The Dark Lady, Soothsayer, Oracle,* and *Prophet.* In 1989, he won the Hugo Award for his novelette "Kirinyaga," written for Orson Scott Card's anthology *Eutopia.* That story established the background for this year's colorful and affecting Nebula finalist, "For I Have Touched the Sky."

"Of all the books and stories I have written to date," Resnick reports, "I think this one is my favorite.

"I got the idea for it during one of my recent trips to Africa, when I watched women carrying heavy loads of firewood on their backs while their unencumbered men walked imperiously ahead of them. Cars and buses sped past them; planes flew overhead; young boys, their ears tied in to Walkmans, trotted by. And yet they labored, as they have labored for centuries, uncomplaining, almost oblivious to the enormous changes in their surroundings.

"Or *were* they oblivious?

"As I watched them, I wondered if any of them ever longed for something more: if they wondered what *my* life was like, if they were curious about why so many of their sisters had moved to Nairobi and Dar Es Salaam and Kampala, if in the privacy of their minds they ever tried to imagine what life might become if they were freed of their daily drudgery. . . ."

There was a time when men had wings.

Ngai, who sits alone on His throne atop Kirinyaga, which is now called Mount Kenya, gave men the gift of flight, so that they might reach the succulent fruits on the highest branches of the trees. But one man, a son of Gikuyu, who was himself the first man, saw the eagle and the vulture riding high upon the winds, and spreading his wings, he joined them. He circled higher and higher, and soon he soared far above all other flying things.

Then, suddenly, the hand of Ngai reached out and grabbed the son of Gikuyu.

"What have I done that you should grab me thus?" asked the son of Gikuyu.

"I live atop Kirinyaga because it is the top of the world," answered Ngai, "and no one's head may be higher than my own."

And so saying, Ngai plucked the wings from the son of Gikuyu, and then took the wings away from *all* men, so that no man could ever again rise higher than His head.

And that is why all of Gikuyu's descendants look at the birds with a sense of loss and envy, and why they no longer eat the succulent fruits from the highest branches of the trees.

WE HAVE MANY birds on the world of Kirinyaga, which was named for the holy mountain where Ngai dwells. We brought them along with our other animals when we received our charter from the Eutopian Council and departed from a Kenya that no longer had any meaning for true members of the Kikuyu tribe. Our new world is home to the maribou and the vulture, the ostrich and the fish eagle, the weaver and the heron, and many other species. Even I, Koriba, who am the *mundumugu*—the witch doctor—delight in their many colors, and find solace in their music. I have spent many afternoons seated in front of my *boma*, my back propped up against an ancient acacia tree, watching the profusion of colors and listening to the melodic songs as the birds come to slake their thirst in the river that winds through our village.

It was on one such afternoon that Kamari, a young girl who was not yet of circumcision age, walked up the long, winding path that separates my *boma* from the village, holding something small and gray in her hands.

"*Jambo*, Koriba," she greeted me.

"*Jambo*, Kamari," I answered her. "What have you brought to me, child?"

"This," she said, holding out a young pygmy falcon that struggled weakly to escape her grasp. "I found him in my family's *shamba*. He cannot fly."

"He looks fully fledged," I noted, getting to my feet. Then I saw that one of his wings was held at an awkward angle. "Ah!" I said. "He has broken his wing."

"Can you make him well, *mundumugu*?" asked Kamari.

I examined the wing briefly, while she held the young falcon's head away from me. Then I stepped back.

"I can make him well, Kamari," I said. "But I cannot make him fly. The wing will heal, but it will never be strong enough to bear his weight again. I think we will destroy him."

"No!" she exclaimed, pulling the falcon back. "You will make him live, and I will care for him!"

I stared at the bird for a moment, then shook my head. "He will not wish to live," I said at last.

"Why not?"

"Because he has ridden high upon the warm winds."

"I do not understand," said Kamari, frowning.

"Once a bird has touched the sky," I explained, "he can never be content to spend his days on the ground."

"I will *make* him content," she said with determination. "You will heal him and I will care for him, and he will live."

"I will heal him and you will care for him," I said. "But," I added, "he will not live."

"What is your fee, Koriba?" she asked, suddenly businesslike.

"I do not charge children," I answered. "I will visit your father tomorrow, and he will pay me."

She shook her head adamantly. "This is *my* bird. *I* will pay the fee."

"Very well," I said, admiring her spirit, for most children—and *all* adults—are terrified of their *mundumugu*, and would never openly contradict or disagree with him. "For one month you will clean my *boma* every morning and every afternoon. You will lay out my sleeping blankets, and keep my water gourd filled, and you will see that I have kindling for my fire."

"That is fair," she said after a moment's consideration. Then she added: "What if the bird dies before the month is over?"

"Then you will learn that a *mundumugu* knows more than a little Kikuyu girl," I said.

She set her jaw. "He will not die." She paused. "Will you fix his wing now?"

"Yes."

"I will help."

I shook my head. "You will build a cage in which to confine him, for if he tries to move his wing too soon, he will break it again and then I will surely have to destroy him."

She handed the bird to me. "I will be back soon," she promised, racing off toward her *shamba*.

I took the falcon into my hut. He was too weak to struggle very much, and he allowed me to tie his beak shut. Then I began the slow task of splinting his broken wing and binding it against his body to keep it motionless. He shrieked in pain as I manipulated the bones together, but otherwise he simply stared unblinking at me, and within ten minutes the job was finished.

Kamari returned an hour later, holding a small wooden cage in her hands.

"Is this large enough, Koriba?" she asked.

I held it up and examined it.

"It is almost too large," I replied. "He must not be able to move his wing until it has healed."

"He won't," she promised. "I will watch him all day long, every day."

"You will watch him all day long, every day?" I repeated, amused.

"Yes."

"Then who will clean my hut and my *boma*, and who will fill my gourd with water?"

"I will carry his cage with me when I come," she replied.

"The cage will be much heavier when the bird is in it," I pointed out.

"When I am a woman, I will carry far heavier loads on my back, for I shall have to till the fields and gather the firewood for my husband's *boma*," she said. "This will be good practice." She paused. "Why do you smile at me, Koriba?"

"I am not used to being lectured to by uncircumcised children," I replied with a smile.

"I was not lecturing," she answered with dignity. "I was *explaining*."

I held a hand up to shade my eyes from the afternoon sun.

"Are you not afraid of me, little Kamari?" I asked.

"Why should I be?"

"Because I am the *mundumugu*."

"That just means you are smarter than the others," she said with a shrug. She threw a stone at a chicken that was approaching her cage, and it raced away, squawking its annoyance. "Someday I shall be as smart as you are."

"Oh?"

She nodded confidently. "Already I can count higher than my father, and I can remember many things."

"What kind of things?" I asked, turning slightly as a hot breeze blew a swirl of dust about us.

"Do you remember the story of the honey bird that you told to the children of the village before the long rains?"

I nodded.

"I can repeat it," she said.

"You mean you can remember it."

She shook her head vigorously. "I can repeat every word that you said."

I sat down and crossed my legs. "Let me hear," I said, staring off into the distance and idly watching a pair of young men tending their cattle.

She hunched her shoulders, so that she would appear as bent with age as I myself am, and then, in a voice that sounded like a youthful replica of my own, she began to speak, mimicking my gestures.

"There is a little brown honey bird," she began. "He is very much like a sparrow, and as friendly. He will come to your *boma* and call to you, and as you approach him he will fly up and lead you to a hive, and then wait while you gather grass and set fire to it and smoke out the bees. But you must *always*"—she emphasized the word, just as I had done—"leave some honey for him, for if you take it all, the next time he will lead you into the jaws of *fisi*, the hyena, or perhaps into the desert where there is no water and you will die of thirst." Her story finished, she stood upright and smiled at me. "You see?" she said proudly.

"I see," I said, brushing away a large fly that had lit on my cheek.

"Did I do it right?" she asked.

"You did it right."

She stared at me thoughtfully. "Perhaps when you die, I will become the *mundumugu*."

"Do I seem that close to death?" I asked.

"Well," she answered, "you are very old and bent and wrinkled, and you sleep too much. But I will be just as happy if you do not die right away."

"I shall try to make you just as happy," I said ironically. "Now take your falcon home."

I was about to instruct her concerning his needs, but she spoke first.

"He will not want to eat today. But starting tomorrow, I will give him large insects, and at least one lizard every day. And he must always have water."

"You are very observant, Kamari."

She smiled at me again, and then ran off toward her *boma*.

SHE WAS BACK at dawn the next morning, carrying the cage with her. She placed it in the shade, then filled a small container with water from one of my gourds and set it inside the cage.

"How is your bird this morning?" I asked, sitting close to my fire, for even though the planetary engineers of the Eutopian Council had given Kirinyaga a climate identical to Kenya's, the sun had not yet warmed the morning air.

Kamari frowned. "He has not eaten yet."

"He will, when he gets hungry enough," I said, pulling my blanket more tightly around my shoulders. "He is used to swooping down on his prey from the sky."

"He drinks his water, though," she noted.

"That is a good sign."

"Can you not cast a spell that will heal him all at once?"

"The price would be too high," I said, for I had foreseen her question. "This way is better."

"How high?"

"*Too* high," I repeated, closing the subject. "Now, do you not have work to do?"

"Yes, Koriba."

She spent the next few minutes gathering kindling for my fire and filling my gourd from the river. Then she went into my hut to clean it and straighten my sleeping blankets. She emerged a moment later with a book in her hand.

"What is this, Koriba?" she asked.

"Who told you that you could touch your *mundumugu's* possessions?" I asked sternly.

"How can I clean them without touching them?" she replied with no show of fear. "What is it?"

"It is a book."

"What is a book, Koriba?"

"It is not for you to know," I said. "Put it back."

"Shall I tell you what I think it is?" she asked.

"Tell me," I said, curious to hear her answer.

"Do you know how you draw signs on the ground when you cast the bones to bring the rains? I think that a book is a collection of signs."

"You are a very bright little girl, Kamari."

"I *told* you that I was," she said, annoyed that I had not accepted her statement as a self-evident truth. She looked at the book for a moment, then held it up. "What do the signs mean?"

"Different things," I said.

"*What* things?"

"It is not necessary for the Kikuyu to know."

"But *you* know."

"I am the *mundumugu*."

"Can anyone else on Kirinyaga read the signs?"

"Your own chief, Koinnage, and two other chiefs can read the signs," I answered, sorry now that she had charmed me into this conversation, for I could foresee its direction.

"But you are all old men," she said. "You should teach me, so when you all die someone can read the signs."

"These signs are not important," I said. "They were created by the Europeans. The Kikuyu had no need for books before the Europeans came to Kenya; we have no need for them on Kirinyaga, which is our own world. When Koinnage and the other chiefs die, everything will be as it was long ago."

"Are they evil signs, then?" she asked.

"No," I said. "They are not evil. They just have no meaning for the Kikuyu. They are the white man's signs."

She handed the book to me. "Would you read me one of the signs?"

"Why?"

"I am curious to know what kind of signs the white men made."

I stared at her for a long minute, trying to make up my mind. Finally I nodded my assent.

"Just this once," I said. "Never again."

"Just this once," she agreed.

I thumbed through the book, which was a Swahili translation of Victorian poetry, selected one at random, and read it to her:

> Live with me, and be my love,
> And we will all the pleasures prove
> That hills and valleys, dales and fields,
> And all the craggy mountains yields.
> There will we sit upon the rocks,
> And see the shepherds feed their flocks,
> By shallow rivers, by whose falls
> Melodious birds sing madrigals.
> There will I make thee a bed of roses,
> With a thousand fragrant posies,
> A cap of flowers, and a kirtle
> Embroider'd all with leaves of myrtle.
> A bed of straw and ivy buds,
> With coral clasps and amber studs;
> And if these pleasures may thee move,
> Then live with me and be my love.

Kamari frowned. "I do not understand."

"I told you that you would not," I said. "Now put the book away and finish cleaning my hut. You must still work in your father's *shamba*, along with your duties here."

She nodded and disappeared into my hut, only to burst forth excitedly a few minutes later.

"It is a *story!*" she exclaimed.

"What is?"

"The sign you read! I do not understand many of the words, but it is a story about a warrior who asks a maiden to marry him! She paused. "*You* would tell it better, Koriba. The sign doesn't even mention *fisi*, the hyena, and *mamba*, the crocodile, who dwell by the river and would eat the warrior and his wife. Still, it is a story! I had thought it would be a spell for *mundumugus*."

"You are very wise to know that it is a story," I said.

"Read another to me!" she said enthusiastically.

I shook my head. "Do you not remember our agreement? Just that once, and never again."

She lowered her head in thought, then looked up brightly. "Then teach *me* to read the signs."

"That is against the law of the Kikuyu," I said. "No woman is permitted to read."

"Why?"

"It is a woman's duty to till the fields and pound the grain and make the fires and weave the fabrics and bear her husband's children," I answered.

"But I am not a woman," she pointed out. "I am just a little girl."

"But you will become a woman," I said, "and a woman may not read."

"Teach me now, and I will forget how when I become a woman."

"Does the eagle forget how to fly, or the hyena to kill?"

"It is not fair."

"No," I said. "But it is just."

"I do not understand."

"Then I will explain it to you," I said. "Sit down, Kamari."

She sat down on the dirt opposite me and leaned forward intently.

"Many years ago," I began, "the Kikuyu lived in the shadow of Kirinyaga, the mountain upon which Ngai dwells."

"I know," she said. "Then the Europeans came and built their cities."

"You are interrupting," I said.

"I am sorry, Koriba," she answered. "But I already know this story."

"You do not know all of it," I replied. "Before the Europeans came, we lived in harmony with the land. We tended our cattle and plowed our fields, we produced just enough children to replace those who died of old age and disease, and those who died in our wars against the Maasai and the Wakamba and the Nandi. Our lives were simple but fulfilling."

"And *then* the Europeans came!" she said.

"Then the Europeans came," I agreed, "and they brought new ways with them."

"Evil ways."

I shook my head. "They were not evil ways for the Europeans," I replied. "I know, for I have studied in European schools. But they were not good ways for the Kikuyu and the Maasai and the Wakamba and the Embu and the Kisi and all the other tribes. We saw the clothes they wore and the buildings they erected and the machines they used, and we tried to become like Europeans. But we are not Europeans, and their ways are not our ways, and they do not work for us. Our cities became overcrowded and polluted, and our land grew barren, and our animals died, and our water became poisoned, and finally, when the Eutopian Council allowed us to move to the world of Kirinyaga, we left Kenya behind and came here to live according to the old ways, the ways that are good for the Kikuyu." I paused. "Long ago the Kikuyu had no written language, and did not know how to read, and since we are trying to create a Kikuyu world here on Kirinyaga, it is only fitting that our people do not learn to read or write."

"But what is good about not knowing how to read?" she asked. "Just because we didn't do it before the Europeans came doesn't make it bad."

"Reading will make you aware of other ways of thinking and living, and then you will be discontented with your life on Kirinyaga."

"But *you* read, and you are not discontented."

"I am the *mundumugu*," I said. "I am wise enough to know that what I read are lies."

"But lies are not always bad," she persisted. "You tell them all the time."

"The *mundumugu* does not lie to his people," I replied sternly.

"You call them stories, like the story of the lion and the hare, or the tale of how the rainbow came to be, but they are lies."

"They are parables," I said.

"What is a parable?"

"A type of story."

"Is it a true story?"

"In a way."

"If it is true in a way, then it is also a lie in a way, is it not?" she replied, and then continued before I could answer her. "And if I can listen to a lie, why can I not read one?"

"I have already explained it to you."

"It is not fair," she repeated.

"No," I agreed. "But it is true, and in the long run it is for the good of the Kikuyu."

"I still don't understand why it is good," she complained.

"Because we are all that remain. Once before the Kikuyu tried to become something that they were not, and we became not city-dwelling Kikuyu, or bad Kikuyu, or unhappy Kikuyu, but an entirely new tribe called Kenyans. Those of us who came to Kirinyaga came here to preserve the old ways—and if women start reading, some of them will become discontented, and they will leave, and then one day there will be no Kikuyu left."

"But I don't want to leave Kirinyaga!" she protested. "I want to become circumcised, and bear many children for my husband, and till the fields of his *shamba*, and someday be cared for by my grandchildren."

"That is the way you are supposed to feel."

"But I also want to read about other worlds and other times."

I shook my head. "No."

"But—"

"I will hear no more of this today," I said. "The sun grows high in the sky, and you have not yet finished your tasks here, and you must still work in your father's *shamba* and come back again this afternoon."

She arose without another word and went about her duties. When she finished, she picked up the cage and began walking back to her *boma*.

I watched her walk away, then returned to my hut and activated my computer to discuss a minor orbital adjustment with Maintenance, for it had been hot and dry for almost a month. They gave their consent, and a few moments later I walked down the long winding path into the center of the village. Lowering myself gently to the ground, I spread my pouchful of bones and charms out before me and invoked Ngai to cool Kirinyaga with a mild rain, which Maintenance had agreed to supply later in the afternoon.

Then the children gathered about me, as they always did when I came down from my *boma* on the hill and entered the village.

"*Jambo*, Koriba!" they cried.

"*Jambo*, my brave young warriors," I replied, still seated on the ground.

"Why have you come to the village this morning, Koriba?" asked Ndemi, the boldest of the young boys.

"I have come here to ask Ngai to water our fields with His tears of compassion," I said, "for we have had no rain this month, and the crops are thirsty."

"Now that you have finished speaking to Ngai, will you tell us a story?" asked Ndemi.

I looked up at the sun, estimating the time of day.

"I have time for just one," I replied. "Then I must walk through the fields and place new charms on the scarecrows, that they may continue to protect your crops."

"What story will you tell us, Koriba?" asked another of the boys.

I looked around, and saw that Kamari was standing among the girls.

"I think I shall tell you the story of the Leopard and the Shrike," I said.

"I have not heard that one before," said Ndemi.

"Am I such an old man that I have no new stories to tell?" I demanded, and he dropped his gaze to the ground. I waited until I had everyone's attention, and then I began:

"Once there was a very bright young shrike, and because he was very bright, he was always asking questions of his father.

" 'Why do we eat insects?' he asked one day.

" 'Because we are shrikes, and that is what shrikes do,' answered his father.

" 'But we are also birds,' said the shrike. 'And do not birds such as the eagle eat fish?'

" 'Ngai did not mean for shrikes to eat fish,' said his father, 'and even if you were strong enough to catch and kill a fish, eating it would make you sick.'

" 'Have you ever eaten a fish?' asked the young shrike.

" 'No,' said his father.

" 'Then how do you know?' said the young shrike, and that afternoon he flew over the river, and found a tiny fish. He caught it and ate it, and he was sick for a whole week.

" 'Have you learned your lesson now?' asked the shrike's father, when the young shrike was well again.

" 'I have learned not to eat fish,' said the shrike. 'But I have another question.'

" 'What is your question?' asked his father.

" 'Why are shrikes the most cowardly of birds?' asked the shrike. 'Whenever the lion or the leopard appears, we flee to the highest branches of the trees and wait for them to go away.'

" 'Lions and leopards would eat us if they could,' said the shrike's father. 'Therefore, we must flee from them.'

" 'But they do not eat the ostrich, and the ostrich is a bird,' said the bright young shrike. 'If they attack the ostrich, he kills them with his kick.'

" 'You are not an ostrich,' said his father, tired of listening to him.

" 'But I am a bird, and the ostrich is a bird, and I will learn to kick as the ostrich kicks,' said the young shrike, and he spent the next week practicing kicking any insects and twigs that were in his way.

"Then one day he came across *chui*, the leopard, and as the leopard approached him, the bright young shrike did not fly to the highest branches of the tree, but bravely stood his ground.

" 'You have great courage to face me thus,' said the leopard.

" 'I am a very bright bird, and I am not afraid of you,' said the shrike. 'I have practiced kicking as the ostrich does, and if you come any closer, I will kick you and you will die.'

" 'I am an old leopard, and cannot hunt any longer,' said the leopard. 'I am ready to die. Come kick me, and put me out of my misery.'

"The young shrike walked up to the leopard and kicked him full in the face. The leopard simply laughed, opened his mouth, and swallowed the bright young shrike.

" 'What a silly bird,' laughed the leopard, 'to pretend to be something that he was not! If he had flown away like a shrike, I would have gone hungry today—but by trying to be what he was never meant to be, all he did was fill my stomach. I guess he was not a very bright bird after all.' "

I stopped and stared straight at Kamari.

"Is that the end?" asked one of the other girls.

"That is the end," I said.

"Why did the shrike think he could be an ostrich?" asked one of the smaller boys.

"Perhaps Kamari can tell you," I said.

All the children turned to Kamari, who paused for a moment and then answered.

"There is a difference between wanting to be an ostrich, and wanting to know what an ostrich knows," she said, looking directly into my eyes. "It was not wrong for the shrike to want to know things. It was wrong for him to think he could become an ostrich."

There was a momentary silence while the children considered her answer.

"Is that true, Koriba?" asked Ndemi at last.

"No," I said, "for once the shrike knew what the ostrich knew, it forgot that it was a shrike. You must always remember who you are, and knowing too many things can make you forget."

"Will you tell us another story?" asked a young girl.

"Not this morning," I said, getting to my feet. "But when I come to the village tonight to drink *pombe* and watch the dancing, perhaps I will tell you the story about the bull elephant and the wise little Kikuyu boy. Now," I added, "do none of you have chores to do?"

The children dispersed, returning to their *shambas* and their cattle pastures, and I stopped by Juma's hut to give him an ointment for his joints, which always bothered him just before it rained. I visited Koinnage and drank *pombe* with him, and then discussed the affairs of the village with the Council of Elders. Finally I returned to my own *boma*, for I always take a nap during the heat of the day, and the rain was not due for another few hours.

Kamari was there when I arrived. She had gathered more wood and water, and was filling the grain buckets for my goats as I entered my *boma*.

"How is your bird this afternoon?" I asked, looking at the pygmy falcon, whose cage had been carefully placed in the shade of my hut.

"He drinks, but he will not eat," she said in worried tones. "He spends all his time looking at the sky."

"There are things that are more important to him than eating," I said.

"I am finished now," she said. "May I go home, Koriba?"

I nodded, and she left as I was arranging my sleeping blanket inside my hut.

She came every morning and every afternoon for the next week. Then, on the eighth day, she announced with tears in her eyes that the pygmy falcon had died.

"I told you that this would happen," I said gently. "Once a bird has ridden upon the winds, he cannot live on the ground."

"Do all birds die when they can no longer fly?" she asked.

"Most do," I said. "A few like the security of the cage, but most die of broken hearts, for having touched the sky they cannot bear to lose the gift of flight."

"Why do we make cages, then, if they do not make the birds feel better?"

"Because they make *us* feel better," I answered.

She paused, and then said: "I will keep my word and clean your hut and your *boma*, and fetch your water and kindling, even though the bird is dead."

I nodded. "That was our agreement," I said.

True to her word, she came back twice a day for the next three weeks. Then, at noon on the twenty-ninth day, after she had completed her morning chores and returned to her family's *shamba*, her father, Njoro, walked up the path to my *boma*.

"*Jambo*, Koriba," he greeted me, a worried expression on his face.

"*Jambo*, Njoro," I said without getting to my feet. "Why have you come to my *boma*?"

"I am a poor man, Koriba," he said, squatting down next to me. "I have only one wife, and she has produced no sons and only two daughters. I do not own as large a *shamba* as most men in the village, and the hyenas killed three of my cows this past year."

I could not understand his point, so I merely stared at him, waiting for him to continue.

"As poor as I am," he went on, "I took comfort in the thought that at least I would have the bride prices from my two daughters in my old age." He paused. "I have been a good man, Koriba. Surely I deserve that much."

"I have not said otherwise," I replied.

"Then why are you training Kamari to be a *mundumugu*?" he demanded. "It is well known that the *mundumugu* never marries."

"Has Kamari told you that she is to become a *mundumugu*?" I asked.

He shook his head. "No. She does not speak to her mother or myself at all since she has been coming here to clean your *boma*."

"Then you are mistaken," I said. "No woman may be a *mundumugu*. What made you think that I am training her?"

He dug into the folds of his *kikoi* and withdrew a piece of cured wildebeest hide. Scrawled on it in charcoal was the following inscription:

I AM KAMARI
I AM TWELVE YEARS OLD
I AM A GIRL

"This is writing," he said accusingly. "Women cannot write. Only the *mundumugu* and great chiefs like Koinnage can write."

"Leave this with me, Njoro," I said, taking the hide, "and send Kamari to my *boma*."

"I need her to work on my *shamba* until this afternoon."

"Now," I said.

He sighed and nodded. "I will send her, Koriba." He paused. "You are certain that she is not to be a *mundumugu*?"

"You have my word," I said, spitting on my hands to show my sincerity.

He seemed relieved, and went off to his *boma*. Kamari came up the path a few minutes later.

"*Jambo*, Koriba," she said.

"*Jambo*, Kamari," I replied. "I am very displeased with you."

"Did I not gather enough kindling this morning?" she asked.

"You gathered enough kindling."

"Were the gourds not filled with water?"

"The gourds were filled."

"Then what did I do wrong?" she asked, absently pushing one of my goats aside as it approached her.

"You broke your promise to me."

"That is not true," she said. "I have come every morning and every afternoon, even though the bird is dead."

"You promised not to look at another book," I said.

"I have not looked at another book since the day you told me that I was forbidden to."

"Then explain *this*," I said, holding up the hide with her writing on it.

"There is nothing to explain," she said with a shrug. "I wrote it."

"And if you have not looked at books, how did you learn to write?" I demanded.

"From your magic box," she said. "You never told me not to look at *it*."

"My magic box?" I said, frowning.

"The box that hums with life and has many colors."

"You mean my computer?" I said, surprised.

"Your magic box," she repeated.

"And it taught you how to read and write?"

"*I* taught me—but only a little," she said unhappily. "I am like the shrike in your story—I am not as bright as I thought. Reading and writing is very difficult."

"I told you that you must not learn to read," I said, resisting the urge to comment on her remarkable accomplishment, for she had clearly broken the law.

Kamari shook her head.

"You told me I must not look at your books," she replied stubbornly.

"I told you that women must not read," I said. "You have disobeyed me. For this you must be punished." I paused. "You will continue your chores here for three more months, and you must bring me two hares and two rodents, which you must catch yourself. Do you understand?"

"I understand."

"Now come into my hut with me, that you may understand one thing more."

She followed me into the hut.

"Computer," I said. "Activate."

"Activated," said the computer's mechanical voice.

"Computer, scan the hut and tell me who is here with me."

The lens of the computer's sensor glowed briefly.

"The girl, Kamari wa Njoro, is here with you," replied the computer.

"Will you recognize her if you see her again?"

"Yes."

"This is a Priority Order," I said. "Never again may you converse with Kamari wa Njoro verbally or in any known language."

"Understood and logged," said the computer.

"Deactivate." I turned to Kamari. "Do you understand what I have done, Kamari?"

"Yes," she said, "and it is not fair. I did not disobey you."

"It is the law that women may not read," I said, "and you have broken it. You will not break it again. Now go back to your *shamba*."

She left, head held high, youthful back stiff with defiance, and I went about my duties, instructing the young boys on the decoration of their bodies for their forthcoming circumcision ceremony, casting a counterspell for old Siboki (for he had found hyena dung within his *shamba*, which is one of the surest signs of a *thahu*, or curse), instructing Maintenance to make another minor orbital adjustment that would bring cooler weather to the western plains.

By the time I returned to my hut for my afternoon nap, Kamari had come and gone again, and everything was in order.

For the next two months, life in the village went its placid way. The crops were harvested, old Koinnage took another wife and we had a two-day festival with much dancing and *pombe*-drinking to celebrate the event, the short rains arrived on schedule, and three children were born to the village. Even the Eutopian Council, which had complained about our custom of leaving the old and the infirm out for the hyenas, left us completely alone. We found the lair of a family of hyenas and killed three whelps, then slew the mother when she returned. At each full moon I slaughtered a cow—not merely a goat, but a large, fat cow—to thank Ngai for His generosity, for truly He had graced Kirinyaga with abundance.

During this period I rarely saw Kamari. She came in the mornings when I was in the village, casting the bones to bring forth the weather, and she came in the afternoons when I was giving charms to the sick and conversing with the Elders—but I always knew she had been there, for my hut and my *boma* were immaculate, and I never lacked for water or kindling.

Then, on the afternoon after the second full moon, I returned to my *boma* after advising Koinnage about how he might best settle an argument over a disputed plot of land, and as I entered my hut I noticed that the computer screen was alive and glowing, covered with strange symbols. When I had taken my degrees in England and America I had learned English and French and Spanish, and of course I knew Kikuyu and Swahili, but these symbols represented no known language, nor, although they used numerals as well as letters and punctuation marks, were they mathematical formulas.

"Computer, I distinctly remember deactivating you this morning," I said, frowning. "Why does your screen glow with life?"

"Kamari activated me."

"And she forgot to deactivate you when she left?"

"That is correct."

"I thought as much," I said grimly. "Does she activate you every day?"

"Yes."

"Did I not give you a Priority Order never to communicate with her in any known language?" I said, puzzled.

"You did, Koriba."

"Can you then explain why you have disobeyed my directive?"

"I have not disobeyed your directive, Koriba," said the computer. "My programming makes me incapable of disobeying a Priority Order."

"Then what is this that I see upon your screen?"

"This is the Language of Kamari," replied the computer. "It is not among the 1,732 languages and dialects in my memory banks, and hence does not fall under the aegis of your directive."

"Did you create this language?"

"No, Koriba. Kamari created it."

"Did you assist her in any way?"

"No, Koriba, I did not."

"Is it a true language?" I asked. "Can you understand it?"

"It is a true language. I can understand it."

"If she were to ask you a question in the Language of Kamari, could you reply to it?"

"Yes, if the question were simple enough. It is a very limited language."

"And if that reply required you to translate the answer from a known language to the Language of Kamari, would doing so be contrary to my directive?"

"No, Koriba, it would not."

"Have you in fact answered questions put to you by Kamari?"

"Yes, Koriba, I have," replied the computer.

"I see," I said. "Stand by for a new directive."

"Waiting . . ."

I lowered my head in thought, contemplating the problem. That Kamari was brilliant and gifted was obvious: she had not only taught herself to read and write, but had actually created a coherent and logical language that the computer could understand and in which it could respond. I had given orders, and without directly disobeying them she had managed to circumvent them. She had no malice within her, and wanted only to learn, which in itself was an admirable goal. All that was on the one hand.

On the other hand was the threat to the social order we had labored so diligently to establish on Kirinyaga. Men and women knew their responsibilities and accepted them happily. Ngai had given the Maasai the spear, and He had given the Wakamba the arrow, and He had given the Europeans the machine and the printing press, but to the Kikuyu He had given the digging-stick and the fertile land surrounding the sacred fig tree on the slopes of Kirinyaga.

Once before we had lived in harmony with the land, many long years ago. Then had come the printed word. It turned us first into slaves, and then into Christians, and then into soldiers and factory workers and mechanics and politicians, into everything that the Kikuyu were never meant to be. It had happened before; it could happen again.

We had come to the world of Kirinyaga to create a perfect Kikuyu society, a Kikuyu Utopia: could one gifted little girl carry within her the seeds of our destruction? I could not be sure, but it was a fact that gifted children grew up. They became Jesus, and Mohammed, and Jomo Kenyata—but they also became Tippoo Tib, the greatest slaver of all, and Idi Amin, butcher of his own people. Or, more often, they became Friedrich Nietzsche and Karl Marx, brilliant men in their own right, but who influenced less brilliant, less capable men. Did I have the right to stand aside and hope that her influence upon our society would be benign when all history suggested that the opposite was more likely to be true?

My decision was painful, but it was not a difficult one.

"Computer," I said at last, "I have a new Priority Order that supercedes my previous directive. You are no longer allowed to communicate with Kamari under any circumstances whatsoever. Should she activate you, you are to tell her that Koriba has forbidden you to have any contact with her, and you are then to deactivate immediately. Do you understand?"

"Understood and logged."

"Good," I said. "Now deactivate."

WHEN I RETURNED from the village the next morning, I found my water gourds empty, my blanket unfolded, my *boma* filled with the dung of my goats.

The *mundumugu* is all-powerful among the Kikuyu, but he is not without compassion. I decided to forgive this childish display of temper, and so I did not visit Kamari's father, nor did I tell the other children to avoid her.

She did not come again in the afternoon. I know, because I waited beside my hut to explain my decision to her. Finally, when twilight came, I sent for the boy, Ndemi, to fill my gourds and clean my *boma*, and although such chores are woman's work, he did not dare disobey his *mundumugu*, although his every gesture displayed contempt for the tasks I had set for him.

When two more days had passed with no sign of Kamari, I summoned Njoro, her father.

"Kamari has broken her word to me," I said when he arrived. "If she does not come to clean my *boma* this afternoon, I will be forced to place a *thahu* upon her."

He looked puzzled. "She says that you have already placed a curse on her, Koriba. I was going to ask you if we should turn her out of our *boma*."

I shook my head. "No," I said. "Do not turn her out of your

boma. I have placed no *thahu* on her yet—but she must come to work this afternoon."

"I do not know if she is strong enough," said Njoro. "She has had neither food nor water for three days, and she sits motionless in my wife's hut." He paused. "*Someone* has placed a *thahu* on her. If it was not you, perhaps you can cast a spell to remove it."

"She has gone three days without eating or drinking?" I repeated. He nodded.

"I will see her," I said, getting to my feet and following him down the winding path to the village. When we reached Njoro's *boma* he led me to his wife's hut, then called Kamari's worried mother out and stood aside as I entered. Kamari sat at the farthest point from the door, her back propped against a wall, her knees drawn up to her chin, her arms encircling her thin legs.

"*Jambo*, Kamari," I said.

She stared at me but said nothing.

"Your mother worries for you, and your father tells me that you no longer eat or drink."

She made no answer.

"You also have not kept your promise to tend my *boma*."

Silence.

"Have you forgotten how to speak?" I said.

"Kikuyu women do not speak," she said bitterly. "They do not think. All they do is bear babies and cook food and gather firewood and till the fields. They do not have to speak or think to do that."

"Are you that unhappy?"

She did not answer.

"Listen to my words, Kamari," I said slowly. "I made my decision for the good of Kirinyaga, and I will not recant it. As a Kikuyu woman, you must live the life that has been ordained for you." I paused. "However, neither the Kikuyu nor the Eutopian Council are without compassion for the individual. Any member of our society may leave if he wishes. According to the charter we signed when we claimed this world, you need only walk to that area known as Haven, and a Maintenance ship will pick you up and transport you to the location of your choice."

"All I know is Kirinyaga," she said. "How am I to choose a new home if I am forbidden to learn about other places?"

"I do not know," I admitted.

"I don't *want* to leave Kirinyaga!" she continued. "This is my home. These are my people. I am a Kikuyu girl, not a Maasai girl or a European girl. I will bear my husband's children and till his *shamba*, I will gather his wood and cook his meals and weave his garments, I will leave my parents' *shamba* and live with my husband's family. I will do all this without complaint, Koriba, if you will just let me learn to read and write!"

"I cannot," I said sadly.

"But *why?*"

"Who is the wisest man you know, Kamari?" I asked.

"The *mundumugu* is always the wisest man in the village."

"Then you must trust to my wisdom."

"But I feel like the pygmy falcon," she said, her misery reflected in her voice. "He spent his life dreaming of soaring high upon the winds. I dream of seeing words upon the computer screen."

"You are not like the falcon at all," I said. "He was prevented from being what he was meant to be. You are prevented from being what you are not meant to be."

"You are not an evil man, Koriba," she said solemnly. "But you are wrong."

"If that is so, then I shall have to live with it," I said.

"But you are asking *me* to live with it," she said, "and that is your crime."

"If you call me a criminal again," I said sternly, for no one may speak thus to the *mundumugu*, "I shall surely place a *thahu* on you."

"What more can you do?" she said bitterly.

"I can turn you into a hyena, an unclean eater of human flesh who prowls only in the darkness. I can fill your belly with thorns, so that your every movement will be agony. I can—"

"You are just a man," she said wearily, "and you have already done your worst."

"I will hear no more of this," I said. "I order you to eat and drink what your mother brings to you, and I expect to see you at my *boma* this afternoon."

I walked out of the hut and told Kamari's mother to bring her banana mash and water, then stopped by old Benima's *shamba*. Buffalo had stampeded through his fields, destroying his crops, and I sacrificed a goat to remove the *thahu* that had fallen upon his land.

When I was finished I stopped at Koinnage's *boma*, where he offered me some freshly brewed *pombe* and began complaining about Kibo, his newest wife, who kept taking sides with Shumi, his second wife, against Wambu, his senior wife.

"You can always divorce her and return her to her family's *shamba*," I suggested.

"She cost twenty cows and five goats!" he complained. "Will her family return them?"

"No, they will not."

"Then I will not send her back."

"As you wish," I said with a shrug.

"Besides, she is very strong and very lovely," he continued. "I just wish she would stop fighting with Wambu."

"What do they fight about?" I asked.

"They fight about who will fetch the water, and who will mend my garments, and who will repair the thatch on my hut." He paused. "They even argue about whose hut I should visit at night, as if I had no choice in the matter."

"Do they ever fight about ideas?" I asked.

"Ideas?" he repeated blankly.

"Such as you might find in books."

He laughed. "They are *women*, Koriba. What need have they for ideas?" He paused. "In fact, what need have any of us for them?"

"I do not know," I said. "I was merely curious."

"You look disturbed," he noted.

"It must be the *pombe*," I said. "I am an old man, and perhaps it is too strong."

"That is because Kibo will not listen when Wambu tells her how to brew it. I really should send her away"—he looked at Kibo as she carried a load of wood on her strong, young back—"but she is so young and so lovely." Suddenly his gaze went beyond his newest wife to the village. "Ah!" he said. "I see that old Siboki has finally died."

"How do you know?" I asked.

He pointed to a thin column of smoke. "They are burning his hut."

I stared off in the direction he indicated. "That is not Siboki's hut," I said. "His *boma* is more to the west."

"Who else is old and infirm and due to die?" asked Koinnage.

And suddenly I knew, as surely as I knew that Ngai sits on His throne atop the holy mountain, that Kamari was dead.

I walked to Njoro's *shamba* as quickly as I could. When I arrived, Kamari's mother and sister and grandmother were already wailing the death chant, tears streaming down their faces.

"What happened?" I demanded, walking up to Njoro.

"Why do you ask, when it is you who destroyed her?" he replied bitterly.

"I did not destroy her," I said.

"Did you not threaten to place a *thahu* on her just this morning?" he persisted. "You did so, and now she is dead, and I have but one daughter to bring the bride price, and I have had to burn Kamari's hut."

"Stop worrying about bride prices and huts and tell me what happened, or you shall learn what it means to be cursed by a *mundumugu*!" I snapped.

"She hung herself in her hut with a length of buffalo hide."

Five women from the neighboring *shamba* arrived and took up the death chant.

"She hung herself in her hut?" I repeated.

He nodded. "She could at least have hung herself from a tree, so that her hut would not be unclean and I would not have to burn it."

"Be quiet!" I said, trying to collect my thoughts.

"She was not a bad daughter," he continued. "Why did you curse her, Koriba?"

"I did not place a *thahu* upon her," I said, wondering if I spoke the truth. "I wished only to save her."

"Who has stronger medicine than you?" he asked fearfully.

"She broke the law of Ngai," I answered.

"And now Ngai has taken His vengeance!" moaned Njoro fearfully. "Which member of my family will He strike down next?"

"None of you," I said. "Only Kamari broke the law."

"I am a poor man," said Njoro cautiously, "even poorer now than before. How much must I pay you to ask Ngai to receive Kamari's spirit with compassion and forgiveness?"

"I will do that whether you pay me or not," I answered.

"You will not charge me?" he asked.

"I will not charge you."

"Thank you, Koriba!" he said fervently.

I stood and stared at the blazing hut, trying not to think of the smoldering body of the little girl inside it.

"Koriba?" said Njoro after a lengthy silence.

"What now?" I asked irritably.

"We did not know what to do with the buffalo hide, for it bore the mark of your *thahu*, and we were afraid to burn it. Now I know that the marks were made by Ngai and not you, and I am afraid even to touch it. Will you take it away?"

"What marks?" I said. "What are you talking about?"

He took me by the arm and led me around to the front of the burning hut. There, on the ground, some ten paces from the entrance, lay the strip of tanned hide with which Kamari had hanged herself, and scrawled upon it were more of the strange symbols I had seen on my computer screen three days earlier.

I reached down and picked up the hide, then turned to Njoro. "If indeed there is a curse on your shamba," I said, "I will remove it and take it upon myself, by taking Ngai's marks with me."

"Thank you, Koriba!" he said, obviously much relieved.

"I must leave to prepare my magic," I said abruptly, and began the long walk back to my *boma*. When I arrived I took the strip of buffalo hide into my hut.

"Computer," I said. "Activate."

"Activated."

I held the strip up to its scanning lens.

"Do you recognize this language?" I asked.

The lens glowed briefly.

"Yes, Koriba. It is the Language of Kamari."

"What does it say?"

"It is a couplet:

> I know why the caged birds die—
> For, like them, I have touched the sky."

THE ENTIRE VILLAGE came to Njoro's *shamba* in the afternoon, and the women wailed the death chant all night and all of the next day, but before long Kamari was forgotten, for life goes on and she was just a little Kikuyu girl.

Since that day, whenever I have found a bird with a broken wing I have attempted to nurse it back to health. It always dies, and I always bury it next to the mound of earth that marks where Kamari's hut had been.

It is on those days, when I place the birds in the ground, that I find myself thinking of her again, and wishing that I was just a simple man, tending my cattle and worrying about my crops and thinking the thoughts of simple men, rather than a *mundumugu* who must live with the consequences of his wisdom.

VULGAR ART

Orson Scott Card

A resident of Greensboro, North Carolina, Orson Scott Card has established himself over the past decade or so as a true phenomenon in the SF and fantasy fields, a writer who approaches his materials in such a fiercely heartfelt manner that he takes his readers with him on his own otherworldly spiritual journeys. His most acclaimed novels include *Hart's Hope, Songmaster, Ender's Game, Speaker for the Dead* (the last two of which achieved the unprecedented feat of winning back-to-back Hugo and Nebula awards), and the first three books in his projected six-volume Alvin Maker series, *Seventh Son, Red Prophet*, and *Prentice Alvin*, two of which were Nebula finalists for best novel. Card's short fiction has also won readers, awards, and praise.

Beyond prose narrative, Card writes criticism, reviews (most conspicuously in a monthly column, "Books to Look For," in *The Magazine of Fantasy and Science Fiction*), opinion, and satire. He founded the review *Short Form*, a journal devoted to criticism of SF poetry and short fiction, and he still contributes to it a column called "You Got No Friends in This World" as well as a stand-alone supplement, edited by "Chester de Roors," called *The Green Pages*. Today, in fact, it would be hard to find anyone else in the field with a more energetic or controversial presence, not excluding the energetic and controversial Harlan Ellison.

In "Vulgar Art," an address delivered to the Indiana Humanities Council in October 1989, Card argues that elite and popular sorts of art can, and must, cross-pollinate, and that even the latter may be worthy of public funding.

I write in a genre that is pretty much without traditional metaphors. It's one of the first things that literary writers notice when they dabble in the reading of science fiction, that there are very few metaphors. The speech is very plain and simple. And there's good reason for that. Metaphor is a figure of speech that absolutely depends on the audience recognizing that the asserted relationship is *not* real. When you say *this* is equivalent to *that*, the audience must recognize that in fact it is *not* the same thing. Then they look for similarities in order to identify the metaphor.

In speculative fiction, however, you can't be sure that the metaphor is not real. In a fantasy story, the sentence, "Her tear was a jewel on her cheek," is not necessarily received as metaphor. It's just as likely that she could then reach up and take off the jewel, set it in gold, and wear it as a ring, because what seems strange and impossible *can* be real and true within the story.

Recently I taught a class in the science fiction short story, and we faced this problem in a tale by Tom Maddox. There was a sentence in the second or third paragraph—a sentence that would be perfectly all right in any story outside the genre—in which someone arrived at an airport. The author wrote (as best I remember): "The reptile bus slithered out to bring the passengers from the plane." Because this was still early in the story, we didn't yet know the rules of Maddox's world. I was not the only reader in that class who took that second paragraph literally for just a moment, conjuring up the visual image of a large dinosaur with a howdah on its back coming out to bring passengers from the airplane. It took a while for us to realize, "Oh! Oh, that was a metaphor," because in a science fiction story reptile buses might well be "real."

There's another way of seeing this, though: Not that science fiction and fantasy stories *lack* metaphor, but rather that they don't *contain* it. Instead, they often *are* metaphors. I have often given sessions in schools and various other places in which I ask the audience questions and they come up with story ideas by answering them. One of the questions that I ask is, "What should the price of magic be?" If a character gets his magical powers just by waving a wand or making a wish, a fantasy story becomes very boring, because the character has all the power of an omnipotent god and fiction about such a character is intrinsically uninteresting. Magic has to cost something, so its use isn't arbitrary and whimsical.

One of the things that often comes up is that the price of magic is blood. It makes for some really interesting, gruesome stories. The blood of a fly, for example, could be used by a housewife to stop a pot from boiling over. The blood of a deer could be used to become invisible. But the most power would come from the blood of a human being. Perhaps even more from the blood of your own child, as the idea invariably goes in these sessions.

But then I stop and ask, "What does this have to do with the real world? Does power actually work that way in the real world?" The answer is almost invariably, metaphorically, yes. Even in this case. For instance, in the personal lives of politicians, getting power often means sacrificing the interests of their children. Or we can take it on a larger context—that many a politician wins political clout today by borrowing from, or we can say stealing from, the resources of the coming generation, which is another way of bleeding our children for present power. There is a real world correspondence with the workings of fantastic literature, and it is not a trivial one, I think.

Another example that often comes up is that the price of magic is losing parts of your body. Cast a spell, drop a limb. Besides the obvious fact that then power is self-limiting, because after you've used it up there is no more, it also has to do with the reality that the more power you exercise the more you begin to fragment your identity. You do lose parts of yourself, or can, in the real world.

In other words, the inner workings of a fantasy world can stand, metaphorically, for the real world.

Another example, this time from science fiction, is a novel by Arthur C. Clarke, *Rendezvous with Rama*. A huge alien craft enters the solar system, and of course we humans have to launch an exploratory mission to try to determine what's going on, what this strange spaceship is here for. The explorers go inside and discover that as it orbits the sun a vast array of life springs forth inside this artificial habitat, but there's no sign of intelligent beings, nobody that we can meet, nothing we can make sense of, no language we can translate. Just a whole bunch of life.

Humans explore from one end of this great ship to the other, never meeting another sentient creature. And then, at the very end, all of a sudden the huge alien craft starts moving; it's leaving, and the humans barely escape to return to Earth and report. They never understood a thing that was going on inside it.

Now, a lot of readers were outraged by this novel because it made no sense. What was it about? But that was part of the point. Because it was a truly alien artifact, it *made no sense*. There *was* no explanation.

There *is* no way to understand what a truly alien mind is about. Why did they create this thing? Why did it come here? Why didn't it stay? Why did it leave? There's no explanation that makes any sense at all to us.

But the story can also be interpreted metaphorically. We are born into *this* world and struggle to make sense of it to the end of our life. And, generally speaking, we die without ever really being sure what's going on. We do, however, know one thing: It *will* go on without us, as it went on before we came, just as that space craft went on its merry way whether the human beings explored it or understood it or not.

Science fiction and fantasy, then, by allowing or even requiring the writer to create worlds or universes that are contrary to reality, encourages the story to take place inside a metaphorical world.

Now, what is the process of metaphor? You're familiar with it in almost every art, but especially in language. The process involves perpetual surprise. Unlike things are juxtaposed, equivocated. A familiar thing is presented out of place, and we derive meaning from that misplacement, because it surprises us, but we recognize the rightness of it, too (or we do if a metaphor is successful). It isn't a factual connection, but it is or might be a *true* one. And so we respond to a powerful metaphor by saying, "I never saw it that way before," "I never thought of it that way before," "It *is* like that."

Metaphor, however, is only one of the devices that artists use to bring their audience an experience of strangeness. Strangeness is one of the fundamental appeals of art. An attraction to strangeness is part of being primates. Look at the behavior of our distant cousin, the chimpanzee. When you study chimps in the wild, you find that lone males go out foraging, looking for food. (By the way, they have an interesting way of immediately sizing up a tree. If it's got food enough for only one chimp, they somehow forget to call anyone else. But if it has too much to exploit alone, *then* suddenly they remember they're part of a larger community and start calling and hooting. Amazing, watching chimps, how much their behavior resembles fourth grade.)

When a stranger, a human observer, approaches a chimpanzee, the chimp's first response is the normal animal response to strangers, which is: back off. But most chimps don't back off too far—just far enough that the chimp feels safe. Then he watches, *has* to keep watching, can't *stop* watching. And the longer the human observer sits there doing nothing that's particularly threatening, the more the chimp sidles around, explores, watches, pretends to be busy doing something else, but keeps glancing over at the human to see what in the world this strange thing is. And eventually, as long as the human does nothing to alarm him, the chimp ends up almost in the human's lap—because we primates are obsessed with strangeness. Fascinated by it. Drawn to it.

And yet, we're also terrified by it. One of the things that makes us individuals is that none of us has exactly the same mix of attitudes. Our attitude toward strangeness varies between fear and fascination. Our attitude toward familiar things varies between a sense of safety and utter boredom. I think this may well be one of the sources of intelligence in primates, that we *do* have that fascination with strangeness that allows us to be creative, to embrace change. And yet we also have that need for security that causes us to constantly retreat back to something that's stable, to hang on to public memory, to hang on to our identity.

We're all different in our need for strangeness versus familiarity, and our need is situational. Like people, world explorers, who go to Hong Kong and eat at McDonald's. We're that way about our art. We want art to reassure us and surprise us, to comfort and challenge us.

Some examples from literature. Take glitzy romance. The strangeness in the story comes from the life of the rich, whom most of the readers of course will *never* meet—actually, usually, the writers have never met truly rich people either until *after* they have several bestsellers. And strangeness comes from the exotic locales where the story takes place. So there *is* some sense of strangeness there. But there is also plenty of solid familiarity in the formulaic story, particularly in the constant reassurance that rich people are really much more miserable than the rest of us, and that *good* people always end up with better lives than bad people. Very comforting. So the readers get a pleasing mix: strangeness—something new, a little risky, a little dangerous, I'm in a new place; and yet a familiar repetition—something comforting, stable, to reaffirm the readers' contentment with their role in the world.

Now, those not in the audience for glitzy romances don't value the strangeness. We tend to see only the familiar element, the repetition. And it's easy to notice that the strangeness in a glitzy romance comes only within a very safe compartment. That is, we know that *almost* everything is going to be safe; the reader is putting at risk only *this* much.

But that's true of every kind of art. We never put *everything* at risk. We *always* compartmentalize it, and say, "*Inside* this box you can do whatever you want, but *outside* this box, don't mess with things. It scares me. It bothers me. I don't like that. I'm not comfortable with it." It's true of serious fiction, just like any other genre.

Let me give you an example. A writer named Patricia Geary came up through the academic-literary genre and wrote stories that, by any standard, are beautifully written. I think, in particular, of a novel of hers called *Strange Toys*. It's a strong, realistic, powerful depiction of a sick family, with a charming and weird little girl in the center of it. But it literalizes its metaphors the way that fantasy does. That is, the author doesn't say, "The kids have certain rituals in their lives that they regard as being like magic in giving them control over the world." Instead, the author says, "The rituals that these girls perform *do* control reality, and the magic works." So the metaphor becomes part of the reality of the story, and the *story* is metaphor, rather than *containing* metaphors.

An astonishing thing happened as soon as she started using that technique. Nobody wanted her fiction. A superbly talented writer, but she couldn't get published because while her stories were challenging and strange and innovative in a genre that prides itself on rewarding innovation—but she did not innovate within the safe box. If she'd written her stories in present tense, that would've been no problem. Probably she could have published them if they'd been written in *conditional* tense; but because she wrote them using literalized metaphors after the manner of fantasy, they didn't get published until somebody walked across the hall at Bantam and handed *Strange Toys* (or perhaps the novel before it) to the fantasy editor. Suddenly her books found a home—the strangest home she'd ever imagined. The critics within that field immediately embraced her because they were prepared to receive experimentation in *that* box.

Why did the serious fiction community reject her works? Because it did *not* repeat the old, familiar experiments. The voice was not quirky, the language was not extravagantly metaphorical, but instead brought in a technique that was strange in unexpected ways. No one knew what to do with it. Thus, just as the readers of glitzy romance accept strangeness only in landscapes, never in the manner of writing or even in story line, so also the readers of serious fiction celebrate strangeness only in certain familiar areas: voice and style and that old favorite, metaphors. The very process, in fact, of noticing and decoding metaphor and symbol within fiction becomes, itself, a safe, reassuring ritual. Just like romance readers settling down to see where Judith Krantz will take them this time.

Now, if you're an admirer of serious literature, you may resent this comparison, but I assure you that, from an anthropological viewpoint, the patterns within these communities are identical. Indeed, what I'm doing now *is* a kind of metaphor, a juxtaposition of two things you thought were unconnected. With any luck, it will be a strange and challenging idea: that Krantz and McInerny, L'Amour and Updike, King and Bellow *may* fulfill identical roles within the communities they write for.

Such an assertion outrages some people the way others would be infuriated if I equivocated, say, the cross, the crescent, and the hammer and sickle. Or if someone put a crucifix in a jar of urine. For those who think that Jesse Helms is an idiot for hating that, remember that he's not the only one who responds with visceral resentment when his icons are challenged. It's good to remember how Patricia Geary was treated when she challenged certain assumptions.

I'd like to look at the process whereby yesterday's strangeness becomes today's safe haven. From about 1910 on, *all* the traditional arts began to pursue a similar kind of strangeness: a rejection of the previous protocols of communication. Music began rejecting harmony, melody, even tonality. Visual art began to reject realism and, finally, representation at all. Literature began to reject clear, straightforward narrative that involved the reader emotionally, and began instead to praise fiction and poetry that needed to be decoded, that encouraged distance.

In *all* of these serious arts there was a rejection of immediate communication with and emotional involvement of the audience. Once, now—once—these innovations were strange and challenging. But now, all these experiments are older than my parents; yet they are still being called experimental. And daring; yet they're all safely contained within the same box.

This has happened before. In Elizabethan England, *true* literature, *serious* literature, was poetry. The vulgar audience could only understand the theatrical stage—it was the artistic equivalent of bear-baiting. Yet it was the stage that produced most of the greatest works of the age.

In the Augustan age in England, *true* art was high tragedy, following the illusive unities. Vulgar romances were despised. But it was out of the romantic, not the tragic tradition that the novel arose—with all of its prosaic crudeness—and, eventually, triumphed.

In each case, "high" art, "serious" art had stopped attempting to communicate with the unschooled public. In each case, the public embraced those "low" artists who tried to speak to them. And in each case, out of the "low," "vulgar," "popular" tradition came most of the great achievements of the age.

It's happening *now*. In America, "serious" art has lost almost all connection with the mass audience—but *not* because the mass audience is not hungry for art. The common folk read and cry over *Gone with the Wind*, they hang works by Norman Rockwell or Frank Frazetta or Roger Dean in the kitchen, they listen to Paul Simon or Bonnie Raitt or Sting, and they watch Spielberg's movies and "L.A. Law" and "Roseanne." Far from being insensitive to art, the common people are insatiable. People with no money for food will still spend money on art. And since the "serious" artists won't give it to them, they'll get it from someone else.

The mass audience rejects "serious" art precisely because "serious" art has rejected *them*, removing the very things they valued most: the melody, the sense and logic from music; the visual images and implied story and character from the visual arts; the story and clarity from fiction and poetry.

I wish I had a dollar for every university writing teacher who has said, "We're not going to talk about plot in this course, because I don't really understand *that*. We're going to talk about style." It's like an art teacher saying, "I don't know much about the human figure, so in *this* class we'll concentrate on color mixing and brush strokes."

Just as the vulgar audience ignores works that are clearly not intended for them, so the elite audience ignores works that don't address the issues that they've learned to think of as worth addressing. Now, in the spirit of laissez-faire, why should anyone complain about the situation? The elite is happy with *its* art, the common folk are happy with theirs; so what? No harm done.

I don't think so.

This situation fosters a couple of dangerous illusions. First, the artistic elite assumes, in their ignorance, that popular art is all the same. You see one, you've seen 'em all. But it isn't true. In fact, the common people are very alert to qualitative differences in the art that they embrace. And they almost *never* praise a work merely because they think they *ought* to.

I have a very good friend who works as a fireman. Formerly, he was a dental technician. He hangs wallpaper to make money in his spare time. A couple of years of college is all the formal training he's had. Yet he's one of the most discerning readers that I know. He cares very much about which writers are good and why they're good. He thinks clearly and originally about why some books are better than others. He never mouths learned platitudes and clichés, because he never studied them in school, as far as I know. But I learn more about critical theory, I am more challenged by conversing with *him* than I have been in most of my graduate literature courses.

He is not unique. I've had similar experiences over and over again with untrained readers who nevertheless think through the experience of literature and derive their own ideas about what is good and what is bad fiction.

If all popular art were the same, then it would all sell the same, but it doesn't. And it isn't because of hype, either. Stephen King was not hyped until after the popular audience had discovered him. Rock groups are *all* hyped, but there's no discernible connection between the hype and the success of some and the failure of others.

The popular audience is just as critical and just as discerning as the elite audience. They just use different standards. They have different values. So the elitists are deluded when they think all popular art is the same.

The second illusion is: the artistic elite assumes that popular art is always familiar and repetitive. And much popular art *is*, in fact, predominantly familiar. But then, much "serious" art—perhaps *just* as much serious art—is astonishingly and depressingly repetitive, and just as reassuring and comforting to its audience.

However, much in popular art is also surprising and challenging, and it's often strange in ways and in areas that are themselves surprising to that artistic elite. So the elite, when they do look at vulgar art, often assume that they're seeing junk when, in fact, they simply don't understand what they're seeing.

Let me give you a personal example. (Of course, I start with the assumption that my *own* work is *not* junk—a delusion that many of us who do art for a living thrive on—and I really have no intention of taking seriously anyone who challenges this. So my personal example may not prove my point to your satisfaction; but I'm sure you can find *other* examples that do.) I was having a conversation with a well-known poet who is himself a champion of storytelling and communication in poetry, which makes him kind of a lone wolf. He read the first volume of my Alvin Maker series, a book called *Seventh Son*, and talked to me quite frankly afterwards. He said, "I just *really* didn't care for it, because all this magic kind of stuff—anything can happen, so why should I care what *does* happen?"

I was astonished, because I'd spent the first five chapters very carefully delineating the rules of that universe, so that any fantasy or science fiction reader would know exactly what could and could not happen in this world. We *all* do that. That's how speculative fiction works. It's very rare for a book to get past an editor and appear in the bookstores without having resolved that issue. It's one of our basic techniques, and I do it as well as anyone. How could he say that "anything" could happen in my book?

Finally it dawned on me that it wasn't that I had failed; he simply didn't realize that he was receiving those clues. He had never read fantasy of this kind—contemporary prose fantasy. So he was completely unfamiliar with the protocols of reading speculative fiction; he did not recognize how invisibly and economically a science fiction and fantasy writer establishes alternate realities. Those techniques were wasted on him as a reader. They were strange, and so he rejected them instead of exploring and learning them.

What's more important is that they were also unavailable to him as a writer. Had he wanted to write a fantasy, he would not have had the tools, or at least *that* tool. He didn't know it existed, even though he had read a book that used it.

Ignorance is loss. And the artistic elite, by ignoring vulgar art, is losing the ability to reach a popular audience even if they tried.

A classic example in my field is Gore Vidal's venture into science fiction, with a novel called *Kalki*, one which I hope most of you have forgotten. It's cruel of me to remind you of it. It was an embarrassing book, at least to anyone who knew how to read or write science fiction, because Vidal was venturing into an area where many, many talented writers had built upon each other's work and established a whole language of communication; in trying to re-invent the wheel, he proved that he was incapable of duplicating the work of fifty years of science fiction writers. The result was a pretty shabby book.

Not all serious literary writers who have ventured into science fiction fail. John Hersey, for instance, passes back and forth between science fiction and literary fiction. *The Child Buyer, White Lotus, My Petition for More Space*—they are clearly science fiction, and brilliantly done. But no one cares that much about the difference. The man knows how to do both things at the same time.

James Clavell's *Shogun* is, in its own way, a world creation book, very similar to the novel *Dune* in many of the science fiction techniques he uses. But those tools, so useful both inside and outside the genre of speculative fiction, are unavailable to those artists who never look beyond the surface of a vulgar art.

But the danger of the present situation goes beyond the illusions. Despite, or perhaps *because* of, its ignorance of the vulgar art that it despises, the artistic elite often feel a missionary zeal to save the popular audience from popular art. The elite decries the popular taste and longs to force its own preferred pieces on the vulgar audience, in order to *elevate* and improve them. In doing so they provide modern examples of the attitude of many Christian missionaries in the Americas and Polynesia and Africa, so convinced of the superiority and rightness of their dogma and ritual that they never even questioned whether they ought to destroy the indigenous beliefs and practices and writings.

(That, by the way, was another metaphor. It may challenge and offend some who are committed to "serious" art—it is not a pleasant thing to be compared to the average priest in the Americas in 1512.

But I urge you to examine the metaphor; it will tell you something true.)

Culturally, the artistic elite in America too often approaches the indigenous popular art of the American people with all the tender mercy of the Inquisition. The question is not whether to root it out, but merely how. The very use of the term *serious art* is one of the most damning evidences of this attitude. I chose the term, instead of using the ones I usually use, because I prefer to use the language of the community whose attitudes I'm attacking.

"Serious" literature, indeed. Do they think that the rest of us are kidding? I'm as serious in creating my stories as they are in writing theirs. For them to call themselves "serious literature" and speak of bringing art to the masses is as arrogant and ignorant and elitist as it was when Columbus said of the native Americans, "They have no language," and spoke of teaching them to speak, when what he meant was teaching them to speak Spanish. (Another metaphor; but it fits snugly.)

Just as our work has often been sneeringly dismissed as *sci-fi*, we in the speculative fiction community often refer to literary fiction as *li-fi*. It's a petty revenge for a thousand insults, and it changes nothing. But like the Br'er Rabbit stories among American slaves, it *does* make us feel better. (That's another extravagant simile, of course, but see if it might not contain some truth.)

The cultural imperialism of the artistic elite manifests itself at two levels: the private and the public.

You can find cultural imperialism in small, private acts, like when a teacher or librarian sneers at a student's taste in books. "Why are you still reading those Harlequins?" they ask, and make the students ashamed. How *dare* they? They cannot guess what private hunger those despised books might be satisfying. The same person would never dream of saying, "You must eat like me, and dress, and walk, and work like me in order to be a worthwhile person." So, why must the student "read like me"?

Another example of private tyranny: the teacher who forces eleventh graders to read *Moby Dick* or college freshmen to tackle *As I Lay Dying* when they are not prepared to understand it or experienced enough in life to care about it even if they did.

When I was a graduate assistant at Notre Dame, we were given a great deal of freedom in designing our own freshman comp and lit course. I did what made sense to me. I wanted to teach principles of criticism along with teaching writing, and so I gave them Robert Cormier's book *I Am the Cheese*, which you will not find in the literature section of the bookstore. It's in the young adult section. It's a children's book. It is also a gripping mystery, a *passionate* book.

It is structurally so complex, with shifting points of view and alternating timelines, that it would be daunting to try to decode them without a lot of help from a teacher. But the complexity was so smoothly handled by the writer that it was absolutely invisible to the students when they read.

Almost every student read it in one night. They sat down to begin reading the assigned work, and couldn't stop. They came back to me in class and said, with shock, "I *liked* this book. I *loved* this book." It was a foreign experience to them. They had almost never been required to read a book that they could love.

The next book I gave them was *The Princess Bride* by William Goldman, in the days before the movie was made. And again they couldn't stop reading it. They told me they laughed all the way through it except when they cried. And yet I was able to take them through extremely complex analyses of structure and irony, because this also is a really strange, interesting, difficult book to parse. Artistically it is so complex that I could barely touch on what was going on, yet they began to discover a lot of wonderful things about how stories work; but I believe they could only discover these things because the story actually worked for them from the beginning. We could agree on that. Because we all shared the experience of being profoundly moved by both of those stories, we could start analyzing how it was done.

Then I gave them a third work, and with no discussion, assigned them to write about it. *King Lear*. The results were much better than I ever expected. I had expected pleas for help. What I got was startlingly original interpretations and analyses of what's going on in *King Lear*, on many, many levels. Only a couple of them, English majors both, gave me anything that I had ever heard before. Yet everything the others gave me was at least interesting, usually valid, sometimes wonderful. It was an approach that worked, because the authors of all three works had never forgotten that they were trying to communicate with an audience that wanted a wonderful story.

There was another grad student that same year who was determined to give these kids *literature*. After a semester of abstruse texts,
he ended up with an extremely rebellious class of students who had
learned almost nothing about literature. All done with the best intentions: They were going to learn *literature* if it killed them.

The teachers who assign work that is unreadable, at least at the
age of the students and with the level of preparation that they had,
often have the *best* intentions; they would simply be ashamed to teach
works that students might actually have read voluntarily for pleasure.

But the conclusion many such abused students reach after trips
to museums to see incomprehensible art, or after being forced to
read boring or impenetrable literary works, or listen to utterly incomprehensible, anti-melodic music—the conclusion they reach is, "If I
like it, it must not be good; and if it's *good*, I'm not going to like it."

Now, if we have a vast number of people who never read for
pleasure in American society, at least part of the blame must rest
with those who made their youthful experiences so unpleasant. They
seek and find their stories elsewhere.

Then there's the danger from public acts. In America today, we
generally use the taxation power, when it touches art at all, to support
artists who are producing works that only a tiny minority of Americans
actually *want*. Now a great case can be made, I think, for public
funding of ballet and opera, because these arts *can't* exist without
career performers, who can't *be* career performers without getting
paid—and that takes money. So public funding of ballet and opera
makes sense, the way funding museums does, for the preservation of
an art.

But it is harder to understand, in the fields of music composition,
two-dimensional and three-dimensional visual arts, fiction, and poetry,
why there should be public funding at all. Those arts can be produced
for a very modest investment in material—plus a much greater investment in *time*, but that does come free to the artist, as a general
rule. Once produced, these arts can be offered to the public at large,
which will very democratically reward the artists whose work they
want more of.

The role of the government, here, is quite puzzling, until you
observe the general pattern of how the public monies are disbursed.
In most cases, it is given exclusively to the less successful practitioners

of elitist art. The masses are being taxed to pay for art that is explicitly designed *not* to appeal to or communicate with them.

A member of that vulgar audience might well ask, "Why should I be taxed to pay for publication of a book that I don't want to read?" or, turning the question around another way, "Why are my tax monies taken by a committee of elitists and used to subsidize their friends, people who often do art that seems as formulaic and repetitive to *me* as my westerns or romances or mysteries might seem to *them*?"

Now, I know the most common answer. The most common answer is that horror and romance and western writers don't need subsidies. I mean, look at the way Louis L'Amour, Stephen King, and Judith Krantz *sell*.

But my answer to that is, "Look how John Updike sells." It's hardly fair to compare the *least* successful practitioners of elitist art with the *most* successful practitioners of popular art. There's big money at the top of almost every genre. But for every starving young writer who aspires to be the next John Updike, there's at least one other starving writer who aspires to be Stephen King. The one writer gets just as hungry as the other, the one is just as sincere and passionate and serious about his art as the other—and also probably as egotistical and vain and desirous of fame and fortune as the other—so why are most literature subsidy programs designed to benefit the one while the other can go hang himself?

I wait in vain for an answer. I've waited for a long time for an explanation of why one artistic community is *better* than another.

I've heard members of the elite point out all the failings of Stephen King, pointing out why his work is so bad when measured against the standards of the literary elite. But I assure you, the contemporary fantasy community has critics who can wax just as eloquent in pointing out the glaring deficiencies of Saul Bellow when measured by the standards set by Stephen King. It depends upon what you want fiction to do, and the argument always boils down to some tautology, like this: "*This* kind of work is worthy because we of the literary elite approve of it; and we are of the literary elite because we approve of this kind of work."

Still I wait in vain for a demonstration of how even bad elitist art is intrinsically better for the American people than the best popular art. Yet most art funding programs are run as if that statement were already proved and didn't even need to be discussed.

The thing that I find most painful here is that the division between "serious art" and "popular art" is so useless—and so unnatural, really. This division between serious and popular art (or *elitist* and *vulgar* art, to use the more loaded terms) is not unique to America, but nowhere else is the hostility between them so fierce. I think part of the reason for this is that in other countries, the artistic communities are also forced to deal with the *American* cultural invasion, while in America we're not. So even the despised genres are encouraged in other countries if only to have a homegrown product. The elitists hold their noses when they touch the work of local popular artists, but still they say: "Hey, it may be junk but at least it's not *American* junk."

The fact remains, though, that the masses throughout the world are faunching after American art. American art exports make a fair run at balancing out the trade deficit; but, oddly enough, what the other countries want is not the art of the American elite, by and large. It's American *popular* art that is reshaping the world.

Or perhaps that's not so odd. The power to change the world rests in the hands of the artists who attempt to communicate with the world. That is so obvious as to hardly need saying, and yet it clearly *does* need saying.

The greatest danger from the fierce division between the vulgar audience and the artistic elite is that if the artistic elite actually does have something of value to offer, it is not being received and will not be received until the artistic elite stops being an elite and starts trying to reach the general audience again.

The real lesson from the story of *Piss Christ* and Jesse Helms is not that public art is in danger from the Philistines (though it is). It's that the art that has been publicly funded shows little discernible reason why the public should fund it. The people have already voted against this sort of art in the bookshop and the gallery and the record store. Public funding of that rejected art has all the earmarks of a coup designed to keep the defeated party in office after all. (That's another metaphor, but see if there might not be truth in it.)

I think the real need in American arts and letters is for the wall to be torn down between elite and popular art. Instead of celebrating tiny variations in a sea of numbing sameness, the elite should be encouraged to open itself to the other genres. They should embrace true strangeness. The elite should be encouraged to try to find out what it is that popular artists are doing that allows them to speak to the people.

And I assure you that it's not because they're pandering to the lowest level of the people, though some do that. There are at least as many members of the artistic elite who pander to the basest instincts of the elite audience, too. But the best of each genre can learn from the best of the others.

The elite should also explore and try to find out what they are doing as an artistic elite that makes the public reject them. They should ask, "What can we learn from each other? How can we communicate with a larger audience without weakening or trivializing the truth of our work?"

I think it can be done. I think it *is* being done. But those who have the responsibility for disbursing public funds should encourage those artists in any genre who are trying to open their art to the public, who have respect for talent and vision in many genres. If you don't understand another genre and yet have responsibility for judging its worthiness in order to disburse funds fairly, then you owe it to the public that you serve to educate yourself or consult with those that do understand that genre.

Those who are part of the academic and artistic elite need to open themselves to strangeness, to be at least as open to other arts as they wish the general public were open to the arts that they approve of. If your critical theory has nothing to say about Stephen King or Margaret Mitchell, then it's not a general theory at all, but rather a special case.

And if your art support program benefits only artists who do a certain kind of art, which is challenging only in predictable, familiar ways, then don't congratulate yourself on supporting art. On the contrary, you are fossilizing it.

We're all here because we *care* about art and literature, and because we put time and effort into producing it and supporting it. And I say it *is* worth doing, as long as we do it with open minds.

I've taken you through a metaphoric process today. I've shown you familiar things, perhaps in strange contexts. I hope you'll explore the metaphor, and see if there might not be truth in it.

Michael Bishop

Michael Bishop, in his third and final year as editor of the annual *Nebula Awards* anthology, doesn't usually refer to himself in the third person. Here, he adopts that odd conceit to preserve from introduction to introduction a certain symmetry and to avoid appearing immodest. His novels include *No Enemy But Time, Who Made Stevie Crye?, Ancient of Days, Unicorn Mountain,* and *Philip K. Dick Is Dead, Alas. Blooded on Arachne, One Winter in Eden,* and *Close Encounters with the Deity* are his short story collections. He has edited two independent anthologies, *Changes,* with Ian Watson, and *Light Years and Dark,* winner of *Locus*'s best-anthology-of-the-year award for 1984.

Of the following story, Bishop says, "An ommatidium is one of the facets of the compound eye of an insect like the dragonfly. My intent was to write a linear narrative in segments mirroring the faceted structure of such an eye. A quasi-Ballardian approach. I rarely do hard SF stories, but this is one, even though it has a mystical element that some may view as at odds with its focus on a science like nanotechnology. Finally, 'The Ommatidium Miniatures' contains a small bow—by way of an outright theft—to the late James Blish's 1952 story, 'Surface Tension.' "

"A Is for Aphid." Emmons could never recall his mother without thinking of the ABC books of microscopic phenomena that she had compiled to amuse him during long summer afternoons on Tybee Island. A microscopist of acknowledged creativity, Kathleen Emmons had published one of these books under the off-putting title *An Abecedary of the Near Invisible.* To almost everyone's surprise, it became a best-seller. For the next few years you couldn't find a home with elementary-school-age children anywhere in the country without a copy of her book lying on a coffee table or sticking out of a bookcase.

"A Is for Aphid," it asserted. And on the facing page, looking to young Emmons more like bug-eyed outer-space monsters than like microscopic insects, a herd of potato-shaped aphids elephant-walked

200

the magnified branch of a muscadine vine. Deeper into the picture book, you learned that "D Is for Diatom," "M Is for Microchip," "R Is for Rotifer," and you saw the stunning micrographs illustrating these statements. But the siphon-nosed aphids at the outset of his mother's book were the creatures that had fascinated Emmons as a boy. Thus, he'd leapt at the invitation of International MicroDyne and begun preparing for his drop-down. He had done so not only to test the minute engines of the company's new technologies but also to solder a spiritual link with his past—when, once upon a time, *he'd* been small: an embryonic personality struggling to creep out from the shadows thrown by his mother's success and his father's international reputation.

The Incredible Shrinking Man. On the seventh floor of the IMD Sensor and Actuator Center in a northern suburb of Atlanta, Emmons sat in a conference room watching a video of a 1957 sci-fi flick he had previously avoided having to see. Watching this movie was one of the weirder requirements of the field-test training that McKay had masterminded for the pilot of the company's first microremote; and as Scott Carey, the movie's common-man protagonist, shrank to the size of a three-year-old boy, a mouse, and, finally, a bipedal cockroach, Emmons's attention wobbled.

"I can't believe you've never seen this," said McKay, leaning into him in the carpeted dark and flinching when Carey stabbed his straight pin up into the belly of an attacking spider. "It's a certifiable classic."

But Emmons thought it smart to refrain from confessing that he hated the movies, that he had always hated the movies, and that he was grateful to his parents for encouraging him to develop other interests; he kept his eyes—not his mind—on the oversized screen and said nothing. McKay, a personnel rather than a research-and-development specialist, sincerely believed that even MicroDyne's brightest technicians could benefit from the psychological training provided by a sci-fi "classic" like *The Incredible Shrinking Man*, and when an executive of his rank took that sort of tack, what else could you do but comply?

"To God There Is No Zero." For now, high on the screen, Scott Carey, who had squeezed into his garden from a window ledge in the base-

ment, was gazing at the impossibly distant stars and all the muddled galaxies. "That existence begins and ends," said the actor Grant Williams in the film's final voice-over narration, "is man's conception, not nature's. And I felt my body dwindling, melting, becoming nothing. My fears melted away, and in their place came acceptance. All this vast majesty of creation, it had to mean something. And then I meant something, too. Yes, smaller than the smallest, I meant something, too. To God there is no zero. I still exist!"

And B is for bullshit, thought Emmons, for it appeared to him that all he had seen in the film—denial, alienation, degradation, struggle—refuted Carey's concluding cry of existential yea-saying; indeed, the hero's fears about his own insignificance, and life's ultimate meaninglessness, were *underscored* by the fact that Carey was going to go on shrinking forever.

Being There. McKay had the lights brought up. He still got a boost from the film's upbeat gloss on the existential ramifications of littleness.

"Going down isn't easy," he told Emmons. "It's different from light microscopy, different from electron microscopy, and different from doing hands-on manipulations with a stereo-microscope assist. *Being there*—down among the dust mites, so to speak—is an *intenser* sort of microscopy, Emmons. Even if, on the literal level, you're operating a tiny waldo, doing watchmaker tasks with silicon pincers the size of an amoeba's paws.

"You have to overcome the possibility of 'dimensional shock' and take your bearings from the point of view of a nematode, say, or a spider colt. You have to learn to see again, at what I like to call 'ground zero.' Theoretically, it seems smart to work your way to the needed redimensionalization slowly. Which is why I've asked you to watch *The Incredible Shrinking Man* and then to discuss it with me."

Emmons discussed the film with McKay, certain that his boss was enjoying their talk—as he had the movie—immeasurably more than he was.

Frogs and Philistines. During their talk, McKay noted that Science— Emmons could hear the capital—had long ago declared that certain species of frog could not see anything in their environment inapplicable to their day-to-day existence. They were selectively blind to whatever failed to advance their survival or immediate well-being. The nonessential was invisible to them. A dragonfly at mealtime would loom like a helicopter, but an animal neither edible nor threatening—a wading heifer, for example—would splash by unregarded.

Scowling, McKay noted that some human philistines had a similar trait; namely, an inability to see anything that so much as hinted at parentheticality or irrelevance, *i.e.*, the microscopic.

Emmons's mind cast back to his mother's abecedaries: McKay was preaching to the converted. If A wasn't for "aphid," then it was for "amoeba"; if F wasn't for "follicle," then it was for "flea." The naked human eye could not distinguish two dots less than a tenth of a millimeter apart, but from an early age he had trained himself to see all that the human eye *could* see.

How, then, was he either a frog or a philistine?

His mother had helped make him sensitive to the invisible—the infusoria in a vial of creek water—and his father, whose namesake Emmons was, had made these lessons stick by seeing to it that he often felt like a mere protozoan. In fact, of late Emmons secretly saw himself as someone whom others did not fully register: a spear carrier in a play or some anonymous urban scarecrow sleeping in the gutter.

F Is for "Father," F Is for "Flea." The Emmonses' beach house on Tybee Island had always been full of dogs: Newfoundlands, poodles, Russian wolfhounds. It had also been full of fleas.

As McKay lectured, Emmons recalled his father striding shoeless in his tennis whites over the rattan mats on their concrete porch. Fleas jumped from the mats onto the damp cotton of his father's sweat socks, where their hard little bodies took on the instant visibility of commas or periods. His father picked off each flea with his thumb and forefinger and dropped it into the hot tapwater in an otherwise empty fish tank.

Lying on their pinched sides, the fleas kicked pathetically on the surface. Finger-jabbed, they spiraled, still kicking, to the bottom, where, eventually, the kicking ceased.

The elder Emmons, who seldom played very long with his namesake because his son usually netted more shots than he returned, would spend the rest of the morning decoying, seizing, and dunking fleas, moving from spot to spot on the mats to entice fresh generations of vermin to spring onto his socks. This intellectual celebrity, the computer scientist and backdoor cosmologist who had extended and redeemed his once-discredited mentor Edward Fredkin's science of "digital physics," would scold young Emmons for failing to capture fleas, too.

To the world at large, he held up the dictum that the universe is a computer—that atoms, electrons, and other subatomic particles are built from infinitesimal bits of information; that reality is grainy; and that there exists a single underlying programming rule to account for the movement and purpose of each of its constituent grains—but to his twelve-year-old son on Tybee, in the microcosmos of his family's summer retreat, he preached filial devotion, a more disciplined forehand smash, and the philosophical-cum-recreational benefits of flea-tweezering.

Microscopic Rain and a Midget's Parasol. "In a sense," McKay was saying, "Carey was lucky. He shrank by degrees, with plenty of chances to make adjustments."

Emmons, returning from his flashback, became aware of the dense particulate rain in his boss's strangely appointed office. Decay products from the radioactive gases thrown off by the ceiling tiles and the Sheetrock walls rained down as an invisible but inescapable fallout. The air was afire. It fell in charged veils, sleeting, draping, folding back on itself to repeatedly stipple his boss with iotas of disintegrating matter. Also, the molecules on the surface of McKay's aircraft carrier of a desk were migrating aside to allow the falling particles to penetrate and rape it.

A guilty horror seized Emmons as he watched the rain, a shower clearly imperceptible to McKay, who was jawing about "acclimating declensions" and giving odd examples:

"The smallest adult human being recorded, Emmons, was a Mexican midget called Lucia Zarate. At seventeen, Señorita Zarate stood two feet and two inches tall and weighed not quite five and a half pounds. This nineteenth-century freak could have stepped from one of the Montgolfiers' balloons, popped a parasol, and floated safely to earth. On her trip down, she could have leisurely scrutinized a torrent of high-altitude plankton: pollen grains, lichen fragments, the spores of fungi, bacteria, algae, and so forth. If MicroDyne could bring off that easy a drop-down, Emmons, you'd have no sweat accepting your littleness."

But Emmons kept thinking how handy the señorita's parasol would have been: a shield against the invisible deluge.

"Let's Get Small." McKay's office was a museum of the minute. It contained an elegant miniature of the living room of the Tybee Island beach house—down to a baby baby grand piano, an itsy-bitsy computer station, a dinky fireplace with even dinkier andirons and grates, a collection of foraminifer shells, and a gallery of framed Kirkuchi patterns (diffraction images of various alloy particles as created and photographed inside a transmission electron microscope) no bigger than postage stamps.

A newt-sized plastic doll of Emmons's canonized father sat in a wicker rocker in this mock-down of their old beach house, gazing at the Kirkuchi patterns and thinking godly thoughts. McKay paid no attention to these items, he'd seen them so many times before, but Emmons knew that this miniature architectural tribute to his father had triggered his flashback as surely as had McKay's jabber about frogs and philistines. The urge seized him to grab the father doll and pop it between his fingernails as if clicking the carapace of a flea— but, even as a tiny doll, his father remained a Micromegas in Emmons's view, and he couldn't do it.

Elsewhere in McKay's office there were Lilliputian cathedrals, miniature divans, Tinker Toy forts, and a display case containing gnat robots, beetle jeeps, electrostatic motors, and microdozers. The spiders that had draped some of these furnishings with gauze were living creatures, just like Emmons, but everything inanimate in the room mocked him by seeming more cunningly made.

"Ever see a tape of Steve Martin doing his classic 'Let's Get Small' routine?" McKay had just asked. "God, I love that routine. Think 'high' for 'small.' You'll get a grip on microminiaturization as a kind of occupational addiction. Look around. You can see why a shtick like that would appeal to me. . . ."

Inadequacy, Impotence, Insignificance: A Tract. That evening, in his apartment, Emmons worried that even his competence as a microremote engineer hadn't given him the sense of self possessed by a pompous company shill like McKay. Would going down—getting smaller—do the trick?

If H isn't for "humility" (an abstract noun), then it's for "hydra" (a tube-shaped freshwater polyp with a mouth at one end ringed by tentacles). And another definition of hydra is "a multifarious evil not overcome by a single effort." How to cope with the fact that the hydra he'd been struggling to defeat wasn't any sort of evil, but rather the achievements of a mother who'd classified over a thousand species of nematodes and a father who'd led the world's scientific community toward the one computational Rule governing every nanometer of space and perhaps explaining everything?

Forget that Fredkin's Rule—as his father had dubbed it—was still incompletely teased out. Forget that many scientists still blasted both the elder Emmons and the late Fredkin as, at best, "inspired crackpots." *Emmons* was now an Olympian name. Although the son bearing it was proud of his name, he was also cowed by it, mindful of the meagerness of his own efforts in comparison to his parents'. He seemed doomed by the scale of their reputations to fall on his face in any attempt to match them. He was too small to rival their successes, a bacterium in a life-extinguishing drop of acid: Scott Carey with a Ph.D. in microengineering.

"It's a Didinium-*Eat*-Paramecium *World."* Germaine Bihaly, who lived across the complex's parking lot, showed up at his door with a tray of Cantonese carryout boxes, each one a small soggy chalet packed with steamed chestnuts, sweet-and-sour meats, plump shrimp, or vivid strings of slime defying identification.

"Share?" she said.

Emmons let her in. Bihaly was a travel agent, whom he had met over the telephone while booking a flight to a sensor-and-actuator conference in Berkeley. Later, he had coincidentally found her to be one of his neighbors.

They ate Chinese sitting on the ad sections from the *Atlanta Constitution.* Emmons explained why he felt like the incredible shrinking man and told her how, as part of his training, he'd had to watch an old sci-fi flick and then listen to McKay gab about its applicability to the piloting of microremotes.

Unsympathetic, Bihaly said, "Hey, Emmons, it's a *Didinium*-eat-*Paramecium* world," a joke between them ever since he had shown her his mother's sequential micrographs of a predatory ciliate seizing and absorbing another ciliate species nearly twice the *Didinium*'s size. Wasn't he a big boy? Couldn't he take care of himself in the sharkish corporate world?

Later, Emmons, frightened and tentative, hovered over Bihaly's body like a gar above the remains of a hammerhead's kill.

The Night Testimony of Leeuwenhoek. Bihaly stayed anyway, and Emmons dreamed that he was an animalcule in a moist cavern among a population explosion of such creatures, all fidgeting, feeding, and reproducing in a balmy darkness not unlike that of MicroDyne's company pool.

What most upset Emmons about his presence among these nameless microorganisms was the heightening of his own namelessness by their large numbers. The indeterminacy of the Where in which he and all the other tiny beasties multiplied also bothered him. But, at last, a voice spoke over, around, and through him—like God making a proclamation—and he knew that he and the bacteria around him were cliff-dwelling on the speaker's gums.

"I dug some stuff out of the roots of one of my teeth," boomed the dead Dutch lens grinder and scope maker, Anton van Leeuwenhoek, Emmons's host. *"And in it I found an unbelievably great company of living animalcules, amoving more nimbly than I had seen up to now. The biggest sort bent their bodies into curves in going forwards, and the number of animalcules was so extraordinarily great that 'twould take a thousand million of some of them to make up the bulk of a coarse sand grain."*

In his sleep, Emmons shriveled.

"Indeed, all the people living in our United Netherlands are not as many as the living animals I carry in my mouth." Emmons had once read that Leeuwenhoek attributed his lifelong ruddy health to a hot Ethiop beverage—coffee—that "scalded the animalcules" in his

mouth. Emmons's arms reached out for Germaine Bihaly, but they could not find her.

Artificial Fauna in a Day-Care Zoo. For the past seven months, Emmons had stopped nearly every morning on the edge of the day-care courtyard. He watched the kids swarm over the fiberglass backs of pink dinosaurs and the extruded-foam statues of giraffes.

Today, he saw a mechanical crane lowering into the courtyard an armored monster so much like a menacing alien crab that most of the kids dashed into the arms of day-care workers to escape it. Emmons knew it for the jungle-gym simulacrum of a dust mite, magnified thousands of times. Its body plates and serrated front claws were gigantic. Detracting from its realism, size aside, was the absence of magnified counterparts for the carpet fibers, hair strands, and skin flakes that cling to living dust mites.

"Educational, don't you think?" said McKay, appearing behind Emmons as if from nowhere.

Emmons stayed mute. He imagined the kids climbing on the dust mite like parasites on parasites, *ad infinitum*. A team of workmen positioned the yawing statue on its base, and Emmons wondered if possibly there weren't a few situations in which it might not be so bad to be parasitized.

The Relativity of Time Consciousness. "When you're down there, Emmons, you'll feel like the Methuselah of the microverse. That's because your eyes and hands will be electronically plugged into the ommatidia and manipulators of your remote. Generations will come and go, but you'll endure.

"Your consciousness—unlike poor Scott Carey's—will be up here in the Sensor and Actuator Center with me, President Sawyer, and the kids out there in the courtyard, but you'll be interacting with critters for whom a second may be an hour and a day a lifetime. That could rattle you."

McKay pointed to the hummingbird feeder on the far edge of the fiberglass zoo and to the ruby-throats hovering about it.

"Those guys have a metabolic rate higher than that of any other bird or mammal, Emmons. About twelve times that of a pigeon, about a hundred times that of an elephant. A second for a hummingbird is equivalent to two or three minutes for a whale. Just imagine what an hour down in the microdimensions could be, and remember that as you observe and actuate, okay?

"You've got to have this conception of yourself as being in two places at once, but you've got to subordinate your real-world self to the one on microsafari. Otherwise, you'll screw up. We don't sweat the screw-ups for MicroDyne's sake, Emmons. One day, we'll mass-produce microbots in the same kind of volume that the folks in Silicon Valley do microchips. It's *your* well-being we're worried about. We don't want to take a raving loon or a mindless artichoke out of actuator harness."

McKay consulted his watch. Less than two hours to drop-down. It would roll around in either an eyeblink or an ice age, depending on which of his anxieties Emmons set his inner clock by.

Telemetry vs. Manned Redimensionalization. Bihaly could not understand why International MicroDyne, or any other multinational mass-producing flea-sized actuators and invisible sensors, thought it necessary to plug the eyes and mind of a human being into the tiny contraptions that were already evaluating the safety of space-shuttle parts, encoding new functions on gallium-arsenide chips, and overseeing the manufacture of other microbots.

"Hell, Bihaly, to boldly go where no one's ever gone before," Emmons told her. "Why weren't we satisfied to fling only a lander at Mars? Why do our astronauts perform EVAs when a machine could do the job a helluva lot more safely?"

Bihaly continued to object. Emmons wasn't going to shrink, not like that guy in the SF film; in fact, he wasn't going to go bodily to the microdimensions at all. But, according to McKay, there was a psychological hazard as forbidding as the prospect of stranding an astronaut on Titan.

"So please tell me," Bihaly said, "why you've chosen to be the first MicroDyne employee to accept the risk?"

"It's pretty simple, really. I want to send back this message to McKay: 'That's one baby step for amoeba-kind, one gigantic step for Yours Truly.' Ain't it a shame the lousy drop-down's not going to be televised?"

The Map Is Not the Territory, the Name Is Not the Thing Named.
McKay took him into the hermetic, dust-free room in which he was
to execute the drop-down and perform his mission. "Dust-free,"
McKay hurried to qualify, in the sense that only the target area—a
bell of clear glass eighteen inches in diameter and six high—contained
any dust, organic debris, or moisture. As for Emmons himself, he
would not really be in this room, but in a nearby operator's booth,
jacked into the microremote prototype beneath the glass bell in the
center of the otherwise vacant floor of this otherwise featureless chamber. In sterile yellow boots and coveralls, the two men stared down
on the bell.

"My Mildendo," Emmons said.

McKay lifted his eyebrows.

"The capital city of Lilliput," Emmons said. He saw that the
dome's inner circle had been quartered into pie wedges of jungle,
desert, ocean, and a landscape of Mondrianesque microcircuitry. It
was a map, a relief map. As a very small boy, he had once taken a
Texaco road map from the glove box of his dad's Audi and studied it
as if it were a two-dimensional kingdom, convinced that the names
of towns were the towns themselves and that dot-sized people really
lived there.

A fantasy that his mother's microscopy had given a credibility
that even beginning grade school hadn't undermined.

Today the fantasy had come true. The map was the territory (even
if the name was still not the thing named). As he and McKay knelt
to examine the bell more closely, Emmons had the unpleasant sensation that he was both a demiurge to this little world and one of its
puny inhabitants.

"O Is for Ommatidia." What must it be like to be a gnat gazing up
through the bell at McKay and him? Would the ommatidia of one of
those tiny insects even register them, or would their images be frag-
mented into so many repeating split screens that the creature's brain
rebelled against the overload?

An ommatidium—as Emmons and half the population of the
United States had learned thirty years ago from *An Abecedary of the
Near Invisible*—is one of the light-sensitive facets of the compound
eye of a fly, a honeybee, or a dragonfly. The dragonfly, his mother's

book had said, has more of these honeycomblike optical drupes than does any other insect, nearly thirty thousand.

Emmons loved the word: *Ommatidium.*

Dragonflies saw the world fractured, divvied up, split-screened to infinity, which, of course, was also the way that Emmons lived his life and saw reality. It was the same discontinuous, grainy, particulate world amplified in his father's brilliant reworking of Fredkin's private science, digital physics. And just as thousands of ommatidia working together brought useful information out of the fundamental graininess of the world, so, too, might Fredkin's Rule precipitate from the countless information bits of the universe one crystalline truth that made perfect sense of the whole.

Emmons said it to himself as a mantra: Ommm-atiddy-*ummm.* Ommm-atiddy-*ummm.* Ommm-atiddy-*ummm.*

"You'll see more when you're down there," McKay said, puffing as he climbed off the floor. "From a human vantage, the bell's pretty damn empty-looking and ordinary-seeming. But there's stuff in there, all right, and you'd best get to it."

Emmons, standing, had a dizzying image of thousands of immense, cockamamie avatars of himself backing away from the dome and fading off into a vast blue muzziness.

Inside the Microtaur. Emmons entered the operator's booth and, with McKay's and two businesslike technicians' help, placed himself in harness.

His invisible vehicle—the one at the very center of the sealed dome—was smaller than a weevil nymph, much too tiny for unassisted detection. Its dimensions qualified it as a micro-, rather than a nano-, technological wonder, but it had not been manufactured by the whittle-away process employed for most of MicroDyne's current wares; instead, it had been drexlered—built up atom by atom—from virtual nothingness, so that it had not only a clear exterior shape under the scanning electron microscope, but also an intricately made interior, or cockpit, with fine one-to-one correspondences to all the controls in the human-scale operator's cab.

Outwardly, the remote resembled a cross between an armor-plated combat vehicle, moving on treads, and an eight-armed crab.

Emmons regarded it as the spider-mite equivalent of a modern tank and the mythological centaur, a kind of high-tech microtaur.

Strapped into his seat and plugged into the vehicle's sensors and actuators, Emmons finally received the signal for drop-down. Obediently, he hit the switches in their proper sequences. *Wham!* Brobdingnagian landscapes bloomed, and he was there, an intruder in the pettiness and majesty of the microdimensions.

Down Among the Dust Mites. "That's one baby step for amoebakind," Emmons said, but the realization that he was moving forward on tiny caterpillar treads made him cut short the guff. He could float, he could tractor, he could shinny, and, by the unfurling of veil-like wings, he could even fly a little, escaping by a hair the fate of insects so nearly weightless that the Brownian movement of random molecular action could buffet them to doom.

What he couldn't do was walk—not as a person walked, anyway—and his first true dimensional shock, all training aside, was the weirdness of this lack. Simulator trials had been helpful, but not wholly to the point. After all, the incredible shrinking man had not had to give up his body as he dropped toward the infinitesimal, only the dumb assumptions that size bestowed dignity, that whatever was small was willy-nilly of no import. The great whales of the seas and the bacterial populations in the human gut, Emmons knew, were . . . well, *equally meaningless lifeforms.*

But not being able to ambulate as human beings usually do—that was a bitch. Down among the dust mites, you had to motor like dust mites. If you didn't do in Rome as the Romans did, you could count on going nowhere but crazy. Frustrated, Emmons slapped at switches like a kid trying to undercut an upright Babel of ABC blocks.

Reverberations from the Voice of God. "Emmons, you idiot, stop that!" McKay thundered from afar. "I can't believe you're behaving this way! You haven't done a blasted thing yet!"

But Emmons could believe it. He was a child again, overwhelmed by his father's disdain, lost in an utterly mystifying world.

"Easy," God advised. "Caterpillar into Quadrant Dust Jungle. We'll try the microchip wirings after you've had a chance to take your bearings there."

Emmons settled down; he headed the microtaur into Quadrant Dust Jungle, treading through a gray tangle of pet hairs, grease-coated cotton fibers, cat-flea eggs, pollen grains, skin scales, severed strands of spider webbing, and lopsided arches of unidentifiable gunk and fuzz.

Initially, this alien landscape fascinated Emmons, more by its grotesquerie than by its "beauty," but the longer he piloted the microtaur the more grim and monotonous it seemed. He was reminded of boyhood car trips across the panhandle of Oklahoma.

Boredom was settling on him when he saw a scale-freckled dust mite micrometering over the detritus-cobbled terrain, and he neared the retiring critter, a sort of cow-cum-crayfish, just to see what it would do.

It sensed the microtaur and switched directions. Thus baited, Emmons caterpillared after the mite, careful not to overtake it in his zeal to enliven things.

Relatively soon, he came among dozens—hundreds—of other such mites grazing through the spun-dust jungle of the quadrant. They were microdimensional cattle, heifers of the waste declensions of the very small.

"Reorient your vehicle and head for the EPROM chips in Quadrant Microprocessor!" demanded God.

Grudgingly, Emmons obeyed.

Taking the Tour. Over a period of days, Emmons's microtaur did a grand promenade of the bell, creeping into the separately sealed Quadrant Microprocessor to perform Herculean cutting, pasting, and wire-connecting labors on the wafers arrayed there, and incidentally clabbering them with debris from Dust Mite Territory.

Never mind, said McKay; it was the execution of the preassigned tasks that mattered, not their ultimate results, for under optimum conditions their results were entirely predictable. It was the doing of them by hands-on intervention at "ground zero" that was being tested.

"A is for A-OK," the godly McKay intoned. "Good job, Emmons."

In the control booth, Emmons took nutrients through IV stylets and fatigue-offsetting electrostimulus through the wires externally mapping his nervous system.

His microtaur entered Quadrant Living Desert, where its treads terraced a landscape of sand grains, humus particles, and buried seeds. Beneath this promise squirmed springtails and earthworms, creatures out of the *Dune* books, while beneath them unraveled miles of fungal mycelium and loop snares.

The microtaur's drexlered claws seized nematodes, tardigrades, and Pantagruelian lice. It brought minute soil samples into its collection baskets, then tractored out of Quadrant Living Desert into its final microenvironment, Quadrant Waterworld.

Here, it unshipped flagellate oars to power it through a realm of rotifers, ciliates, and diatoms.

Despite his various energizing hookups, Emmons was exhausted. He hadn't slept for days. If he failed to get some sleep soon, he would begin—even in this hallucinatory realm—to trip out. McKay and MicroDyne were hard taskmasters. He hated them for protracting his mission and for holding him so long in actuator harness. A pox on the bastards.

A Rendezvous with Mytilina. Emmons's microtaur sculled through Quadrant Waterworld and all its light-shot, alga-forested grottoes, bucking, releasing ballast, sounding, rising again.

Eventually, it neared a branching filamentous tree, jewel-green in the submarine stillness, on which a single crystal rotifer had gingerly perched. By its thornlike toes (resembling paired tails), its red eye-spot (like a speck of blood in a minute package of egg white), and its transparent shell (or lorica), Emmons knew it for a representative of the genus *Mytilina*.

It bobbed in the currents stirred by the MicroDyne vehicle, but otherwise appeared unalarmed, even though Emmons understood that the rotifer was aware of his approach. In fact, it actually wished for him to close with it so that they could converse.

"McKay," he said, activating his throat mike, "this is weird. A goddamn rotifer wants to talk with me."

When no one in the Sensor and Actuator Center replied, Emmons knew that the *Mytilina* had willed his isolation from his co-workers and that a meeting with the creature was inevitable.

"Son," it said. "Son, what do you think you're doing?"

How Can the Perceiver Know That Which Composes Its Apparatuses of Perception? Each separate hairlike process ringing the mouth of the rotifer wiggled at its own ever-altering rate. The sound waves generated by these "smart" vibrations belled out through the water, colliding with, building upon, or subtly damping one another as the *Mytilina* itself required, so that by the time the shaped wave-front struck the sensors of his vehicle, it was—Emmons could think of no other appropriate term—"recognizable human speech." On the other hand, Emmons realized that the speaker was actually either God (not McKay & Friends, but the Living God) or his own celebrity father in the guise of a microorganism.

"Maybe this is just my way of trying to help deduce the Rule," Emmons replied. "Didn't you always claim that the basic units of reality are very small, that the universe only seems continuous because we can't see the parts from which it's made? It's like a pointillistic painting by Seurat seen from a long way away. Walk closer and you see the dots. The same with Sunday's funnies. Take a magnifying glass and you'll see the specks of colored ink making up Linus's security blanket."

The crimson eye-spot of the bobbing rotifer pulsed, growing and shrinking at the whim of some inner cadence.

"Derek," it said, "can eyes composed of the smallest units in existence perceive those units? Do you really believe such a situation possible or likely?"

(Either the Deity or my dad is scolding me, Emmons thought. Give heed.)

"Remember," the *Mytilina* said, wobbling on its algal perch. "If the universe is a computer, everything happening as a result of its existence is innately incapable of understanding that it runs at the *direction* of that computer. The software, Derek, can't know the hardware—just as ommatidia the size of the smallest grains comprising reality can never see those grains. Put another way, they can never know—perceive—themselves."

Know Thyself. The rotifer talked to Emmons for mind-made ages; the purpose of the mystic computer of the universe—to answer the question posed by its hidden creator—was obvious. But both the answer and the question itself remained obscure to the universe's sentient representatives because the algorithmic program running to provide the answer was still in process. Not even God—as the *Mytilina* itself could attest—had the answer yet, and no one could guess how much longer the program had to run before it burped out its solution.

Emmons's head began to ache. Other "wheel animalcules" drifted into view, curlecuing toward his father's emerald tree like pixels filling a computer screen.

"Join us, Derek," the rotifer said. "Escape that shell you're hiding in and join us here in Quadrant Waterworld."

It confessed that although he might never learn the question God had posed the universe, being too small to perceive anything that vast, and too integral a part of the program in process to have an objective vantage on it, he might yet learn a few things that would repay him for slipping out of harness into the amniotic warmth of the very small.

Emmons, in the submerged microtaur, saw this as the best offer he'd had in years. Doggedly, he started to prise up electrodes, unplug jacks, strip away wiring, and pull out IV stylets. Free at last, he would crawl into the ejection tube and shoot himself into the tiny water world now harboring both his father and God.

Z Is for Zero, Which to God Does Not Exist. McKay ordered two burly technicians into the barricaded control booth. But before they could restrain him, Emmons—sweaty, pop-eyed, thick-tongued—fell back into his padded chair as if siphoned of all memory and will. The operator's cab was a shambles. (His microremote yawed in an emerald orchard of algae and glassy rotifers.) Feverishly, McKay and his cohorts worked to revive Emmons.

Bihaly's appearance wasn't providential—she had been worrying about the drop-down—but McKay's decision to let her in before the company doctor arrived may have been. "Rick," she said, using her private diminutive. "Rick, look at me."

Emmons's eyes opened. Above him, the faces of Bihaly, McKay, and the doctor orbited one another like the kaleidoscope jewels. He felt nothing—not relief, gratitude, or panic—only a fine, pervasive nothingness drifting through him like pollen through the foliage of evergreens. So what? Nothingness was okay. It might even be survivable. To God, after all, there was no zero.

Emmons had been down for slightly more than four hours, a fact McKay's blurred watch face withheld from him. Again, no matter. Eventually, his eyes would adjust. Maybe, when they did, Bihaly, who had called him back from that which cannot see itself, would still be there and, with her, he would try to understand all that had ever happened to him.

THE GREAT NEBULA SWEEP

Paul Di Filippo

In *Nebula Awards 24*, Paul Di Filippo appeared with an original essay on the unsung contributions to the SF-and-fantasy fields of Theodore Geisel (a.k.a. Dr. Seuss), "My Alphabet Starts Where Your Alphabet Ends." Di Filippo's novels, none yet published, include *Harp, Pipe, and Symphony; El Mundo Primero; Ciphers; Spondulix: A Romance of Hoboken*; and, in progress, *Fuzzy Dice*. A search through the card catalog of the Providence, Rhode Island, library and another through *Books in Print*, reports Di Filippo, reveal that the title *Fuzzy Dice* is his and his alone. I can't speak for others, but *I* would pay to read a novel by that name.

Di Filippo's short fiction *has* been published—in *Unearth, Twilight Zone, Fantasy & Science Fiction, New Pathways, Amazing Stories, Night Cry*, George Zebrowski's *Synergy, Pulphouse*, and *Mirrorshades: The Cyberpunk Anthology*. His nonfiction regularly appears in *SF Eye*, Charles Platt's *SF Guide, New Pathways*, the SFWA *Bulletin*, and elsewhere. His story "Kid Charlemagne" was a Nebula finalist for best short story of 1987.

"The Great Nebula Sweep" pokes sardonic fun at Nebula Mania, a malady that afflicts a good portion of the membership of SFWA every spring. Paul's essay/story, or story/essay, is original to this volume.

A review of **Mega-Awesome SF: The True Story Behind *Forever Plus!***, by Amber Max (Serconia Press, 1994, 334 pages, $29.95, ISBN 0-14-009692-2).

We all hoped that we had heard the last about the Great Nebula Sweep scandal. But now we must contend with this book.

The first notice anyone received of the existence of *Mega-Awesome SF* was through the "Today" show. In her interview with Deborah Norville, Amber Max, archetypical Valley Girl, seemed more intent on promoting herself than disclosing any new information. Her mantra—"I rilly, rilly wrote all these pages myself!"—did little to inspire confidence that her book would be of any value.

Opening the book to the first chapter certainly did not dispel my worst fears. Entitled "Amber's Totally Fabulous Guide to Life," this preface is all gossip and beauty tips. I was almost tempted to toss the book without reading further.

I'm glad, however, that I persisted, for in the next chapter— "Riding My Harley"—we begin to reap fresh, hitherto unavailable insights into the actors in the Great Nebula Sweep.

At their first encounter—a literal collision in the local Waldenbooks, midway between the SF and aerobic-video sections, during February 1990—Amber Max was nineteen, and Harley Prout was twenty-five. Employed by Chipco, the enormous computer conglomerate, Harley was also a lifelong reader of SF. He had for many years harbored secret hopes of becoming a published writer himself. But a decade of unanimous and unmitigated rejection had finally convinced him that he was an utter literary incompetent.

Making up his mind at last to succeed by computer trickery where he had failed with talent, and urged on by the mischievous and adoring Amber Max, Harley sought a cybernetic solution.

Harley was currently working on neural networks for his employer. These computer constructs were intended to mimic the functioning of the human brain more closely than conventional programs. Capable of heuristic fuzzy logic and parallel processing, neural networks offered the promise of replicating human mental abilities more closely than mere serial machines.

Using advanced Chipco hardware and unlimited company time, Harley set out to teach a neural network of unprecedented complexity the rules for producing an SF masterpiece.

In a process known as "training up the system," he started out by feeding the neural net—which had English-parsing abilities—the raw texts of all Nebula and Hugo winners, as well as the texts of all other ballot entries. He followed this up by giving it the voting statistics that had produced the winners. Learning of a poll Ben Bova had conducted among SFWA members to learn what selection criteria they employed in selecting award-winners, Harley obtained, through judicious bribes, the poll results from Galileo Marketing Systems, along with their secret multidimensional scaling techniques. These too were fed to the network.

It was now early spring 1991, and the current Nebulas were about to be awarded. Harley let his system peruse the contestants and make its choices. The network replicated the exact vote distribution the members of SFWA later produced.

Amber reports that Harley was overjoyed. " 'This is the key,' he told me. 'On the lowest level, writing is just the random generation of words. The secret lies in discriminating which words are the best. And I've got that power of discrimination now.' "

Securing an ultrasophisticated, text-generating program analogous to the famous RACTER, Harley wired it in a feedback loop with his neural network. He set the parameters of the network to maximum and turned the whole thing loose. The network inspected the text produced by the generator and passed only that which met its Nebula standards. The approved text was fed back to influence subsequent choices.

Amazingly, a coherent short story began to emerge. Reading it, Harley wept, and Amber exclaimed, "Holy shit, Harley, this is better'n *Star Wars!*"

Harley knew that his story was guaranteed to sell. He was reluctant to submit it under his own name, however, convinced that because of his reputation it would languish unread in the slushpile. That was when the crucial decision was made to use Amber's name on the byline.

All the story lacked was a title. Harley ran a simple subroutine that permuted all previous Nebula titles, and passed the choices on to the judgment of the network.

DOORS OF REPENTENCE, BLIND CONCILIATOR, ENEMY CLAW, SLOW PASSENGERS, A LETTER FROM THE KING OF SAND, DANCING CHICKENS AND UGLY DEERS, GOD SONG, BORN WITH THE SHADOWS, THE QUICK-ENING FLUTE, CATCH THAT HANGMAN, CHILDMANCER, MOTHER TO DRAGONS, THE FOUNTAINS OF SALIVA, DREAM OF THE LEFT-HANDED SNAKE, HARD BLOOD, THE VISION SOLUTION, THE PLANNERS OF TIME, THE GIRL WHO FELL INTO THE UNICORN TAPESTRY, A HELIX OF MIST, A DOG'S OPINION, PRESS LOVE OR DEATH, REVOLUTION MAN, ENDER IS FIVE, A TIME OF WORLDS, RINGWAY . . . All these and more met the thumbs-down from the network. Then came the winner: FOREVER PLUS!

As Amber records: "Harley said anyone could see it was a natural. 'The all-purpose ambiguity, the notion of one step beyond eternity, appealing to the immature desire for immortality, the exclamation point—it's perfect!' I just said, 'It's short and rad and real nineties, dude. I like it!' "

It was now the end of August 1991. Harley mailed the story out under Amber's name to the highest-paying market, where its publication would be sure to attract the most attention: *Omni* magazine. The story was purchased immediately. Further, it was slated to appear as soon as possible, in the first issue of 1992. This initial sale, however, was merely the first step in Harley's master plan to conquer the SF field. The next stage involved setting the network to churning out two longer versions of the syncretic masterpiece: a novelette and a novella.

Like the Kennedy assassination or the first moon landing, the publication of "Forever Plus!" in the January 1992 issue of *Omni* is an event emblazoned on the memories of all who read it. Entire issues of fanzines were devoted to heaping laurels on this one story. Professional reviewers everywhere climaxed in fits of critical ecstasy. Editors begged the unknown Amber Max for more of her work. Looking back on the short story version of *Forever Plus!* now, even after the secret of its origin has been exposed, one is still hard put to dislike or resist it. Scientific tests have revealed that, like the "fatal joke" of the Monty Python skit, the text is so constructed as to have actual neurological impact on the mind of anyone conditioned by years of reading SF.

In Chapter Five, " 'Way Off the Applause Meter," we finally learn what it felt like to be on the receiving end of all this adulation. "It was rilly, rilly super. We were like, 'Hey, more champagne, waiter!' " But, as Amber details, the buzz did not last long. Almost immediately, Harley had to buckle down to implementing his plan of conquest. "He was mega-anal, like. I just couldn't get him to kick back."

The novelette version of the story was dispatched to Axolotl Press, which of course immediately snatched it up. The limited signed chapbook was released by early March. The reaction to this version was even stronger, if possible. As "Forever Plus!" grew and grew in length, it promoted heavier and heavier semiotic meltdown in the brains of its readers.

By May a Tor SF Double featuring the brand-new novella version of "Forever Plus!" on one side was available. For the companion work, Tor editors, knowing it would make little difference what they bundled with Amber's masterpiece, had hurriedly grabbed the first piece moldering in the slushpile, a novella by the legendary eccentric Gerry Saint-Armand, Providence recluse in the Lovecraft tradition. The Double went through six printings before the official publication date, incidentally making Saint-Armand more money than had all of his previous sales combined.

By the time the novella saw print, the network had produced a 500,000-word definitive version of *Forever Plus!* Amber was represented now by the new firm of Meredith-Macauley-Heifetz. They auctioned off the manuscript to Bantam/Foundation for ten million dollars. Bantam had the book in print by August, a simultaneous release in hardcover, trade, and mass-market paperback. It was the first SF novel in a single volume to top a thousand pages.

To recount the long and intricate plot of *Forever Plus!* for an audience already intimately familiar with it would be pointless. Suffice it to note that by choosing an immortal protagonist, particularly one whose immortality resulted from jumping into a new body upon the expiration of each old one, Harley was able to move through an enormous range of times, milieus, and viewpoints. Opening with the protagonist yet an infant, the novel manages to traverse all the usual Misunderstood Child Prodigy terrain so beloved by SF readers. After this archetypal prologue comes the Awakening Adolescent, the Sensitive Youth, the Competent Man, the Wise Elder, the Disembodied Psyche, and, in a daring shift of viewpoint, the Oppressed Female. Afterward, the cycle repeats with variations extending into the nonhuman. Meanwhile, we have passed through Comet Strike, Realpolitik Scenario, Nuclear War, Nuclear Winter, Psychic Mutants, Eco-catastrophe, New Dark Ages, Gradual Renaissance, Expansion into the Solar System, Generation Ships, Discovery of FTL, the Backwards Colony, First Contact, Interspecies War, Galactic Empire, Collapse of Empire, Stagnation, and End of Time. Indeed, the protagonist survives the Big Crunch of an entropic universe to preside godlike over the birth of a new plenum!

By now, *Forever Plus!* was the literary equivalent of Beatlemania or *Thriller*-era Michael Jackson fever. The blurbs on later editions reveal a kind of shared madness.

"I am caught like a fly in Amber's prose. This is Pure Story." Orson Scott Card.

"John Campbell would have kissed her, then married her!" Algis Budrys.

"This is not a novel, it's Life itself! *Forever Plus!* forever more!" Faren Miller.

"Scientifically impeccable. Can Amber Max be housing the souls of Heinlein, Herbert, and Hawking?" Tom Easton.

"Signifier and signified are unified in a deconstructed hyperreality." Samuel Delany.

"I have ceased working on *The Pressure of Time*. Amber Max has said it all." Thomas Disch.

"Amber Max is not an absolute Goddess of Literature. But in this age of clones and computer simulations, she ineluctably approaches that state, arguably." John Clute.

This last quote, as Amber reports in Chapter Eight, "Cut Me Some Slack, Dude!" caused quite a bit of trouble between her and Harley. "He like totally freaked out. ' "Simulations," ' he kept muttering over and over. ' "Simulations." The synchronicity is too weird. He must know. . . . And Jesus, I'm sick of reading your name! I can't stand being unknown. We've got it all, but it's all different than I thought it would be. I wanted to be famous, but instead everybody thinks it's you.' Then he got like totally paranoid and started raving. 'Clute must know the secret. That phrase must be a hidden message to me. He's gonna spill the secret and screw us out of the awards. I'll kill him, I swear it. Gimme that phone!' I had to wrestle it away from him and he only calmed down after playing six hours of Nintendo."

The publication of each new version of *Forever Plus!* was immediately followed by a flood of Nebula recommendations from the members of SFWA. By late summer of 1992, it was clear that all versions would easily make the final Nebula ballot.

At the Worldcon in Orlando that Labor Day, *Forever Plus!* fever was at an incredible pitch. Amber Max, discreetly accompanied by the seemingly insignificant Harley Prout, made her first public appearance. Mobs swarmed around her.

When, on the final day, a representative from the Lucas-Spielberg studio made the announcement that the film of *Forever Plus!* was already in production, the crowd erupted and trashed the entire hotel in its exuberance. The movie was released in time for Christmas, making it eligible for the freshly reinstated Dramatic Production Nebula.

Nineteen-ninety-three broke with *Forever Plus!* mania unabated. The Nebula voting was a mere formality. *Forever Plus!* won in every category, sweeping the board.

At the Nebula Banquet—well, here's Amber:

"I was wearing like this ultra-chic dress from Azzedine Alaïa with my Manolo Blahnik heels. I got up to make my fifth acceptance speech when Harley went apeshit. 'Don't listen to her! I wrote it, me, Harley Prout! Or my program did, which is the same thing!' He tried to rush the stage, but security got to him first. All I could think was, God, my feet are so-o-o-o sore in these shoes! It's like, why now, Harley?"

After the banquet Harley was not to be found. Amber went back home to wait for his return. Now things began to go sour.

The people assigned to translate *Forever Plus!* for foreign editions found that it was impossible to capture the magic that had made it work in English. The neurological effect proved to be language-specific. The whole pretense shattered when, in December of 1993, Harley himself released the machine-code for his neural network to every BBS and publication from *Byte* to *Popular Computing*. Amber's tearful confession on "Entertainment Tonight" finally disillusioned the last of her fans.

The controversy that ensued was enormous. Amber was stripped of all her awards. Publishers tried to reclaim their monies, but Amber was smart enough to hire the law firm of Holland, Dozier, and Holland to represent her, and managed to hold on to it all (minus legal fees, of course).

In her final chapter, "Harley, Come Home," we are presented with a portrait of a repentant, faithful, wiser Amber, longing patiently and publicly for the return of "my Silicon Valley squeeze, my gnarly circuit-bender, my rad lad, the one and only Harley Prout—before the money's all gone."

AT THE RIALTO

Connie Willis

Connie Willis has appeared in every number of the *Nebula Awards* volumes that I've edited: "Schwarzschild Radius" (23), "The Last of the Winnebagos" (24), and "At the Rialto" (25), a cleverly comic look at physicists and particle physics. Ms. Willis won a pair of Nebulas in 1982, for short story ("A Letter from the Clearys") and novelette ("Fire Watch"). She has also won two Hugo Awards. Her books include *Lincoln's Dreams* (John W. Campbell Memorial Award); *Water Witch* and *Light Raid*, with Cynthia Felice; a collection, *Fire Watch*; and her most recent novel, *Doomsday Book*.

Of this award-winning novelette, Ms. Willis writes: "People reading 'At the Rialto' might assume it a mere Flight of Fancy, but it is firmly based on Scientific Fact. Everything I have written about Forest Lawn and quantum theory and Frederick's of Hollywood is Absolutely True—taking into account Heisenberg's Uncertainty Principle, of course; my favorite exhibit of Historical Interest at the Frederick's museum is the one on undergarments of the Fifties, entitled 'Nose Cones and Guided Missiles.'

"Physicists really do hold conferences in cities in Wisconsin, Spencer Tracy and Katharine Hepburn really don't have a square (neither does Harrison Ford, a situation that should be remedied immediately), and Californians really do eat things like free-range bean curd for breakfast. I have of course taken Artistic License here and there. The concession stand at Grauman's Chinese does not sell jujubes, there are at least six charming men in the universe, and the real Tiffany was, as hard as this may be to believe, even dumber."

"Seriousness of mind was a prerequisite for understanding Newtonian physics. I am not convinced it is not a handicap in understanding quantum theory."

Excerpt from Dr. Gedanken's keynote address to the 1989 International Congress of Quantum Physicists Annual Meeting, Hollywood, California

I got to Hollywood around one-thirty and started trying to check into the Rialto.

"Sorry, we don't have any rooms," the girl behind the desk said. "We're all booked up with some science thing."

"I'm with the science thing," I said. "Dr. Ruth Baringer. I reserved a double."

"There are a bunch of Republicans here, too, and a tour group from Finland. They told me when I started work here that they got all these movie people, but the only one so far was that guy who played the friend of that other guy in that one movie. You're not a movie person, are you?"

"No," I said. "I'm with the science thing. Dr. Ruth Baringer."

"My name's Tiffany," she said. "I'm not actually a hotel clerk at all. I'm just working here to pay for my transcendental posture lessons. I'm really a model/actress."

"I'm a quantum physicist," I said, trying to get things back on track. "The name is Ruth Baringer."

She messed with the computer for a minute. "I don't show a reservation for you."

"Maybe it's in Dr. Mendoza's name. I'm sharing a room with her."

She messed with the computer some more. "I don't show a reservation for her either. Are you sure you don't want the Disneyland Hotel? A lot of people get the two confused."

"I want the Rialto," I said, rummaging through my bag for my notebook. "I have a confirmation number. W37420."

She typed it in. "Are you Dr. Gedanken?" she asked.

"Excuse me," an elderly man said.

"I'll be right with you," Tiffany told him. "How long do you plan to stay with us, Dr. Gedanken?" she asked me.

"*Excuse* me," the man said, sounding desperate. He had bushy white hair and a dazed expression, as if he had just been through a horrific experience or had been trying to check into the Rialto.

He wasn't wearing any socks. I wondered if *he* was Dr. Gedanken. Dr. Gedanken was the main reason I'd decided to come to the meeting. I had missed his lecture on wave/particle duality last year, but I had read the text of it in the *ICQP Journal*, and it had actually seemed to make sense, which is more than you can say for most of quantum theory. He was giving the keynote address this year, and I was determined to hear it.

It wasn't Dr. Gedanken. "My name is Dr. Whedbee," the elderly man said. "You gave me the wrong room."

"All our rooms are pretty much the same," Tiffany said. "Except for how many beds they have in them and stuff."

"My room has a *person* in it!" he said. "Dr. Sleeth. From the University of Texas at Austin. She was changing her clothes." His hair seemed to get wilder as he spoke. "She thought I was a serial killer."

"And your name is Dr. Whedbee?" Tiffany asked, fooling with the computer again. "I don't show a reservation for you."

Dr. Whedbee began to cry. Tiffany got out a paper towel, wiped off the counter, and turned back to me. "May I help you?" she said.

Thursday, 7:30–9 P.M. *Opening Ceremonies.* Dr. Halvard Onofrio, University of Maryland at College Park, will speak on the topic, "Doubts Surrounding the Heisenberg Uncertainty Principle." Ballroom.

I finally got my room at five after Tiffany went off duty. Till then I sat around the lobby with Dr. Whedbee, listening to Abey Fields complain about Hollywood.

"What's wrong with Racine?" he said. "Why do we always have to go to these exotic places, like Hollywood? And St. Louis last year wasn't much better. The Institut Henri Poincaré people kept going off to see the arch and Busch Stadium."

"Speaking of St. Louis," Dr. Takumi said, "have you seen David yet?"

"No," I said.

"Oh, really?" she said. "Last year at the annual meeting you two were practically inseparable. Moonlight riverboat rides and all."

"What's on the programming tonight?" I said to Abey.

"David was just here," Dr. Takumi said. "He said to tell you he was going out to look at the stars in the sidewalk."

"That's exactly what I'm talking about," Abey said. "Riverboat rides and movie stars. What do those things have to do with quantum theory? Racine would have been an appropriate setting for a group of physicists. Not like this . . . this . . . do you realize we're practically across the street from Grauman's Chinese Theatre? And Hollywood Boulevard's where all those gangs hang out. If they catch you wearing red or blue, they'll—"

He stopped. "Is that Dr. Gedanken?" he asked, staring at the front desk.

I turned and looked. A short roundish man with a mustache was trying to check in. "No," I said. "That's Dr. Onofrio."

"Oh, yes," Abey said, consulting his program book. "He's speaking tonight at the opening ceremonies. On the Heisenberg uncertainty principle. Are you going?"

"I'm not sure," I said, which was supposed to be a joke, but Abey didn't laugh.

"I must meet Dr. Gedanken. He's just gotten funding for a new project."

I wondered what Dr. Gedanken's new project was—I would have loved to work with him.

"I'm hoping he'll come to my workshop on the wonderful world of quantum physics," Abey said, still watching the desk. Amazingly enough, Dr. Onofrio seemed to have gotten a key and was heading for the elevators. "I think his project has something to do with understanding quantum theory."

Well, that let me out. I didn't understand quantum theory at all. I sometimes had a sneaking suspicion nobody else did either, including Abey Fields, and that they just weren't willing to admit it.

I mean, an electron is a particle except it acts like a wave. In fact, a neutron acts like two waves and interferes with itself (or each other), and you can't really measure any of this stuff properly because of the Heisenberg uncertainty principle, and that isn't the worst of it. When you set up a Josephson junction to figure out what rules the electrons obey, they sneak past the barrier to the other side, and they don't seem to care much about the limits of the speed of light either, and Schrödinger's cat is neither alive nor dead till you open the box, and it all makes about as much sense as Tiffany's calling me Dr. Gedanken.

Which reminded me, I had promised to call Darlene and give her our room number. I didn't have a room number, but if I waited much longer, she'd have left. She was flying to Denver to speak at C.U. and then coming on to Hollywood sometime tomorrow morning.

I interrupted Abey in the middle of his telling me how beautiful Racine was in the winter and went to call her.

"I don't have a room yet," I said when she answered. "Should I leave a message on your answering machine or do you want to give me your number in Denver?"

"Never mind all that," Darlene said. "Have you seen David yet?"

"To illustrate the problems of the concept of wave function, Dr. Schrödinger imagines a cat being put into a box with a piece of uranium, a bottle of poison gas, and a Geiger counter. If a uranium nucleus disintegrates while the cat is in the box, it will release radiation which will set off the Geiger counter and break the bottle of poison gas. Since it is impossible in quantum theory to predict whether a uranium nucleus will disintegrate while the cat is in the box, and only possible to calculate uranium's probable half-life, the cat is neither alive nor dead until we open the box."

from "The Wonderful World of Quantum Physics," a seminar presented at the ICQP Annual Meeting by A. Fields, Ph.D., University of Nebraska at Wahoo

I completely forgot to warn Darlene about Tiffany, the model-slash-actress.

"What do you mean you're trying to avoid David?" she had asked me at least three times. "Why would you do a stupid thing like that?"

Because in St. Louis I ended up on a riverboat in the moonlight and didn't make it back until the conference was over.

"Because I want to attend the programming," I said the third time around, "not a wax museum. I am a middle-aged woman."

"And David is a middle-aged man who, I might add, is absolutely charming. In fact, he may be the last charming man left in the universe."

"Charm is for quarks," I said and hung up, feeling smug until I remembered I hadn't told her about Tiffany. I went back to the front desk, thinking maybe Dr. Onofrio's success signaled a change. Tiffany asked, "May I help you?" and left me standing there.

After a while I gave up and went back to the red and gold sofas.

"David was here again," Dr. Takumi said. "He said to tell you he was going to the wax museum."

"There *are* no wax museums in Racine," Abey said.

"What's the programming for tonight?" I said, taking Abey's program away from him.

"There's a mixer at six-thirty and the opening ceremonies in the ballroom and then some seminars." I read the descriptions of the seminars. There was one on the Josephson junction. Electrons were able to somehow tunnel through an insulated barrier even though they didn't have the required energy. Maybe I could somehow get a room without checking in.

"If we were in Racine," Abey said, looking at his watch, "we'd already be checked in and on our way to dinner."

Dr. Onofrio emerged from the elevator, still carrying his bags. He came over and sank down on the sofa next to Abey.

"Did they give you a room with a semi-naked woman in it?" Dr. Whedbee asked.

"I don't know," Dr. Onofrio said. "I couldn't find it." He looked sadly at the key. "They gave me 1282, but the room numbers only go up to seventy-five."

"I think I'll attend the seminar on chaos," I said.

"The most serious difficulty quantum theory faces today is not the inherent limitation of measurement capability or the EPR paradox. It is the lack of a paradigm. Quantum theory has no working model, no metaphor that properly defines it."
Excerpt from Dr. Gedanken's keynote address

I got to my room at six, after a brief skirmish with the bellboy-slash-actor who couldn't remember where he'd stored my suitcase, and unpacked. My clothes, which had been permanent press all the way from MIT, underwent a complete wave function collapse the moment I opened my suitcase, and came out looking like Schrö-dinger's almost-dead cat.

By the time I had called housekeeping for an iron, taken a bath, given up on the iron, and steamed a dress in the shower, I had missed the "Mixer with Munchies" and was half an hour late for Dr. Onofrio's opening remarks.

I opened the door to the ballroom as quietly as I could and slid inside. I had hoped they would be late getting started, but a man I didn't recognize was already introducing the speaker. "—and an inspiration to all of us in the field."

I dived for the nearest chair and sat down.

"Hi," David said. "I've been looking all over for you. Where were you?"

"Not at the wax museum," I whispered.

"You should have been," he whispered back. "It was great. They had John Wayne, Elvis, and Tiffany the model-slash-actress with the brain of a pea-slash-amoeba."

"Shh," I said.

"—the person we've all been waiting to hear, Dr. Ringgit Dinari."

"What happened to Dr. Onofrio?" I asked.

"Shhh," David said.

Dr. Dinari looked a lot like Dr. Onofrio. She was short, roundish, and mustached, and was wearing a rainbow-striped caftan. "I will be your guide this evening into a strange new world," she said, "a world where all that you thought you knew, all common sense, all accepted wisdom, must be discarded. A world where all the rules have changed and it sometimes seems there are no rules at all."

She sounded just like Dr. Onofrio, too. He had given this same speech two years ago in Cincinnati. I wondered if he had undergone some strange transformation during his search for room 1282 and was now a woman.

"Before I go any farther," Dr. Dinari said, "how many of you have already channeled?"

"Newtonian physics had as its model the machine. The metaphor of the machine, with its interrelated parts, its gears and wheels, its causes and effects, was what made it possible to think about Newtonian physics."

Excerpt from Dr. Gedanken's keynote address

"You *knew* we were in the wrong place," I hissed at David when we got out to the lobby.

When we stood up to leave, Dr. Dinari had extended her pudgy hand in its rainbow-striped sleeve and called out in a voice a lot like

Charlton Heston's, "O Unbelievers! Leave not, for here only is reality!"

"Actually, channeling would explain a lot," David said, grinning.

"If the opening remarks aren't in the ballroom, where are they?"

"Beats me," he said. "Want to go see the Capitol Records Building? It's shaped like a stack of records."

"I want to go to the opening remarks."

"The beacon on top blinks out Hollywood in Morse code."

I went over to the front desk.

"Can I help you?" the clerk behind the desk said. "My name is Natalie, and I'm an—"

"Where is the ICQP meeting this evening?" I said.

"They're in the ballroom."

"I'll bet you didn't have any dinner," David said. "I'll buy you an ice cream cone. There's this great place that has the ice cream cone Ryan O'Neal bought for Tatum in *Paper Moon*."

"A channeler's in the ballroom," I told Natalie. "I'm looking for the ICQP."

She fiddled with the computer. "I'm sorry. I don't show a reservation for them."

"How about Grauman's Chinese?" David said. "You want reality? You want Charlton Heston? You want to see quantum theory in action?" He grabbed my hands. "Come with me," he said seriously.

In St. Louis I had suffered a wave function collapse a lot like what had happened to my clothes when I opened the suitcase. I had ended up on a riverboat halfway to New Orleans that time. It happened again, and the next thing I knew I was walking around the courtyard of Grauman's Chinese Theatre, eating an ice cream cone and trying to fit my feet in Myrna Loy's footprints.

She must have been a midget or had her feet bound as a child. So, apparently, had Debbie Reynolds, Dorothy Lamour, and Wallace Beery. The only footprints I came close to fitting were Donald Duck's.

"I see this as a map of the microcosm," David said, sweeping his hand over the slightly irregular pavement of printed and signed cement squares. "See, there are all these tracks. We know something's been here, and the prints are pretty much the same, only every once in a while you've got this," he knelt down and pointed at the print of John Wayne's clenched fist, "and over here," he walked toward the box office and pointed to the print of Betty Grable's leg, "and we can figure out the signatures, but what is this reference to 'Sid' on all these squares? And what does this mean?"

He pointed at Red Skelton's square. It said, "Thanks Sid We Dood It."

"You keep thinking you've found a pattern," David said, crossing over to the other side, "but Van Johnson's square is kind of sandwiched in here at an angle between Esther Williams and Cantinflas, and who the hell is May Robson? And why are all these squares over here empty?"

He had managed to maneuver me over behind the display of Academy Award winners. It was an accordionlike wrought-iron screen. I was in the fold between 1944 and 1945.

"And as if that isn't enough, you suddenly realize you're standing in the courtyard. You're not even in the theater."

"And that's what you think is happening in quantum theory?" I said weakly. I was backed up into Bing Crosby, who had won for Best Actor in *Going My Way*. "You think we're not in the theater yet?"

"I think we know as much about quantum theory as we can figure out about May Robson from her footprints," he said, putting his hand up to Ingrid Bergman's cheek (Best Actress, *Gaslight*) and blocking my escape. "I don't think we understand anything *about* quantum theory, not tunneling, not complementarity." He leaned toward me. "Not passion."

The best movie of 1945 was *Lost Weekend*. "Dr. Gedanken understands it," I said, disentangling myself from the Academy Award winners and David. "Did you know he's putting together a new research team for a big project on understanding quantum theory?"

"Yes," David said. "Want to see a movie?"

"There's a seminar on chaos at nine," I said, stepping over the Marx Brothers. "I have to get back."

"If it's chaos you want, you should stay right here," he said, stopping to look at Irene Dunne's handprints. "We could see the movie and then go have dinner. There's this place near Hollywood and Vine that has the mashed potatoes Richard Dreyfus made into Devil's Tower in *Close Encounters*."

"I want to meet Dr. Gedanken," I said, making it safely to the sidewalk. I looked back at David. He had gone back to the other side of the courtyard and was looking at Roy Rogers's signature.

"Are you kidding? He doesn't understand it any better than we do."

"Well, at least he's trying."

"So am I. The problem is, how can one neutron interfere with itself, and why are there only two of Trigger's hoofprints here?"

"It's eight fifty-five," I said. "I am going to the chaos seminar."

"If you can find it," he said, getting down on one knee to look at the signature.

"I'll find it," I said grimly.

He stood up and grinned at me, his hands in his pockets. "It's a great movie," he said.

It was happening again. I turned and practically ran across the street.

"*Benji Nine* is showing," he shouted after me. "He accidentally exchanges bodies with a Siamese cat."

Thursday, 9–10 P.M. "The Science of Chaos." I. Durcheinander, University of Leipzig. A seminar on the structure of chaos. Principles of chaos will be discussed, including the Butterfly Effect, fractals, and insolid billowing. Clara Bow Room.

I couldn't find the chaos seminar. The Clara Bow Room, where it was supposed to be, was empty. A meeting of vegetarians was next door in the Fatty Arbuckle Room, and all the other conference rooms were locked. The channeler was still in the ballroom. "Come!" she commanded when I opened the door. "Understanding awaits!" I went upstairs to bed.

I had forgotten to call Darlene. She would have left for Denver already, but I called her answering machine and told it the room number in case she picked up her messages. In the morning I would have to tell the front desk to give her a key. I went to bed.

I didn't sleep well. The air conditioner went off during the night, which meant I didn't have to steam my suit when I got up the next morning. I got dressed and went downstairs. The programming started at nine o'clock with Abey Fields's Wonderful World workshop in the Mary Pickford Room, a breakfast buffet in the ballroom, and a slide presentation on "Delayed Choice Experiments" in Cecil B. DeMille A on the mezzanine level.

The breakfast buffet sounded wonderful, even though it always turns out to be urn coffee and donuts. I hadn't had anything but an ice cream cone since noon the day before, but if David were around, he would be somewhere close to the food, and I wanted to steer clear of him. Last night it had been Grauman's Chinese. Today I was likely to end up at Knott's Berry Farm. I wasn't going to let that happen, even if he was charming.

It was pitch-dark inside Cecil B. DeMille A. Even the slide on the screen up front appeared to be black. "As you can see," Dr. Lvov said, "the laser pulse is already in motion before the experimenter sets up the wave or particle detector." He clicked to the next slide, which was dark gray. "We used a Mach-Zender interferometer with two mirrors and a particle detector. For the first series of tries we allowed the experimenter to decide which apparatus he would use by whatever method he wished. For the second series, we used that most primitive of randomizers—"

He clicked again, to a white slide with black polka dots that gave off enough light for me to be able to spot an empty chair on the aisle ten rows up. I hurried to get to it before the slide changed, and sat down.

"—a pair of dice. Alley's experiments had shown us that when the particle detector was in place, the light was detected as a particle, and when the wave detector was in place, the light showed wavelike behavior, no matter when the choice of apparatus was made."

"Hi," David said. "You've missed five black slides, two gray ones, and a white with black polka dots."

"Shh," I said.

"In our two series, we hoped to ascertain whether the consciousness of the decision affected the outcome." Dr. Lvov clicked to another black slide. "As you can see, the graph shows no effective difference between the tries in which the experimenter chose the detection apparatus and those in which the apparatus was randomly chosen."

"You want to go get some breakfast?" David whispered.

"I already ate," I whispered back, and waited for my stomach to growl and give me away. It did.

"There's a great place down near Hollywood and Vine that has the waffles Katharine Hepburn made for Spencer Tracy in *Woman of the Year.*"

"Shh," I said.

"And after breakfast, we could go to Frederick's of Hollywood and see the bra museum."

"Will you please be quiet? I can't hear."

"Or see," he said, but he subsided more or less for the remaining ninety-two black, gray, and polka-dotted slides.

Dr. Lvov turned on the lights and blinked smilingly at the audience. "Consciousness had no discernible effect on the results of the experiment. As one of my lab assistants put it, 'The little devil knows what you're going to do before you know it yourself.' "

This was apparently supposed to be a joke, but I didn't think it was very funny. I opened my program and tried to find something to go to that David wouldn't be caught dead at.

"Are you two going to breakfast?" Dr. Thibodeaux asked.

"Yes," David said.

"No," I said.

"Dr. Hotard and I wished to eat somewhere that is *vraiment* Hollywood."

"David knows just the place," I said. "He's been telling me about this great place where they have the grapefruit James Cagney shoved in Mae Clark's face in *Public Enemy.*"

Dr. Hotard hurried up, carrying a camera and four guidebooks. "And then perhaps you would show us Grauman's Chinese Theatre," he asked David.

"Of course he will," I said. "I'm sorry I can't go with you, but I promised Dr. Verikovsky I'd be at his lecture on Boolean logic. And after Grauman's Chinese, David can take you to the bra museum at Frederick's of Hollywood."

"And the Brown Derby?" Thibodeaux asked. "I have heard it is shaped like a *chapeau.*"

They dragged him off. I watched till they were safely out of the lobby and then ducked upstairs and into Dr. Whedbee's lecture on information theory. Dr. Whedbee wasn't there.

"He went to find an overhead projector," Dr. Takumi said. She had half a donut on a paper plate in one hand and a Styrofoam cup in the other.

"Did you get that at the breakfast buffet?" I asked.

"Yes. It was the last one. And they ran out of coffee right after I got there. You weren't in Abey Fields's thing, were you?" She set the coffee cup down and took a bite of the donut.

"No," I said, wondering if I should try to take her by surprise or just wrestle the donut away from her.

"You didn't miss anything. He raved the whole time about how we should have had the meeting in Racine." She popped the last piece of donut in her mouth. "Have you seen David yet?"

> Friday, 9–10 P.M. "The Eureka Experiment: A Slide Presentation." J. Lvov, Eureka College. Descriptions, results, and conclusions of Lvov's delayed conscious/randomed choice experiments. Cecil B. DeMille A.

Dr. Whedbee eventually came in carrying an overhead projector, the cord trailing behind him. He plugged it in. The light didn't go on.

"Here," Dr. Takumi said, handing me her plate and cup. "I have one of these at Caltech. It needs its fractal basin boundaries adjusted." She whacked the side of the projector.

There weren't even any crumbs left of the donut. There was about a millimeter of coffee in the bottom of the cup. I was about to stoop to new depths when she hit the projector again. The light came on. "I learned that in the chaos seminar last night," she said, grabbing the cup away from me and draining it. "You should have been there. The Clara Bow Room was packed."

"I believe I'm ready to begin," Dr. Whedbee said. Dr. Takumi and I sat down. "Information is the transmission of meaning," Dr. Whedbee said. He wrote "meaning" or possibly "information" on the screen with a green Magic Marker. "When information is randomized, meaning cannot be transmitted, and we have a state of entropy." He

wrote it under "meaning" with a red Magic Marker. His handwriting
appeared to be completely illegible.

"States of entropy vary from low entropy, such as the mild static
on your car radio, to high entropy, a state of complete disorder, of
randomness and confusion, in which no information at all is being
communicated."

Oh, my God, I thought. I forgot to tell the hotel about Darlene.
The next time Dr. Whedbee bent over to inscribe hieroglyphics on
the screen, I sneaked out and went down to the desk, hoping Tiffany
hadn't come on duty yet. She had.

"May I help you?" she asked.

"I'm in room 663," I said. "I'm sharing a room with Dr. Darlene Mendoza. She's coming in this morning, and she'll be need-
ing a key."

"For what?" Tiffany said.

"To get into the room. I may be in one of the lectures when she
gets here."

"Why doesn't she have a key?"

"Because she isn't here yet."

"I thought you said she was sharing a room with you."

"She *will* be sharing a room with me. Room 663. Her name is
Darlene Mendoza."

"And your name?" she asked, hands poised over the computer.

"Ruth Baringer."

"We don't show a reservation for you."

*"We have made impressive advances in quantum physics in the
ninety years since Planck's constant, but they have by and large been
advances in technology, not theory. We can only make advances in
theory when we have a model we can visualize."*
                                  Excerpt from Dr. Gedanken's keynote address

I high-entropied with Tiffany for a while on the subjects of my
not having a reservation and the air conditioning and then switched
back suddenly to the problem of Darlene's key, in the hope of catching
her off-guard. It worked about as well as Alley's delayed choice
experiments.

In the middle of my attempting to explain that Darlene was not the air-conditioning repairman, Abey Fields came up.

"Have you seen Dr. Gedanken?"

I shook my head.

"I was sure he'd come to my Wonderful World workshop, but he didn't, and the hotel says they can't find his reservation," he said, scanning the lobby. "I found out what his new project is, incidentally, and I'd be perfect for it. He's going to find a paradigm for quantum theory. Is that him?" he said, pointing at an elderly man getting in the elevator.

"I think that's Dr. Whedbee," I said, but he had already sprinted across the lobby to the elevator.

He nearly made it. The elevator slid to a close just as he got there. He pushed the elevator button several times to make the door open again, and when that didn't work, tried to readjust its fractal basin boundaries. I turned back to the desk.

"May I help you?" Tiffany said.

"You may," I said. "My roommate, Darlene Mendoza, will be arriving some time this morning. She's a producer. She's here to cast the female lead in a new movie starring Robert Redford and Harrison Ford. When she gets here, give her her key. And fix the air conditioning."

"Yes, ma'am," she said.

"The Josephson junction is designed so that electrons must obtain additional energy to surmount the energy barrier. It has been found, however, that some electrons simply tunnel, as Heinz Pagel put it, 'right through the wall.' "

from "The Wonderful World of Quantum Physics," A. Fields, UNW

Abey had stopped banging on the elevator button and was trying to pry the elevator doors apart. I went out the side door and up to Hollywood Boulevard. David's restaurant was near Hollywood and Vine. I turned the other direction, toward Grauman's Chinese, and ducked into the first restaurant I saw.

"I'm Stephanie," the waitress said. "How many are there in your party?"

There was no one remotely in my vicinity. "Are you an actress-slash-model?" I asked her.

"Yes," she said. "I'm working here part-time to pay for my holistic hairstyling lessons."

"There's one of me," I said, holding up my forefinger to make it perfectly clear. "I want a table away from the window."

She led me to a table in front of the window, handed me a menu the size of the macrocosm, and put another one down across from me. "Our breakfast specials today are papaya stuffed with salmonberries and nasturtium/radicchio salad with a balsamic vinaigrette. I'll take your order when your other party arrives."

I stood the extra menu up so it hid me from the window, opened the other one, and read the breakfast entrees. They all seemed to have cilantro or lemongrass in their names. I wondered if radicchio could possibly be Californian for donut.

"Hi," David said, grabbing the standing-up menu and sitting down. "The sea urchin pâté looks good."

I was actually glad to see him. "How did you get here?" I asked.

"Tunneling," he said. "What exactly is extra-virgin olive oil?"

"I wanted a donut," I said pitifully.

He took my menu away from me, laid it on the table, and stood up. "There's a great place next door that's got the donut Clark Gable taught Claudette Colbert how to dunk in *It Happened One Night*."

The great place was probably out in Long Beach someplace, but I was too weak with hunger to resist him. I stood up. Stephanie hurried over.

"Will there be anything else?" she asked.

"We're leaving," David said.

"Okay, then," she said, tearing a check off her pad and slapping it down on the table. "I hope you enjoyed your breakfast."

"Finding such a paradigm is difficult, if not impossible. Due to Planck's constant the world we see is largely dominated by Newtonian mechanics. Particles are particles, waves are waves, and objects do not suddenly vanish through walls and reappear on the other side. It is only on the subatomic level that quantum effects dominate."
Excerpt from Dr. Gedanken's keynote address

The restaurant was next door to Grauman's Chinese, which made me a little nervous, but it had eggs and bacon and toast and orange juice and coffee. And donuts.

"I thought you were having breakfast with Dr. Thibodeaux and Dr. Hotard," I said, dunking one in my coffee. "What happened to them?"

"They went to Forest Lawn. Dr. Hotard wanted to see the church where Ronald Reagan got married."

"He got married at Forest Lawn?"

He took a bite of my donut. "In the Wee Kirk of the Heather. Did you know Forest Lawn's got the World's Largest Oil Painting Incorporating a Religious Theme?"

"So why didn't you go with them?"

"And miss the movie?" He grabbed both my hands across the table. "There's a matinee at two o'clock. Come with me."

I could feel things starting to collapse. "I have to get back," I said, trying to disentangle my hands. "There's a panel on the EPR paradox at two o'clock."

"There's another showing at five. And one at eight."

"Dr. Gedanken's giving the keynote address at eight."

"You know what the problem is?" he said, still holding on to my hands. "The problem is, it isn't really Grauman's Chinese Theatre, it's Mann's, so Sid isn't even around to ask. Like, why do some pairs like Joanne Woodward and Paul Newman share the same square and other pairs don't? Like Ginger Rogers and Fred Astaire?"

"You know what the problem is?" I said, wrenching my hands free. "The problem is you don't take anything seriously. This is a conference, but you don't care anything about the programming or hearing Dr. Gedanken speak or trying to understand quantum theory!" I fumbled in my purse for some money for the check.

"I thought that was what we were talking about," David said, sounding surprised. "The problem is, where do those lion statues that guard the door fit in? And what about all those empty spaces?"

Friday, 2–3 P.M. *Panel Discussion on the EPR Paradox.* I. Ta-kumi, moderator, R. Iverson, L. S. Ping. A discussion of the latest research in singlet-state correlations including nonlocal influences, the Calcutta proposal, and passion. Keystone Kops Room.

I went up to my room as soon as I got back to the Rialto to see if Darlene was there yet. She wasn't, and when I tried to call the desk, the phone wouldn't work. I went back down to the registration desk. There was no one there. I waited fifteen minutes and then went into the panel on the EPR paradox.

"The Einstein-Podolsky-Rosen paradox cannot be reconciled with quantum theory," Dr. Takumi was saying. "I don't care what the experiments seem to indicate. Two electrons at opposite ends of the universe can't affect each other simultaneously without destroying the entire theory of the space-time continuum."

She was right. Even if it were possible to find a model of quantum theory, what about the EPR paradox? If an experimenter measured one of a pair of electrons that had originally collided, it changed the cross-correlation of the other instantaneously, even if the electrons were light-years apart. It was as if they were eternally linked by that one collision, sharing the same square forever, even if they were on opposite sides of the universe.

"If the electrons *communicated* instantaneously, I'd agree with you," Dr. Iverson said, "but they don't, they simply influence each other. Dr. Shimony defined this influence in his paper on passion, and my experiment clearly—"

I thought of David leaning over me between the best pictures of 1944 and 1945, saying, "I think we know as much about quantum theory as we do about May Robson from her footprints."

"You can't explain it away by inventing new terms," Dr. Takumi said.

"I completely disagree," Dr. Ping said. "Passion at a distance is not just an invented term. It's a demonstrated phenomenon."

It certainly is, I thought, thinking about David taking the macro-cosmic menu out of the window and saying, "The sea urchin pâté looks good." It didn't matter where the electron went after the collision. Even if it went in the opposite direction from Hollywood and Vine, even if it stood a menu in the window to hide it, the other electron would still come and rescue it from the radicchio and buy it a donut.

"A demonstrated phenomenon!" Dr. Takumi said. "Ha!" She banged her moderator's gavel for emphasis.

"Are you saying passion doesn't exist?" Dr. Ping said, getting very red in the face.

"I'm saying one measly experiment is hardly a demonstrated phenomenon."

"One measly experiment! I spent five years on this project!" Dr. Iverson said, shaking his fist at her. "I'll show you passion at a distance!"

"Try it, and I'll adjust your fractal basin boundaries!" Dr. Takumi said, and hit him over the head with the gavel.

"Yet finding a paradigm is not impossible. Newtonian physics is not a machine. It simply shares some of the attributes of a machine. We must find a model somewhere in the visible world that shares the often bizarre attributes of quantum physics. Such a model, unlikely as it sounds, surely exists somewhere, and it is up to us to find it."
Excerpt from Dr. Gedanken's keynote address

I went up to my room before the police came. Darlene still wasn't there, and the phone and air conditioning still weren't working. I was really beginning to get worried. I walked up to Grauman's Chinese to find David, but he wasn't there. Dr. Whedbee and Dr. Sleeth were behind the Academy Award Winners folding screen.

"You haven't seen David, have you?" I asked.

Dr. Whedbee removed his hand from Norma Shearer's cheek.

"He left," Dr. Sleeth said, disentangling herself from the Best Movie of 1929–30.

"He said he was going out to Forest Lawn," Dr. Whedbee said, trying to smooth down his bushy white hair.

"Have you seen Dr. Mendoza? She was supposed to get in this morning."

They hadn't seen her, and neither had Drs. Hotard and Thibodeaux, who stopped me in the lobby and showed me a postcard of Aimee Semple McPherson's tomb. Tiffany had gone off duty. Natalie couldn't find my reservation. I went back up to the room to wait, thinking Darlene might call.

The air conditioning still wasn't fixed. I fanned myself with a Hollywood brochure and then opened it up and read it. There was a map of the courtyard of Grauman's Chinese on the back cover. Deborah Kerr and Yul Brynner didn't have a square together either, and Katharine Hepburn and Spencer Tracy weren't even on the map. She had made him waffles in *Woman of the Year*, and they hadn't even given them a square. I wondered if Tiffany the model-slash-actress had been in charge of assigning the cement. I could see her looking blankly at Spencer Tracy and saying, "I don't show a reservation for you."

What exactly was a model-slash-actress? Did it mean she was a model *or* an actress or a model *and* an actress? She certainly wasn't a hotel clerk. Maybe electrons were the Tiffanys of the microcosm, and that explained their wave-slash-particle duality. Maybe they weren't really electrons at all. Maybe they were just working part-time at being electrons to pay for their singlet-state lessons.

Darlene still hadn't called by seven o'clock. I stopped fanning myself and tried to open a window. It wouldn't budge. The problem was, nobody knew anything about quantum theory. All we had to go on were a few colliding electrons that nobody could see and that couldn't be measured properly because of the Heisenberg uncertainty principle. And there was chaos to consider, and entropy, and all those empty spaces. We didn't even know who May Robson was.

At seven-thirty the phone rang. It was Darlene.

"What happened?" I said. "Where are you?"

"At the Beverly Wilshire."

"In Beverly Hills?"

"Yes. It's a long story. When I got to the Rialto, the hotel clerk, I think her name was Tiffany, told me you weren't there. She said they were booked solid with some science thing and had had to send the overflow to other hotels. She said you were at the Beverly Wilshire in Room 1027. How's David?"

"Impossible," I said. "He's spent the whole conference looking at Deanna Durbin's footprints at Grauman's Chinese Theatre and trying to talk me into going to the movies."

"And are you going?"

"I can't. Dr. Gedanken's giving the keynote address in half an hour."

"He is?" Darlene said, sounding surprised. "Just a minute." There was a silence, and then she came back on and said, "I think you should go to the movies. David's one of the last two charming men in the universe."

"But he doesn't take quantum theory seriously. Dr. Gedanken is hiring a research team to design a paradigm, and David keeps talking about the beacon on top of the Capitol Records Building."

"You know, he may be onto something there. I mean, seriousness was all right for Newtonian physics, but maybe quantum theory needs a different approach. Sid says—"

"Sid?"

"This guy who's taking me to the movies tonight. It's a long story. Tiffany gave me the wrong room number, and I walked in on this guy in his underwear. He's a quantum physicist. He was supposed to be staying at the Rialto, but Tiffany couldn't find his reservation."

"The major implication of wave/particle duality is that an electron has no precise location. It exists in a superposition of probable locations. Only when the experimenter observes the electron does it 'collapse' into a location."

"The Wonderful World of Quantum Physics," A. Fields, UNW

Forest Lawn had closed at five o'clock. I looked it up in the Hollywood brochure after Darlene hung up. There was no telling where he might have gone: the Brown Derby or the La Brea Tar Pits or some great place near Hollywood and Vine that had the alfalfa sprouts John Hurt ate right before his chest exploded in *Alien*.

At least I knew where Dr. Gedanken was. I changed my clothes and got in the elevator, thinking about wave/particle duality and fractals and high entropy states and delayed choice experiments. The problem was, where could you find a paradigm that would make it possible to visualize quantum theory when you had to include Josephson junctions and passion and all those empty spaces? It wasn't possible. You had to have more to work with than a few footprints and the impression of Betty Grable's leg.

The elevator door opened, and Abey Fields pounced on me. "I've been looking all over for you," he said. "You haven't seen Dr. Gedanken, have you?"

"Isn't he in the ballroom?"

"No," he said. "He's already fifteen minutes late, and nobody's seen him. You have to sign this," he said, shoving a clipboard at me.

"What is it?"

"It's a petition." He grabbed it back from me. " 'We the under-signed demand that annual meetings of the International Congress of Quantum Physicists henceforth be held in appropriate locations.' Like Racine," he added, shoving the clipboard at me again. "*Unlike* Hollywood."

Hollywood.

"Are you aware it took the average ICQP delegate two hours and thirty-six minutes to check in? They even sent some of the delegates to a hotel in Glendale."

"And Beverly Hills," I said absently. Hollywood. Bra museums and the Marx Brothers and gangs that would kill you if you wore red or blue and Tiffany/Stephanie and the World's Largest Oil Painting Incorporating a Religious Theme.

"Beverly Hills," Abey muttered, pulling an automatic pencil out of his pocket protector and writing a note to himself. "I'm presenting the petition during Dr. Gedanken's speech. Well, go on, sign it," he said, handing me the pencil. "Unless you want the annual meeting to be here at the Rialto next year."

I handed the clipboard back to him. "I think from now on the annual meeting might be here every year," I said, and took off running for Grauman's Chinese.

"*When we have that paradigm, one that embraces both the logical and the nonsensical aspects of quantum theory, we will be able to look past the colliding electrons and the mathematics and see the microcosm in all its astonishing beauty.*"

Excerpt from Dr. Gedanken's keynote address

"I want a ticket to *Benji Nine*," I told the girl at the box office. Her name tag said, "Welcome to Hollywood. My name is Kimberly."

"Which theater?" she said.

"Grauman's Chinese," I said, thinking, This is no time for a high entropy state.

"Which theater?"

I looked up at the marquee. *Benji IX* was showing in all three theaters, the huge main theater and the two smaller ones on either side. "They're doing audience reaction surveys," Kimberly said. "Each theater has a different ending."

"Which one's in the main theater?"

"I don't know. I just work here part-time to pay for my organic breathing lessons."

"Do you have any dice?" I asked, and then realized I was going about this all wrong. This was quantum physics, not Newtonian. It didn't matter which theater I chose or which seat I sat down in. This was a delayed choice experiment and David was already in flight.

"The one with the happy ending," I said.

"Center theater," she said.

I walked past the stone lions and into the lobby. Rhonda Fleming and some Chinese wax figures were sitting inside a glass case next to the door to the rest rooms. There was a huge painted screen behind the concessions stand. I bought a box of Raisinets, a tub of popcorn, and a box of jujubes and went inside the theater.

It was bigger than I had imagined. Rows and rows of empty red chairs curved between the huge pillars and up to the red curtains where the screen must be. The walls were covered with intricate drawings. I stood there, holding my jujubes and Raisinets and popcorn, staring at the chandelier overhead. It was an elaborate gold sunburst surrounded by silver dragons. I had never imagined it was anything like this.

The lights went down, and the red curtains opened, revealing an inner curtain like a veil across the screen. I went down the dark aisle and sat down in one of the seats. "Hi," I said, and handed the Raisinets to David.

"Where have you been?" he said. "The movie's about to start."

"I know," I said. I leaned across him and handed Darlene her popcorn and Dr. Gedanken his jujubes. "I was working on the paradigm for quantum theory."

"And?" Dr. Gedanken said, opening his jujubes.

"And you're both wrong," I said. "It isn't Grauman's Chinese. It isn't movies either, Dr. Gedanken."

"Sid," Dr. Gedanken said. "If we're all going to be on the same research team, I think we should use first names."

"If it isn't Grauman's Chinese or the movies, what is it?" Darlene asked, eating popcorn.

"It's Hollywood."

"Hollywood," Dr. Gedanken said thoughtfully.

"Hollywood," I said. "Stars in the sidewalk and buildings that look like stacks of records and hats, and radicchio and audience surveys and bra museums. And the movies. And Grauman's Chinese."

"And the Rialto," David said.

"Especially the Rialto."

"And the ICQP," Dr. Gedanken said.

I thought about Dr. Lvov's black and gray slides and the disappearing chaos seminar and Dr. Whedbee writing "meaning" or possibly "information" on the overhead projector. "And the ICQP," I said.

"Did Dr. Takumi really hit Dr. Iverson over the head with a gavel?" Darlene asked.

"Shh," David said. "I think the movie's starting." He took hold of my hand. Darlene settled back with her popcorn, and Dr. Gedanken put his feet up on the chair in front of him. The inner curtain opened, and the screen lit up.

Richard Grant

Richard Grant is an ambitious and talented young writer with an admirable track record. His novels include *Saraband of Lost Time*, which was a runner-up for the 1985 Philip K. Dick Award; the lovely *sui generis* fantasy *Rumors of Spring*; the Nabokovian *Views from the Oldest House*; and a new SF novel, *Through the Heart*, that he calls a straightforward tale with a single narrative consciousness and an uncluttered plot line.

Lately, Grant has begun to write essays—at once theoretical, pragmatic, and impassioned—about SF writing.

"A work of fiction is a continuum created by its sentences."

With this startling but apt definition as fuel, Grant takes us on the following thoughtful and thought-provoking trip—a journey into the heart of how fiction is made, what it can mean, how it is experienced, and why the best of it is so powerful and enriching that it can actually change lives. In spite of a quibble or two with certain of Grant's opinions, I find myself hear-hearing his essay's primary argument and admiring both its eloquence and its civilized tone. Moreover, Grant offers a challenge to every caring would-be writer of science fiction, speculative fiction, fantasy, magic realism, technosurrealism, or whatever-monicker-it-has-today, that our field ignores only at its peril.

If you've made it through Vladimir Nabokov's *Ada*, you will have deduced, as young Van does, three main facts (though not the same ones as the naked protagonist): It gets easier after the first two chapters. It contains some of the best eroticism in literature. And it is a masterwork of science fiction, a story set in a world that is an artistic sibling of our own, with efficient trains but no electricity, where Russia is "a quaint synonym of Estoty," where all the days are long and all the nights are luminous—a *haut monde*, expatriate's Lake Wobegon.

I mention this not to claim any new territory for our expansionist genre but by way of establishing an æsthetic reference point. I want to expound a theory of fiction, and in particular of science fiction, that is somewhat at odds with the prevailing way of thinking. I do not argue that the orthodox position is wrong, or that my theory is better. I merely suggest that there is more than a single approach to fiction, and therefore more than a single standard by which the quality of a work of fiction may be judged. Perhaps if we can realize this, we can come a little closer to understanding the literary mainstream, and to understanding how people in the mainstream perceive us.

Let us call the orthodox theory of science fiction the SF Standard. John Shirley has defined the tenets of the Standard (which he calls the Clarion/Milford Standard) as follows:

1. "Well-rounded" characterization.
2. Clear sentence structure.
3. Ideas supported by strong internal logic.

All of which, as Shirley says, "is either harmless or to the good, but it's hardly a world-class goal." I would say that none of this constitutes a goal at all, but simply a method. The SF Standard, as one might expect, addresses itself to the question of *how* to write, not the more fundamental question of *why* to write.

For many science fiction writers, of course, this question has at least one obvious answer: To entertain.

Yes, well, but. Some of us are highly entertained by seed catalogs. What we mean to say is, we write fiction in order to tell a story.

And what is a story? A story is, you know, kind of like a plot. You've got this main character, see, and you've got this conflict, and you've got this resolution at the end. This is a story. This is what Ursula Le Guin calls the Story of the Hero. Such a story, as Le Guin notes, obeys clear laws: ". . . first, that the proper shape of the narrative is that of the arrow or spear, starting here and going straight there and *thok!* hitting its mark (which drops dead); second, that the central concern of narrative, including the novel, is conflict; and third, that the story isn't any good if he [the hero] isn't in it."

This suggests that the SF Standard should be amended so as to specify that one of the "well-rounded" characters be a hero, and that it should include a further point:

4. Conflict.

To which I would add one more, though perhaps it is stating the obvious:

5. A fictional world, differing in some respect from our own (for otherwise the story would not be science fiction).

Five things, then, make up the SF Standard.

ONE NOTES a certain roundness to this. The purpose of a story is to entertain, and the way to entertain is to tell a story. This is, on the face of it, a fully satisfying æsthetic, a sufficient answer to the question *why*, for it underlies the great body of fantasy and science fiction.

To be sure, one does hear certain other and more high-minded responses, chiefly from the "What if?" contingent. We write, these worthies say, in order to pose important questions about the future of society. We write in order to sound a warning. We write in order to give hope. We write in order to change the course of events.

And how do we do this? Why, by telling a good story, of course. By creating well-rounded characters. By using our fictional worlds to support our ideas. And so we are back around the campfire again, listening to the exploits of some hero, or some anti-hero, some reluctant hero, some unlikely hero. And then the monster reared its head. And then the maiden shrieked. And then the coked-out virtual punk emulation from Hell hurled his nuclear-tipped psi-ray superconducting wetware shaft, which self-iterated through cybertime and *thok!* hit the adroitly foreshadowed climax of the plot (causing the reader to drop five bucks for the paperback).

Ah, that was a good one. Please pass the mastodon.

It must have been somewhere in high school—I'm thinking maybe ninth grade—that we were given the basic tools of literary criticism. It would have been early in the year, before we had gotten far through that godawful anthology of boring writers whom no one has ever voluntarily read. *The Experience of Literature*, this might have been called. At the beginning of the book was a chapter written by one of its editors, the same humorless pedagogue who thought it would be a real good idea for you to read "The Chrysanthemums" by John Steinbeck; this chapter was called The Elements of a Story. And on that day, hovering before the dusty void of the blackboard, the teacher rattled them off: Character. Plot. Setting. Style. Theme. (This one you especially hated, as it tended to give rise to essay questions. What is the author's theme? Support your answer. 15 pts.)

These, we were told, are the elements. The elements of a story. We did not enjoy that lesson nor the months of tedious discussion that followed. (The *setting* of this story is the Salinas Valley. The author's *theme* is Deception.) But neither did we bother to question it. It seemed reasonable to us that a story should have "elements." Just two periods ago we had been sitting in Chemistry class, where a large glossy paper chart, torn at the edges and stained with something yellow, displayed the Periodic Table of the Elements, a daily reminder that everything in the world is made up of smaller parts. It seemed quite reasonable to us that a story should have "elements," like everything else. Besides, and more importantly, this way of looking at fiction made it possible to sustain a class discussion. It gave us a model, we would say now, without which it would have been hard to analyze a story, to explain it, to break it down into bite-sized ideas that could be written on a blackboard (and which later would pop up on a test).

Without the notion of "elements," without this model or this paradigm, we young readers would have confronted a story in much the way the author had confronted it: as an inchoate body of words and sentences and paragraphs, a vat of incidents, images, quotations, spontaneous outpourings, afterthoughts, fears, morals, passions, ideals . . . the exact formula changes from story to story, of course, and even more so from one writer to the next. But this is perhaps too much to explain in fifty minutes to ninth-graders, and anyway it may be missing the point. We are looking for general truths and not for the myriad unique considerations that pertain to a single case. Our task— like that of our colleague in Chemistry—is an enumeration of the constituents. Like our colleague in Physics, we are concerned with unified theories, principles that hold sway in all realms and at all levels of complexity. It may be true that John Steinbeck should be read differently than Djuna Barnes, Charlotte Brontë than Lord Dunsany, but we insist—as we feel we must insist, for otherwise all is anarchy—that the same "elements" are integral to each, that Character Plot Setting Style Theme are the quarks, the DNA, of literary reality.

Maybe they are. It's a reductionist age, or at any rate the end of one. Committing to memory the Elements of a Story did enable most of us to get through (or around) *The Experience of Literature* and out into the broad corridors of adult life, where we have read, for the most part, only what we have chosen to read, unless we've managed to pick up some pocket change writing book reviews. (And if so, then quite likely we've taken out and sharpened the contents of our ninth-grade schoolbag.) Some of us have even become writers ourselves. And therewith lies the problem—the true, insidious Horror of High School English.

IT CANNOT have escaped your attention, I hope, that the Elements of a Story bear a striking resemblance to the five points of the SF Standard. There is some change in terminology—*ideas*, I think, is a preferable substitute for *theme*—but for the most part we are dealing with parallel models, compatible paradigms. What has happened is clear. Yesterday's ninth-graders have grown up, and their reading habits have changed, but their understanding of fiction has not evolved very much at all from that overheated classroom on that clear October afternoon. We memorized the words on the blackboard, we passed the test, and now when we sit down to write that lesson remains with us. We think, Who are my characters, What is the plot, What is the central idea. We contemplate the "voice" of the narrative, a sophisticated new way we have of talking about style. As science fiction writers we are especially careful about the details of our imaginary worlds—we may even go in for something called "world-building"—which only means that we give more attention to setting than other writers do.

But why do we write this way? Because it is the only way we know.

But what is this that we "know"? It is a model, it is a unifying theory, it is a reductionist view of literature; it is something we were taught in English class.

But what does this model mean? What purpose does it serve? *Is it really true?*

Well, you know, there are problems with models of any kind. They are like metaphors—without which, as Susan Sontag points out, we could not talk about anything. They are "true" to the extent that they enable us to make meaningful statements about the thing under discussion, and they are "false" to the extent that they distort or oversimplify the actual state of affairs. The model in question is a modern, rational one: any given work of fiction may be understood by reference to the "elements" it comprises. This model was very useful for high school English, for it brought a sense of order to things. It made it possible for the teacher to explain to Richard why "The Chrysanthemums" was a good story, an important story, and that if Richard thought otherwise, he was wrong. C-minus.

In the world outside the classroom, however, the model may be less satisfactory. Like Newtonian physics, it may be valid only within certain limits. To go beyond those limits—to escape that overheated classroom—we may need a larger, more encompassing theory. Let me summarize my case:

1. The SF Standard is a useful (and obviously successful) theory of writing. It is not, however, the only possible theory.

2. It suffers from being relatively primitive and thus overly general; it does not provide a means of distinguishing between moderately effective stories and brilliant artistic achievements.

3. It suffers from the problems of reductionist theories in general: it focuses on small or concrete things at the expense of great or transcendent ones. It would lead us, for example, to think that *Little, Big* is flawed because many of its characters are implausible, or *Gravity's Rainbow* because its plot dissolves into absurdity.

4. It gives us a distorted sense of values, by emphasizing a few specific attributes and ignoring all others.

5. It makes a mediocre work assembled according to the orthodox formula appear to be more important or worthwhile than a brilliant work composed according to some other standard.

6. It is intended to help young writers tell the difference between bad fiction and good; therefore it provides no clue whatsoever as to what makes great fiction great. How could it? Very few ninth-graders are ready for *Ulysses* or *Parade's End*.

7. And this brings us to the last, and saddest, shortcoming of the Standard: it limits the achievements of talented writers. It teaches them how to become "pros" but not how to become truly distinguished authors. Thus it condemns them to a secondary status, at best, in the literary world, where it is commonplace—and has been for nearly a century—to find fiction of considerable merit that violates some or

all of the Standard's tenets. What is this stuff, and what's so good about it? Well, let's just say that you probably didn't read any of it in high school.

IN HIGH SCHOOL, it's cool to hate English class. It's cool to sneer at anything called "literature" (as in *The Experience of . . .*) and anything that is said, by anyone in a position of authority, to be Good. Well, good.

The trouble is, once you're no longer in high school, once you've become a writer or a critic or a discriminating reader, hating literature isn't cool anymore. Because now we're not talking about withered prose embalmed in textbooks, but rather the stuff that's in the dorm room of your more intelligent type of English major. This English major friend may share your enjoyment of *Neuromancer* (which you've read because you're fairly certain, what with the drugs and all, that it can't be Good or literary or anything like that) but he enjoys *Tristram Shandy* as well, in fact may actively prefer it, inasmuch as the author's contempt for orthodoxy is more absolute. You decline to borrow it, though, for it is old and long and conspicuously artsy—all Penguin paperbacks are artsy—and anyway, when you ask your friend what it's about, he hasn't got a ready answer. It's about, um . . . well actually it isn't *about* anything, really. I mean, it hasn't actually got much of a plot. . . .

You smile politely. More literary crap, you think. Then you go back to your room and read *Speaker for the Dead*.

Well, there's nothing wrong with reading Gibson and Card. But there is something wrong with *not* reading Sterne. And there is definitely something wrong with despising everything that is identified as literature. The only thing accomplished by this is an impoverishment of the genre, a failure to appreciate how great and how funny and how exhilarating fiction can be. The ironic result of this is that science fiction has come to be less like literature and more like *The Experience of Literature*. That book was boring, it was terrible, but it is all we know.

Here is what we must do, then. We must put that classroom behind us. We must exorcise the Horror of High School English and bring about some compromise between science fiction—or more particularly, the SF Standard—and its ancient enemy, literature. We must devise a new paradigm, a more shrewd and inclusive one.

We must bring art back from its long exile.

AS A NOTION of how to proceed, let us think more closely about the old idea of "elements," the units of which all things are comprised. Ninth-grade English teachers told us there were five of them, and so, coincidentally, did ninth-century alchemists, who called them Air, Fire, Earth, Water, and the Quintessence, which may be identified with the *æther*. Now we know that things are a bit more complicated than that. Or perhaps they are more elegantly simple. We might say that there are many more elements than five, dozens of them, fascinating in their interrelationships, their artful asymmetries. Or we might say that in fact there is only a single component after all, a single ground or field not entirely unlike the *æther*, from which all things arise.

Let us proceed, then, as follows.

Let us first reject reductionism, the notion that one can understand a work of fiction by taking it apart and scrutinizing its components. One can as easily discover what makes a woman beautiful by subjecting her to vivisection. We will, in our new theory of literature, think of fictional works as complete, organic wholes, whose components—if we must number them—are many more than five.

Let us, secondly, consider fictional works individually, with as little preconception as we can manage to bring to bear. Let us not embrace (or reject) a novel because it has the whiff of cyberpunk about it, or because its author is named Updike (or Sterling), or because it was published (or not published) as a genre book, or a mainstream book, or a Vintage Contemporary.

Let us, thirdly, meditate for a while on the notion that there is an underlying unity or interconnectedness in fiction, as there is in reality at large, and that we may be able to read a book with at least part of our mind on this level, experiencing the thing as it is—a continuum created by its sentences—without trying to disassemble or analyze or classify it overmuch. Some works and some writers seem to demand such an approach: Beckett, Robert Aickman, M. John Harrison, most myths, ancient and otherwise, and the growing number of books which cause reviewers to mutter that ritual phrase, "hard to categorize."

Let us, fourthly, try to remember what we were talking about before we got carried away there. Ah, yes: Nabokov. The Grand Exile.

Ada is a great novel and a science fiction novel, of sorts, but it is not a novel of ideas, nor does it have believable characters (they are much too delightful), nor does its shining landscape give evidence of "world-building," nor (as you will realize, who have gotten bogged down in Chapter 2) does it have an especially fleet-footed plot. What makes it so good, then? Figuring this out certainly requires some kind of new paradigm, for the book obviously fails all the examinations of ninth-grade alchemy.

The altered reality of *Ada* has a particular relationship to the thing we mean when we say "the real world." This relationship—that of a brother or a sister—is important to the novel, as it is important to many novels, especially science fiction novels; indeed, the book is suggestively subtitled *Or Ardor, a Family Chronicle*, and the exhilarating love story at its center is an incestuous one. Let's take a closer look at these amorous siblings: objective reality and artistic reality.

We tend to think, we sci-fi homeboys, that what we write has something to do with the world outside our computers. We think, some of us, that we are performing an act that we call "extrapolating." Others of us, more shy or perhaps more sly, do not hope or claim to foresee the future, but rather to alter it; by calling attention to the fact that, let us say, a world governed by Jimmy Swaggart would not be altogether cool, we hope that readers will slap their foreheads, exclaim "What was I thinking?" and nominate John Shirley for President.

Still others of us choose a more elliptical route. We create fictional worlds that are clearly—often bizarrely—different from the world described daily in *The New York Times*. Thus we draw the reader's attention to certain things that the two far-apart worlds manage to have in common. (Perhaps the women in both places continue to do most of the cooking.) In this way we hope to shed light, if not tears, upon what we hold to be universal or timeless truths (e.g., that the men are out sticking their nuclear-tipped psi-ray superconducting wetware shafts into things, as is [or is not] right and proper).

And there are, of course, other strategies we employ, for other purposes. But all these cases, the varying connections between our make-believe worlds and the objective world, the *New York Times* world—the crutch for people who can't handle science fiction—are alike in this way: they reflect an idea which I will simply and modestly call the Great Collective Unconscious Unifying Idea of All Science Fiction. This notion is, to wit:

There is such a thing as Realism.

That is, it is possible to write realistically. It doesn't take much imagination. All you have to do is write things down the way they happen. Anybody can do that. Anne Tyler does that, and she's just a housewife. Therefore what we're doing is Very Different from what those other writers do.

In fact, I do not subscribe to this notion. I think the whole Great Collective business is a misunderstanding. I don't think any such thing as realism has ever existed or ever shall, in this or any other literature. Try writing some, if you doubt it. Try to make an incident, a conversation, a day at the office, anything, feel on paper the way it feels in life. It can't be done, except now and then in flashes, epiphanies, moments that vanish as quickly as they are perceived. The world is a much stranger place than your ninth-grade English teacher (or the author of *Mind Children*, but that's another essay) would lead you to believe. Reality is not a simple concept, nor is the illusion of realism a facile literary achievement.

Any work of fiction presents for us a vision of an altered reality, a created or imaginary world, if only in the sense that the writer has employed such devices as a limited point-of-view, beginning and ending at arbitrary points, confining the story to the realm of That Which Can Be Described—indispensable features of fiction, every one, though none is shared by reality. This does not mean that fiction is in some sense a failed enterprise, that art is necessarily inferior to life. Both can be awful and both can be wonderful.

So all fiction is speculative fiction; all fictional worlds are visionary. Thomas Hardy's Stonehenge is as purely imaginary as Marion Zimmer Bradley's. Dickens' London is as dark and fantastical as Hambly's, or Ackroyd's. The desolate landscape of *A Canticle for Liebowitz* is much like the terrain explored by writers like Kem Nunn in *Unassigned Territory* and Joy Williams in *Breaking and Entering*. The same people drift from place to place, too, in this netherworld: the "checkered individual" in Bulgakov's *The Master and Margarita* reappears as the Checkered Demon of Zap Comix fame, then finds employment as accountant to a scatterbrained aristocrat in a recent fantasy novel.

We're all making this up. And what we're making up, specifically, is not just an altered or fictional reality. It is specifically an artistic reality, a reality created by artifice, because that is what "art" means, and all that it means, whether we choose to identify it as such or prefer some euphemism like "entertainment." Art may be terrible—as its sibling, life, may be also—but as Shelley sez, that is for some future jury to decide.

I WOULD NOT be speaking bluntly like this, using the A-word, except that I am fairly confident that none of the hyper-pious SF faithful—among whom, I gather, "art" is a term of derision—will have made it this deeply into the discussion. But art, you see, is what I now must talk about. The world of *Ada* is the world of art, a sibling of the world of life, equally strange, and with a strong familial resemblance. We learn this from the book's first sentence, an inversion of the famous opening line of *Anna Karenina*, more artsy stuff; only in *Ada* it is the unhappy families who (like many SF novels) are all alike. From there the sibling worlds separate, though they can never bear to remain apart for long. They come together—I believe that phrase is apt—again and again, each trying to possess the other, to merge, to become one world, but that of course cannot be. Their intimate congress has a thrilling sense of wrongness about it.

Nabokov, in this novel, fairly spells it out. The illusions, the hallucinations, the whimsical or horrifying fancies with which the characters in *Ada* are visited are nothing more or less than the common features of this, the parallel story in which we live. And the fictitious places and people of our world are the everyday features of that other one. Here is a specimen passage:

> "Space is a swarming in the eyes, and Time a singing in the ears," says John Shade, a modern poet, as quoted by an invented philosopher ("Martin Gardiner") in *The Ambidextrous Universe*, page 165. Space flutters to the ground, but Time remains between thinker and thumb, when Monsieur Bergson uses his scissors.

Naturally I did not follow all this when I read *Ada* at the age of seventeen. And yet reading that novel was certainly the most exciting and important experience I had ever known as a reader of fiction. Truly, it changed my life.

This makes me question one of the central tenets of the Standard: that a work of fiction must make sense, or as Shirley says that it must contain "ideas supported by strong internal logic." Perhaps this point is valid in a general way. Yet it seems to confuse the problem of analyzing a book—as, for instance, in ninth-grade English class—with the actual experience of reading it. I did not know or care, when I was seventeen, what the "ideas" of *Ada* were, much less what (if anything) they were supported by. I have since given a great deal of thought to the marvelous coherence of the novel, but I have done this long after the fact of reading and being moved by it.

The tendency of the orthodox school is to believe that reading is a purely rational undertaking, that through the enlightened use of such modern analytic tools as the Elements of a Story we can understand what the book is about, what motivates its characters, how its fictional world operates, and on and on, down to the finest resolution possible with the instruments at hand. Should a work of fiction not withstand such scrutiny, should it fail some test of logical consistency, then it will not fare well with science fiction folks—notwithstanding that it may contain some of the greatest sentences in the language, or scenes of such startling power as to change forever a seventeen-year-old boy's life.

Young Vlad Nabokov, son of a liberal legislator in the short-lived Russian Republic, was banished forever from his homeland, the Russia of Tolstoy and Gogol, at the same time, and to the same place, that Russia itself was banished. They both found refuge in art, a realm abundant enough to sustain them for most of a century. John Shade, the real poet laureate of this unreal world (and a character in Nabokov's *Pale Fire*), wrote a poem that begins:

> I was the shadow of the waxwing slain
> By the false azure of the windowpane.
> I was the stuff of ashen fluff, and I
> Lived on, flew on, in the reflected sky.

The poem's commentator, a demented English prof who believed himself to be the exiled king of Zembla, "a distant northern land," found in these lines the key not only to Shade's life but to his poetry. The image of a bird dying as it smacks into the glass, then taking up a new existence in "the reflected sky," struck this commentator as quite appealing, quite apt. The professor knew the window well: it was the one through which he spied on Shade at work in his study, writing the poem. Some glass act. A fictitious poet, writing a real poem, is watched by a man who thinks he's a king, and who has invented for himself a lost kingdom, with all the usual attributes of "world-building." The two men, and the two worlds, are separated by a window which reflects and distorts but also permits observation, most particularly of the act of creativity, the poet's flight into the false azure—the haven of exiles, of poets, of cyberpunks—the netherworld of art.

There is (as a younger colleague of Shade's has discovered) more than one history of the world, because there is more than one world. Two, at least: *this* one, and the one we imagine. *That* world is the one where the sky is the color of television, tuned to a dead channel, where for a long time I used to go to bed early, where all unhappy families are alike, where the enemy's gate is down, where all winters should be so warm, all nights so black, all headlights so dazzling. The realms of fiction are innumerable, but they belong to the same reality, the same artistic continuum. And it is a real place—as real as this one, anyway—because it really exists, in every way except the physical. And even in this regard, the window opens eerily; for Life imitates Art, as any English major knows. So real spaceships sport fictional names, Scorpions prowl the streets of decaying cities, imaginary poets are quoted in real books.

A work of fiction, I have said, is a continuum created by its sentences. This continuum gives rise to the experience of reading the work, and it must provide the underpinning—the unified field, as it were—of our new theory of fiction.

The paradigm that underlies the SF Standard (the five elements, ideas "supported by" internal logic) is a physical one. It gives us a materialist view of art, just as orthodox science gives us a materialist view of life. It considers a work of fiction as though it were a physical thing, a structure to be "supported," which can be dismantled and analyzed and thus—in theory, at least—completely understood.

In fact, a *book* is a physical thing, but the experience of reading it is not. And it is the *experience* that is important; for otherwise, why do we read? Why do we, as writers, seek to entertain? Not, surely, so that our readers can enjoy a rousing discussion, afterward, about our theme, our plot, our setting. We want our readers to talk, but what we want them to say is something along the lines of, "This is a great book." In other words, "Reading this book was a great experience." We understand that fiction can be thought about (and ought to be, by the author at least) in an analytical way. And yet we also know that during the act of reading, a work of fiction is experienced as a whole, complete, undivided thing—as, for example, one experiences a piece of music as a unified composition, even though one knows that the actual sound is made by musicians toodling and thwacking at their respective instruments, producing waveforms that smack into one's ear.

In this respect, the continuum created by a work of fiction is more like a field than an agglutination of particles. When we read fiction, we experience this field directly. It is generated by the flow of words, the images, the feelings they evoke, the interplay between the fictional world and the objective one. This field coexists with the field already present in the reader's mind, creating as it were an æsthetic interference pattern, a jostling and commingling of experience. If the fiction is good (and if our own ability to read it, our general level of literacy, is sufficiently high) then the experience can be rich and interesting. Afterward, if we like, we can try to figure out why we had this experience, how specifically the work succeeded or failed. We can round up the usual suspects, Character Plot Setting Style Theme, or we can seek some new model upon which to base our discussion.

I will suggest one model myself, and a term to describe it. The idea that two fields may interact, and that the resulting interference pattern may be physically represented, is not, of course, new. We know all about holograms, in which we experience the interaction visually; hence "-gram." Though we must be mindful that we are speaking metaphorically (but so are the Standardites, with their "elements"), let us consider the interaction of two fields of consciousness—

the reader's and the writer's—taking place through the medium of a work of fiction. I propose that we think of a work of fiction as a *holotext*, which I define as a continuum of words in which the whole is present in every part.

This seems true to the experience of reading. When we read a book we experience it as a continuous, indivisible flow. The fictional world is created anew for us with every sentence. Thus every sentence bears the full load of the finished work for as long as it is in the mind of the reader. (This gives us new insight into why such things as long digressions, bad puns, lifeless dialogue are so disruptive: because they puncture the continuum of the holotext.) A fictional work is successful if its holotext is intense—boldly colored, sharply contoured, emotionally charged—if, in other words, the interaction between reader and writer is especially strong.

Notice, please, that this has nothing to do with themes, or with ideas supported by strong internal logic. Logic, or its absence, has much more to do with how a reader feels after finishing a story than during the experience of reading itself. Some stories, including much of the oral tradition, may deliberately not make any ordinary kind of sense, because it is their purpose to jolt the reader or the listener out of his normal frame of mind; such stories are among the most powerful of all works of fiction.

A trip to a fictional world is not a rational experience; it is a *trip*, it is an altered state of consciousness. The alteration is brought about by interaction between two fields: that of life and that of art, the transcendent firmament, where FTL warships flit from star to star while John Shade's waxwing blithely twitters, happy to see them gone.

IN *ADA*, there is a bit of introspection near the end. One of the amorous siblings, now an old man, discusses a book on which he has been working.

> "My aim was to compose a kind of novella in the form of a treatise on the Texture of Time, an investigation into its veily substance, with illustrative metaphors gradually increasing, very gradually building up a logical love story, going from past to present, blossoming as a concrete story, and just as gradually reversing analogies and disintegrating again into bland abstraction."

"I wonder," said Ada, "I wonder if the attempt to discover those things is worth the stained glass."

And there, you see, very neatly, is why fiction is no more a rational game than life is. The poor author, a reasonable chap, has laid out the plan for a book—the book we have almost finished—only in the end he finds himself upstaged by his lovely sister, the artistic one, whose mind is clearly somewhere else. It is hard to explain why Ada's remark makes the passage feel magical, spring from the page; certainly it does not depend on making sense, i.e., on the reader knowing what stained glass she is talking about. I suspect the passage works because it is surprising, and because in some way it is beautiful. Beauty, as a goal of fiction, or as an absolute value, has seldom been touched upon by the SF Standard. And yet it has almost always been bound up in our idea of art, even if occasionally in a negative sense—as with, say, certain mid-century painters, from whose work beauty is purposefully banished. It crops up, like the poppies of Flanders, in the darkest of post-Holocaust worlds. I doubt that one could fashion a satisfying theory of fiction that did not take the special nature of beauty, its immanence, its redemptive quality, into account.

I take comfort from this. I have not written, myself, to satisfy any well-defined æsthetic, but I find that as I have continued to write and to read I have evolved one. I suspect that some of it is applicable to the work of other writers, though I'm not sure how many. Perhaps all of them. Here, anyhow, by way of summary, is my own credo, as it stands.

I no longer believe that the characters in my fiction have anything to do with people in real life. I believe they are the descendants of other characters in other books. In many cases their names and their manner of speaking and their physical characteristics reflect this.

I do not believe anymore that the imagined worlds of my fiction are "extrapolations" of any real world, nor that they ought to be. To the extent that they exist in an imaginary future, in a place that bears some resemblance to North America, they are not historical descendants of our world, but *literary* descendants of our *culture*. I am not particularly interested in exploring future politics, or economics, and above all not technology. (It is my belief that "hard" science, the science of inanimate things, has already passed its brightest hour, and that neither hardware nor software nor wetware nor ware of any kind will have an importance in the daily lives of our grandchildren that is comparable to that of other, softer things: their feelings, their taste in music, the contents of their gardens.)

What interests me today, and what I suppose will interest people several hundred years from now, is not how the world is organized or how wars are fought or how many planets have been terraformed. What is of interest, I think, is *how life feels*—what it is like to live in this place at this time, looking at this scene outside my window, sleeping with this person, reading this book (or watching this holo-cube, or enjoying this bracing hallucination).

I do not worry much about making things make sense. Many writers do, and the results are unconvincing. That a fictional world is rich, that it is complex, that it is full of contradictions, that it allows us an occasional glimmering insight into lives that seem real, that seem worth living—these achievements are much more valid to me than any effort to imagine how we are going to interact with the household computer, or what kind of vehicle we will drive to the spaceport bar. Who cares? Objects, in general, occupy rather little of my attention at present, and I suspect they will hold no more fascination for my grandchildren.

At the center of my system of values is art; and I find, as I have mentioned, that the idea of art is closely connected with the idea of beauty, though the precise connection seems open to debate. Just as my characters are derived not from people but from other literary personages, and my fictional worlds are derived not from our world but from our culture, so the prose in which these things are embodied is derived from the books that I have read. On this point, I'm sure I am in abundant company. We all strive for a style and a voice of our own, but the very nature of our struggle—our ambitions, our understanding of the possibilities of language—is either expanded or limited by our experience as readers.

Here I think we see the SF Standard at its feeblest. The goal (again, from Shirley's definition) of "clear sentence structure" seems to me absolutely the lowest conceivable ambition that a writer can sustain. Clear sentences are admirable things, I suppose, but they bring to mind the *très* Sixties notion that The Purpose of Writing is to Communicate. There are many things that writing can do—hearten, inform, sexually arouse, terrify, admonish, amuse—and these things are *not* subsumed by the notion of "communicate," any more than the things that sentences can be—melodious, oppressive, energized, strenuous, didactic, exhilarating—are implied by the word "clear." Ideas are contained in words, as we ought to know, and if we are going to talk about writing as though we were a bunch of ninth-graders, then the sad issue of this discussion should come as no surprise.

Let's grow up, then. At least let's get out of high school and proceed to college. If we are going to be writers, let's read the work of good writers, wherever we find them, and let's learn from them what we can. Let's read Shakespeare and Austen and Dickens and Eliot; let's read Pynchon and Bowen and Gaddis and Tyler. Let's look for new writers—Jaimy Gordon, Kem Nunn, Susanna Moore. And by all means let's read our colleagues in SF, whether or not they are published with genre imprints on the spine.

If we are going to be critics, our task is even more exacting. It is not important, or even desirable, that a critic should knock himself out reading every new book that comes his way. This has the unhappy effect of making lightweight, easily digestible works seem better, from our haggard critic's point of view, than works that are subtle or complex or otherwise out of the ordinary. The critic's time would be much better spent in dipping into the more important works of literary theory and criticism. Really, there are not all that many of them, and the significant ones are quite approachable. The list might begin with Aristotle's *Poetics*—it's a teenie weenie essay, and you'll never be puzzled by odd uses of words like "tragedy" and "comedy" again—and continue through Shelley's theory of the sublime, Coleridge's musings on the imagination, Matthew Arnold, and perhaps the essays of T. S. Eliot. Now we have arrived at an era in which all of us should feel at home. We can read with ease and enjoyment Edmund Wilson, Northrop Frye, I. A. Richards (whose errors some of our critics seem destined to repeat), and then we bound into the present with the likes of Leslie Fiedler, Susan Sontag, John Updike, John Clute, and Ursula K. Le Guin.

As with all lists, these are not comprehensive; nor is there a need to read everyone on them. If you are a conscientious writer, however— and even more so if you are a critic—not having read at least some of the writers on *both* lists is a grave omission, a failure to do justice to yourself and to your readers . . . and to art, if we care about such things. And if we do not, then science fiction will continue to be scorned by the literary world at large. If we do not write with the same breadth of vision, the same depth of experience, or the same confident and invigorating mastery of prose as our peers in other fields, then we will inevitably lose readers, especially young ones. Worse, we will lose writers. We will no longer attract those gifted, restless, obsessive souls, hungry for intellectual excitement, who have not ceased to believe in such things as poetry and beauty and truth, who have not acquired the trick of self-deception so adroitly practiced by many "SF pros." These writers—the great authors of the next generation—will wander elsewhere. And we will have no one to blame but ourselves.

John Crowley

The distinguished body of work that John Crowley has produced since debuting with *The Deep* (1975) is an ornament not simply to the SF field but to all American letters. His other novels include the futuristic fable *Beasts*, the complex and lyrical *Engine Summer*, the World Fantasy Award–winning *Little, Big* (which many regard as his most ambitious and successful work so far), and his byzantine decoding of a secret world, *Aegypt*. A very small portion of his short fiction appears in *Novelty: Four Stories*. He is now at work on a second novel in the tetralogy that began with *Aegypt*, a book called *Love and Sleep*.

"In Blue" did not appear on the 1989 final ballot. I include it as a worthy stand-in for Crowley's novella finalist "Great Work of Time," which appears in Gardner Dozois's best-of-the-year volume and which runs almost twice the length of this fascinating tale—which, as John Kessel has noted, is both intellectually stimulating and emotionally affecting. "And it's real science fiction, too," Kessel observes.

Crowley himself says, "There was a brief moment some twelve years ago (maybe such a moment comes to most people who write science fiction) when I thought I had truly imagined one way in which the future might view the world: that I had thought up a new science, or a new scientific attitude. I was very gratified, then, when chaos theory and related breakthroughs came along: they were far more rigorous than anything I had imagined and lacking the human reference, but were strikingly like what I had glimpsed, what I have called 'act-field theory' in the story 'In Blue.'

"There's more to the story than act-field theory. It's also an attempt to construct a society utterly different from our own but which the reader cannot determine to be either 'good' or 'bad'—just as we cannot possibly make such a simple determination about the society we live in now.

"It's also the saddest story I've ever written."

The route they took every morning from their dormitory to the project's buildings took them through very old parts of the city. They

IN BLUE ◆ 269

crossed a square where weeds grew up between enormous paving stones, a square so vast it could diminish even the long, square-columned, monolithic buildings that bordered it. The square was usually deserted and silent; not even the indigenous population of the city, descendants of those who had built this square or at least of men and women who had inhabited it when it was still a living place, ever came here much. It was too open, too lifeless: or rather it had a life too large, too intimidating; nothing could be done with it. The new populations of the city, the squatters and refugees, also rarely came here; probably most of them weren't even aware of its existence.

Hare's group passed out of the square beneath an arch the height of ten men and as thick as a room. Looking up as they passed under it, Hare could see that the honeycomb pattern of its vaulting was distorted deliberately to make the arch seem even higher, even more intimidating than it was. The hexagons high up, in the center of the arch, were actually smaller than the ones on the sides, lower down; the circles inscribed inside the hexagons were really ovals, making the center of the curve of the arch seem to retreat into a space within itself, a space that could not exist, a space into which Hare's heart seemed to be drawn.

Then he had passed under the arch and moved on with the others.

Why had they done it that way? Every morning he wondered. Why had it occurred to anyone to expend so much ingenuity on a trick like that, who had then been willing to take the trouble to execute it? Slaves. But they must have been skilled nonetheless, and proud of their skills. The effort of it, the enterprise of it, at once oppressed and lightened him, drawing his mind apart.

He looked back, as he always did, to see the whole of it, and to study the band of letters that ran across the top. Each letter must have been a meter long; between the words there were diamond-shaped stops as large as a hand. But what were the words? What was the language? He tried to memorize the first few letters, as he always did, but as always by the time he reached work he would forget their exact shapes.

He turned away. One or two of the others had also glanced back, to see what it was that Hare looked at, but they couldn't see it, and looked curiously at Hare; the woman who worked beside him at the project smiled at him, enjoying his oddness. Hare returned the smile and looked ahead.

Farther on were narrow streets, and these, too, contained fragments of the ancient city, not ruins so much as antiquities in the process of being packed up in new construction. That the old cornerstones and bits of columned fronts were being preserved in this way was an illusion; the incremental plan for new housing, for places to put the thousands who were coming in from the countryside, made it necessary to squeeze modular units wherever Applications determined they could go, leaving the old disorder to be carted away later. Hare supposed it wouldn't be long before the gray boxes, which stacked to any height, which could be piled up anyhow wherever there was room, would spill out into the square, growing with the shy persistence of ivy, higgledy-piggledy, full of children, strung with lines of laundry and hung with gaudy hectoring posters in country dialects. In these streets the uniform units had already climbed above all but the tallest of the older buildings, their zigzag stairways like ivy's clutching roots.

Through the open doors of some units, Hare's group passing by could glimpse women at stoves, or nursing children; more often, though, doors and shutters would be quietly closed as the group passed, the faces that looked out suddenly occluded by a door. These country people were shy; if they found themselves observed, they would turn away, or even cover their faces with their hands. Had they used to do so in their old home places? Where Hare had grown up, people had been friendly and talkative. He thought it must be the city, the sight of strangers, cadre in Blue who had an uncertain but real control over their lives. When Hare's group came upon children playing in the labyrinthine streets, they would stop playing and withdraw into doorways or behind pillars, silent, their dark eyes large; they wouldn't come out though Hare's group waved and called to them.

It was a problem in figure-ground mechanics, Hare thought: that the cadre in Blue knew themselves to be the servants of masters, the people; but the people thought that the servants were their masters—and of course there were instances when the servants did seem to be directing the lives of their masters. It must be hard for them, Hare thought: the uniforms of Blue meant survival, food, shelter, help, and before them even the grown-ups were as shy as children offered sweets or kindnesses by great strangers.

But most of Hare's group had, like Hare, also come here from the country or from small towns, and also felt themselves to be displaced—perhaps that's why they smiled and waved at the elusive children of the altered streets, and why they talked little or in low voices as they walked through this many-layered necropolis where the living trod on the dead, who when they had lived had trod on other dead. Hare, in the city, felt for the first time sharply how many more dead there are than living.

The dead had carved in stone; the living wrote on paper. The long, bannerlike posters were everywhere, explaining, exhorting, encouraging: not only explaining how not to waste water, but why it was important that water not be wasted. Some were torn off in midsentence, by hands or wind; kindly teachers whose mouths were suddenly stopped.

"Look," Hare said to the woman who walked next to him. He read from a poster: " 'If you don't know how to read, begin learning now.' "

"Yes," the woman said. "There's a lot of illiteracy still."

She took the hand of the woman next to her, who smiled without looking at her. Hare said nothing.

HARE'S WORK at the project was the preparation of training manuals, introductory lessons in act-field theory and social calculus. Presently he was working on an introduction to coincidence magnitude calculations.

It was not difficult work; it was far less demanding than the work for which Hare had been trained, and for which he had shown such early promise in school, when it was thought that he might be one of those few who could alter the calculus that altered the lives of men and women. When he walked the long halls of the project building, he passed the open doors of rooms where men and women sat together, without tools beyond a terminal or a pad or without even those, men and women at work on that calculus; Hare, as he passed their doors, hearing their low voices or their laughter, could almost see the networks of their thought growing. If they caught sight of Hare, they might wave, for he had worked with some of them in these rooms and in rooms like these in other places. Then he passed on, through other rooms, meeting rooms and commissariats and the communications annex, to the cubicles where work like his was done. Beyond these cubicles lay the maintenance sheds, the shops and warehouses. Then that was the end. Hare, sitting down at his work station and turning on the dim light above it, wondered how long it would be before he was shifted that one last degree.

Not long, he thought. He wasn't sure he could even complete the manual he was working on in any form that could be submitted. And beyond the maintenance sheds, the shops and warehouses? Only the world that Hare's manuals taught about: life: the whole act-field. He would most likely go on moving, as he had moved, by degrees down from the highest realm of thought about it, to a mere place in it: or no place.

He opened the composer on his desk and retrieved the notes he had made the day before.

"Introduction. Definitions. Description of contents. Figure-ground mechanics a necessity for coincidence magnitude calculation. Probabilities and how they differ from coincidence magnitudes: example. Problems and strategies: synchronicity, self-reference paradoxes, etc. Conclude introduction: importance of coincidence magnitude calculation to the social calculus, importance of the calculus to act-field theory, importance of act-field theory to the Revolution."

He considered these notes for a long time. Then, keyed to the line about the difference between probabilities and coincidence magnitude, he wrote this:

"Example:

"It was once believed that no two snowflakes are exactly alike. More properly we can say that the probability of any two snowflakes' being exactly alike is very low. The fall, at the same moment, of two snowflakes that are exactly alike, and the fall of those two snowflakes on this word 'snowflake' that you are now reading, would be a coincidence of a probability so low as to be virtually incalculable.

"But the *magnitude* of the coincidence, if it were to be calculated by the methods you will learn here, would not be high.

"This is because coincidence magnitude is a function of *meaningfulness* as well as of probability. We know that only acts (as defined by the special and general act theories) can have meaningfulness; an act's meaningfulness is a function of its definition as an act, a definition made possible by the infinitesimal social calculus. An act bearing high meaningfulness and low probability generates a high coincidence magnitude. To calculate meaningfulness against probability, and thereby arrive at the magnitude of the coincidence, requires that coincidence magnitude calculation be operable within act-field theory as a *differential* social calculus.

"Act-field theory predicts the occurrence, within any given parameters of the field, of coincidences of a certain magnitude. It is said to *account for* these. The appearance within those parameters of coincidences greater in magnitude than the theory accounts for is a coincidence of implicitly high magnitude, generating its own parameters in another dimension, parameters calculable within the theory, which then *accounts for* the higher level of coincidence. The generation of such new parameters is called an *implicit spike*, and the process is itself *accounted for*."

Here Hare's thought branched.

"Implicit spikes," he wrote, and then erased it.

"Act-field theory, then," he wrote, and erased that.

Whichever way his thought branched it seemed likely to take him to the tolstoy edge.

Once (Hare had no conception of how long ago, but long ago) they had thought that if the position and velocity and mass of every atom in the universe could be known, at some given moment, then the next moment and thus each succeeding moment could be predicted with certainty. Of course such complete knowledge could not be assembled, no computer could be built large enough to contain all the facts, or to calculate with them; but if they could be. And then they learned that the universe was not made like that at all, that only probabilities of states and events could ever be known with certainty, and that the very act of measuring and perceiving those probabilities entailed altering them. Some people (Hare had heard) had gone mad when this was proven, out of the awful loss of certainty, the loss even of the possibility of certainty. Others rejoiced: the loss of false certainty made real knowledge possible. The calculations began again, and were fruitful. The universe of events danced inexhaustibly, and the mind could dance with it, if it would.

And there had also been a time (the same time, perhaps; the same olden days) when people had thought that history might also be calculated: that if the weather and the size of harvests and the productivity of factories and the rate of invention and every other possible variable could be known; though it could not be, and every hurt every person had suffered, every belief or thought each one had—every man's position and mass and velocity—then it could be known with certainty why every event that happened had happened, and what would happen next.

But the human universe was no more like that than the universe of stars and stones. Such calculations would fail not because they were impossibly difficult but because no such certainties as were aimed at could possibly exist. It could not even be determined what units were to be measured—human acts—and where one stopped and another began. All conceivable plans for making the measurements met a mirror paradox, a self-reference, an infinite regression: the tolstoy edge.

But only give in to that; only rejoice in it; only be not surprised to find that the points plotted on your graphs make a figure like your own face, and the calculations begin again. And are fruitful: the special theory of acts, empty now of any concrete content, defines an act, the definition including the meaningful activity of looking for such a definition; the general theory defines their entrainments, heterarchies, and transformations. Act-field theory creates a virtually infinitely dimensional simplex for operating in, and the infinitesimal social calculus separates the inseparable, one act from another, dissolving in its simplicity the self-reference paradox as completely as the infinitesimal calculus in mathematics had dissolved the paradoxes of division that had plagued it for so long. And the social calculus makes possible the Revolution: once frozen before the infinite divisions of distance to be crossed before the target is reached, the Revolution now is loosed by the archer's fingers and leaps the distance into the unfigurable, ultimately unknowable heart of man.

And how could he, Hare, sitting here now, know all that, know it so well that when he was a boy he had in one tiny way added to it (some refinements of figure-ground mechanics for which he had won a prize in school), how could he sit here now before it and be unable to describe it? How could it ever make him afraid?

And yet he could not bring himself to continue.

He leaned back in his chair, which groaned beneath his weight. He pressed a key on the composer and held it down, and letter by letter his story about the snowflakes was removed from the screen.

HARE SAT at lunch with Dev, a woman of about his age. He didn't know her well, but she for some reason chose him to talk to. She ate little, and seemed to be full of a story she both wanted to tell and didn't want to tell, about a young friend of hers, and their friends, whom Hare didn't know. Hare listened, nodding, sympathetic, for the woman felt some grief, a grief that the story she told should have revealed; but the way she told it made it impossible to understand. She said "you know" several times, and "all that kind of thing," and waved her hand and shook her head as at a cloud of gnatlike complications that she could see in her story but couldn't or wouldn't describe. Hare lost the thread; there were too many "she's" in the story for him to remember which was which.

"So we all *did* go swimming," the woman said. "That night, by the bridge where there's the embankment. Well, I said I'd go. And then she said she and her new friend, the other one from the one she came with, the one she'd just met, didn't want to—but they said, Oh, come on, everybody needs to cool off. You know."

Hare was listening carefully now.

"So they all took their clothes off. And they're really very young." She laughed. "And, well. With *her* it never bothered me, but you know they can be so unkind, or no, not that, I just couldn't. I mean I'm too old really for those games they play, you know? Girls together, like in school. You get beyond that kind of thing. I laughed about it, you kids go ahead, I just like to watch, I'm an old grandma. And they just let me sit."

Hare put down his bowl. He was smiling, too, and nodding, as though sharing with the woman this amusing part of the story, where she'd tried to act her age with offhand grace; and trying to feel the other feeling that the woman felt: exclusion from happy comradeship, and jealousy; and trying also to transmute his own sudden strong feelings, by careful attention to her, into sympathy. He shook his head, smiling at how life sometimes goes on.

"Kids," she said. "At that age you just don't care."

Hare wanted to ask: What did they do together in the water? But he could not have asked this and maintained his air of casual interest; and he thought that if she told him he would not understand her answer rightly anyway, because what the young women did together in the water would be three times masked from him: by their own young feelings, by the feelings of the woman who watched them from the bank, and worst of all, by the obstruction of his own feelings, so irrelevant to the young women in the water and what they did together, and yet so fierce.

"I know what you mean," he said, remembering a day in spring years ago, when he was at school.

The school Hare had gone to as a boy was built in the shape of a T. In one branch of the T the girls were taught by female teachers; in the other branch the boys were taught by men. Where the branches met, the corridor of Hare's part ended, crossed by the corridor of the girls' part running at right angles. Going from class to class, coming near this juncture, boys could watch the girls walking in their part: books under their arms, or held up before them, embraced in that way that girls so often held their books but boys for some reason never did; talking together in groups or walking singly. Glances and waves could be passed from one part to the other, and brief conversations held there. There was a gymnasium in the school—Hare could not remember now just how it attached to the body of the school building—where alternately through the day boys' and girls' exercise classes met; it could also be filled with folding chairs when visiting cadre came to lecture. For these events the boys used one half of the floor, and the girls the other, separated by a wide aisle.

On fine days, after they had had their lunch, older students who had permission from their teachers were allowed to walk outside for a while on a strip of pavement that ran before the wide back doors of this gymnasium, to talk and smoke cigarettes. There was a proctor to watch them, but he usually absented himself. These were good students; they were being given a taste of the sort of privileges cadre had, and that they themselves might someday have. The boys understood that, and talk was usually serious. On a burning spring day, a first summer afternoon, Hare was walking with three or four other boys, smoking and talking. They were all laughing too loud, because of the day, and the sun, and summer coming. Then—either blown open by a gust of wind because they hadn't been properly closed, or opened from within by someone on purpose to bring cool air into the hot gymnasium—the double doors of the gymnasium opened.

There was a girls' class in progress. A girl Hare knew slightly, a cheerful laughing girl, stood framed in the doorway, legs wide apart, hair lifted by the sudden inrush of air. She wore only a band across her breasts and a sort of strap around her waist and between her legs. She waved to Hare, surprised but unashamed. Beyond her, in the comparative darkness of the gymnasium, were the others in the class. There were mats laid out on the floor. Two girls on each mat were wrestling; some wore the same breast band that the girl standing in the doorway wore, some who didn't need them yet didn't. Those not wrestling stood to watch the others. Hare saw all this in a moment. The girls within shouted and laughed, the wrestlers stopped and looked, some of the girls ran to hide. Around Hare the boys were laughing. Hare only stood staring, become eyes, his heart become eyes, his hands and mouth become eyes. Then the girl pulled the doors shut with a boom.

The boys around Hare laughed together, pummeling each other and shouting in an excess of energy, until the proctor came smiling to see what was up, what the joke was. Hare turned away from the closed doors, feeling an almost unbearable sense of loss and exclusion; feeling withered and desiccated within, made old, by loss.

Hare wanted to ask the woman Dev if that was what she had felt by the river, watching her friend and the other young women: that sense of loss and exclusion.

But it couldn't be. Because she had, once, herself been one of those girls on the mats, among others. She had always been in the other part. The young woman swimming with the others was her friend; they were all her friends. Hare couldn't imagine then what she felt, whether her feelings were of the same kind as his, or a different kind altogether, and whether it hurt as much, or more, or less: her loss of what he had never had.

"I know what you mean," he said again.

WILLY SAID TO HIM: "You look tired. You always look tired now. You look as though someone knew something terrible about you, and you were afraid he was going to tell all your friends, and you can't stop worrying about it. But I know everything about you, and there isn't anything terrible at all."

Willy shared Hare's room in the dormitory building where the project staff were housed. Willy wasn't exactly cadre, he hadn't much education, he was good with his hands and worked in the project maintenance shops. But Hare, when he saw that he wouldn't be able to have a room of his own because the project staff had grown too large, had got Willy into his room. Willy didn't mind living with project cadre, he had no sense of inferiority, and everybody liked Willy, his goodness, his jokes, his sympathy with everyone. Willy got along.

Though they had often lost touch in the intervening years, Hare had known Willy since school. Willy was four years younger than he, and at summer work-camp when Hare was proctor, Willy, alone and unhappy at his first camp, had adopted Hare to be his friend and protector. He'd sneak out of his own bunk with the young children and make his way to Hare's bed, shyly but insistently climbing in with him. Hare, half asleep, didn't resist the boy's affection; he was embarrassed to find him there in the morning, as immovable as a log in his deep childish sleep, and the other proctors made fun of him, but they were jealous, too, that Hare had someone so devoted, to run errands for him; once there had been a fight with another proctor over Willy. Willy understood—he always understood the context, the human net of desires and fears, the act-field, in a concrete way that Hare never would—and after that when he crept into bed in Hare's cubicle, he would be silent; would lie with Hare almost not moving, and with his face pressed into the hollow of Hare's shoulder would masturbate him with small motions, sometimes seeming to fall asleep amid it. When Hare made noises, Willy would whisper *shhh* in his ear, and giggle.

Willy called it playing. He always did. It was more intense pleasure than eating, without that daily compulsion but no less automatic; as refreshing as football or hard calisthenics, but imbued with affection and intimacy. The continuum in Willy from simple affection and shared good times to those cryings-out, those spasms, was unbroken; it had no parts; it was the social calculus in reality, and Hare loved it in Willy and envied him for it.

Because for all he, Hare, knew the integral social calculus, in him there was such a division. There was a breaking into parts, as in the

oldest and wrongest paradoxes; an infinite number of discrete distances to cross between himself and what he desired.

"It's because I want the other," he told Willy when long ago he'd
tried to say it in words. "You want the same. So it wouldn't occur to
you."

"That's not it," Willy said, laughing. "Because I've been with
women, too. I bet more than you have. I like people, that's the
difference. You have to like people. If you like people, they'll like
you back. Men or women. If you're interested in them, they like you
for it. It's simple."

Hare had laughed, too, shame-faced, uneasy with the humility
he had to learn in order to take advice from the boy whom he'd
protected and taught. Pride: it was a fault cadre were liable to, he
knew, a fault that must be erased. Why shouldn't he take advice from
Willy? While Hare had grown up in the thin atmosphere of schools,
study camps, and project dormitories, Willy had been moving in the
sea of the people, the endless flux of the Revolution, with all its
accidents and coincidences. Never cease learning from the people:
that was a maxim of the Revolution grown old and unfeelable for
Hare.

But he had tried to learn. He had tried to meld himself with the
common play of desire and pleasure, hope and disappointment, pleasure and work. He became, or seemed to become, wise; became
someone to whom others told stories, because of his calm, sensible
sympathies. The endless voices: Hare heard stories everywhere,
people told him of their plans and desires, Hare nodded and said *I
know what you mean.*

But he had no stories himself that he could tell.

THE DORMITORIES where the cadre that worked in Hare's project lived
were modular, like the people's housing, though the units were
smaller. Above the communal facilities, the refectories and common
rooms and work stations, the units were bolted on seemingly at random; but in fact Applications worked and reworked the building's
program to assure that every unit got as much sun and air, as many
windows, as short a walk to toilets, as possible; and so optimized along
many dimensions it accreted as complexly and organically as a coral
reef, and with the same stochastic logic.

Toward the summer's end the man who had lived alone in the unit next to Hare and Willy was shifted to another project. The people associated with his part in the project gave him a farewell party in one of the common rooms. They gave him a few small gifts, mostly jokes relating to work, and they ate cakes and drank tea spiked with some alcohol someone had got from the dispensary. Willy, to whom things like this were important, who remembered the birthdays of many people, had spent some time decorating the corner of the room where they sat, and he gave the departing man a real gift, an antiquity he'd found somewhere in the city and made a box for in the shop. The antiquity, a small white-enameled cube of thin metal, had a little door in the front that opened to show an interior space, and four red spirals symmetrically painted on its top, and representations of dials or knobs here and there. It was passed from hand to hand, everyone marveling at how old it must be and wondering what it might have been for. Willy was pleased with the effect. The man who was leaving was very touched, even surprised, Hare thought, and embraced Willy; and then, somewhat clumsily, all the others. Then the party was over.

The next week two young women came to live together in the empty room.

They were young, in training in the project, and inseparable; shy amid new people, but making their way together. Hare talked with them now and then when he found himself opposite them at dinner. They weren't sisters, though they looked enough alike to be sisters: both dark, with luminous eyes and full, childlike yet maturely sensual faces. Their light clothes of Blue (they had come up from a project in the south) revealed them as though without their knowledge or consent. They had a funny way of finishing each other's sentences. When Hare came upon one of them alone and began a conversation with her, she talked of little but her friend, her opinions and feelings, and kept looking around to see if she had come. When at last her friend appeared, a calm joy transformed her face. Hare watched her, his polite smile stuck on his face: watched love come and settle on her features and in the repose of her body.

Because they lived next to him, because he could hear through the thin wall the indistinct murmur of their voices and the sounds of their movements, Hare thought often about the two of them. The time he spent alone in his room was punctuated by the small sounds they made: a laugh over some joke Hare couldn't hear; obscure sounds of things moved or handled. Without willing it, he found himself growing alert to these sounds, his attention pricking up at them like a dog's ears. When Willy was also in the room, Hare paid no attention to the next room; his and Willy's noises drowned them out. But alone he listened; even held still to listen, found himself making the silent movements of a spy with his glass or his book, so as not to miss— What? he asked himself; and went on listening.

There was a night when loud scrapings, sounds of effort, laughter, business, went on some time next door; something bumped against Hare's wall. He could make nothing of all this until, after general lights-out, he climbed into bed and heard, close by him and more distinctly than before, the sound of their voices, the jounce and squeak of their bed.

They had shifted the few furnishings of their room, and moved the bed they shared from the far side of the room up against the wall that divided their room from Hare's, the same wall against which his own bed was placed. It was as though the three of them were now in the same bed, with the thin wall between them dividing it in two.

Hare lay still. There were long silences; a word from one of the two of them, a brief answer; the noise of the bed when one of them moved. He heard one of them get up, the pat of her naked feet on the floor; she returned, the bed spoke. With slow care he rolled over in his bed so that he lay next to the wall. Still he could hear no intelligible voices, only the sounds of their speech. But now, with the lights out, alone next to them close enough to touch them but for the wall, he knew he must hear, hear it all.

His mouth was dry, and there was a kind of intense constriction in him. Where had he once heard that you could eavesdrop on an adjoining room by putting a glass against the wall, and listening as though to a megaphone? He only thought about this for a time, lying still; then he slid from the bed, lit his night-light, and took his glass from the sink. His knees were watery-weak. The feelings he felt didn't seem to him to be sexual, weren't like the feelings caused by sexual fantasies, they were more dangerous somehow than that; and yet he knew now what he wanted to hear. He got silently back into bed; he placed the glass against the wall, and his ear against the glass, his heart beating slow and hard.

There was a sort of roar, like the sound of the sea in a shell, the sound of his own blood rushing; then one of the two women spoke. She said: "When the first boy has passed the last marker."

"All right," said the other. "I don't know."

Silence.

What were they talking about? They were together, in bed. Lights were out. They might still have a night-light on: that he couldn't tell. He waited.

"Last boy passes the first marker . . . ," said the second who spoke.

"No," said the first, laughing. "*First* boy passes the *last* marker. You got the last boy."

More silence. Their voices were distinct, and not far away, but still remote, as though they spoke from the bottom of a clear pool. Hare knew he could listen all night long, but at the same time he grew horribly impatient. He wanted a sign.

"I don't like that one. Let's do another."

"You're just lazy. Listen again."

"Oh, let's stop."

Hare understood then. They were solving a puzzle, the kind printed in the back pages of mathematical journals. Aimlessly, without paying it much attention, they were working out a relay-race problem. Hare did them himself sometimes, when he had nothing better to do.

How could that be? They had one another, they were alone in a room, in a bed, they loved each other, they were free, free together in circumstances so enviable that desire only to be a witness of it, only to know a little of it, had driven Hare to this shameful contrivance, the glass against the wall, the wanting ear against the glass: and they were working out—or not even really bothering to work out—a puzzle in a magazine. But why would they? How could they?

He lowered the glass from the wall. Desire must not be what he thought it was: if its satisfaction was always present, it must grow blunted, it must not even be often thought of. That must be so. If you lived with the one you loved you did puzzles, had arguments, sometimes made love, slept. Couldn't he have supposed that to be so? It was obvious. Desire was a wholer, though not a larger, thing than the thing that was within himself. Of course it must be: and that cut him more deeply than anything he had expected to overhear.

There was further talk from the next room. He picked up the glass and listened again, willing them to show each other love, for his sake. But the talk was unintelligible to him now, private, or perhaps directed at something visible to them alone: anyway, meaningless. Then speech grew infrequent. Still he listened. Then, when silence had gone on so long that it might as well have been an empty room he listened to, he gave up, exhausted by the effort of attention; no doubt they slept.

Hare didn't sleep. He lay awake, feeling irremediably cheated, cheated of their desire. He wouldn't have minded the hurt he would have suffered that their desire faced away from him, so long as he could have witnessed it; yet even that they had withheld from him— not even on purpose, not conscious of him at all, having no intention toward him whatever.

On other nights he listened again. He sometimes heard things he could interpret as lovemaking if he chose to, but nothing clear enough to gain him what he wanted—entrance, commonality, whatever it was. When he slept with Willy, he made a joke of it, telling Willy in a whisper that the two could be heard; Willy smiled, intrigued for a minute, then bored when nothing immediately amusing could be heard; then he slept. Desire kept Hare awake beside him. Desire lay heavily in him: his own, the two women's desire that faced away from him. Desire seemed lodged hard in his throat and gut, distorting his nature and his natural goodness, something foreign, not a part of him, which yet cut every part of him, like a knife he had swallowed.

That month when Willy was moved to the night shift and Hare saw him only at dinner and for a few moments when Hare was preparing to leave for the project and Willy had just returned, Hare felt a certain relief. He couldn't have stopped, now, listening to the undersea sounds that came through his drinking glass, and of course he couldn't do it when Willy was present—but it was more than that. He couldn't have put Willy out of his room, that would have been like cutting a lifeline, but he couldn't now have him nearby either.

His presence was like a reproach, a sign that what had become of Hare need not have happened.

HISTORY NO LONGER EXISTED. Hare had had to reinvent it.

On his free days he would find excuses to avoid the communal activities of the dormitory, the classes and criticism sessions and open committee meetings, and with a tablet and pencil he would wander in old parts of the city, working and dreaming—working by dreaming—over this invention of his, history.

On a bench in a crowded park he sat opposite a great and now unused building, fronted with fluted pillars and crowned in the middle of its roofline with complex statuary, a group of men and women victorious or defeated, winged infants, and horses, which seemed to be bursting out of the unknowable old interior into the air of the present.

The building was a favorite of his, partly because it was still whole, partly because the present had not been able to think of a use for it, but mostly because as he sat before it—closing one eye, then the other, measuring with his thumb and with lengths of the pencil held up before him—he saw most clearly the one sure fact he had learned about the past. The past thought in geometry: in circles, sections of circles, right triangles, squares, sections of squares. The building before him was nothing but an agglomerate of regular geometrical figures, cut in stone and overlaid with these striving figures continually trying, but never succeeding, in bursting them apart. He imagined that the whole structure—even the fluting of the pillars, the relation of different bits of molding to one another—could be expressed in a few angles, in small whole numbers and regular fractions. Even the statues, with their wild gestures and swirling draperies, were arranged in a simple rhythm, a graspable hierarchy.

He thought it was odd that it should be so; and he thought it was odd that he should derive so much pleasure from it.

Why had the past thought that the world, life, should be pressed into the most abstract and unliving of shapes—the regular geometrical solids that were foreign to all human experience? Except for a few crystals, Hare thought there were no such things in the world. The mind contained no such shapes; the shapes the mind contained, if they were to be projected into the world, would look like—they *did* look like—the clusters of people's housing that crept up to the edges of this park. They would look like the stacked, irregular dormitories Hare had lived in for years, restless accumulations always seeking optima, the result of a constant search amid shifting variables. Those were the mind's shapes, because the computers that designed the dormitories and the people's housing contained and used the logic of the mind: contained it so completely that the shapes that lay within the human mind, truly there in the resulting structures, were no more immediately apparent there than the shapes of the mind are in a casual conversation, with all its strategies, accommodations, distributions, and feedback loops.

But this building was part of the past. The past wasn't like the present. The past hadn't understood the shapes the mind naturally contained, it had no way of ascertaining them—no mirror as the present had in its big, linked computers; the past had longed for absolutes, for regularities foreign to the mind's nature, and (if the stories Hare had heard were true) had enforced them brutally on a heterarchical world. What peace, then, when all those hierarchies, when the very striving for hierarchy itself, had been dissolved in the Revolution! Peace; Perpetual Peace. The false and hurtful geometries had bent and melted and yielded to the unpredictable, immense stochastic flow of the act-field, leaving only a few memorials like this building, obdurate things caught in the throat of time.

Afternoon sunlight fell slantwise across the broad face, coloring its gray stone pink. There was a band of tall letters, Hare saw, running across the whole length of it, obscured by dirt: the light had cleansed them for a moment, and Hare, with many glances from his tablet to the building, copied them:

° IAM ° REDIT ° ET ° VIRGO ° REDEUNT ° SATURNIA ° REGNA °

He closed his tablet, and rose.

In the broad avenue that led away from the park and the building, people went by, an endless stream of them, bicycles and trucks, cadre in Blue, children and workers and country people. Two young women, one in shorts pedaling a bicycle, the other half-running beside her, holding with one hand the teetering bicycle that tried to match her slower pace. Both young, and smiling; they smiled at Hare when they saw that he watched them—happy, it seemed to him, and proud of their young health and beauty on a summer day. He smiled for them, paying them the compliment of being proud of it, too.

The people were a corrosive against all hierarchies.

Still smiling, Hare followed the avenue to where the cathedral stood on a square of its own. Its high doors stood open on this day; in winter they were closed, and only a small wicket let people in and out. And for whom had these immense doors been built, then, what beings needed such a space to go in and out by? As he passed through, he looked up at the ranked carvings of figures, human but attenuated and massed like a flight of birds, that swooped up the sides of the archway, ascending toward those seated at the top like a committee. Who were they all? The dead, he thought.

The interior of the church had been cleared of its benches. The great floor was being used (though vast spaces rose unused and useless overhead) as a clearing house for newcomers to the city. Groups of people stood before long tables waiting for housing and ration allocations. The sound of their footsteps, of the answers they gave to questions asked of them, even the taps of a pencil or the click of a terminal, rose into the upper volume of air and came to Hare's ears magnified and dislocated from their sources. Behind the tables low walls of board had been set up all along the stone walls of the church, whether to protect the walls, the windows and statuary, or simply for a place to pin up directions and information, Hare didn't know. He walked, head bent back, trying to follow the lines of the arches into the upper dimness. This, he thought, more than the other building across the park, mirrored the mind: the continual exfoliation of faces, birds, flowers, vines; the intersecting curves of vaulting, like the multiplane ellipsoids of a whole-program simplex; the virtually infinite reaching-away of it all into unseeable darkness. The colored, pictured glass, like the bright but immaterial reflections of the world in the thinking brain.

It wasn't so, though, really. His eyes, growing accustomed to the dimness, began to follow the lines of arches into the circles out of which they had been taken. He measured the regular spaces between pillars, and counted the repeated occurrences of squares, rectangles, triangulations, symmetries.

It was breathtaking how they had bent and tortured those simple ratios and figures into something that could approximate the mind.

He felt a fierce joy in the attempt they had made, without understanding why they had made it. He thought this church must have been built later than the less complex but also somehow more joyful building beyond the park. He wondered if there was a way of finding out.

The low wall of flimsy board closed off some deep recesses even more full of figuration and glittering metalwork than the body of the church: like hollows of memory, if this were a mind, memory at once bright and dark. Peering into one such recess, Hare could see the statue of a woman atop a sort of table heaped up with what looked like gilt bushes. She wore robes of blue and a crown, a crown circled with pearls; some of the pearls had come out, leaving dark holes like caries. She stood beneath a little vaulted dome; a band of mosaic around the dome made letters, letters like those across the top of the arch he passed under every day, or the facade of the building down the avenue. He opened his tablet to a clean page and carefully copied the letters:

°° A ° V ° E ° E ° V ° A °°

Ave Eva. "Ave Eva," he said aloud.

The woman's face—modest, with lowered eyes, despite her crown—did not look to Hare like the Eva he knew, his Eva. And yet he thought she did look, in her self-contained remoteness, a little like the Eva he sometimes dreamed of: dreams from which he would awake in a sweat of loneliness and cold loss.

He went out of the church.

No: now the building down the avenue, washed in sun, looked far the younger of the two, cheerful and new. Older or younger? He thought about it, blinking in the sunlight.

It seemed there ought to be enough of the past to make an act-field in itself; it rose vastly enough in Hare's mind, teasing him with limitless complexity. But it wasn't so. Even if everything that could be known about the past were known, it would still be far too thin to make an act-field. Even now, in order to construct a human act-field, the Revolution's computers ingested so much random matter that it was hard to find room in them for ordinary computations, food production, housing allocation: and even so, what the computers possessed was only a virtuality—a range of acts that was virtually but not truly infinite; enough for the Revolution's work, but still only a shadow cast by the immensity of the real act-field in which the people lived.

And history—out of which all old theories about society had been made—was a shadow of a shadow, so thin as to be for the program's purposes nonexistent. The whole of the past was less nutritious to the browsing search programs than the most meager meal of daily motions, truck accidents, school schedules, dew point, paper consumption, hospital discharges, decibel levels. The kinds of postulates that could be derived from history would not be recognized within act-field theory as postulates; out of the paucity of history, closed systems only could be constructed, those hurtful tautologies that ended in *ism*, once thrust onto the world like bars—systems less interesting than common arithmetic.

Hare knew all that. It didn't matter that the past was made of stone, and the present of thin walls of board bolted and stapled over it: history was a dream. History was Hare's dream. He didn't expect to learn from it; he knew better than that; he meant only to escape to it for a while.

Amid the crowds of the people; mounting up old stone steps, cut beside narrow cobbled streets; moving with the traffic along the broad avenues bordered with shuttered buildings; in the center of the great square, measuring its size by the diminution of a lone bicycle progressing toward the mouth of a far arch, Hare was in history, and his heart was calm for a while.

HARE WONDERED if the magnitude of the coincidence that had brought him together with Eva could be calculated, and if it were, what the magnitude would be. To daydream in that way meant to suspend his own knowledge of how such calculations worked—they could never work backward, they were abstracting and predictive; they could never calculate the magnitude of coincidences that had actually occurred. And Eva herself would have hated it that he should try to calculate her, predict her, account for her in any way.

Outlaw in a world without law, how had she come to be the way she was? Remembering the distances within her eyes, or waking from a dream of her regard turning away from him, he would think: she was trying to go far off. Loving Hare had not been a stopping or a staying but had been part of that going; and when he had explained to her that no, she couldn't go far off, didn't need to, and couldn't really even if she wanted to, then she went farther off by not loving him any longer—walking away, wearing her pregnancy like defiance, not hearing him call to her.

Hare sat at his desk at the project, looking at the notes for his manual on coincidence magnitude calculation, but thinking of Eva and the years since, years in which an automatic grasp he had once had of the Revolution's principles had weakened, a gap had opened between himself and his work, and the project that had been so eager to get him had begun to have difficulty finding something he could do. Eva had thought she could walk away from the world; Hare, standing still, had felt the world move away from him, grow less distinct, smaller.

No, that wasn't possible either. And any work he could do had its real importance to the Revolution, the same real importance as any other work; work for the Revolution had all the same formal properties and was all included; what it consisted of hour to hour didn't matter, it was all accounted for.

Importance of coincidence magnitude calculation to the social calculus. Importance of the calculus to act-field theory. Importance of act-field theory to the Revolution.

When Hare had been in school, that had been part of every lecture, on no matter what topic: its importance to the Revolution, its place in Revolutionary thought. Even in those days the boys hadn't listened closely; the Revolution was too old; it was either self-evident or meaningless to say that a thing was important to the Revolution, because there wasn't anything that was not the Revolution. *Dedicate yourself daily to the work of the Revolution,* said the tall letters that ran above the blackboards in his classroom. But that was like saying, Dedicate yourself to the activity of being alive: how could you do otherwise? If act-field theory, which lay at the heart of the Revolution and all its work, meant anything, then no act—no defiance of the Revolution, no grappling to oneself the principles of it, no ignoring or rejecting of it—could be not part of it. If any act could be not part of the Revolution, if any act could be conceived of as being not governed by act-field theory, then the field would dissolve; the Revolution would founder on the prediction paradox. But act-field theory was precisely the refutation of that paradox.

It was what he could not make Eva see. She was haunted by the thought that all her acts were somewhere, somehow, known in advance of her making them, as though the Revolution hunted her continually.

Importance of act-field theory to the Revolution. Hare twisted in his chair, linked his hands, changed the way his legs were crossed. The morning sped away.

There was a woman he had known in cadre training, at summer camp, in those days of night-long earnest conversations in screened wooden common rooms, conversations that absorbed all the sudden feelings of young men and women for the first time thrust into daily contact. She had believed, or had told Hare she believed, that there was no such thing as act-field theory. She was sure, and argued it well, that for the Revolution to succeed, for the people to live within it happily and take up their burdens and do their work, it was only necessary for the people to believe that the theory *did* work. Once-upon-a-time, she said, social theories made predictions about behavior, and thus could be disproved or weakened or shown to be self-contradictory when behavior was not as the theory predicted, or when unwanted results arose when the theory was applied. But act-field theory simply said: whatever you do, whatever comes about in the whole act-field, is by *definition* what act-field theory predicts.

Every shocking or astonishing turn of events; every failed harvest, street riot, cadre shake-up; every accident or reversal in every life, are all as act-field theory says they must be. They are all accounted for, every spike, every rising curve, every collapse. And when the Revolution has swept away those failed and hurtful systems that attempt to predict and direct the future, there is nothing left to rebel against, nothing to complain of. There is Perpetual Peace. Street riots slacken in force, go unnoticed, are aberrations that have been accounted for even before they occur; the people go to work, harvests are steady, cadre do their jobs, there are no longer shake-ups and purges, none at least beyond those that have been accounted for. The Revolution is permanent. In the midst of its eternal mutability and changefulness, society no longer needs to change, or to hope for an end to change either. Life goes on; only the hierarchies are gone.

She said she didn't object to any of that. She felt herself to be in training precisely to do that work, to maintain the illusion that act-field theory governs human life in the same way that axioms govern a mathematical system. She felt (Hare remembered her uplifted face, almost aglow in the dark common room, long after lights-out) that there could be no higher a task than to dedicate oneself to that work, which was cadre's work within the Revolution. Act-field theory dissolved social truisms like an acid, but it itself could never be dissolved; its works were its truth, the happiness of the world was its truth, the Revolution was its truth.

Hare listened, warmed by her certainty, by the strength of her thought; and he smiled, because he knew what she did not know. He had been where she couldn't go. She was no mathematician; she had not, as he had, just completed a multiplane ellipsoidal simplex and entered it onto the central virtual act-field and seen—he *saw* it, saw it like a landscape full of unceasing activity—the interior of the Revolution's data base, virtually as limitless as the actual act-field it reflected: and then saw it, at the bidding of his program, turn and look at itself.

How could he communicate that mystery? Ever since, as a schoolboy, he had learned that there are problems—in topology, in chaos description, in the projection of fractals—problems with true and verifiable solutions that only computers can construct, and only other computers verify, Hare had known how it was that computers could truly contain a virtual act-field, an image of the world larger than he could access within himself. He could put real questions about the world to the computers and receive real answers, answers not he nor any human mind could predict, answers only the computers themselves could prove true.

There *was* an act-field, and a theory by which it could be constructed. Just as Hare knew there was an interior in the young woman who sat beside him, which he could apprehend through her words and through the strength of her thought touching him as he listened and looked, an interior bounded by the planes of her pale temples and the warm body real beneath her clothes of Blue, so he knew truth to be contained within the interiors of the Revolution's computers: truth both unbounded and boundless, endless by definition and somehow kind.

He remembered that feeling. He remembered it, but he no longer felt it. He could not ever, knowing what he knew, think as that woman had, that act-field theory was a lie or a kind of trick. He imagined, guiltily, what a relief it might be to think so, but he could not. But act-field theory no longer seemed to him kind, as it once had. It seemed to be hurting him, and on purpose.

But if act-field theory underlay the Revolution, and the Revolution could not hurt him or anyone, then act-field theory could not hurt him.

He sat back, his hands in his lap, unwilling to touch the keys of the composer, reasoning with himself—tempted to reason with himself, as a man with a wound is tempted to probe it, pull at the scab, pick at the hurt flesh.

He *did not need to feel* these things, he told himself. He did not need to write an introduction to his manual. It needed none. Of course any part of act-field theory could be introduced by an explanation of all of it, but no part *needed* such an introduction. The project knew that. Certainly the project knew that. In fact the project had given him this job precisely because it would not require him to think about the whole of act-field theory, but only about the simple mechanics of its application. And yet the fact that he could no longer think clearly about the whole (which was why he was here now before this antiquated composer) meant that when he was confronted with this simple introduction, he felt like a man confronted with a small symptom, not in itself terrible, not even worth considering, of a fatal systemic disease.

Perhaps, though, the project *had* thought of all that; perhaps it had put him here, in this cubicle, and presented him with the concrete, the explicit and fearful consequences of act-field theory, to punish him for no longer being able to think about the theory itself: for betraying, through no fault of his own, the Revolution. No fault of his own: and yet he felt it to be his fault.

No, that was insane. If the Revolution was not always kind, it was never vindictive, never; for a heterarchy to be vindictive was a contradiction in terms: the Revolution could not be if it could be vindictive.

Unless there was a flaw in the theory that underlay the Revolution, act-field theory, which made heterarchy in the world conceivable, which made the integral social calculus possible and therefore all the daily acts and motions of the human world, including his sitting here before his unwritable manual.

But there could be no flaw in act-field theory. Hare knew that as well as he knew that he was alive. Act-field theory proved that all possible disproofs of act-field theory were themselves provable parts of act-field theory, just as were all other acts. It was not even possible for Hare to consider act-field theory without the act of his considering having been accounted for by the theory.

All possible strategies for avoiding paradox within act-field theory were also parts of the theory; they were acts the theory defined. Just as his sitting here pursued by paradox was defined and accounted for.

Hare had entered into an infinite-regression fugue; the taste of infinity was in his mouth like metal. That which had freed the world held Hare like a vise, like a cell in which a madman runs eternally, beating his head first on one wall, then the other.

HARE GOT PERMISSION to go and visit Eva and his son in the country. It was never hard to get such permission, but it was often hard to find transportation for such a purely personal trip. Hare's cadre status was no help; in fact it was considered not quite right for cadre to be seen traveling for private reasons. It didn't look serious; it could seem like unearned privilege and might be offensive to the people. Hare learned of a convoy of trucks that was taking young people out of the city to help with the harvest, and he was promised a ride on one of these.

When Willy returned from his night shift, he shook Hare awake, and as Hare, yawning and blinking, dressed, Willy undressed and climbed into the warmth Hare had left in the hollow of the bed. Hare went out into the empty, frosted streets, still tasting the dream from which Willy had awakened him.

Hare wondered if there were different names for different kinds of dream. This dream had been the kind where you seem to be telling a story to someone, and at the same time experiencing the story you are telling. Hare had been telling a story to Willy, a shameful and terrible secret that he had always kept from him, but which he had to confess to him now because Willy wanted to play. He had to confess how when he was a boy—and here he seemed not only to remember the episode but to experience it as well—when he was a boy, he had cut off his penis. He had done it deliberately, for what seemed like sufficient and even sensible reasons; he had kept the cut-off penis in a box. He saw himself opening the box in which he had kept it, and looking at it: it was erect but dead-looking, white, the veins in it pale. As he looked at it, the dream rising away from him, he realized how stupid he had been—how horribly stupid to have done this irrevocable thing that could never, ever be repaired, why, why had he done it— and as he contemplated the horror, Willy's hand awoke him. Relief of the purest kind washed over him, the dreadful burden fell away: it was all a dream, he hadn't done it at all. He grasped Willy's hand and laughed. Willy laughed, too. "Just a dream," Hare said.

Hare walked through the streets to the truck depot, shivering, feeling alternately the horror of the dream and the relief of waking. He had been distant with Willy lately: he ought to stop that, there was no reason for it.

Young men and women, students and younger cadre, filled the open trucks, mostly in Blue, mostly laughing and pleased at the prospect of a day in the country. Hare found the driver who had promised him a ride, and he was helped into the truck by several hands. The convoy started its engines, and as dawn threw long bars of sun between the buildings, they drove out of the city. The young people in Hare's truck began to sing, their strong high young voices clear, and the truck's engine a bass accompaniment to their song. It was stirring.

More somber, across the bridge, were the wide tracts of old city suburbs, long straight streets crossed by dirt roads where pools of water colored with oil stood in the truck ruts. Children, who perhaps belonged to the flowerets of modular housing growing over the dumps and shacks and abandoned factories, looked up to watch them pass. The young people stopped singing and began to find places within the truck's bed where they could sit comfortably through the long ride. Some opened books or journals they had brought. Some of the women lit cigarettes, though none of the men did.

Almost all the boys Hare had known who smoked cigarettes gave them up at a certain age, once out of school, but many women didn't. Women who smoked were of a certain kind, Hare thought; or at least they all seemed to roll and smoke their cigarettes in the same way, with the same set of gestures. Like that one, sitting with another out

of the wind in the shelter of the cab: tall, lean, her hair cut short and
carelessly, she used her cigarette in a curt, easy way, dangling it in
her long hand that rested over her knee, flicking it now and then with
her thumbnail. She rolled it within her fingers to lift it to her lips,
drew deeply though it had grown almost too short to hold, and grace-
fully, forcefully, two-fingered it away over the truck's side, at the same
time dismissing the smoke from herself through mouth and nostrils.
The hard way she smoked seemed like the mark of a sisterhood; her
friend beside her smoked in much the same way, though not tempered
by the grace, the young eyes, or the kind smile that this one paid to
Hare when she caught him studying her. Hare returned the smile,
and the woman, still smiling, looked away, running her hand through
her hair.

Hare laughed, enjoying the way what she did to mask herself,
the smoking, revealed her to him. Young: when she was older, and
more practiced, it wouldn't reveal her, but just now, in this morning,
it did. Perched on the truck's scuppers, among youth—among the
unmarked who desired so much to be marked, and in their desire,
showing their tender just-born selfhoods the more cleanly, the more
tartly to his senses—Hare for a moment felt how well after all the
world is put together, and how well the people in it fit into it: a
seamless act-field into which, no matter what fears he felt, Hare too
fitted: into which even his fears of not fitting also fitted in the end.

He thought of Eva.

The truck left him off at a bare crossroads, where it turned toward
the broad garden lands. He walked the two or three miles to the
cadre crèche where Eva lived and worked, and where their son was
growing up: three years old now. Hare had with him some books for
Eva—she always complained there weren't enough, or the ones she
could get weren't interesting—and a gift for his son, which Willy had
made: a nesting set of the five regular geometric solids, all inside a
sphere. They could be taken apart, and with some trouble, put back
together again.

IT HAD NEVER BEEN the case that anyone, any bureau or person or
committee, ever forbade a marriage or some permanent arrangement
between Eva and Hare. There was no committee or person who could
have done that. Eva believed from the beginning, though, that such

a barrier existed; it made her at once fearful and angry. Hare couldn't convince her that, whatever stories she may have heard, whatever rumors circulated, cadre weren't forbidden to regularize affairs like theirs. "They don't want it," Eva would say. "They don't care about anyone's happiness, so long as the work gets done. They never think about anything but the work." And Hare could not make her believe that, in the very nature of the Revolution, there was no "they," there could not be a "they" of the kind she feared and hated.

Certainly there was a tedious set of procedures that had to be gone through, but none of them were restrictive, Hare insisted, they were only informational. Many different people, yes, had to be informed; Hare and Eva's plans had to be passed outward into wider and wider circles of diffusion, first to the proctors and flow people at the project, then to the committee representatives at the dormitory, then the neighborhood and city committees; eventually the whole Applications system would have to be informed—would in the course of things become informed even if they only made their intentions known to the first levels of this diffusion. And it was true that in some ways they, Hare and Eva, would stick out: the two of them would make a spike within the regularities of cadre life, which was almost entirely unmarried, assumed to be celibate out of dedication and the pressure of work, and communal in ways that made strong pacts between individuals unusual; which meant that strong pacts between individuals upset people who were upset by unusual things. But why, Hare asked Eva, shouldn't the two of them be an oddity? Didn't she know that such oddities, such spikes, were implicit in the forms of communal life if that life isn't imposed by a hierarchy, is not tyrannical, is chosen, is the Revolution itself? They are assumed; they are already accounted for.

She did know that. But when Hare said—carefully, mildly, without insistence, a plan only for her to consider—that they could make their plans known at the first levels, within the first circles, and see if they were prevented even in the most subtle ways, and at the first signs of such resistance (though he knew there could be no such resistance) draw back if she liked: then she looked away and bit her nails (they were small, and bitten so short that the flesh of her fingertips folded over them; it hurt Hare to look at them) and said nothing.

She wanted something to defy, and there was nothing. She didn't want to hear his explanations of heterarchy, and when he made them, he felt as though he were betraying her.

He knew so much. He knew nothing.

He remembered her face, the day when she told him she was pregnant: her eyes questioning him even as her mouth said she didn't care what he did, this act was hers, she alone had decided on it. She expected some declaration from him, he knew: a denunciation of her for having done this, or a sudden pact offered that he would join her in it, as though joining a conspiracy. It didn't even seem to matter which he did—join her or denounce her. In fact he did neither, not being able to imagine either, not knowing why she should set such terms for him, yet knowing also that it was not really he who was being challenged; and obscurely certain he was failing her by not being able to feel as she did—that her act was a crossroads, a crux, a turning point where a fatal choice had to be made.

He thought: *What if I had pretended to understand?* If she thought she was surrounded by watching authorities, who wanted her not to do what she wanted, if the child had been a defiance of those authorities, then what if he had somehow pretended to join her in her defiance? Would she have believed him? Would she not have gone away? He thought it was possible, and it hollowed his chest to think so.

The cadre crèche was a cluster of low buildings, dormitories, a barn, yards, infirmary, school; beyond were the gardens and fields that the commune worked. In and out the doors, through the halls bright with autumn sunlight, boys and girls came and went, and women tending groups of children. Hare thought this must be a good place for children; it was crowded with the things children like— tools, growing things, farm animals, other children.

He wandered from room to room with his gift and books, asking for Eva. All the men and women who lived and worked in the crèche were parents of children being raised here, but many other children of cadre were here whose parents had chosen not to stay with them. Hare thought of them, the parents, separated also from each other perhaps, attached to faraway long-term projects, or working with the people in distant cities.

It's just hard for cadre, that's all, he thought, very hard. The people acted as they acted, their actions describable by theory but otherwise unbound; for cadre it was different. There were no *theoretical* barriers to their acting just as they would; theoretically, they did exactly that. In practice it was different, or seemed to be different; there seemed to be a gap there, a gap that only kindness and a little good humor could cross. He and Eva were bound by that now, if by nothing else; bound by what separated them, by the whole front of the Revolution sweeping forward at once, which could not be otherwise. With kindness and humor they could cross the gap. It was enough; no one had anything better. It was hard but fair.

In the summer refectory the long tables were now heaped with gourds and vegetables to be put by for the winter; men and women were stringing onions and peppers, hanging up bunches of corn to dry, packing potatoes for storage. Hare stood at the threshold of the broad, screened room filled with harvest, sensing Eva among them before he saw her.

"Hello, Eva."

She turned to find him behind her, and a smile broke on her face that lifted his heart as on a wave. "Hello," she said. "How did you get here?"

"I found a ride. How are you?"

She only regarded him, still smiling; her cheeks were blushed with summer sun, like fruit. "Where's Boy?" Hare asked.

She had called their son only "the boy" or "boy" from the start, refusing to give him any other name; eventually "Boy" had become simply his name, a name like any other.

"He's here," Eva said. She leaned to look under the table at which she sat and called: "Boy! Come see."

He came out from beneath the table, dark curls first, and lifted his enormous eyes (they seemed enormous to Hare) first to his mother, and then to Hare. "Hello," said Hare. "I've brought this for you."

He held out the sphere to Boy, without revealing its secret, and Boy took it from him cautiously; the length of his eyelashes, when his eyes were cast down to study the gift, seemed also extraordinary to Hare. He opened the sphere; inside it was the pyramidal tetrahedron.

"I sent a message," he said. "Didn't you get it?"

"No," she said. "I never to go the terminals. You haven't come to stay, have you?"

"No," he said. "No, of course not."

"You still have work, at the project?"

"Yes." If he had said no, would her face have darkened, or brightened? "It's not the same work."

"Oh."

She had done nothing since he had known her but pose questions he could not answer, problems without solutions; why then did he hunger for her as though for answers, the answers that might unburden him? All at once his throat constricted, and he thought he might sob; he looked quickly around himself, away from Eva. "And you?" he said. "What will you do now?"

Eva was coming near the end of her time at the crèche; she would soon have to decide what she would do next. She couldn't return to work on any of the major projects whose people were housed in the agglomerate dormitories such as Hare and Willy lived in. There were cadre who lived outside such places, among the people, but for the most part they did work for which Eva wasn't trained.

She could also ask to be released from cadre: put off her clothes of Blue and join the people, and live however she could, as they did. She and Boy.

"What will you do?" Hare said again, because she hadn't answered; perhaps she hadn't heard him. Eva only looked down at Boy absorbed in opening the tetrahedron. For a moment it seemed to Hare she resembled the statue of the crowned woman in the cathedral. Ave Eva.

"It might be," he said, "that they would have work for you here, if you asked for it. For another year or more. So that you could stay on here. Isn't that so?"

Boy had turned and stood between his mother's legs, lifting the tetrahedron to her, patient to be helped. Eva only laughed, and picked him up.

"Would you want to do that?" he asked. And just then Boy, in Eva's arms, reached out for him, gleefully, and clambered from his mother to Hare.

The first thing Hare perceived was the boy's weight, much greater than he had expected from the compact miniature body; yet heavy as he was he seemed to fit neatly within Hare's lap and the compass of his arms, as though they were made to go together—which they were, in a way, Hare thought. The second thing he perceived was Boy's odor, a subtle but penetrating odor that widened Hare's nostrils, an odor of skin in part and a sweetness Hare couldn't name. He could almost not resist thrusting his face into the crook of Boy's neck to drink it in.

Eva had begun to talk of her life at the crèche. It was tedious, she said, and every day was much like every other, but she had come to prefer it to the city. All summer, she said, she had worked in the gardens, learning the work with a man who had been a long time in the country, working with the people. He was someone who couldn't be predicted, she said, just as she was herself such a person; someone outside the predictions that were made for everyone, for every person. She had liked talking with him, hearing about other ways of life in other places, other possibilities; after work they had often gone walking with Boy, in the evenings that had seemed to her so huge and vacant here, quiet, as though waiting to be filled.

"As though you could step into them and keep walking away forever," she said.

"Yes."

"That's what he said."

"Yes." But Hare had not been listening; he had been hearing Boy, and feeling him, the solidity of him in his lap. He had begun to imagine what it would be like to live here, as Eva and Boy did. He thought of the passage of days, the work that there would be to do —work which Hare had never done but which he could just now imagine doing. *Have you come to stay?* Eva had asked him, as though it were possible he might. He was Boy's father, after all; he had a place here with him, too. Perhaps, if he did, if he came to stay with Eva and Boy, he might in the course of a year recover the balance he had lost, shake off the lethargy that bound him.

"Would you want to do that?" he asked again.

"Do what?"

"Stay here. If you could."

She looked at Hare as though he had said something not quite intelligible. "I'm not going to stay here," she said.

"Where are you going?" Hare asked.

"I'm going," Eva said. "They can't have me any longer."

"But where?" Hare insisted. "What city? What town? Are you going to look for another project? Are you going to give up Blue?"

She had begun to shake her head, easily but certainly rejecting each of these possibilities. It would not be, her face seemed to say, anything that could be predicted.

"Eva," Hare said. "You know you can't just . . . just fall out of the universe." He had begun to experience an awful swooning vertigo. "You can't, you can't. You'll be alone, you . . ."

"I won't be alone."

"What? What do you mean?"

"I told you," Eva said. "I told you about him. I was telling you all about him. Weren't you listening?"

"Oh," Hare said. "I see."

"You tell me there's no place to go. But there has to be."

"I didn't mean that. I meant—"

"There has to be," Eva said, looking away.

Hare sat still and said nothing further, but it seemed at that moment that the color began to be drained from everything that he looked at: the fruits and orange gourds on the tables, the people in Blue, the colored tiles of the floor. The boy he held, who had a moment ago seemed as large as himself, no, larger, seemed to grow small, distant within his arms, a foreign thing, something not connected to him at all, like a stone. He looked up. Had the sun gone behind clouds? No, it still shone. Where did this awful chill come from? "It's not what I meant," he said again, but did not hear himself speak it; he could only marvel at what had happened, what had happened and would not cease happening. Boy fell silent, and slipped out of his arms to the floor.

"I don't feel well," he said, and stood abruptly. "I'd better go."

Both Boy and Eva were looking at him, curious and not unkind, not kind either; not anything. Their faces were stones or closed doors, the faces of those at accidents or public quarrels. Hare thought he would see such faces if he were to die in the street.

"Do you want to go to the infirmary?" Eva asked.

"No. I'll go."

"Are you sure?"

"I'll go," Hare said. "I'll go. I'll go. I'll go."

HE HAD THOUGHT it was just a story he was being told, about working in the gardens, about summer evenings, empty and vast. He hadn't listened carefully; he hadn't known that there would come this sickening reversal of figure and ground, showing him a story he had not suspected, that he was all unready for. Nothing had been as he thought it was; he had walked into what was the case as into a truck's path.

Hare stood at the crossroads awaiting the trucks returning from the farmlands to the city. The strange gray blindness that had afflicted him at the cadre crèche had not passed, nor had the dreadful stonelike weight in his chest. He patted his chest as he stood waiting, trying to press it down. He thought perhaps he would go to the infirmary when he returned.

It was true what he told her, though, what he knew about heterarchy and she did not, that it was limitless, that it could not be got outside of, that to think about it as though it had an inside and an outside was a kind of pain, the pain of error that is fruitless, unnecessary, because self-inflicted: this conviction that by choice or by some dreadful mistake it is possible to fall out of the universe. Hare knew (it was all that he had ever tried to make her see) that it was not possible to fall out of the universe.

He thought of her and Boy and the man they were going away with. His thought followed them into a featureless stony landscape, without weather or air, under a vault of dun sky. Forever and ever would they be there.

He tried to draw breath deeply, but the painful bolus beneath his sternum seemed to prevent it; he could not get the air he needed.

Perhaps he would die. He wasn't old, but he seemed to be suffering some irreversible debility that quickened almost daily. He could not clearly remember, but he thought he had not really been well since the time when he was a boy and had cut off his penis.

No, that was a dream. Wasn't it? Yes, of course it was. With horror Hare realized that for some hours he had actually been assuming it to be so: that he had done such a thing and was now living with the consequences.

No. He wasn't truly ill. It was only this weather oppressing him, airless and chill, this close vault of dirty sky. He was grievously thirsty. Perhaps he would die.

The trucks surprised Hare, appearing suddenly past sundown; apparently he had been standing and waiting for hours without noticing time pass. He waved. The truck that stopped to pick him up was not the one that had brought him out; the young people who helped him in were not the same, were not the cheerful boys and girls who had sung children's songs and talked and laughed. These looked at Hare in silence, their faces in the twilight pale and reserved.

Hare thought he should explain himself to them. Perhaps he could ask them for help. He opened his mouth, but his throat was so dry and constricted that no words came out; he gaped foolishly, he supposed, but no one smiled. He forced his throat to open, and a gout of language came out that Hare did not intend or even understand.

He had better not talk more, he thought. He sought for a place to sit down; the silent young people drew away from him as he crept toward the shelter of the cab. He supposed that after all no one had heard the nonsense he had spoken, not over the noise of the truck's engine: an awful imploding roar that grew steadily worse, sucking the air from Hare's mouth and the thoughts from his head. He leaned against the cab, his hand hanging loosely over his knee; with his thumbnail he flicked the fragment of cigarette he held between his fingers. He was certain now that he would die of his old wound, or, far worse, that he would live forever. Forever and ever. "Ave Eva," he said, and a woman laughed. Hare laughed, too. The words seemed the only thing that could relieve his thirst. *Ave Eva*, he said again, or thought he said, unable any longer to hear himself under the withering roar. *Ave Eva. Ave Eva. Ave Eva. Ave Eva.*

THE COMMITTEE had high seats behind a long desk. This was not so that they sat above those who came before them to be examined—Hare's guard explained this to Hare—but so that everyone in the room could see them clearly. The committee leader had a seat on one side, and before her she had some dossiers and some things taken from Hare's room, including the sketches of old buildings and the attempts Hare had made to decipher their inscriptions. Hare found it hard to recognize these things; when the committee leader held up a sketch and asked Hare if he had made it, he couldn't answer.

He tried to answer; he opened his mouth to answer, but could not make an answer come out.

The committee was patient. They listened to testimony about Hare, what he had done, how he had been found. They rested their cheeks in their hands, or they leaned back in their chairs with their hands folded in their laps; they asked gentle, unsurprised questions of the people who came before them, trying to get a clear story. When there seemed to be a contradiction, they would ask Hare what had happened. Hare opened his mouth to answer; he thought he could answer, possible answers occurred to him, then other possibilities, opening and branching like coincidence-magnitude calculations, switching figure and ground. Still he thought he could answer, if he could only say everything at once, describe or state the whole situation, the whole act-field, at once; but he could not, so he only struggled for a while with open mouth while the committee waited, watching him. Then they returned to questioning the others.

The two women who lived in the dormitory room next to Hare described how he had got into their room late at night: how he had forced his way in, though talking all the time very strangely and gently, about how he meant them no harm, wanted only to explain. They told (interrupting each other, finishing each other's sentences, until the committee head had to speak sharply to them) of their fear and confusion, of how they had tried to get out of the room, how Hare had prevented them. A torn nightdress was shown to the committee. The committee talked among themselves about attempted rape, asking questions that embarrassed the two women, but asking them so gently that answers were got at last.

Some others from the dormitory described how they had come to the women's room, and their struggle with Hare. They were eager to explain how or why it was that they had let Hare go, had not apprehended him and taken him then and there to security or to the committee representative. The committee head, not interested in hearing this, kept guiding the witnesses back to the facts of Hare's struggle: what weapons he had had, how he had behaved, what he had said.

Willy came in. He wanted to go and stand next to Hare, but the committee asked him to stand where the other witnesses had stood; and all through his story he kept looking at Hare, as though pleading

with him to say something, to behave in some way that Willy understood. Hare saw that Willy's hands shook, and he wanted to take his
hand, to say something to calm him, but he couldn't move. His guard
sat behind him with his hands in his lap and probably wouldn't have
prevented his going to Willy or speaking to him, Hare thought; but
he couldn't do it, any more than he could answer the committee's
questions.

Much of Willy's story was taken up with how tired and upset
Hare had been before this incident, the bad dreams he had had, the
troubles at the project. Hare couldn't remember any of the things
Willy told about—any more than he could remember going into the
women's room, or fighting with the people in the dormitory—but it
seemed to him that the more that Willy, with every kind intention,
tried to explain away Hare's behavior, the worse it looked to the
committee. It sounded as if Willy knew something really terrible about
Hare, and out of love was covering it up.

But Willy had once said to Hare that he knew all about him, and
there wasn't anything terrible.

Hare wanted to say that, more in Willy's defense somehow than
his own, but he could not.

Then, as Willy told about going out after Hare, and searching
the city for him, Hare began to remember something of the events
that were being told to the committee. In the same way that a dream
that is forgotten on waking can be brought into the mind, disconnected
but vivid, by some event of the day, some word or sight, Hare caught
sight of bits of the story he had been in. When Willy told of finding
him at last, huddled on the wide steps of the building whose inscription
he had copied out, he remembered. Not how he had come to be
there, or what had happened to him before, but that alone: Willy's
hand on his shoulder, Willy's face before him, speaking to him. And
he knew also, with a deep horror that deafened him to the committee's
further proceedings, that that had not happened yesterday, or the day
before, but weeks ago; and he remembered nothing at all of what
had happened between then and now.

The committee leader was speaking, summing up the committee's
findings. The case was really out of their provenance, she thought,
and should probably not have been brought before the committee.
She asked Hare if he had anything further to say.

The guard behind Hare leaned forward and tapped Hare's shoulder. Hare stood.

"Do you have anything you want to say?" the committee leader said again, patiently and without insistence.

"It's hard," Hare said. This came out of his mouth as though it were a stone he had dislodged from his throat, not like something he had decided to say. "It's very hard!"

He looked at the faces in the room, the committee, his neighbors, Willy. He knew, suddenly, that they would understand: they must, for they were all engaged with Hare in this hard thing together. "We all know how hard it is," he said. "The work of the Revolution. To grasp its principles isn't easy. To *live* them isn't easy. I've tried hard. We all have." They would understand how he had stumbled, they must; they would help him to rise. Together, in the face of the awful difficulties of the Revolution, they would go on. If he could lean on them, then as soon as he regained his feet, he could try again to be someone on whom others leaned. He smiled, and waited for their smile in return. "It's hard, always grappling with these difficulties. Act-field theory: that's hard to think about." He shook his head in self-deprecation. "Oh, I know. And the duties of cadre. The duty to *understand*. The committee knows how hard it is; everyone knows. I only want to say that I've tried. I want the committee to understand that. The committee understands. You understand."

He stopped talking. The circle of faces around him had not changed. It watched him with what seemed to him a terrible reserve, and something like pity. He knew he had not been recognized. He said, to the calm, closed face of the committee head: "Don't you think it's hard?"

"No," she said. "Frankly, I don't."

Frankly. Hare could not stand up any longer; his knees were unable to support him. Frankly. She had spoken with that remote, unmoved concern, the remote concern with which an adult will speak to a child in moral difficulties, difficulties the adult doesn't feel; without anger, with some impatience, without collusion: collusion would be inappropriate. Hare knew himself to be absolutely alone.

He had stopped speaking. After a moment the committee head gave the committee's resolution. Hare was to be remanded to a hospital. The committee head said she was sure that with rest and attention, Hare would return to normal. When he was better, they might have another meeting, and consider what amends Hare might be able to make for his behavior, if any were thought to be necessary then. Her last words to Hare were the usual formula spoken at the end of committee deliberations, when disposition of someone's case was made. She said: "Did you hear that?"

IN THE SPRING, discharged from the hospital, Hare was given a paper with an address on it, an address in an older part of the city where he had used to go often, to look at buildings.

It was strange to be once again alone on the street. Not often in the last months had he been alone at all, and never on the street. Except that a thin rain was falling, cold and hastening, he might have wandered for a while through the squares and alleys of the quarter; they seemed at once new and familiar to him, and the sensation of walking there was both vivifying and sad: the mixture of emotions made him feel painfully alive, and he wondered how long it would persist. But he turned up his collar and went on to the building to which he had been sent.

It was an old one, and one he remembered. He had stood before it more than once, feeling with his sight and his sense of proportion the curves of its stonework and its iron window-grilles. He had used to look in through the barred glass doors, down a long marble-floored hall bordered by columns, but he had never dared to go in. He went in now. There was an aged doorkeeper who took Hare's paper, made a remark about the rain and shuddered as though it were he who was wet and not Hare, and entered something on the terminal before him. He waited for a reply in the display, and when he had it, he left the little cage or box that was his station and led Hare down the long hall, past the columns pinkish and blue-veined like the legs of old people, to a tall open door. He waited for Hare to enter, then closed the door behind him.

The big room was empty. There was only a work station—a desk and two chairs, a terminal, a pile of printouts and other papers—which stood in the center of the floor, or not quite in the center, as though whoever had placed them there hadn't known that the room had a center. It did, though: it was clearly marked by the radiating diamonds of the parquet floor; it was plumb with the central diamond-shaped pendant of the chandelier, a multitiered forest of swagged lights and what seemed to be strings of jewels, that hung from the center of the ceiling above. Hare looked up at it as he crossed the floor to the desk; it swung around its axis, or rather seemed to swing, as he moved. He sat down in the chair beside the desk, crossed his hands in his lap, and waited. He didn't know who it was he waited for, or what disposition would be made of him now; he only supposed, with a sort of automatic humility he hardly even recognized in himself any longer, that whomever he waited for would be wiser than himself, would be able to see him clearly and know what was best.

That was one thing he had come to learn, over the last months— not how wise others were, but how unwise he was himself. He had learned to trust those who trusted in the world in a way that he could not: that way he hoped he might once again come to trust in the world himself. And even if he could not—even if there remained in him always some fatal mistrust—still there was no better thing that he could do: nothing else at all that he could do.

It hadn't been easy, learning that.

In the first weeks of his stay in the hospital, he had mostly been aware of the difference between himself and others, both those in difficulties like himself, and those attempting to help them. It seemed to him important, desperately important, to make those differences clear: to explain what it was in him that made him unlike others and unable to be as they were. It frightened him to be among so many who were bewildered, hurt, angry, or sad, not because he was not all these things himself, but because he felt himself to be unimaginable to them; and it frightened him more to be with the staff, because he could not define for them, in any way that he felt they could truly grasp, the perplexities within himself that made him unlike them: made him unwise, unwhole, divided and in pain, as they were not.

They were not even cadre for the most part, the staff, not anyway in the wing to which Hare was moved after a series of tests had determined there were no metabolic disorders at the root of his condition. (He had briefly hoped that some such disorder would be discovered, to relieve him of the awful burden of finding the explanation elsewhere. But there was none.) In his wing were those whose troubles were unanalyzable, and the staff there were only kind, only experienced and sympathetic, only set to watch the disorders take their course, and give what common help they could. And how could Hare explain to them—heavy women who nodded and patted his hand, male nurses who spoke in banalities—about act-field theory, its unchallengeable truth, its danger to him?

He knew so much. In his long, long silences his own explanations were his only occupation, and seemed to him all that sustained him over an abyss. He knew, with great precision, what stood between him and happiness; he knew quite well that he did not need to feel as he did, that just beyond his feelings, just past his really quite simple and explainable error, lay the real world, which he could reach if he could only stop making this error, or even stop explaining the error to himself: but when he tried to say these things aloud, to explain this predicament to the nurses and the staff or the other patients, the explanations hurt him; and the real world, as he talked, grew more fearsomely remote.

The explanations broke, in the end, like a fever. Then there were tears, and shameful incontinence of grief, and helplessness; no help at all but kindness and attention, the help of those who knew how little help they could be.

He had not believed it was possible to fall out of the universe: yet he had experienced exactly that. He had fallen out of the universe into explanations of why he could not fall out of the universe. And he had to reach for the hands of those who could not even envisage such a thing and be drawn back in. In the common rooms, with their old furniture worn and stained as though by the sorrows of those who used it; in the kitchens, where he clumsily helped with meals; in the winter yards and the crossing paths of the grounds, he would be swept by waves of healing integration, unwilled, as though some severed part of him were drawing back within him: waves of feeling that left him weak and still afraid of the strange things he contained. When those diminished, too, like the terrible explanations, then he was empty. He looked around himself at the world and knew that though he did not know it, it knew him. He ate its nourishing breakfasts, blinked in its watery winter sunlight, joined its talk tentatively, washed its dishes with humility. He could not fall out of it.

Willy, who had visited him weekly, bringing good food and (what Hare hungered more for) stories of the people Willy knew, came on a spring day to take him away. In his dossier, encoded now with thousands of others in the hospital's records, the course of his illness and its resolution were charted, he knew; and when the magnitude of his difference from others was accounted for, his absolute otherness factored in, they were exactly as act-field theory predicted. It was all right.

All right. He sat, hands folded in his lap, waiting beneath the chandelier.

When a dark woman in Blue of about his own age came through the far double doors, Hare stood. The woman waved to him apologetically across the vast room, picking up a folder from a cart of them by the door; smiling, she crossed the geometrical floor to where Hare stood.

Among cadre there was no rank, and therefore no marks of rank beyond the simple clothes of Blue they all wore. But subtle distinguishing marks had nevertheless arisen; Hare knew that the cluster of pens in this woman's pocket meant heavy responsibilities. There was more, though. In the last months the faces of those he met were often charged for him with intense but imaginary familiarity; and yet about this woman he was sure.

"I know you," he said.

She raised her eyebrows. She didn't know him.

"Yes," Hare said. "Years ago." He named the study camp where in the summer of Hare's seventeenth year they had known one another, studied together, hiked together. As he spoke, he remembered the summer darkness of the common room where late at night they had talked.

"Oh, yes," she said. "Yes, yes, I remember now. A long time ago." She smiled, remembering. "A long time."

She had opened Hare's dossier, and now drew out the drawings of buildings and the calculations of their geometries that Hare had made. The last time Hare had seen them was when he stood before the committee: so long ago.

"Do you know why you do this?" she asked. "Copy these things?"

"No. I like them, I like to look at such places, old places, and wonder how they came to be; what the people thought and felt who built them."

"History," she suggested. "The past."

"Yes."

"That interests us, too," she said. "My project, I mean."

"Oh," said Hare, not knowing what else to say. "Is yours . . . is it an Applications project?"

She smiled. "No," she said.

"Oh."

She rested her cheek again in the palm of her hand. "I think," she said, "that long ago there was another time like this one, when people lived in places whose history they didn't know, whose history they had forgotten. They had lost history because they knew so little. They called that ignorance 'darkness,' and when they began to relearn history, they called that knowledge 'light.' But we're in darkness, too. Not because we know so little, but because we know so much. It's not different."

"Knowing everything is not different from knowing nothing," Hare said. "Is that what you mean?"

She quoted an old principle of act theorists, one that had become an adage of Revolutionary cadre: "We seek no solution—only knowledge of the problem."

She turned to the drawing of the building opposite the cathedral, whose lettering Hare had copied out. Her finger touched the words.

"Do you know what they mean?" Hare asked her.

"No," she said. She folded her hands before her. "When you went out to do these things . . ."

"It was always on my own time," Hare said. "On free days."

"Did you tell anyone where you were going, what you were doing?"

"Not usually. Not all of it." Hare stared down at the hat he held in his hands. He felt, like an old secret wound, his taste for history, like a peasant child's taste for eating dirt.

"It must have seemed," she said, "that you were leading a double life. Did you feel that way? That you were leading a double life?"

At her words hot tears rose to Hare's eyes with awful quickness, and he felt for a moment that he would sob, as he had sobbed so often at just such small remarks that winter. A double life: a life inside, and another outside, between which Hare was pulled apart.

"Will you go on doing this, now?" the woman asked gently, her eyes watching Hare's evident distress.

"I don't know," he said. He looked up. "I want to help," he said.

"I want to do useful work. I know that I haven't been much help for a long time, but I'm stronger now. I want to be of use."

She turned over the picture, and pushed the pile toward Hare. For a moment he didn't understand that she was giving them back to him. "I think your project made a mistake when they removed you from the work you'd been doing," she said.

"You do?"

"I think the better thing would have been to release you from cadre altogether." She rested her cheek again in the palm of her hand. "What do you think?"

A storm of shame arose within Hare, a storm that made the dreadful imploding roar he had first heard in the truck returning from the country. It broke so quickly over him that he had to suppose he had all along been expecting precisely these words to be said to him. Through its great noise he could not hear his own answer: "I'll do as you think best," he said. "Whatever you think."

"Go to the people," the woman said.

Hare covered his eyes. "I'm not good for much," he said. "There's not much I know how to do."

"What I suggest is this," the woman said. "You'll get a ration card and find a place in the city. Then—go on with what you did. I mean the drawings and the investigations you liked. History."

Hare listened.

"If you would," she said, "I would like you to come back here, now and then, and talk to me—to my project—about what you are doing."

"That would be all right?" Hare said. "I could do that?"

"You can do as you like," she said. "You can go back to your project, too."

"No," Hare said, feeling a strange warmth at his breastbone. "No. I'll do as you say."

"I don't know what we can learn, but I think . . . well." Her humorous eyes regarded him steadily. "Anyway there's probably nothing better for you to do. You are an oddity, aren't you?"

"Yes," Hare said.

"Did you think the Revolution was not large enough to contain you?"

"No," Hare said, "I didn't think so." But he had: he understood at that moment that he had thought exactly that.

She took a card from his dossier and handed it to him. "Take this to Applications, in the old cathedral," she said. "They'll tell you what to do. Come back here when you like. I'll be glad to see you."

She stood; Hare's interview was evidently at an end. He twisted the hat he held in his hands.

"I was remembering," he said, "something you told me. That summer, when we met at study camp." He felt his heart fill with a familiar apprehension. "You said . . . We were talking about act-field theory, which I was working on then, and you told me you believed that there was no such thing really as act-field theory at all; but that so long as everybody believed there was such a theory, and cadre believed that it worked, then it *did* work."

"Yes?"

"Yes." Dreadful as the danger Hare felt himself to be in, narrow as the ledge he stood on, he had to ask: "Do you still think that?"

"No," she said. Her smile hadn't passed, but it had changed, as though she not only shared a memory with Hare, but a joke as well; or a secret. "No, I don't."

HARE WALKED through the old quarter of the city, not feeling the thin rain soaking through his shoes. He seemed to himself to be naked but warm, to be already not in Blue, and walking in the world for the first time, as though his feet created it step by step: the world he had fallen out of, the world into which Eva and Boy had gone. He laughed, in fear and hunger for it.

His desire was not what he had thought it to be: his desire for history, for Eva, for Boy, none of it was what he thought it was. He knew nothing, nothing of the world he walked in; but he might learn.

What a strange, what a foolish error for him to have made, Hare thought. If he were called again before the local committee to make restitution for the trouble he had caused, he could tell them: he had come, without knowing it, to see the world in hierarchies. He, with his years of training, his excellent education, had built hierarchies in his heart. He had not known it until he had been asked to resign from cadre and had been overcome with shame: as though to be in

Blue were better than to be not in Blue, to be cadre better than to be among the people.

He had believed act-field theory governed the act-field, and not the reverse. But the act-field governed. In the computers of the Revolution, as in the corridors and hollows of Hare's heart and mind, there was only a virtuality, after all; a virtual real-world, and not a whole one. He was inside the act-field and not it inside him; so was the Revolution, and all its work.

"Oh, I see," he said aloud. He had stopped walking. At the end of the street the great square opened, crossed by a single person on foot, a single bicycle. The obscure huge buildings that bordered it were soft in the misty rain. Hare, for the first time, yet not as though for the first time, but as though coming to remember some commonplace thing of enormous, of vital, importance, saw the act-field. Still; calm; with no face, not kind, not cruel, not anything. He reached out with his mind to touch it, but everywhere he touched it, it parted, showing him spaces, interstices, emptinesses formed by the edge of himself facing the sparkling edge of the world.

Hare cried out, as though stung. He felt the sensation of an answer, a sensation like a physical shock. The answer was an answer to a figure-ground problem, the simplest figure-ground problem, a problem solved long ago. The answer was an emptiness, formed by the edges of two questions: but the sensation of the answer was like a bit of light, a point of light lit, flaring fiercely and burning out: a physical sensation, a brief coincidence, an act.

Then it was gone. Hare set out across the square.

YEAR OF THE BAT: SCIENCE FICTION MOVIES OF 1989

Bill Warren

Because the Nebula Award for best dramatic presentation lasted only three years (1973–75), the editors of this annual anthology enlist the aid of Bill Warren to document trends in the making of science fiction films.

The author of *Keep Watching the Skies,* a two-volume study of SF films from 1950 to 1962, Warren often acts as a consultant to those in need of guidance. (While I was writing "The Ommatidium Miniatures," for example, he provided me with valuable information about *The Incredible Shrinking Man.*) He has written for *Starlog, Fangoria, Cinefantastique, American Film,* and other magazines. He was the American correspondent for the French TV series "Fantasy," and he is now the system operator for the "Show Biz Round Table" on the General Electric computer service GEnie.

"In the past," Warren notes, "I've tried to cover every science fiction film released in the U.S. in a calendar year—theatrical releases and videotapes. Because space limitations have forced me to say less about the significant films than I've sometimes wanted to, I am now concentrating on theatrical releases, with only one or two video releases creeping in. This is not to say that there are no worthwhile video releases, only that they are hard to find. I mean, last year I told everyone to catch *Zombie High* . . . but did you? Noooooo."

As a special feature, Warren appends to this year's survey essay a brief summary of prevailing trends among SF films in the 1980s.

The 1980s have ended. Technically, of course, 1990 is the last year of the 1980s, but few other than the pedantic counted it that way. Instead, 1989 was widely viewed and endlessly discussed as the wrap-up of what many called the "Me Decade." I've got mine, Jack, you get yours. (Others had pegged the '70s with that tag.) Trend-watchers were busily examining the movies of 1989 to spot evidence of the

315

acknowledged characteristics of the '80s, as if social trends are directly linked to our arbitrary system of numbering years.

If the "Me Decade" was reaching a self-immolating climax in 1989, why was the biggest hit of the year, and one of the biggest hits of *any* year, about a millionaire playboy so self-sacrificing that he goes out to battle crime personally? In a way it is comforting to realize that a man so selfless, so devoted to helping others, *could* become such a hero to a bunch of yupped-out teenagers whose main idol had been Donald Trump.

However, because I'm criticizing others for reading too much into the (presumed) end of the 1980s, I really should avoid reading too much into the amazing success of *Batman*. After all, if there was any real trend to the year of 1989 in SF movies, it was the futuristic underwater thriller—which floated to the surface, a dead fish, by year's end.

In years past, I have tried to discern any trends visible among the SF movies of a given year, but that's really not germane in 1989— and it can be argued that it never was. While hard-SF movies are in the minority, the genre has become pervasive and calcified. It's here to stay. If there are trends, the most notable, and interesting, may be that there are more and more films in which the distinction between fantasy and science fiction simply does not exist. Some fantasy films, not covered here, incorporate SF elements; a few SF films include some fantasy elements. It's not a matter of technical accuracy, but of how the material is handled. A movie like the fascinating *The Navigator* exists in its own world; it's developed logically, and is realistically handled, but is not based on scientific reality. It would not be better if it *were*.

Initially, I had hoped to make this year's entry a strong platform for advocating the restoration of the Dramatic Presentation Nebula, an award I feel should exist to honor good science fiction writing in films, television, radio, and theater. But this issue is divisive *within* the Science Fiction Writers of America organization, and members of that organization make up only a small percentage of this book's readers (otherwise, we're *all* in trouble), and listing the reasons for the clash would probably bore nonmembers. Therefore, I will limit myself to pointing out a few films I think would have been worthy of being nominated for such an award, had it been presented for the year 1989. (Among them, one not dealt with here: Terry Gilliam's prodigious *The Adventures of Baron Munchausen*.)

A final note before plunging into a discussion of the major science fiction movies of 1989. In previous *Nebula Anthology* reports, I have done my best to cover *every* science fiction movie released in a given year, both theatrically and on videotape. This was not easy, either in tracking down all the films, or in simply sitting through some of them. I saw it as some kind of noble mission that only I could carry on.

I have come to the reluctant conclusion that it's not noble, nor yet a fool's errand, but also isn't necessarily a good idea for this book. Last year's entry, after all, was a long, painful wade through endless lists of awful movies. Now, someone *should* cover SF movies in this manner, and I would like that someone to be me, but the limitations of space and of focus—and of my own tolerance for enduring crap—have at last become clear to me.

Fortunately, the level of crap was pretty low in 1989, which featured several remarkable movies, two of which received little notice upon their initial release, but which are bound to become more and more highly regarded. But the first SF film out of the chute for the year was nothing much, Tri-Star's *DeepStar Six*. The rumors around Hollywood had it that the film was a preemptive strike; allegedly, financing was granted the makers of "Deep Six" (its earlier, better title) if they could get an imitation of *Leviathan* out on the market before *Leviathan* itself. But of course, no one in Hollywood would do that.

DeepStar Six begins well, but the script is undeveloped and the characters unconvincing; even good actors, including Miguel Ferrer, Marius Weyers (the klutz from *The Gods Must Be Crazy*), and Cindy Pickett, have an upstream swim in bringing their roles to life.

Writers Lewis Abernathy and Geof Miller pour *Alien* and *Jaws* into the same pot, mix in a little *Hello Down There* and *The Thing* (either version), and never veer from the standard increasing-in-danger storyline. In the near future (presumably), a U.S. Navy–operated undersea base is commanded by Dr. Van Gelder (Weyers), who hopes to prove that people can live for long periods on the ocean floor. Everyone is overworked, although there are romances among the personnel. When a huge cavern is discovered nearby, Van Gelder orders it collapsed, but it's larger than expected, and an unknown

Something escapes from the cavern and starts killing everyone. (Why? Never made clear.)

This is an acceptable if routine outline for a science fiction/horror adventure. But in terms of exposition, the writers painted themselves into a corner. Everyone aboard the base has been there for a long while—so it's unnecessary for anyone to explain to someone else just what they're doing, but this meant their dialogue is often so loaded with technobabble as to be incomprehensible to the audience; we just don't know what they're doing. The characters are weakly drawn, so we don't have many reasons to *care* about their deaths.

Unfortunately for director Sean S. Cunningham, who keeps things moving briskly, the structure of the film precludes much suspense. Of necessity, the monster has to stay outside the undersea base much of the time. The film insists that it is gigantic, and yet when the base is flooded, it gets in and hides in the water in these necessarily small rooms. The creature, vaguely described as an "arthopod," never seems real, partly because we never have a good idea what it looks like, and partly because what we do see looks rather unlikely. The miniatures of DeepStar itself, the little craft attending it, and the missile base are all convincing enough for a movie. Just not this one.

DeepStar Six was relatively low-budget, but *Leviathan* was expensive ($24 million), with medium-big stars (Peter Weller, Richard Crenna, Lisa Eilbacher, Hector Elizondo), superlative sets (by Ron Cobb), and mostly good special effects. The surprise, and disappointment, wasn't that *Leviathan* is better or worse than the earlier film, but that it is hardly any *different*.

In the near future, an underwater mining team happens upon a Soviet ship, which proves to have been deliberately sunk. Two of the miners, crude Sixpack (Daniel Stern) and luscious Bowman (Eilbacher), drink the contents of a flask found in the ship's safe. They soon develop a strange disease and die; after death, they meld together in a big heap. It turns out the Soviets were experimenting with genetic alteration, hoping to transform people into water-breathers, but instead they got some shapeless thingy that ran amok, leading the Soviets to scuttle their ship. Naturally, this happens again.

The explanations offered in the script by David Peoples and Jeb Stuart are tenuous at best, and infernally confusing at worst. The monsters—there are ultimately several of them—drink blood, apparently change shape, gain the minds of those they devour, and reproduce from small chunks. All this is contrived for horror effect, but the traits don't add up to anything.

George Cosmatos directed, competently enough. In fact, everything about the film is competent except the derivative, muddled script. It's so routine, so predictable, that halfway through the press screening I felt like switching to another channel. Films like this are more annoying than low-budget misfires like *DeepStar Six*. The film cranks up the editing toward the apocalyptic climax, Jerry Goldsmith's good score provides a driving rhythm, the cast acts up a storm, but the movie just lies there. Like so many other films, *Leviathan* is ultimately just another imitation of *Alien*.

The underwater biggie was *The Abyss*, courageous, beautifully realized, well acted, exciting, tense—and familiar and inconclusive. At the end, a gigantic alien spaceship rises from the ocean depths, bearing sunken ships, an underwater mining rig, and other objects on its vast surface. But all this turns out to be a mere device for reuniting separated lovers. The audience wanted and deserved more than that. Writer-director James Cameron's heart was in the right place, but his mind was full of the familiar and banal.

The setup: it's the good old near future again. When a U.S. submarine encounters something moving impossibly fast in an undersea trench near the Bahamas, it collides with the wall of the trench and sinks. *Deepcore*, an experimental undersea oil drilling rig, bossed by Bud Brigman (Ed Harris) and designed by Lindsey (Mary Elizabeth Mastrantonio), his soon-to-be-ex-wife, is the only underwater device that can reach the area where the sub went down before a major tropical storm strikes. A group of Navy Seals, commanded by Lt. Coffey (Michael Biehn), is sent down to take charge of operations. Coffey, already bitter and acid, takes an armed nuclear weapon aboard *Deepcore*, then goes mad from the physiological stress in adjusting to the depths.

When they arrive at the lip of the abyss, strange things begin happening. The crew encounters glowing objects, or creatures, which zip off at great speed. Lindsey sees a vast, manta ray–like object, and then, in one of the most magical special effect sequences I have ever seen, a long, thick tendril made of water comes into *Deepcore* to see *her*. The water tendril was done via computer animation, and is one of the greatest effects in movie history.

The Abyss is an almost-wonderful entertainment. The first third of the film is tense, exciting fun—fast, suspenseful, and involving. In a short time, Cameron, Harris, and Mastrantonio have made us care for the two leads, without forcing an "aw, they should get back together" reaction. Mastrantonio is great, and the excellent effects won the Oscar, but there are problems.

The film, which would have been better *without* the aliens, becomes diffused by the side issue of Coffey's going bananas. Alan Silvestri's music turns treacly and sentimental toward the end, drenching us in angelic voices, when the images are doing enough singing for anyone. And the ending wimps out. We want something grander, more exciting, more conclusive than "Close Encounters of the Damp Kind." Cameron is proficient, particularly with suspense; there are some numbing sequences in *The Abyss*, so tense that you are unaware of anything other than the movie, but he needed to look elsewhere than other movies for inspiration.

The Roger Corman–produced low-budget *Lords of the Deep*, also set underwater in the near future, also dealing with manta-shaped aliens, simply slipped out on videotape, and no wonder. It had nothing to recommend it.

The movie business being what it is, 1989 also brought the usual batch of science fiction sequels. David Cronenberg's *The Fly* was a true horror film—it horrified audiences with its graphic depiction of a man slowly becoming an amalgam of human and housefly—but also a vivid, powerful drama of discovery and alienation. It is, simply, a science fiction classic. *The Fly II* is just another monster movie.

In the original script for *The Fly* (I), before it was revised by Cronenberg for the better, the villain was an Evil Industrialist, a cliché and stereotype. Cronenberg tossed that guy out the window, but here he is in *The Fly II*. Lee Richardson is Bartok, head of a big laboratory somewhere devoted to something or other.

One of his experiments is Martin Brundle, son of the two leading characters in *The Fly*. Because of his aberrant chromosomes and genes, inherited from his flyized father, Martin grows from infancy to adulthood in five years flat. He is also a genius, a trait not ordinarily associated with flies. As an adult, Martin (Eric Stoltz) becomes involved in furthering his father's research into teleporting matter through the air like a TV picture. However, Martin, too, is turning into an amalgam of fly and human. In the meantime, he falls in love with Beth (Daphne Zuniga), apparently the only one of Bartok's lab employees who is not a soulless creep. Martin, abruptly gaining the ability to leap about like a grasshopper, escapes from Bartok, but is returned to the lab, where he cocoons like a butterfly. He erupts as a six-legged, mandible-headed mutant and Wreaks Revenge.

The script was worked on by various writers over the previous two years, including (in order) Mick Garris, brothers Jim and Ken Wheat, and finally Frank Darabont. But these writers, who have turned out good work in the past and no doubt will in the future, seem to have been forced to follow this poorly conceived plot. Darabont tried to create a betrayed father-son relationship between Martin and Bartok, but first-time director Chris Walas, a superlative special-effects technician, lost that somewhere, and some of his scenes are incoherently cut; frequently, Walas couldn't seem to find the right locations for the camera.

The real problem with *The Fly II* is the central difficulty with most movies today: it was conceived as a product, and talented people were forced to follow the company line. Cronenberg's *The Fly* was something else entirely: while satisfying the requirements of a science fiction–horror thriller, it also was a character study, a romance, and something of a grotesque comedy. *The Fly II* misses most of this.

The fifth of the *Star Trek* movies was directed by William Shatner who, not surprisingly, directs much as he acts: broadly, emotionally, with a lot of corn, stressed humor, and some extravagant qualities. It's another "*Enterprise* meets God" story, more literally than the others, and though it's not up to the level of *Star Trek IV*, it's fun with lumps in it.

The *Enterprise* crew comes to the rescue when benign fanatic Sybok (well played by Laurence Luckinbill) has seized control of Paradise, the only city on the Planet of Universal Peace. He wants a spaceship, and when the *Enterprise* arrives, Sybok seizes control and heads off for the center of the universe, where he hopes to find God Himself. Sybok, in an unconvincing development, is Spock's elder half-brother.

It turned out that *non*-Trekkies liked *Star Trek V: The Final Frontier* a lot more than the converted, partly because though Trekkies like Captain Kirk, many can't stand William Shatner. Furthermore, the script included noncanonical elements that annoyed them. Also, the special effects are highly variable. There's a great shot of a shuttlecraft zooming out of a moonlit Yosemite Valley, and the "God" scenes toward the end are satisfactory. But the planet where "God" lives looks like a Christmas tree ball wrapped in cellophane. It wouldn't have passed muster in *Queen of Outer Space*, much less a multimillion-dollar movie of today.

Other than the James Bond movies, the Star Trek movies are really the only series now going in the old-fashioned sense of the word. People used to love series movies, things like the Andy Hardy films, the Charlie Chan mysteries, the Tarzan adventures—not because they showed audiences something new, but because they *didn't*. Audiences wanted to go back to that place again, with those people, and have a similar adventure. And in fulfilling our expectations for a Star Trek movie, *Star Trek V* was reasonably satisfying.

Shatner was one of the co-authors of the story, with producer Harve Bennett and David Loughery, who wrote the final script. As a director, Shatner has his cameraman (Andrew Laszlo) try some big ideas and though not all work, he deserves praise for working hard to make this look like a *movie* and not a TV show. Although I found *Star Trek V: The Final Frontier* entertaining enough, all too many didn't, and it was the least successful of any of the Trek features. It took a long while for Paramount to decide to do *Star Trek VI*.

Back to the Future Part II began immediately where the first film left off, as Doc Brown (Christopher Lloyd) arrives breathlessly in the DeLorean time machine—now also capable of flight—to whisk Marty McFly (Michael J. Fox) and his girlfriend Jennifer (now played by Elizabeth Shue) off to the future. The original film's ending was not really a setup for a sequel, just a riding-off-into-the-sunset last burst of excitement—but here's the sequel, nonetheless.

Not as good as the first movie, *BTTF II*, as it's called by its fans, is broader, more cartoony. Director Robert Zemeckis, who did the first one, is fast and imaginative, and the script by Bob Gale is full of invention and clever ideas involving time travel. It lacks the odd poignancy which the first fleetingly grazed, and the movie suffered for the lack.

In the original, Marty was accidentally whisked back to 1955, where he accidentally interfered with the meeting of his parents, and so had to get them back together. The first dealt with the parents and Marty's dad's lifetime *bête noir*, Biff Tannen (Thomas F. Wilson), but in a real sense, *II* only has three characters: Marty, Doc, and Biff.

We're in 2015 long enough for a few good gags, a cloud of flying cars, and a restaging of the skateboard scene from the original, this time with flying skateboards and Biff's even more horrible grandson Griff (also played by Wilson). These future scenes were mostly to satisfy the setup in the last scene of the first movie, because about a third of the way into the film, Zemeckis and Gale go for the limit, as far as time travel stories are concerned. They introduce the idea of paradox.

While Marty and Doc are occupied elsewhere, Biff sneaks off in the flying time machine with an almanac of sports scores, and gives it to his younger self in 1955. So that when Marty and Doc return to 1985, it is not the 1985 they left. In *this* 1985, Biff is the richest— and most vulgar—man in the world, having turned Hill Valley into a cross between *Blade Runner*, Las Vegas, and Hell (if that isn't redundant). He used the almanac to make a fortune; he even ended up married to Marty's mom after his dad died (in this timeline).

To undo this, Marty and Doc can't go to the future, for as the film ingeniously points out, the future of *this* 1985 isn't the same as the one they just left. So they have to go back to that same night in 1955 and get the book away from Biff—without being seen by anyone, including Marty, back there already (from the first movie). Are you following all this?

Back to the Future Part II has the Zemeckis trademarks of speed and action, plus as many tucked-in, over-your-shoulder gags as a Will Elder comic book. It's brisk, fun, and good-natured, but that alternate 1985 is scary—it's so convincingly grim and unpleasant, and Thomas F. Wilson so brutally confident, that the film has some trouble recovering. But these scenes, as bleak as they are, are the best part of the film. Zemeckis and Gale assured everyone that this movie stands on its own, but it really doesn't—it's a second act, though a good one.

And as it turned out, it was more satisfying than *Part III*, the last act, filmed back to back with *II* and released in the summer of 1990.

Honey, I Shrunk the Kids, with the goofiest title since *I Was a Teenage Werewolf*, was in no danger of being overlooked, but no one expected this entertaining variation on *The Incredible Shrinking Man* to turn out to be the sleeper of the summer. It's funny, exciting, handsomely produced, and novel. It's also a sweetly clean movie, not compromised, but a true family movie—and it made a fortune.

Rick Moranis is Wayne Szalinski, who's sure that he can find a way to create a ray that will shrink things, and as the title says, the machine shrinks Wayne's kids Amy (Amy O'Neill) and brainy little Nick (Robert Oliveri), as well as neighbor kids Ron Thompson (Jared Rushton) and his older brother Russ (Thomas Brown). They end up, as a disgusted Ron puts it, the size of boogers, less than a quarter of an inch tall. Unaware of this, and frustrated by rejection by the scientific community, Wayne smashes the ray machine, then unknowingly sweeps the kids up with the debris and throws them into the garbage in the alley.

All the kids have to do is to walk to the Szalinski house through the ill-kept back yard. Of course, it is now, because of their size, a four-mile hike through a towering jungle of grass. And when Wayne and his wife realize that he has, indeed, shrunk the kids, they have to try to rescue the itsy-bitsy brats before they're stepped on or eaten by a passing bug.

The special effects are splendidly realized by a huge crew; the most impressive are the stop-motion sequences involving several arthopods: a bee, a friendly ant, and a hostile scorpion. Joe Johnston was a production designer for LucasFilm for several years—he designed Yoda, among other things—and makes a pleasing directorial debut here. The opening scenes are a little slower than one would like, and the cartoony tone of the scenes involving the adults doesn't jibe with the more straightforward approach taken to the characterization of the children. The plotting inventively pairs the children up in unexpected ways: the bratty neighbor boy with the teenage girl, for example, much to the benefit of the story. The movie plays fair with the premise: it is authentic science fiction. The original screen story was by Stuart Gordon, Brian Yuzna, and Ed Naha; Naha wrote the final script with Tom Schulman, and it's good enough that I would have liked to see it nominated for a (hypothetical) Dramatic Presentation Nebula—though not necessarily *win* the award. (I do not always consider the best film of a year also the best *written*.)

The distributors of *Bill and Ted's Excellent Adventure* had no faith in the movie; it sat on the shelf for several months, before being kind of tossed out the front door. And it became a genuine hit—the audience found the movie, and they responded. It's both clever and dopey, clever in its premise and in its willingness to try to say something within its clownish premise, and dopey because the premise really is pretty silly.

Bill (Alex Winter) and Ted (Keanu Reeves) are San Dimas, California, teenagers, who dream of becoming a hit band under the name Wyld Stallyns. They're so soaked in their dreams and in their friendship with each other that they haven't any brain room left over for stuff like school. But a big history final, in the form of a lecture by each student, is coming up, and if they don't pass it, Ted will be sent off to military school, and Wyld Stallyns will never be.

The failure of the group to form is potentially so catastrophic to the peaceful society of the future, which is based entirely on the philosophy of Bill & Ted (Be Excellent to Each Other, and Party On, Dudes), that George Carlin is sent back with a time machine in the shape of a phone booth to help Bill & Ted pass their history exam. This involves zooming in and out of the circuits of time, and picking up a passel of real historical figures, including Napoleon, Billy the Kid, Socrates, Freud, Beethoven, Joan of Arc, Genghis Khan, and Lincoln.

The script by Chris (son of Richard) Matheson and Ed Solomon is wittily conceived, in that it is the ultimate adolescent dream, beyond sex, beyond dreams of avarice: Bill & Ted aren't just *successful*, they will be the most important dudes who ever lived. But they never lose their blithe innocence, and that makes them charming, even endearing. Admittedly, they are also a little wearisome to spend an entire movie with, since they never vary, and are essentially the same kid.

Stephen Herek directed, and gets everyone through the film, but never works up much of a head of steam; he's unable to make the big climax as showy as one would like. Also, it does require Bill & Ted to suddenly *really* know a lot about history, which they must have picked up by simple proximity to the historical figures. Some convoluted fun is had with time travel, and the whole film is pleasant enough for what it is.

It was a good year for science fiction comedies, with the preceding two and Julien Temple's wide-eyed spoof of America, *Earth Girls Are Easy*. The script is by Julie Brown, Charlie Coffey, and Terrence E. McNally; it has plenty of cute ideas, but only a faint story—and what there is, is familiar and routine. But the movie is not about the story; it's about pop culture and the San Fernando Valley.

Geena Davis is tall, beautiful and talented, and the best thing about this cheerfully silly musical. She can seem ditzy and intelligent simultaneously, which comes in handy here. She's a manicurist at the Curl Up & Dye salon, about to be married to a self-absorbed doctor (Charles Rocket), who has lost interest in her. (I consider that fantasy.) She quarrels with him, tosses him out of the house, smashes up his playthings, and throws a bowling ball through his computer.

Meanwhile, up there in space is a Buck Rogers–styled ship, a big, plastic, toy-like rocket crewed by furry aliens, blue Mac (Jeff Goldblum), red Wiploc (Jim Carrey), and yellow Zebo (Damon Wayans). Wiploc and Zebo spy on Geena, and accidentally crash their spaceship in her swimming pool. (They enlarge whenever they leave the ship, shrink when they return.) The water makes it impossible for the ship to take off, so the pool has to be drained—but that takes a full day, so there she is, a Val with three fuzzy aliens on her hands. Naturally, being a beautician, she has them shaved, and they all come out gorgeous. The movie then just marks time until the end; we know that our heroine and Mac will fall in love and that she will dump the duplicitous doctor once and for all.

Co-writer Julie Brown is also a costar, and gets to do some of her own songs, the best of which is "'Cause I'm a Blonde," an anthem for airheads. Brown is funny and spoofy, and I would have been glad to see a lot more of her. But that would have meant less of Davis, and I couldn't have stood for that.

The sassy movie saunters along, stuffed with little and big gags (a nightclub called "Deca Dance"), more songs, some funny side characters, including the ultimate surfed-out pool cleaner (Michael McKean), bright colors, and terrific designs. Structurally, it's a mess, but it's also clever and entertaining.

For years, hard-core science fiction aficionados have been hoping for an SF movie written by a Real Science Fiction Writer; if one were given the chance, the theory went, he or she would show Hollywood how it should be done. So some were pinning hopes on *Millennium*, adapted from his own short story, "Air Raid," by an authentic science fiction writer, John Varley, who has won both top awards in the SF field, the Hugo and the Nebula.

As an airliner is about to crash, a doomed crewman sees something odd about the passengers. Bill Smith (Kris Kristofferson), a crash investigator, is puzzled by the cockpit recording in which the crewman screams, "They're all dead!" He later meets the alternately shy and aggressive Louise Baltimore (Cheryl Ladd), who after fleeing him, shows up again and seduces him, then vanishes. Later, Smith finds an odd device which temporarily paralyzes him, and again encounters Louise—who clearly has never met him before.

Louise is from a thousand years in the future, a world so destroyed by pollution and environmental damage that people have become sterile. The dialogue nicely sketches in a believable, if horrible, future world, but we never see it, just the giant lab (or whatever) housing the time machine. To save humanity, they have been going into the past and snatching hundreds of people who would not be missed, because without the intervention of the time travelers, they would die in crashing aircraft. This is to avoid paradoxes.

But after carefully explaining all this, the consequences of the paradox are so illogical as to seem arbitrary. Apparently paradoxes don't alter the future, they shake it up. Little paradoxes cause "time-quakes" but apparently no changes. A big enough paradox will destroy it. Furthermore, the romance between Bill Smith and Louise is awkward and schmaltzy—a major shame, because, to my great surprise, Cheryl Ladd is fine as Louise. However, she's not served well by the fish-out-of-water humor coloring her first/second encounter with Bill. Ladd comes close to making these scenes work, however, and her performance here may have changed some minds about her. She's not just a TV star; she's a talented actress.

Apparently director Michael Anderson was anxious about exposition, and we're given too much of it, both by scientist Daniel J. Travanti and robot Robert Joy, who delivers the movie's absolutely awful last line. Anderson directed one Oscar-winning movie, *Around the World in 80 Days*, but since then, for the most part his movies have been drab and uninteresting. *Logan's Run*, his other major SF film, suffers from much of the same literalness and caution as *Millennium*. When a movie company invests in a film like this, why do they so often hire a tired, ordinary old director like Anderson or Richard Fleischer? It's as if because they directed a few SF movies, they are cursed to direct more forever. Someone younger, more hip to the SF jive, would have been far more appropriate. Then *Millennium* might have been something memorable rather than the disappointment it is.

Communion didn't convince me that writer Whitley Strieber (played by Christopher Walken) was spirited away from his upstate New York cabin by blue gnomes and pink sprites, presumably aliens. The film opens well, to a haunting, bluesy jazz theme by Eric Clapton, as the camera moves slowly over night-lit Manhattan. And Walken is terrific as Strieber, completely believable as a writer from the moment we see him, however quirky he seems. Director Philippe Mora creates a mood of apprehension rather than dread.

Strieber, his wife Anne (Lindsay Crouse), their young son (Joel Carson), and two friends head for that cabin in the wilderness, but though their performances and the script are highly naturalistic, Mora uses looming or low camera angles to create a sense of disquiet, and the realistic tone of the script clashes with the horror-movie style of photography. At the cabin, as in Strieber's best-selling book of the same name, Strieber witnesses some scant elements of oddness, a bright light, a big eye peeking around a doorway, the impression that something touched his forehead. In a return visit to the cabin, he becomes so deranged that he almost shoots his wife.

When he visits psychiatrist Dr. Janet Duffy (Frances Sternhagen), hypnosis brings it all out at once. He was abducted from his cabin that night by hooded blue dwarves and slender, graceful creatures with big eyes, and taken up to what seems to be a spaceship. He's kept by them in a near-dream state, speaking in disjointed phrases, watching what goes on around him with interest but no involvement. This revelation doesn't help, though; he's still anguished. So finally he drives back up there, walks into the spaceship, and talks to a duplicate of himself disguised as a magician. The audience stares, agape. The story concludes with Strieber accepting the reality of what happened and preparing to write a book about his experiences.

Mora feels he has preserved the ambiguity present in Strieber's book—he hopes it remains unclear as to whether Strieber experienced all this, or really was on the verge of a breakdown. But there *is* no ambiguity in Strieber's book—it's obvious he feels that this was not only real but that it began in his childhood. Aside from the poor alien effects, *Communion* is technically a handsome achievement, but the script lets the production down. It becomes increasingly diffuse, even wandering, and though we can see from Walken's performance that *Strieber* is satisfied with what happens, the audience isn't likely to be. It's like half of a story, in which not only do we not know the other half, but we *never will*.

The Australian *Young Einstein* is a real departure for film biographies. It's the first not merely to ignore accuracy, but to assault it with cream pies. How you respond to the film depends largely on your tolerance for Silly, and willingness to put up with some boring scenes to wait for the good stuff.

In 1905, Albert Einstein (Yahoo Serious) is the skinny, bushy-headed son of poor but honest Jewish Tasmanian apple farmers. Bert is brilliant, he admits, and is forever cobbling together inventions to test theories he has just now devised. For example, his father finally reveals that the Einsteins have always been brewers of fine beer, but despairs of getting bubbles into beer. Bert turns his genius intellect to this task, and in splitting a beer atom discovers not only atomic energy, but a way to bubblize beer.

He heads off to Australia to patent his beer-atom-splitting formula, $E = MC^2$, and there he makes an enemy of stuffy Preston Preston (John Howard), falls in love with Marie Curie (Odile De Clezio), invents rock 'n' roll, the electric guitar, and surfing, and is thrown into a lunatic asylum where he rescues some kittens about to be baked into a pie. At the climax, Bert races off to France to find Marie and stop Preston Preston from blowing up Charles Darwin (Basil Clarke) and other scientific notables with an atomic beer-bubblizing chamber.

Young Einstein is the kind of thing you dream up during late-night college-age bull sessions, adding more and more stupidities and silly twists until you and your friends are helpless with laughter. The next day, you tell someone who wasn't there about this great, funny thing you heard, and they stare at you blankly. *Young Einstein* is a you-hadda-be-there story. It tries to get by on sheer zaniness of conception, but it needed to be directed in a zany fashion as well, and it simply isn't. There's no energy to the film, no sense of pace. There are some good slapstick gags here and there, but they aren't directed like slapstick; for all the zest of the direction, they might as well have been doing Eugene O'Neill.

The film is harmless, though, and Yahoo Serious himself has some charm, though he does tend to be too aware of this charm. He has a nice turn in utter self-involvement, and can seem both stupid and brilliant at the same time. He wrote and directed the film, which grew from a modestly budgeted outing to the erratically epic movie it is now.

Cyborg was one of the last gasps of Cannon Pictures, but few other than its investors were sorry to see the company go under. From its beginning until its demise, Cannon released a string of projects that should never have been begun, or which were doomed by compromise, poor scripts, or inappropriate directors. This one was just another variation on *The Road Warrior*, which, in terms of the sheer number of its clones, may be the most imitated movie in history. Although there aren't any fanged, cannon-equipped cars in *Cyborg*, the setting is the standard junk-apocalypse future, with lots of rapacious thugs dressed in leather and metal brutalizing the innocent and unprotected. One of these is a cyborg (Dayle Haddon), sent out by doctors in Atlanta to find a cure for the plague that's ravaging the world. No explanation is offered as to why she had to be a cyborg to do this.

Despite the title, however, she's not the main character, who's Gibson (Jean-Claude Van Damme), a loner and defender of the helpless. Apparently not long before the movie starts—there are too many flashbacks—his newfound family was wiped out by a blue-eyed, black villain called Fender (Vincent Klyn), who has captured the cyborg. Gibson is reluctant to get involved, but agrees to assist another woman (Deborah Richter) in getting to Atlanta to help the cyborg.

This was one of several movies intended to turn Van Damme into a Schwarzenegger-like action hero, but while he has the right physique and a good, movie-star face, he lacks Schwarzenegger's charm and sense of humor. The movie plods along from one repetitious fight to another, mostly designed to show off Van Damme's abilities as a kickboxer, but he hadn't developed much of a following, and *Cyborg* was a flop.

The movie was directed by Albert Pyun, an earnest but smug director, who is a little clearer in his intentions here than in such previous disasters as *Alien from L.A.* and *Radioactive Dreams.* He would have been better off if he had allowed some conscious humor to creep in. Then again, the climax, with Fender and Gibson squaring off in a rainstorm while literally growling at each other, is so absurd that perhaps it was intended to be funny. This is the most violent movie ever written by a person named Kitty (Chalmers, in this case), but that is not a recommendation.

I don't blame Walter Koenig for his disappointment when his first starring film, *Moontrap*, went straight to videotape, because it's good enough that it could easily have worked out in theatrical release. The low-budget film was directed by Robert Dyke, who already is a better director than many established directors working on about the same budget. He knows the right angles to choose, and never relies on the standard master shot/two shot/closeup rhythm that too many use as a crutch. He blocks out scenes with imagination and taste, and knows how to use editing for impact and to fool the viewer into thinking the movie is more expensive than it is. He blunders at times, but he's promising and astute.

Koenig is Jason Grant, a present-day space shuttle pilot who's always wished he could have gone to the Moon. His copilot and best friend is Commander Ray Tanner (Bruce Campbell), who's younger and more dashing, and who also longs to go to the Moon. They get their chance when they discover a quarter-mile-long spaceship in a decaying Earth orbit; aboard it, Jason finds a coppery pod and a desiccated human corpse 14,000 years old. There was evidence the ship had been on the Moon, but how they found the precise crater it was launched from is unexplained and unexplainable. When the pod pops open and constructs a big killer robot-like thing out of itself, machinery, and human body parts, NASA is persuaded to send the last remaining Apollo capsule to the Moon, manned by Grant and Tanner. There, they find a woman (Leigh Lombardi) in suspended animation, and more alien machines. The climax takes place on another alien ship on its way to take over the Earth.

The script by Tex Ragsdale could have been better; the basic

332 * NEBULA AWARDS 25

storyline is serviceable enough, but he uses some genuinely bad ideas, particularly the utterly predictable and utterly tiresome "horror continues" ending. Not everything in the story is explained, and that's fine with me; I like some elements of mystery left. I presume that Ragsdale and Dyke did *have* an explanation in mind, and I hope that they don't think they *did* explain everything. Not everything works; the music is unimaginative, Campbell is a bit over the top, Koenig slightly too rehearsed, but those are not important flaws. It's worth seeking out on videotape—where it was apparently quite popular, at least popular enough for a sequel to be announced.

The design of the unusual New Zealand film *The Navigator* resembles a cross between the medieval movies of Monty Python and Ingmar Bergman—and, oddly, the movie plays rather like one, too. It's austerely beautiful, amusing, and unique in its plot.

England in 1348 is suffering from the Black Plague. An isolated village fears the plague, which hasn't arrived in their area yet. They live a bare-bones existence, apparently getting by on mining; it's winter, and the snow is deep. (The sequences in the village are almost all in stark black and white.) Young Griffin (Hamish McFarlane), who has occasional prophetic visions, is horrified when his older brother Connor (Bruce Lyons) returns from "the outside world" with bad news—the plague does seem to be on its way toward them. Griffin tells the others that his visions have revealed that if they use an odd piece of mining equipment and descend into the Earth, they will find a celestial city with a tall church spire, upon which they must place a newly forged copper cross. By doing this, their village will be spared the plague—but he doesn't tell them that his dreams also reveal that one of them must fall from the steeple and die.

Connor, Griffin, and four other villagers begin their perilous descent, and eventually emerge in *modern-day* Auckland (the film is now in color). To these isolated, primitive men, the 1988 city is not one whit stranger than they expect the outside world to be, and though it is a place of wonder, they take it in their stride. Things seem to climax at a church steeple, they return to their town and time, and a logical ending to the adventure. Logical and tragic.

The Navigator has the texture of a legend. Director Vincent Ward co-wrote with Kely Lyons and Geoff Chapple. His control of the medium is so strong, his narrative drive so clear, and his work with the actors so expert that there's a chance that Ward will be one of the great directors of the 1990s.

One of the most impressive aspects of the movie is its strong, clear narrative, as precise and uncluttered as a Western, and as easy to follow, despite what seems at first to be an incoherent opening. There's a warmth in the telling, and an involvement with believable characters that's unusual for a film with so peculiar a storyline. Ward adds little details that emphasize the folk-tale aspects of the film: a winged, scythe-wielding skeleton flies past the opening to their tunnel; in New Zealand, the cross they carry perfectly fits a mold that an Auckland foundry already has handy. There's a bit with a gauntlet that could have been found in a classical folk song.

Ward doesn't sacrifice coherency for profundity, nor does he sacrifice profundity for thrills. Though the film is, at last, not great, it is a unique, haunting story, and will be fondly recalled for years by those who see it. Whether it's really science fiction, science fantasy, "magic realism" or something else remains for others to decide, but if the Nebula Award were still given for Dramatic Presentation, this would have been on my list of nominees.

As would *Miracle Mile*. Steve De Jarnatt's script floated around Hollywood for nine years or so, and frequently turned up in lists of the best unfilmed movies. De Jarnatt, whose only previous film as director was the mediocre *Cherry 2000*, was determined that his pet *Miracle Mile* be filmed correctly. He bought it back, found financing, and directed it himself.

And in this awesomely accomplished movie, De Jarnatt lived up to his goals: this is American independent moviemaking at its best. As both writer and director, this is a triumph for De Jarnatt. He deals here with tricky subject matter, the kind of thing that has defeated long-established professionals. The film is about a nuclear attack on Los Angeles.

On the stretch of Los Angeles' Wilshire Boulevard known as the Miracle Mile, near the tar pits, swing trombonist Harry (Anthony Edwards) meets the girl of his dreams, waitress Julie Peters (Mare Winningham). The film seems to be setting itself up as a gentle, wise modern-day romance (and, bizarrely enough, that's what it remains, though that's not all it is), as we see a nicely paced montage of first impressions. Harry arranges to meet Julie when she gets off work, but he oversleeps, and she goes home, disappointed. Harry arrives at the restaurant, where he absently answers a ringing pay phone. It's a panic-stricken guy in a North Dakota missile silo, who misdialed. America has launched an attack on the Soviet Union, and within seventy minutes, the missiles will fall on Los Angeles.

Making arrangements with a steely Yuppie (Denise Crosby) he encounters to join her on a jet out of L.A., Harry rushes off to get Julie. But just getting to her is a struggle, involving stolen cars, explosions, the police, and other obstacles. But amid this expertly managed mounting suspense, De Jarnatt always keeps track of the human element. The characters are ordinary people, but realistic and sympathetic. There's even time for humor, as when Harry frantically wheels the Valium-doped Julie toward a heliport in a shopping cart.

From the moment of the phone call on, *Miracle Mile* increases steadily in tension—it is the first time I can recall in all my years of moviegoing in which my mouth literally went dry from so much suspense. *Everything* in this film works, the evocation of time and place, the production design, the simple but believable effects. By including humor, De Jarnatt allows us to think it's possible that Harry and Julie will get away, which only cranks the tension up more. It's funny, intelligent, satiric, sarcastic, shocking, and somehow deeply satisfying. Even at the end, when there is no way out for anyone, as nuclear bombs set the palm trees of Los Angeles afire, as Harry and Julie sink into the tar pits in a destroyed helicopter, the film somehow manages to make a positive statement about love and the human condition. They will die, they know, but they will someday be found as diamonds, eternal, beautiful and precious.

A lot of people hated *Batman*, but I loved it even before it made approximately one squillion dollars. It's a dark, delightful, intriguing, and exciting adventure. I was constantly surprised, fascinated, involved. The expected weaknesses—expected by me, anyway—weren't there. Those that were there didn't seem as important to me as the movie's virtues.

The least important aspect of *Batman*, and admittedly its weakest element, is the story. It's set early in Batman's career, as he prowls Gotham City catching criminals the overworked cops (some of them are corrupt) can't catch. We meet Batman, then his love interest, reporter Vicki Vale, and Bruce Wayne, millionaire playboy, Batman's true identity. We also meet Jack Napier (Jack Nicholson)—the right-hand man to Gotham City crime boss Grissom (Jack Palance); Jack is given to purple suits and is already a crazy. Grissom engineers a police attack on the ambitious Napier. Batman is on the scene, and accidentally drops Napier into a vat of chemicals. Napier emerges with chalk-white skin, red lips in a permanent grin, and green hair—and a totally mad, brilliant mind: the Joker. He and Batman are soon opponents, as the Joker tries to take over Gotham City.

That's the setup, but the movie is not the setup. The movie is the performances, Tim Burton's imaginative direction, the conflict between the characters as established in the script by Sam Hamm and Warren Skaaren, the brilliant production design by Anton Furst, and the rich, Max Steiner–like score by Danny Elfman.

Jack Nicholson is fine as the Joker, but I didn't expect the *discipline* Nicholson brought to the role. His performance seemed out of control to some, though it's anything but. Nicholson never loses sight of the fact that the Joker is both cause and effect, that mad Napier lives behind that blanched face. He cavorts and jitterbugs his way through the movie, twirling out of scenes in insane pirouettes, laughing at his own brilliance, murdering simply to show who's boss. He declares himself the "world's first fully functioning homicidal artist," and we can believe *he* believes it. The Joker is indeed a clown, and is almost always funny—Nicholson delivers the throw-away lines as if they were his own improvised ad-libs (and maybe some were). His Joker is insane, he is a killer, and he is unpredictable. He's actually frightening. He is such a powerful opponent for Batman that it seems at least possible the Joker could win. And critics of the film thought it was overbalanced on the Joker's side.

But he is up against Michael Keaton as Batman. In hiring Mr. Mom, Batfans thought Warner Bros. were going against their promise that this would be a *serious* Batman movie. Well, serious it is (though often funny), and one of the most serious elements is Keaton. I never dreamed he had this range. Some accused him of underplaying the role, but that's not it. The Joker has allowed his derangement to spill out into the public. Bruce Wayne has bottled up his problems, turned inward and focused upon that which changed his life, the murder of his parents (by Napier, in fact).

Essential to Burton's conception of Batman and the Joker is the wonderwork of Anton Furst. His Gotham City, a grimy, seething hellhole, with dark corners and looming walls, a New York run riot without building codes, a place where, as Jack Napier says, decent people shouldn't live, is part Oz, part the Los Angeles of *Blade Runner*, and a large part Fritz Lang's monumental city of the future, Metropolis. This smoky, fetid sewer of a city not only needs Batman, it *generates* him—and the Joker as well. (They were created by the city, and by each other.) It's a triumph of the imagination that validates Batman the character and *Batman* the movie.

The movie divided audiences; some hated it, and their complaints have some justification—but I think this may even be some kind of *great* movie. Just what kind I must admit I have not decided. But I do know this: I think it is the best dramatic realization of a comic book so far.

THE 1980s BEGAN for science fiction films with imitations of and sequels to movies of the late 1970s. Series like *Superman, Star Wars*, and *Star Trek* continued, helping make the 1980s the decade of the sequel. There are a lot of little trends in terms of content for the decade, as it became increasingly clear that while Hollywood realized that SF is a marketable commodity, they don't know whom to market it *to*.

Adults? No, the failure of Kirk Douglas' two 1980 SF movies, *The Final Countdown* and *Saturn 3* seemed to show that. (But didn't executives notice that, in particular, *Saturn 3* did open well? Meaning that audiences *did* want to see SF—but a better movie than that one.)

Well, maybe SF movies really were the new Westerns, and with *Outland* being a modest success in 1981, that idea seemed to have some validity. Again, its initial grosses were a lot better than later on; the idea that perhaps the movie was in the right genre but simply not *good* enough has no validity in Hollywood.

The most significant year for SF in the decade of the '80s was 1982, when *E.T.* was released, and *The Road Warrior* (*Mad Max 2*) finally opened in the United States. Not only was *E.T.* a phenomenon, the biggest money-making film in movie history, but *The Road Warrior* was also a hit, and generated dozens of imitations and one sequel. But few really tried to imitate *E.T.* because it was made by Steven

Spielberg, and moviemakers just don't know why his films are popular. (Later in the decade, when his popularity fell off, I'm sure many in Hollywood were relieved; he was just a flash in the pan, after all.)

Also that year, the movie that will almost certainly ultimately be judged the best SF film of the 1980s was released, and was not a success. But *Blade Runner* later turned a profit from videotape sales and rentals, apparently the first movie to do so, and that in itself had a great effect on how movies were made and marketed from then on. John Carpenter's *The Thing* didn't do well either, but slowly developed a cult reputation, primarily for its imaginative, ghoulish special effects by Rob Bottin.

But these films had little impact on the trends in the remainder of the decade. *The Terminator* in 1984 did, however, not just in suggesting that action films and SF could be blended, but in establishing Arnold Schwarzenegger not only as a highly "bankable" star, but also as one who gladly appeared in SF movies. His later *Predator* and *The Running Man* were modestly successful in the U.S., but smash hits overseas; 1990's *Total Recall* was also a hit in America. The financial failures of *2010* and *Dune* in '84 "proved" to Hollywood that SF movies based on novels were not good investments.

By 1985, Hollywood decided that the real target audience for SF was teenagers, so having such movies *starring* teenagers were surefire hits—and not just SF, but fantasy films as well. But of the big onslaught of teens-and-fantasy films of that year, only *Back to the Future* and *Teen Wolf* (both starring Michael J. Fox) were really hits; most of the others faded fast.

In 1986, *The Fly* and *Aliens* were hits. Consequently, James Cameron, who directed the latter (and *The Terminator*), later received a huge budget for *The Abyss*. But instead of giving David Cronenberg more money for films he wanted to make, Hollywood decided that it wasn't his genius that made *The Fly* work, it was The Fly, and so made *The Fly II*. Cameron played the game the Hollywood way; Cronenberg was just too weird.

In 1987, everyone was shocked; only *RoboCop*, of the SF movies of the year, really did well. *Harry and the Hendersons* and °*Batteries Not Included*, which everyone expected to be hits, flopped; so did the much better *Innerspace*. So it had to be action + SF, that was the formula. And 1989 gave us Hollywood's currently traditional action genre, odd-partner cop thriller, paired with SF, in *Alien Nation*, and a nation yawned.

Science fiction drives the money guys in Hollywood bananas. They *know* it has its audience, but they are going crazy trying to find it. Right now, they think it is action and SF that is the key, but they still don't get it. The action + SF movies that made tons of money were, by and large, *good movies* that blended the SF and thrills intelligently. Hollywood has forever been convinced that quality is not a salable commodity, and as we move into the 1990s, do not expect that to change.

APPENDIXES

ABOUT THE NEBULA AWARDS

A Nebula Awards banquet takes place every spring, its location alternating between New York City and the West Coast. The twenty-fifth annual Nebula Awards were presented at the traditional banquet, held on April 28, 1990, at the Hyatt Regency Embarcadero in San Francisco, California.

Since 1965, the Nebulas have been given for the best novel, novella, novelette, and short story published during the preceding year (see Introduction for word lengths defining each category). An award for Best Dramatic Presentation first given in 1973 lasted three years, the membership later voting to restrict the Nebula to published literary works.

The Grand Master Nebula Award goes to a living author for a lifetime's achievement. This award is bestowed no more than six times in a decade. In accordance with SFWA bylaws, the president, who traditionally consults with past presidents and the board of directors, nominates a candidate. This nomination then goes before the officers; if a majority agree, that candidate becomes a Grand Master. To date, ten writers have received the Grand Master award: Robert A. Heinlein (1974), Jack Williamson (1975), Clifford D. Simak (1976), L. Sprague de Camp (1978), Fritz Leiber (1981), Andre Norton (1983), Arthur C. Clarke (1985), Isaac Asimov (1986), Alfred Bester (1987), and Ray Bradbury (1988).

This year's Nebula Awards volume is the twenty-fifth entry in a unique series.

PAST NEBULA AWARD WINNERS

1965

Best Novel: *Dune* by Frank Herbert
Best Novella: "The Saliva Tree" by Brian W. Aldiss
  "He Who Shapes" by Roger Zelazny (tie)
Best Novelette: "The Doors of His Face, the Lamps of His Mouth"
  by Roger Zelazny
Best Short Story: " 'Repent, Harlequin!' Said the Ticktockman" by
  Harlan Ellison

1966

Best Novel: *Flowers for Algernon* by Daniel Keyes
  Babel-17 by Samuel R. Delany (tie)
Best Novella: "The Last Castle" by Jack Vance
Best Novelette: "Call Him Lord" by Gordon R. Dickson
Best Short Story: "The Secret Place" by Richard McKenna

1967

Best Novel: *The Einstein Intersection* by Samuel R. Delany
Best Novella: "Behold the Man" by Michael Moorcock
Best Novelette: "Gonna Roll the Bones" by Fritz Leiber
Best Short Story: "Aye, and Gomorrah" by Samuel R. Delany

1968

Best Novel: *Rite of Passage* by Alexei Panshin
Best Novella: "Dragonrider" by Anne McCaffrey
Best Novelette: "Mother to the World" by Richard Wilson
Best Short Story: "The Planners" by Kate Wilhelm

1969

Best Novel: *The Left Hand of Darkness* by Ursula K. Le Guin
Best Novella: "A Boy and His Dog" by Harlan Ellison

Best Novelette: "Time Considered as a Helix of Semi-Precious Stones" by Samuel R. Delany
Best Short Story: "Passengers" by Robert Silverberg

1970

Best Novel: *Ringworld* by Larry Niven
Best Novella: "Ill Met in Lankhmar" by Fritz Leiber
Best Novelette: "Slow Sculpture" by Theodore Sturgeon
Best Short Story: No award

1971

Best Novel: *A Time of Changes* by Robert Silverberg
Best Novella: "The Missing Man" by Katherine MacLean
Best Novelette: "The Queen of Air and Darkness" by Poul Anderson
Best Short Story: "Good News from the Vatican" by Robert Silverberg

1972

Best Novel: *The Gods Themselves* by Isaac Asimov
Best Novella: "A Meeting with Medusa" by Arthur C. Clarke
Best Novelette: "Goat Song" by Poul Anderson
Best Short Story: "When It Changed" by Joanna Russ

1973

Best Novel: *Rendezvous with Rama* by Arthur C. Clarke
Best Novella: "The Death of Doctor Island" by Gene Wolfe
Best Novelette: "Of Mist, and Grass, and Sand," by Vonda N. McIntyre
Best Short Story: "Love Is the Plan, the Plan Is Death" by James Tiptree, Jr.
Best Dramatic Presentation: *Soylent Green*

1974

Best Novel: *The Dispossessed* by Ursula K. Le Guin
Best Novella: "Born with the Dead" by Robert Silverberg
Best Novelette: "If the Stars Are Gods" by Gordon Eklund and Gregory Benford

Best Short Story: "The Day Before the Revolution" by Ursula K. Le Guin

Best Dramatic Presentation: *Sleeper*

Grand Master: Robert A. Heinlein

1975

Best Novel: *The Forever War* by Joe Haldeman

Best Novella: "Home Is the Hangman" by Roger Zelazny

Best Novelette: "San Diego Lightfoot Sue" by Tom Reamy

Best Short Story: "Catch That Zeppelin!" by Fritz Leiber

Best Dramatic Presentation: *Young Frankenstein*

Grand Master: Jack Williamson

1976

Best Novel: *Man Plus* by Frederik Pohl

Best Novella: "Houston, Houston, Do You Read?" by James Tiptree, Jr.

Best Novelette: "The Bicentennial Man" by Isaac Asimov

Best Short Story: "A Crowd of Shadows" by Charles L. Grant

Grand Master: Clifford D. Simak

1977

Best Novel: *Gateway* by Frederik Pohl

Best Novella: "Stardance" by Spider and Jeanne Robinson

Best Novelette: "The Screwfly Solution" by Raccoona Sheldon

Best Short Story: "Jeffty Is Five" by Harlan Ellison

Special Award: *Star Wars*

1978

Best Novel: *Dreamsnake* by Vonda N. McIntyre

Best Novella: "The Persistence of Vision" by John Varley

Best Novelette: "A Glow of Candles, a Unicorn's Eye" by Charles L. Grant

Best Short Story: "Stone" by Edward Bryant

Grand Master: L. Sprague de Camp

1979

Best Novel: *The Fountains of Paradise* by Arthur C. Clarke
Best Novella: "Enemy Mine" by Barry Longyear
Best Novelette: "Sandkings" by George R. R. Martin
Best Short Story: "giANTS" by Edward Bryant

1980

Best Novel: *Timescape* by Gregory Benford
Best Novella: "The Unicorn Tapestry" by Suzy McKee Charnas
Best Novelette: "The Ugly Chickens" by Howard Waldrop
Best Short Story: "Grotto of the Dancing Deer" by Clifford D. Simak

1981

Best Novel: *The Claw of the Conciliator* by Gene Wolfe
Best Novella: "The Saturn Game" by Poul Anderson
Best Novelette: "The Quickening" by Michael Bishop
Best Short Story: "The Bone Flute" by Lisa Tuttle*
Grand Master: Fritz Leiber

1982

Best Novel: *No Enemy But Time* by Michael Bishop
Best Novella: "Another Orphan" by John Kessel
Best Novelette: "Fire Watch" by Connie Willis
Best Short Story: "A Letter from the Clearys" by Connie Willis

1983

Best Novel: *Startide Rising* by David Brin
Best Novella: "Hardfought" by Greg Bear
Best Novelette: "Blood Music" by Greg Bear
Best Short Story: "The Peacemaker" by Gardner Dozois
Grand Master: Andre Norton

1984

Best Novel: *Neuromancer* by William Gibson
Best Novella: "PRESS ENTER ■" by John Varley

* This Nebula Award was declined by the author.

Best Novelette: "Bloodchild" by Octavia E. Butler
Best Short Story: "Morning Child" by Gardner Dozois

1985

Best Novel: *Ender's Game* by Orson Scott Card
Best Novella: "Sailing to Byzantium" by Robert Silverberg
Best Novelette: "Portraits of His Children" by George R. R. Martin
Best Short Story: "Out of All Them Bright Stars" by Nancy Kress
Grand Master: Arthur C. Clarke

1986

Best Novel: *Speaker for the Dead* by Orson Scott Card
Best Novella: "R & R" by Lucius Shepard
Best Novelette: "The Girl Who Fell into the Sky" by Kate Wilhelm
Best Short Story: "Tangents" by Greg Bear
Grand Master: Isaac Asimov

1987

Best Novel: *The Falling Woman* by Pat Murphy
Best Novella: "The Blind Geometer" by Kim Stanley Robinson
Best Novelette: "Rachel in Love" by Pat Murphy
Best Short Story: "Forever Yours, Anna" by Kate Wilhelm
Grand Master: Alfred Bester

1988

Best Novel: *Falling Free* by Lois McMaster Bujold
Best Novella: "The Last of the Winnebagos" by Connie Willis
Best Novelette: "Schrödinger's Kitten" by George Alec Effinger
Best Short Story: "Bible Stories for Adults, No. 17: The Deluge" by
    James Morrow
Grand Master: Ray Bradbury

Permissions Acknowledgments

Bulletin of Science Fiction Writers of America (Spring 1990). Reprinted by permission of SFWA and the authors.

Previously unpublished comments by Elizabeth Ann Scarborough, Gardner Dozois, Robert Frazier, Bruce Boston, John M. Ford, and John Crowley in the headnotes to their contributions are all copyright © by the individual contributors and are used by their permission. The excerpt from Damon Knight's autobiographical essay in the introduction to "What Is Science Fiction?" is used with his permission.